Huddud's House

Huddud's House

A novel

by Fadi Azzam

translated by Ghada Alatrash

Interlink Books
An imprint of Interlink Publishing Group, Inc.
Northampton, Massachusetts

First published in 2024 by

Interlink Books
An imprint of Interlink Publishing Group, Inc.
46 Crosby Street, Northampton, MA 01060
www.interlinkbooks.com

Cover design by Harrison Williams

Library of Congress Cataloging-in-Publication data available.
ISBN-13: 978-1-62371-115-3

Printed and bound in the United States of America

To Adad Azzam

Here, in Huddud's House, you will find the secrets behind your name.

Acknowledgements

Our deepest and heartfelt thanks to Heather Janbay and Dr. Kristina McGowan (both American-born and native English speakers) for their nuanced reading of *Huddud's House*, sentence by sentence and word by word—Heather, who read with her cutting American lens, and whose reading was informed by a knowledge of Arabic that she speaks in the same dialect as the author; and, Kristina, whose edits and suggestions were invaluable, and who was at times consumed by one sentence for an entire day (or more); your line: "I am cheering you on, waiting for you at the finish line" was an incredibly inspiring drive in what seemed like an endless marathon in this journey of translation. We cannot thank the two of you enough.

With you, we can now present this work to our English readers.

Fadi Azzam and Ghada Alatrash

"Love is a kind of warfare."
—Ovid

"Indeed, God did not create the world except through love, and divine love is the scandal of time. Love is a small death."
—Sheikh al-Akbar Muhyiddin Ibn Arabi

1

Fidel

Dubai, the beginning of 2011

Next to Burj Al-Arab on Jumeira Beach, a group of young men in swimsuits sat around a table under an umbrella and contemplated the sea in wonder. One of them was smoking a hookah, his breath taken by what he saw. Another repositioned himself in his seat and took off his sunglasses to get a better look. And a third gasped in disbelief at what he was seeing. They seemed to be staring at a group of women emerging from the water in their bikinis, their bodies slender, swaying gracefully and coquettishly.

Whispering and giggling as they strolled by, the women noticed the men's stupefaction. But the young men continued to look ahead, their eyes focused instead on something on the sea, paying no heed to the young women in bikinis. The women then turned their heads and were also overcome with the same astonishment as they caught sight of three luxurious yachts leisurely passing by.

At that moment, Fidel shouted angrily, "Sto-o-o-p!"

The expressions suddenly vanished from the faces of the film crew and were replaced by silent looks of resentment. Fidel approached the work team and demanded that the scene be reshot, while the fifty technicians and crew members scurried like bees in a beehive. His mobile rang.

"Hello, Dr. Omran," he said in a friendly tone. "No, it's impossible for me to leave the set. Can this wait until tomorrow?" After a pause, he continued, "OK then, it would be easier for you to come my way and we can talk. I'm not too far from you. I will send you my location." Half an hour later, Dr. Omran, a businessman, arrived at the site where Fidel Abdullah was filming.

"Half an hour break!" Fidel announced through a microphone, and turned to Omran. "Welcome, Dr. Omran."

"Hello, our great and busy film director," replied Dr. Omran.

"I will always make myself available for you," he said warmly. "So, tell me, what is it that cannot wait until tomorrow?"

"I understand that you are in charge of all the marketing for our hospitals in the Gulf, and I need you to go to Damascus and help with the launch of our new hospital, Sama Al-Sham, which will be happening in two weeks. It's currently run by an important friend, Dr. Sa'ad. But honestly, I especially need you to run the campaign side of things and to promote the hospital for the purposes of tourist medical treatment. It will be the first of its kind in the Middle East, both in quality and price."

"Did I hear you say Damascus?"

"Yes, Fidel."

"Well, I may not have told you this earlier, Doc, but I'm not allowed to go to Damascus. I'm on the wanted list and my name is flagged by national security."

"What are you talking about? What did you do?"

"It's a long story, from more than eighteen years ago, before I left for the UK."

"Listen, Fidel. I may not know you on a personal level, but what I do know through the work you've done for us as well as for others is that you are quite talented and well respected. What a shame it is that you are able to visit all other countries but not your own homeland!"

"You're telling me! Go tell the Mukhabarat.[1] They have no mercy, and they won't allow for the mercy of Allah to descend," Fidel said with a bitter laugh.

"Would you give me permission to get a feel for the situation? I have some close friends there who we could ask about any safety concerns

---

1   The Mukhabarat, also known as the General Intelligence Directorate (GID), is the intelligence agency of Syria.

or risks if you were to visit Syria. Can you send me your personal information?"

Fidel, showing clear signs of distress and eager to change the subject, said, "I thank you with all my heart, but as much as I hate to say it, I don't think there is any hope. I've tried more than once, to no avail. Regardless, I will go ahead and text you my information."

Fidel Al-Abdullah. Birthplace: Rif Dimashq, August 21, 1974. Father's name: Tawfeeq. Mother's name: Fatima.

Omran's visit left Fidel in a bad mood, and he turned the remaining work hours into a living hell, barking out orders and demanding retake after retake. He ended his day accompanied by one of the women who worked as a model in the company's commercials, and they headed together to his apartment in Jumeira Lake Towers. He knew that nothing could extinguish his internal fire except for a wild night like the ones he skillfully produced.

2
Fadl and Fidel

"Fidel. I will name him Fidel," yelled my father after having been informed by the midwife that his newborn was a healthy baby boy who showed no signs of Down's syndrome.

It was a sultry day in the summer of 1974, in a quiet village on the outskirts of Damascus.

Irritated by the announcement, my uncle Sheikh Mahmoud objected, "But Fidel is a Christian name."

"No, my dear. I am naming him after the great Fidel Castro. He wasn't Christian, nor does he know your God!" responded my father, as he headed to fill the arak[2] glasses for his Communist friends, who had come to celebrate the arrival of a healthy heir after two healthy girls and one son with Down's.

My mother was accustomed to the madness of my father, Mr. Tawfeeq Al-Abdullah, the loud Communist math teacher. She whispered apologetically in her brother's ear. Meanwhile, my uncle sought God's forgiveness and Allah's protection from an accursed Satan as he listened to the blasphemy of his hard-headed brother-in-law. He lifted me up, blessed me, and prayed to God that his nephew would become a righteous person.

"His name will be Fadl, as he is indeed a blessing from the Almighty God."

---

2   Arak is an alcoholic drink. In Syria, arak is typically made from fermented grapes distilled to create a clear, colorless, high-proof spirit.

And so it was that I grew up with two names: a name that reflected my father's deep desire for me to become a lawyer like Castro, and the other name embodying my mother's prayers to see me turn into a sheikh like her brother.

By the age of ten, my uncle was set on teaching me to recite the Holy Quran, while my father fueled my imagination with stories about Guevara and Castro, and taught me to recite freedom songs for revolutionaries across the world. Indeed, every discussion between my father and uncle ended up with my father throwing insults at religions and my uncle angrily swearing and threatening that my father, along with his Communist, atheist and arrogant friends, were bound to burn in the fires of hell, and only then would they realize God's power and wonders.

But it wasn't God who answered Sheikh Mahmoud's prayers; the Syrian Mukhabarat did instead. They detained my father, a member of the leftist opposition, for four years. During these years, my mother took advantage of my father's absence, and with the help of my uncles, they made a young sheikh out of me.

My father was the first to discover my gift for drawing, but my mother turned it into calligraphy after my uncle convinced her that personification through drawing was haram.[3] And so, I memorized half of the Quran and more than two hundred hadiths. I read Ibn Hisham's *Seerah*, Abu Al-Faraj Al-Isfahani's *Kitab Al-Aghani*, and Ibn Malik's *Al-Alfiyya*. I became the school's little genius in Arabic, history, and religion. By the time I was in high school, I became the young imam of the town, just as my mother had always dreamt, with a beard that was never touched by a razor blade. But my name, as per my ID and as documented in the civil records, continued to carry that leftist ring: Fidel.

My father looked twenty years older after his release from prison. They extinguished his fire but failed to break his spirit. Most painful for him was seeing what I had become. He felt betrayed, stabbed in the back. He couldn't express his anger or complain, as was his habit, for my uncles

---

3   Haram is an Arabic term used to describe anything that is forbidden or prohibited in Islamic law. Haram is the opposite of halal, which refers to things that are permissible under Islamic law.

had looked after his home during his long absence and spared us the humiliation of being in need or asking others for help.

He was kicked out of school and dismissed from teaching, deemed a danger to the next generation. So, he went back to work on his land, one that bordered our home, and did so tirelessly. Each morning, while my mother, two sisters and I woke up for the dawn prayer, we heard him mumbling endless curses to the gods of the skies and demons on earth. Gradually, he turned into a silent loner, digging and tilling a dead wasteland, planting a few bushes in its barrenness. He ate alone, worked alone, and barely talked to anyone. The jug of arak accompanied him each evening as he sat to drink it by the side of the house or on the rooftop. He seldom visited anyone nor was visited by anyone.

With the collapse of the Berlin Wall and the beginning of the perestroika movement, the red dream also dried up and turned a dull yellow. But out of stubbornness, and to be spiteful, he enlarged a photo of Marx, hung it in the guest room and centered it between my mother's embroidered wall hangings with the slogans "God and Muhammad" and "God is the light of the heavens and the earth." And like all arak addicts, he turned thin and scrawny, his face wrinkled and his teeth eroded.

I earned high marks on my baccalaureate exam. After my uncle pledged to fund my postgraduate studies at Al-Azhar University, I announced that I would major in Islamic Sharia. My father refused to congratulate me.

Even though I was angry at him for his atheism, drunkenness, and way of life, I did not want to hurt him. So I decided to honor him as a father and said, "Very well, father. I will study law as you wish, but this will not change who I am."

A smile of gratitude appeared below the deep grooves under his black hollow eyes. He whispered in a broken voice, "May God bless you, son. I can now rest in peace," as if finally surrendering to the believers who took advantage of him in what he considered to be his weakest spot, his son.

I vividly recall that day, July 13, 1992, when we woke up and didn't find him. We didn't think much of it at first, until he returned in a taxi later that afternoon and called out my name to help him unload the groceries.

There was a slaughtered lamb along with bags filled with presents. Once he distributed some of the meat to the neighbors, he gathered my sisters together, kissed them for the first time ever, and gave each of them a dress, a pair of shoes, and a box of accessories. He bought a new dress for my mother as well as a brocaded *abaya*. She never ended up wearing it, but kept it lovingly in her closet. He took me aside and placed a watch with a silver band on my wrist, but quickly discovered that it was not working. He cursed the People's Republic of China and their corrupt communism, pulled it off my wrist and shook it, hoping to get the main spring to start, but was unable to. He then placed it on the floor and stomped and smashed it, cursing the son of a bitch who tricked him into buying it. After he calmed down, he pulled out 3,000 lira from his pocket and said to me, "I wish I had more, my dear lawyer, but this is all I have."

He invited some of his old friends over for a barbecue that he promised to prepare with his own hands, as if he was getting back to his old self again, regaining his strength and humor. My mother didn't even complain on that day, and a smile also returned to her face. To everyone's surprise, after the guests left, he helped her with the dishes and in cleaning the kitchen. He held her hand, kissed it, and said, "Indeed you're a great woman to have put up with me for all these years."

And, for the first time ever, we watched our father playing teasingly with my sisters, showing affection and kindness. He also gave my brother Fida a bag full of toys and clothes. He then took me aside and said, "I may have been the worst father in the world, but one day you will understand. You will understand that the God that they are trying to convince you of collaborates with the lowly bastards of Al-Baath. Had he really existed, he would have heard the screams of the forty thousand victims in Hama who were killed at the hands of the butcher and would not have left him unpunished; but instead, he's blessed him and left him perched over our throats." [4]

He then continued in a calmer tone, "Son, you are free to choose as you wish, but I am grateful that you have made one dream of mine come

---

4   The Baath Party has been the ruling party in Syria since 1963.

true. I no longer have any dreams. All of my dreams have been shattered and stomped upon, except for when you agreed to study law. This is my only victory in life and I do not want to lose it. And even though I was frustrated with you as you decided to become religious before giving life a chance, this does not change the fact that I am proud of you.

"Let me tell you something. Faith has nothing to do with being religious. Being religious is about finding a way to God, while being faithful is about standing up for what is righteous and good and living with the beautiful spirit of God in you. It is difficult to explain, and I also know that it is just as difficult to understand. But I deeply believe that if there were psychiatric hospitals in Jerusalem, Meccah, and Damascus during the time of the prophets, they would have placed them in these hospitals, and we would have been spared all this nonsense. I am a communist because it is the only choice a person has as the world becomes too American, Baathist, and Islamist. I may not have been a good father, but you can be proud of one thing—that you had an honorable and honest dad who was true to himself and never stole or betrayed those who trusted him."

"Father, please don't talk like this." I felt an urge to hug him, and I did. I whispered, "You are the most honorable father in the world, and I, your son Fidel, am so proud of you." And we embraced.

He held me tight against his chest, and for the first time in my life, I felt strong and safe. It was a moment that I would come to cherish deeply. It was an embrace that made up for years of loss and misunderstandings. We stayed in one another's arms for a few seconds before he turned back into his old self and said, "Alright, get lost now. You're turning into a drama queen."

He then took his cassette player, bottle of arak, and tobacco, and went behind the house, where he usually worked. He sprayed the trunks of his beloved trees with the water hose, replaced the batteries of the cassette player with new ones, and set it on the edge of a high rock, played an audiocassette of Asmahan, and went about watering the trees.

As we sat and watched him from a distance, it looked like he was talking with the trees. My mother said, "Something does not feel right. Your father has either gone crazy or he has found his way to God. Either way, my heart is not at peace. God help us!"

We watched as he found a seat under the big apricot tree, rolled a cigarette, and began to slowly smoke it while sipping from his large arak glass, contemplating the sunset.

As the sun disappeared and the purple horizon faded away, he drank half a liter of arak and smoked half of his cigarettes, which he had rolled with a pinch of DDT spray, the deadly insecticide he used for tree mites.

By the time darkness fell, he was fully poisoned while Asmahan's voice resounded across that mellow, pale evening: "Oh don't put any blame on me, my dear homeland. Don't be saddened. Blame only those who have betrayed you."

We rushed him to the hospital. They tried to save him, but the physician told us that my father opened his eyes only once, to say, with difficulty, "I beg of you, doctor, just let me go."

"It may have been possible to save him, but this was the first time in my life that I saw a patient who did not want to live. He was begging to die," said the physician.

And he died.

The model listened to Fidel as he told this story late into the night. When she pointed out that it was getting late and that he had drunk almost half a liter of Absolut vodka, he just stared at her, as if surprised by her presence. "Remind me of your name?"

"You can call me anything you like," she answered flirtatiously. Then she moved to embrace him, unaware that she was about to awaken a monster. He pushed her away violently and headed to the closet where he stored a collection of whips, masks, and sex toys, each chosen with great care. He selected a bamboo stick with a well-garnished grip and turned to her with a stoic face and red drunken eyes that looked lifeless and demonic.

He ordered her to take off her clothes. When she resisted, he pounced on her, continuously whipping her thighs and buttocks, lashing her mercilessly and tearing her underwear to pieces. Meanwhile, as her pain turned into muffled cries, he held her down and fucked her violently.

Before she could even begin to regain her composure, he placed a stack of money in her hand and told her to get out. She put on her clothes quickly. These brutal encounters with him were familiar by now, but she was always handsomely paid. She stuffed the five thousand dirhams in her purse and, attempting to reestablish decorum, said, "Whenever you feel like talking about your father, I am available."

He pushed her out, locked the door, returned to the couch, and fell into a deep slumber.

3
Dr. Anees, London

"We're done," said Dr. Anees to his assistants. He pulled off his medical mask and gloves, washed his hands without looking up at the mirror, and walked down a long hallway at Royal Chelsea Hospital, leaving his team behind to wrap things up after nine continuous hours of meticulous labor.

Having made sure that his open-heart patient was no longer in a critical state, he assigned the on-call team to take over, feeling a mixture of sadness and pride. He craved an ice cream cone and oud music. He informed the patient's wife that the surgery went well and that her husband was stable, repeating the same phrases he had used hundreds of times before. He then walked to the end of the hallway to his office. Once inside, he opened the mini fridge, took out a small chocolate and vanilla ice cream cone and savored it slowly while enjoying the delicious pain he felt in his temples. He leaned his head back and listened to Mounir Bashir's music, a ritual he performed after every successful surgery. It was a ritual that even London couldn't take away from him.

The nurse entered and presented him with the most recent vital signs, assuring him that the patient was doing well. He then opened the drawer of his desk, took out his phone, and found four messages from his English wife, Hannah. A cloud of anxiety hovered over his head.

Any disruption to Dr. Anees Alaghwani's routine would turn his precisely calculated system into chaos. He quickly became anxious, his usually orderly mind assuming the worst. His body was overcome with shivers and bursts of cold sweat.

His wife, Hannah Roger, a general practitioner who worked at Willesden Medical Centre, knew this about her husband and had been trying to help him overcome this problem throughout the twenty-two years of their marriage. Hence, finding four messages from her added to his distress. Their tone was worrisome—the first: *Urgent, call as soon as you can*; the second: *Very urgent*; the third, with a tone of self-blame: *Don't worry. It's nothing important. When you're done with your surgery, please call me*; and the fourth: *All is well. Sorry for bothering you, but when I got home, I found a voice message on the answering machine from a man who seemed to be calling from Syria and speaking in Arabic. It sounded urgent. That's all. X.*

He let out a sigh of relief as he read the last message. As long as his son Sami was well, there was nothing urgent to worry about. He turned off the loud music and phoned her. She immediately apologized for her persistence but expressed her concern. "I don't know how he got our home number, but the fact that he left a voice message worried me."

"Don't worry. I'm on my way."

He hung up and thought back to his last visit to Syria a few months earlier, when he learned of the passing of his uncle Badr Al-Deen 'Amara.

After the death of his uncle, he lost all ties with his country, for he had no other close relatives left in Syria. Most of them had emigrated long ago, back in the eighties. He wondered what a call from Damascus could mean. No one had his home phone number except for a few of his close friends. How had this mysterious caller gotten his number?

Briefcase in hand, he left the hospital in his brand new 2011 Land Rover. After the holiday season, London was congested and sluggish, but he didn't mind that it got dark early, for that helped him switch off after a long day of heart surgery, intensely fixated on open chests. Arriving at Willesden, he pulled into the garage, reached for his briefcase, and entered the kitchen through the side garage door, announcing, "I'm home."

No one answered. He took out a jug of carrot-and-orange juice from the fridge and poured himself a glass. He then played the message on the answering machine and looked out through the window at his backyard. The fox was visiting once again; he smiled joyfully as he watched it and listened to the calm voice on the machine.

"Sorry to bother you, Dr. Anees. I am a lawyer from Damascus, Rajeh Al-Agha, and I would appreciate it if you would call me back right away on the same number I am calling from. It's concerning an important matter that is of great interest to you. I got your telephone number from Dr. Sa'ad Al-Deen. Please give me a call at your earliest convenience, and thank you."

Hannah walked in, kissed him on the cheek as usual and asked, "Do you know him?"

"Not yet, but I know the person who gave him our number," he answered calmly, as he dialed the number. As the phone line rang on the other side, their anxiety escalated.

"Good evening, this is Dr. Anees."

"Hello Dr. Anees. I was expecting your call."

"How may I help you, Mr. Rajeh?"

"Well, our office is responsible for the devolution of the estate of your late uncle Badr Al-Deen 'Amara. You and your sister are the only next of kin and inheritors. As a matter of fact, according to the will, your uncle's home, known as "Huddud's House," is in your name. So, you will need to either appoint a lawyer to represent you or come to Damascus for a few days so that we can finish all procedures."

The news exceeded all of his expectations; he would have never guessed that his cold uncle was this generous.

"Unfortunately, I only found out about my uncle's death a few months ago. Regardless, I would rather not come."

"We actually have an immediate buyer for the house, but we will need you to appoint a representative to act on your behalf and then we can take care of the rest."

"Just out of curiosity, Mr. Rajeh, much is the house worth?"

"Approximately, fifty to sixty."

"Are you aware that a plane ticket to Damascus costs more than sixty thousand lira?" replied Dr. Anees sarcastically.

"Fifty to sixty million lira, Dr. Anees. We're talking about more than a million dollars."

Shocked, he stared silently at Hannah, who was listening to the conversation on the speaker. She could tell that the discussion was about something important, but she couldn't understand what they were saying.

"Hello. Hello. Dr. Anees, are you still with me?"

"Yes, yes. Give me until tomorrow and I will get back to you with a decision."

"OK, I will be waiting. Blessings."

He hung up and smiled. "If what this man says is true, then there is one million dollars waiting for me in Damascus." He began to explain to Hannah the story behind Huddud's House and how his uncle meant nothing to him before this phone call.

He tried his best to recall memories of his uncle from his childhood but could only remember a few. His uncle had gone into a state of solitude back in the seventies and did not allow anyone to visit him. He was involved in the process of post-independence policymaking, or so he was told. However, Dr. Anees was never convinced that his uncle was anything but rigid and silently dreadful.

The next day, he called the lawyer back and asked for more details about how long it would take to finalize the paperwork and what was expected of him. The lawyer explained that things could take between three to four weeks, that he would need to provide proof of identity, and that he had the choice of appointing any lawyer as his representative. He also said that the buyer was eager and waiting.

Hannah encouraged him to go, and he made an appointment to meet with the lawyer in person the following week. Taking his face in her hands, she said, "You haven't taken a break in years. Consider it a million-dollar vacation."

"You're right. But first, let's celebrate tonight. Let's go out for a proper meal. You choose the place."

"Oh my," she said. "Dr. Anees himself is asking me out to eat. No, no, I can't believe my ears!"

It was a special night that seemed to revive their cold relationship. They were reminded that they too could do other things besides working and attending medical conferences, like going out to a nice restaurant bustling with pleasures, taking the metro at night, walking and laughing together, and even sleeping together.

4
Fidel

A few days later, Fidel called him back.

"Yes, hello, Dr. Omran."

"My dear Fidel, I am calling to assure you that you are going to be fine. You can choose to go anytime and you will be treated like a VIP. Someone will be waiting for you at the airport, and all it will take is a five-minute visit to a friend's office over a cup of coffee to finish up some routine procedures."

Overcome with a sensation of joy mixed with fear, he replied, "This is great news, but are we talking about *their* kind of five minutes? The last person they invited for five minutes has been drinking his cup of coffee for five years."

"Fidel, get these toxic stories out of your mind. You have my word. And besides, I would not be working with you or your company if, God forbid, you were classified as an enemy of the homeland. Why don't we meet, and you can tell me exactly what this is all about."

Dr. Omran's wife came from a family known for its protective and financial loyalty to the regime. Some have gone as far as to say that Omran was managing the regime's money in the Arabian Gulf, Belarus, and China. As for calling him Doctor, no one knows how that came about. Omran was not a security official but was part of a new class of influential and loyal people who were granted considerable privileges in return for particular services.

Fidel agreed to drop by and take him out, promising to share with him, his trusted friend, the details of his story.

His hope of returning to Damascus awakened many memories in their graves, one from an era that he thought he had buried for eternity. He was willing to do anything for the chance to visit once more in his lifetime, and here was Omran Al-Khallouf renewing his only hope.

They set off in his BMW X6. They crossed Dubai from Sheikh Zayed Road towards Al-Diyafah Street, and from there to Khalid Bin Al-Waleed's Street, arriving at the Old District. He parked in a public lot across from HSBC. Once they stepped out of the car, they were drenched in the humidity of the place. The smell of Dubai was of fermenting organic matter evaporating from its gardens, mixed with the mist of sea air.

They walked to Dubai Creek. Fidel was first to jump onto the ferry, and they crossed to the other bank. He knew the city like the back of his hand. After having been stripped of a homeland and a hometown, he had fallen in love with the charm of Dubai.

Fidel began to tell his story to Dr. Omran. He would later learn that four different Mukhabarat branches had requested his name, and that Dr. Omran would use his story as a part of a report that he would later submit.

"Today, I am Syrian by memory. England did not replace a homeland, for no matter how hard I try, I will always be considered an immigrant carrying a British passport. I pay my taxes in full. In return, the Kingdom offers me protection. In Dubai, I can be both in one, British-Syrian. I have a dream job. I live a life of luxury, a dream for all Europeans. At the same time, I can live an ascetic and simple life in the desert and under the open sky, along with others who are also strangers to the city. I know the city's prostitutes and its finest businessmen. I have befriended its workers and I enjoy the company of beauty queens and celebrities. It's impossible to live this life in any city in the world but here. Dubai's nightlife is world-class, but those who indulge in it have mastered the art of secrecy. Have you come out here before, Dr. Omran?"

"No."

York Club is a four-star hotel and nightclub located in the heart of Dubai. Once they passed through a metal detector, Fidel greeted the security guards, hugged one of the waiters, and flirted jokingly with the female bartender. The ladies of the night were beginning to arrive; they were from the People's Republic of China as well as from other republics of the former Soviet Union, and there were Turks, Iranians, and Ethiopians with Rasta braids. Several of them greeted him by name with kisses and jokes. There was no need to disguise his name because everyone assumed it was fake. He ordered two glasses of cognac and said, "Beer causes a beer belly. Cognac, on the other hand, is the master of all drinks."

Dr. Omran stood contemplating the scene around him. It was difficult to carry on a conversation amid the loud crowd and the roaring desires that surrounded them. Some of the ladies sat at the bar, while others walked around eyeing the customers as they arrived: Arabs, Europeans, Indians, Russians, Turks, and throngs of visitors and residents. Some were there to get a feel for things and have a drink, others were there to enjoy the evening with a woman for as cheap as possible, hoping to make up for their emotional loneliness. The conversation usually began in English—*Where are you from?*

"Your nationality is what determines the bargaining process, where prices can range from fifty to five hundred dollars," explained Fidel. "Arabs usually bargain the most and are the rudest. Older European men are the most generous."

A sensual young blonde girl dressed in seductive clothes came up to him. She had a baby face and stoically cold blue eyes. She hugged Fidel in an amicable manner, and they exchanged a few words in both Russian and English. She then turned to Dr. Omran and greeted him warmly, informing him that this was the first time Fidel had ever brought a friend along.

Right then, a thirty-something woman in a tracksuit with headphones in her ears barged into their conversation. She peered at the golden-haired woman, who anxiously apologized, saying, "I have to go. Let's meet outside of work hours."

Irritated, the pimp said to Fidel, "As usual, you come and waste their time."

"I am not wasting anyone's time. I pay them—I just don't sleep with them."

"Does your friend want to celebrate tonight? I have a fresh group of girls who have just arrived."

"Ask him yourself."

The pimp asked Omran if he was looking for special company for the night.

"It depends on the girl," he said, in a joking tone.

She left for a few moments and returned with a breathtakingly beautiful girl who didn't look a day over twenty. "This is Maria," she said. "She is Ukranian and has only been in Dubai for two weeks. Her price is 2,000 dirhams per night, but because you are a friend of Fidel, you'll get a discount. Let's say 1,500."

"Two weeks is a long time, Boss," Fidel said with a laugh. "And because he is my friend, he won't be paying anything, and Maria will be with the two of us tonight."

"You have until tomorrow afternoon before you'll need to bring her back."

"Done," he promised, placing a bundle of cash in the pimp's hand.

"Do you want to sleep with her?" he whispered to Omran.

"Of course not!" Fidel called out Maria's name, and said, "You are our guest tonight and we would like to invite you out for dinner. We don't want sex. We've already paid your price." Looking confused, she nodded.

"We'll take you to your home so you can freshen up and change into an evening gown. Tonight, you will be our guest of honor, and my friend and I will celebrate you."

"You're exactly what the girls say about you—the prince of Dubai's nightlife," she said, giving him a warm smile.

With a burst of laughter, he replied, "They also say I'm the dumbest customer in Dubai."

Maria played the violin and the piano. She loved Giannini and Mozart. She paid $3,000 to the visa agency, who told her that she would be working as a musician in a reputable hotel. Upon arrival, she learned that slave traders had seized her passport and were demanding $10,000 within three months. In the meantime, they assured her that for the time being she would be working in the oldest profession in the world. Maria shared with them that she was hoping to pay her debt within two months and resume her studies in music, and that this was an experience from which she learned a great deal.

Over dinner at a Moroccan restaurant in Jumeirah called the One and Only, next to Media City, Maria confessed that her situation forced her to mature too quickly and hardened her heart, and repeated that she nevertheless had learned a great deal.

"Sometimes I have to sleep with five men in a day," she admitted.

Cutting his steak, Fidel asked at once, "Do you really want to go back to the university?"

"Without a doubt."

"Then enjoy this last night. As of tomorrow, you are free. I will bring you your passport," he said with certainty.

An Arab band was playing music for Abed Al-Wahab, while Omran sat in astonishment of this strange character named Fidel. They finished their dinner. Maria insisted on staying the night with Fidel, but he instead drove her to her residence, assuring her that he would return the next day at noon to pay her debt in full and promising that this would be her last night in Dubai.

She left the car in a state of disbelief, and before walking away she stood at the window and said, "Please tell me if this is a joke. Don't play with me."

"Tonight is your last night in Dubai, if that's what you really want."

As soon as she left, he called the pimp and told her that he would pay Maria's debt. She explained that things were not that simple, and that she would get back to him once she got in touch with her employer. Thirty minutes later, she called back to inform him of their approval, and they agreed to meet at noon to pick up Maria's passport in exchange for full payment.

"OK, crazy man," laughed the pimp.

Fidel turned to Dr. Omran and told him there was yet another side to Dubai, permeated by silence and serenity, one that he wished to introduce him to once he'd experienced the city's fervorous clamor.

It was almost 4 am. A heavy silence enveloped the city. There was no sound, no cars blowing their horns or merchants shouting at the top of their lungs. The city was muted, its doors shut and its balconies absent of people drinking their coffee. It was a silence that was awe-inspiring. But had Sheikh Muhyiddin Ibn Arabi been summoned, it would have only taken a single glance at the place before he turned away on his camel, muttering, "that which shines cannot be relied upon."

It appeared as if anger had no place in the city, as if this was a peaceful city. No one was interested in sharing anything with anyone. The cars were like locked containers. The luxurious houses were closed spaces, like corked boxes, with no chimneys to breathe in happiness and no outlets to exhale anger or moans. The residents were swollen with silence; they had become increasingly isolated, sitting behind their steering wheels or computer screens, stuck between office and apartment walls, and obsessed with bank accounts. Everything in the city grew amid this silence; even skyscrapers and grand business centers sprouted without noise or disruption. The only sound that could be heard, if one listened closely, was the clicking of calculators.

He drove his BMW to an area called Al-Qouz, where workers congregated. The voices of these workers, who came from Kerala, Bangladesh, and Kashmir, gradually broke the peaceful silence in a city slowly peeking its head up from slumber.

He stopped the car next to one of the camps as workers swarmed toward a line of buses. Blank-faced but strong in body, their clothes gray, they looked as if they had emerged from underground.

"Some of these workers earn less in a month than what Maria makes in half a day," he said, as he turned on the ignition. They headed for the highway towards Rawyet Al-Ain Street, and the city began to disappear behind them, the landscape turning into a desert with reddish sand dunes. He turned onto a side road that stood at the edge of the dunes. "Take off your shoes," he said to Omran.

"Enjoy every footstep," he said, as they made their way barefoot over a dune. "This desert has amazing energy. The spirit of the place resides here. This charming stretch is what I love about this city."

He grabbed a handful of sand and let it seep through his fingers. He contemplated Dubai from a distance, its lights faintly shimmering,

"Dubai is like a handful of sand, impossible to capture. If you see her as a city of money, then that is what she becomes. It is how you see her, a city of pleasure, a city of peace, or a city without spirit. She gives you exactly what you wish to take from her."

"And how do you see her?" asked Omran.

"I don't love or hate her. I simply respect her. She doesn't get into your business as long as you don't interfere in the affairs of her indigenous populations."

"So, you're saying there are two separate parts to the city, one for its citizens and the other for expatriates?"

"Actually, it's more like three, but no one talks about the third Dubai. If only people could be a little kinder to the third part, because without it, Dubai wouldn't be."

"Are you talking about its nightlife?"

"Not at all. Sex work is part of Dubai, like in all other cities, but Dubai happens to be the only Arab city that does not lie about it. There are cities that claim chastity and preach virtuousness but are actually rife with debauchery. I'm talking about a third part of Dubai—made up of the weak, the workers who serve it, build it up, and clean after it. A Dubai that is made up of its servants, drivers, day laborers, and armies of invisible workers."

"This is the leftist speaking in you," Omran snapped slyly. "Now I know why you're wanted in four different Mukhabarat branches!"

It took Fidel a moment to digest what Omran had said. He didn't comment, but with a faint smile, he continued, "Dubai is not yet complete. It will only be complete when it is able to face the facts. If it survives the confrontations, it has the potential to be an ideal city in this world. If it continues to ignore the facts, then it is bound for disaster. At the end of the day, Dubai will pay the price. As for me and the likes of me, all we will have to do is leave."

"But what is the real danger for Dubai?"

"It makes no sense for a city to be the most advanced in marketing, architecture, and technology and still lag behind the rest of the world when it comes to humans and their development. As long as a sorcerer can convince seven out of ten people that he is a friend of the blue jinn and can bring people back from the dead and impregnate the barren, the city will remain in danger."

The only sound to be heard amid the enveloping silence of the desert was the hissing of the sands. It is true that traces cannot be left on sand, but the history of the desert is not read by what's been sketched on its surface, but by what is hidden below. As they sat and listened closely, taking in the beauty, the mystery, and the purity of the air, Fidel Abdullah's voice broke the silence.

"I know that you've been assigned to write a report about me for the Mukhabarat. I'm not interested in pretending that I am patriotic or in praising the regime. All I care about is having the chance to visit my father's grave and to walk at night through the streets of Damascus."

The sand hissed softly at the slightest breeze.

"I am not going to lie to you, Fidel. I have been asked to submit an evaluation on you, not to report you. I am not an informant. I am a businessman, and what I say about you is equivalent to being a guarantor. I have relatives and acquaintances who work with the Mukhabarat. You know what I mean, right?

"They have questions that need answers. Who helped you get out of Syria? They have questions about your English wife, Helen, because according to their sources, she worked for the British Intelligence. And also about your second wife, who is said to be the daughter of one of the heads of an extremist Islamic organization in London. They also want to know about your relationship with Sheikh Ghassan, the imam of the London Muslim Mosque, who is Palestinian. They want to know if you're still in touch with him. To be honest, the report the Syrian Embassy in the UK submitted on you is quite confusing. On one hand, you are presented as an Islamic extremist, and on the other, you are nothing but an opportunist, an alcoholic, and a womanizer. I have used all my influence to secure this trip to Damascus for you, and I must give them something back in return. Fidel, my gut feeling says you are patriotic and that we can work together for the sake of our country. I don't want anything to happen to you, but I don't need a headache because of you either."

Fidel got up, went to the car, and brought back a blue chest that he took on trips. He opened it, took out a thermos, and poured coffee into two cups. Under the faint traces of moonlight and first tidings of dawn, he started to talk.

5

Anees

Dr. Anees reserved his ticket to Damascus on Syrian Airways. Because of his close ties with the Syrian ambassador, he was able to quickly renew his passport at the Syrian embassy. Although he no longer identified as Syrian, he did not care to be considered an Englishman except when it came to technical matters.

He held no strong patriotic feelings for this perplexing place called Syria. Any sort of narrow classification made him feel suffocated, but what bothered him most about the United Kingdom was having to continuously fill out forms that insisted on classifying him according to ethnicity, race, and religion. He was always quick to tick the "Prefer not to say" box. Waiting for his plane at Heathrow, he called Sami, who lived in Edinburgh.

"*As-salamu alaykum*, baba," greeted Sami.

Dr. Anees felt uneasy about the change in Sami's personality in the past two years. He had become deeply involved in religion, seldom returned home on holidays, and spent most of his time with a group of friends involved in charity work for the Muslim community in Britain.

Dr. Anees was not religious. His only recollections of religion were of celebrating the coming of the month of Ramadan with his family. The fragments of memories that remained with him were of the beautiful lanterns with which they decorated their home, his grandfather's fragrance of spice and sandalwood as he took him to the mosque, and the flavor of the most delicious Damascene food and sweets. For Dr. Anees, Ramadan was simply a mixture of aromas and flavors that brought back a distant, happy childhood. But he didn't take a stand against religious people. His relationship with Islam was more of a cultural identity; he neither sought to root it nor cast it off. His main concern was presenting himself as a successful surgeon, a man who dedicated a quarter century of his life to books, references, hospitals, and patients.

Sami spoke Arabic fluently, not only because of Dr. Anees's efforts, but also because Dr. Hannah made sure that her son always attended Arabic classes. However, Dr. Anees was a very strict father, particularly when it came to his son's grades, where he would never accept anything less than an A. At university, Sami defied his father's expectations when he decided to study history and linguistics and later specialized in Islamic studies. Although this course of study was not a great source of pride for Dr. Anees, he had no choice but to trust his accomplished son and embrace the fact that "your children are not your children."[5]

It took him a few minutes to explain the nature of his trip to Sami, who in turn wished his father safe travels, saying, "I wish I could have visited Damascus with you, Dad. Maybe another time." Hearing his son's wish, Dr. Anees felt sad. He had never seriously considered this idea before. Sami's words stayed with him during the flight. His son had grown up too quickly; twenty-two years had passed in the blink of an eye.

A cloud of unexplainable melancholy continued to envelop him. He felt his anxiety escalate as he thought about his return to a homeland of quicksand, a place where he could not be certain where to safely place his foot. At the same time, part of him longed to see the university friends he had left behind. He had seen some of them throughout the years, in Dubai and London, but was always keen to be with them yet again. He wondered which of them kept the memories alive amid the currents of absence. He thought about how even wonderful relationships come to an end, devoured by emptiness and erased with the passing of days, and how friends can seep through our fingers like a handful of sand.

The plane departed, bidding London farewell, and the captain announced that their flight to Damascus would take five and a half hours.

---

5   From *The Prophet*, by Khalil Gibran

As he heard the captain pronounce the name Damascus, Dr. Anees was overcome with a swarm of feelings and memories that he thought were tamed and locked away.

His most recent memories of Damascus were of the year he met Hannah. With her help, he decided to resume his studies in London. They ended up getting married shortly afterward, and quickly and unexpectedly had their son. Gradually, their ideal, quiet life fell into routine and slowly turned into dull repetition. Neither of them cared for a noisy life, both fully devoted to their work. Their work schedules rarely allowed them to cross paths, so they resorted to leaving notes in the kitchen to share the details of their daily lives.

During their ninth year of marriage, while Hannah was in the United States, they endured a yearlong period of distress and silence. Finally, she called him, suggesting that they should rethink their marriage. She had met another man and wanted him to know this before the relationship with this other person evolved.

Dr. Anees received the news calmly. He went to a bar in his neighborhood, had half a glass of beer, and quickly called her back, telling her that he would wait for her. He said he would respect whatever decision she made, but asked that she keep Sami in mind. For the next several days, he tossed and turned in bed in excruciating pain. Finally, his organized mind took hold, and he was able to focus on his work. But ever since, he shielded his heart with a thick layer of indifference and detachment.

Four months later, Hannah returned from the United States. She sent him a message indicating her time of arrival, and also that she missed him and Sami. They waited for her at the airport and went back to home together. He didn't ask about what happened, and neither did she. The subject was never discussed again.

Soon, their intimacy also faded away. They became two distanced bodies brought together by chance, just as they had been before he left.

He reserved a room at Hotel Dedeman for three weeks. The airport had not changed much, its employees with the same long, gloomy faces.

Outside the airport was a huge photo of the young president with "WE LOVE YOU" printed in bold red. Next to it stood a larger photo of his dead father. Anees thought to himself, *It's obviously impossible for this kid to hype himself up without his father's photo next to him; in reality, Hafez never left, and his heavy shadow eternally remains.*

The airport road was poorly paved and edged with dwarfed shrubs. As people prepared to retire for the night, their houses at the entrance of Damascus looked somber. The sight of a lit-up Mount Qasioun took his breath away. He contemplated the streets, unable to feel the old intimacy. Some of the buildings had aged rather tragically. What was new in the city was the horrible traffic jams and the agitating honking of cars.

He opened the window of the car. The air reeked of diesel fumes, and he felt as if he were breathing in the smoke. As he arrived to Al-Baramkeh square, immediately before the President's Bridge, he was taken aback by a scene of dirty raised flags, filthy and crumbling buildings, and eroded walls tarnished with slogans. It was obvious everything had been neglected and that no one cared. A familiar phrase appeared on a wall, one he noticed as he left the country: "There is no life in this country aside from progress and socialism—in the words of the courageous comrade Hafez Al-Assad." But the timeworn phrase had been erased in part to read, "There is no life in this country ... Hafez Al-Assad." *A true reflection of the fact that no matter how powerful or omnipresent a presence may be, everything is bound for decay*, he thought to himself.

As he turned onto the President's Bridge, the Four Seasons Hotel appeared in front of him, overlooking the Barada River. *You leave for twenty-five years only to return and find that your city has been penetrated by hotels standing erect in its center.* He refused to be overcome with grief and was even more determined to leave as soon as possible, no matter the price.

From a sixth-floor balcony, he watched the traffic and city lights. Damascus looked beautiful but also sad. He felt tired after his long journey, and he started to fall asleep soon after dinner. The food had lifted his spirits. Damascene food tickles one's taste buds and fulfills the stomach's desires, boosting the lowest of moods. He changed his mind, and having decided not to sleep, he dialed a friend's number.

"Hello," came from the other side.

"Guess who this is?"

"I'm sorry. Who is this?"

"Is Al-Kamal Café still open?"

"Yes, but who's this again?"

"Aren't you Issa Darwish, who famously said, 'An old patient is better than a new doctor?'"

"No way! Anees?" shouted Issa in disbelief. They agreed to meet in the morning. He turned off the lamp and fell asleep shortly after, overcome by a feeling of affection that he had not had for years.

He felt like a total stranger in a city bursting with life, a suffocated city that was anticipating news about the Arab Spring in Tunisia and Egypt. After breakfast, he went to meet Issa. With every step he took, reflections from the past returned to him with scents and memories. *This city is impossible to forget, and upon returning to it, you feel complete,* he thought to himself. He felt a sense of lightheartedness as his memory guided his steps. He recalled excerpts of poems that he had written during his early days, before he discovered that to live through poetry, with poetry, or for poetry was one of the most difficult and miserable of human experiences.

He felt a mixture of ambiguity and motivating joy. The streets of Damascus were shrouded by January's frigidity, but beneath the surface they burned with embers of accumulated anger that no one had ever expected would erupt one day.

He had lived a serene childhood growing up in the Muhajireen neighborhood. His father passed away early in his life, and his mother remarried and moved to Saudi Arabia. His silent and ambiguous uncle, Badr Al-Deen, took over the family expenses, along with his grandmother. He eventually entered the College of Medicine, where he also met his friends, and began experimenting with poetry. Gradually, this stormy emotional stage ended once he graduated, met Hannah, and traveled to the United Kingdom.

He looked forward to meeting with Issa Darwish and catching up on everything that had taken place in his absence. Issa arrived first. Before entering, he looked closely at Issa through the glass partition. His hair was thick but gray, his round face darker, but his chain smoking and his devotion to reading the newspapers had apparently not changed a bit.

Quietly, he entered with a smile and arms outstretched to embrace his old friend and brother. They stared at one another, tears filling their eyes. They examined the signs of time on one another. Anees took care of his hair. He looked healthy and comfortable, full-bodied and without a belly. Issa began to speak of all that had happened over the years and where everyone had ended up, then he turned to the details of his own experience.

"During my sixth year at the College of Medicine, I was detained. Six years later, I was released, and I continued with my studies and graduate work. I hold a degree in medicine but I don't ever use it, nor does it mean anything to me. I also have three poetry collections. I call them collections, but to be truthful, I laugh at my nonsense. I have been divorced twice, and I am aiming for four divorces. Brother, the Sharia allows for four wives, and so I will give marriage, and divorce, a shot four times."

He carried on, "I am an employee at the Ministry of Health. I work six minutes per day. I go to work, sign in, tell them that I am repulsed by them, and then I leave. At the end of the month, I am paid shit for what I have to put up with, an amount equivalent to getting drunk three times. I am currently working on being a script writer because it's the new thing and it's how they buy writers. I think I'm ready to finally sell my first script. Maybe then I can buy a house. It's time for this Bedouin here to rest. And I am still living in the same home you know. So that is my news."

"And you, Dr. Anees, tell me about you, and what brings you to Damascus after all these years?" asked Issa.

"I am here because of my uncle Badr Al-Deen's will. He left the house for me. I think I will sell it and go back."

"Huddud's House, next to the Al-Jisr Al-Abyad?"

"Yes, that's the one."

"You will definitely find a buyer," Issa said, clearly excited by the news. "All these old Damascene houses are selling quickly and are turned into restaurants and hotels. The reform project has eaten up everything. There are only a few pieces that remain of Damascus before it will be a completely occupied territory. They truly believe that they will remain forever."

Seeing Dr. Anees's smile fade away, he reassured him, "Don't worry. As long as we don't name the older brother or his family, everything else is allowed."

"That's good to know. I can see some real improvements. Today, as I walked downtown, I came across the same brands that we have in London."

"Yes, Doc. Here we earn less than they do in Burkina Faso, and we pay more taxes than you do in Britain. A pair of shoes at a shop downtown is equivalent to a whole month's salary. In other words, the salary of an employee here is worth the same as a shoe," said Issa, with a mix of cynicism and anger.

Anees tried to calm him down. He had not yet rid himself of the paranoia that had long plagued him. Even the walls seemed to have voracious ears that picked up any hint of criticism. He realized that this fear still nested in his consciousness, despite the years.

"Dr. Anees, the true Damascus is dying," said Issa, in a less acute tone. "Truth only dwells in what is happening in the outskirts of the city. The drought during the past three years brought over one million people to Damascus. They left their lands and came from the countryside. Then the regime sold the north to the Turks and the south to mafias."

"Why did you not leave?" Anees asked his friend, hoping to ameliorate the tone of the conversation.

"After all these years, you want me to start over? Where and how? I can't leave Damascus. The day I leave this city, even if just to a nearby town, I know I will feel lost, stripped, and suffocated. I have gotten used to the smell, the people, and even the pain. These things are inseparable from who we are. Living here is like the process of photosynthesis; we exhale our heartbreak, and we receive back the oxygen of hope." He continued, "In Damascus we console one another. Other cities could never tolerate us. We are addicted to Damascus." Changing the topic abruptly, he said, "I was so happy to receive your message, Anees. I got you what you asked for."

He passed him a piece of paper with two numbers—for Abbas Jawhar and Layl Haddad. "They will be very happy to hear from you. Personally, I rarely meet with Abbas. Every once in a while, he comes over late at night for a glass of arak. We don't say a word to one another. He then curses me and leaves. There is nothing left for us to talk about. We are at the point of killing each other at any given moment."

"That bad? What happened? You were joined at the hip in university." They giggled joyfully.

"Today, Abbas is a high-ranking security officer. He has the power to kill you and bring you back to life. I owe to him the fact that I have a job. But we can't get along anymore. I feel ashamed to be with him among our friends. And he feels as ashamed of me with officers and businessmen. He always insults me. He tells me I'm full of shit, and that everyone has their lives worked out except for idiots like me. But I never let it go, and I tell him that at least I can put my head on the pillow and sleep in peace because I don't have blood on my hands, and I'm not a bystander in the face of tyranny. He seldom visits me, but I always leave him the key—"

"Under the plant?"

"Exactly. My God, you still remember?"

"And how is Layl?"

"Like she's always been, as kind as ever. She is married to an oncologist. His name is Adel and they have two children, Mayar and Manar. She is now working at a private hospital."

"Listen Issa, it's almost time for my next appointment with the lawyer and I must go now. I am staying here for two or three weeks. Let's keep in touch. If you know of a trusted lawyer, please let me know."

Issa took out his phone and found the number of a lawyer named Samia Saeed. "She will likely help you, but my advice is that you don't sell it to them."

"Who do you mean by 'them'?"

Issa didn't respond. He looked down at his newspaper and took a sip of the leftover coffee.

6
Fidel

Although he enjoyed telling Omran fragments of his life, there were times when he was no longer addressing Omran but instead speaking to himself, and discovering who he was in the process. His dream of returning to Damascus, laid to rest so long ago, was now becoming a reality, and with it returned the hissing of his past life. As dawn set in, Fidel continued his narrative.

Although I had no choice but to study law, I dedicated my time and efforts to attending lectures of sheikhs, professors, and scholars in the Faculty of Sharia Law, as it was part of the College of Law and happened to be in the same building. I spent most of my time at the library, studying the scholarship that would inform and strengthen my knowledge on my religion and identity.

I met her in the library. She emanated energy and kindness. She was two years ahead of me at the same college. I didn't know how to begin the conversation with her. It was one sentence that opened a window to a new world that would come to change my life. A soft, feminine voice rattled the routine of the place: "Are you studying law to become a lawyer or an officer?"

"Pardon me?" I replied, astonished at the woman standing in front of me with a smile drawn on her tan, blushed face. She wore white pants and a baggy white shirt. Her black hair hung loosely on her shoulders. She repeated the question insistently and added, "You know, no one respects this college because we all know that there is no law or rights here. Most of the students were placed in this college based on their grades and not their desires. Anyway, I am sorry to intrude but I always see you here in the library and it's rare to see students taking things seriously in this college."

I averted my gaze, blaming myself for allowing temptation to get the better of me and thought: indeed, women in the world should be veiled; such provocation could truly lead one astray.

I ended up staying with her until the evening, heedless of all the teachings and warnings I had learned. I couldn't bring myself to leave. We continued to meet day after day; we talked about history, Islam, and society.

Her name was Ruwaida Al-Sha'ir. Her father was a well-known doctor and a socialist. She was an avid reader, fluent in French, a student of law at our university, and studying English at the British Council. I had never come across anyone who spoke with such passion about literature, history, or Islam as she did. She was familiar with every reference I mentioned, she added insight to my own knowledge, and pushed me to expand and diversify my sources. She also introduced me to Sadeq Naihoum's *Islam in Captivity*, a work that shook me to the core.

She was kind, intelligent, and educated. She believed that I had the right to be what I wished to be. I couldn't resist her, and in a matter of a few weeks, I broke several taboos. I visited the university's canteen to drink tea with her, we walked the streets of Damascus together eating corn on the cob, and I enrolled at the British Institute to improve my moderately proficient English skills. Ruwaida helped me; she was understanding of my religious commitments, appreciated my way of life, and changed my perspective on her, someone I considered a shamelessly unveiled, liberated women.

Our relationship was difficult to explain or categorize. We were two friends with very different views on how to live life on Earth and what we thought of the skies, but what brought us together was the way we could be fully with one another. For me, she no longer represented the image of a seductive woman, nor did I represent to her the stereotypical frightening, always-blamed Muslim man. Together we became an exceptional, spiritual energy of work and love.

She discovered my talent for calligraphy and drawing, and I encouraged her skills at organization and the way she stood up for important ethical causes. I never knew exactly how I felt about her. Each experience we lived took us to a deeper level, and this remained the case until the evening she showed up at the university and said, "Come with me."

"Where to?"

"Don't ask. Someone is very interested in meeting you. Bring your artwork. All of it."

I didn't resist. I fully trusted her. She took me to the studio of one of the most famous Syrian artists, Nizar Al-Sakhour. The place smelled of the fermentation of colors, a mixture of Sufi passion and the scent of oils, fabrics, and dyes. There was a huge bookshelf with a great number of books on anatomy, as well as encyclopedias in Arabic, Italian, and English. It was a sanctuary of art, and this old artist was a sensational Sufi. I asked God's forgiveness under my breath when I spotted empty booze bottles and photos of naked women. I felt shame and spiteful jealousy at the sight of a painting on the wall of a naked woman who resembled Ruwaida. After a short conversation, he began flipping through my work. Holding a white piece of paper and a charcoal pen, he pointed at Ruwaida and said, "Love her."

"Pardon me?" I replied anxiously.

"I am telling you that you have ten minutes to love her, or in other words, to draw her."

I obediently complied without stealing a glance at my friend, who stood with her arms crossed at her chest. She looked at me with eyes that were beaming with encouragement. As I drew her, he continued flipping through my sketches. In less than ten minutes, I was finished.

Smoking his cigarette, he studied my sketch and said, "The Faculty of Arts at Damascus University graduates an artist once every five years, a painter every ten years, and one hundred losers every year. You are talented my son, and greatly so. You made a mistake by not studying the arts. You are an artist who lost his way."

That statement was the point when I broke the promise I made to my father, earned the long-drawn disappointment of my uncles, and initiated the catastrophe that befell my life.

I retook the high school baccalaureate exam and entered the College of Arts. As Fadl, I handed a part of me to Fidel, who began to get better acquainted with Damascus, accompanied by an unreserved Ruwaida and her friends, who were bent on changing the country, no matter the price.

I did not enjoy their gatherings. Most of them, with the exception of those given by Ruwadia, had a hostile attitude towards religion. Those in attendance considered it their worst enemy, more abhorrent than tyranny. They cursed God, ridiculed religious people, accused veiled women of backwardness, and deliberately provoked those who fasted during Ramadan.

Once Ruwaida came to see that I was of a different mindset, she was no longer keen to invite me to their meetings or to participate in their activities. But our friendship was separate from all else.

My feelings towards her—a combination of routine, security, and suppressed desires that I strived to sublimate into an exalted friendship—were growing by the day. Occasionally, I would be overcome by feelings of jealousy that I was powerless to subdue. I once confessed this to her. We were in Al-Jahez Park, in central Damascus. We were feeding the ducks during one of our routine weekly dates, and I felt an intense and irresistible desire for her. I reached for the cuff of her shirt and began to pinch and wrinkle it. I wanted to keep us from committing a sin, but at the same time I craved to feel any trace of her. She stared at me in surprise with her kind and meek eyes, and asked, "What's the matter?" Her tone was rather welcoming, not inquisitive.

I was not able to answer. I couldn't gather the courage to tell her that I lusted for her and that I loved her. I had an immense desire to hold her to my chest, or rather for her to embrace me. Unhesitant, she moved closer to me and, with an intense sense of madness, she embraced me. It was then that I first smelled the unforgettable scent of seduction and pleasure. It became entwined in my being. Ever since, I have become an addict of such aromas. She didn't wear perfume, but she had a distinct fragrance from an herbal ointment that she massaged into her skin. As the saying goes, if we took heed, we would find that many a time the nose falls in love before the eyes.

We walked until we came to a tree in bloom that stood under a broken streetlight. I was grateful to whomever had broken it. As she leaned against the tree trunk, I kissed her for the first time. It was the first time I ever stood leaning against a woman's torso, and within a few minutes I felt an explosion between my thighs. Touching Ruwaida, whose essence was like that of a tree, was enough to create a storm, cause my leaves to fall, and create a flood that left my pants wet. I collapsed, as if I were free-falling. All my desire was replaced with chastising guilt and acute embarrassment. She embraced my head tightly and drew it hard against her shoulder, and her earring fell. As I stood entangled in the branches of this woman, I continued to fall silently like her earring to the ground. She kissed my forehead as I bent down to grab the earring. I asked if I could keep it and we continued to walk.

On our way out of and as we got to the gate at the park, she whispered, "Untuck your shirt and cover your pants."

Utterly humiliated, I did as she said, but that spot leaked into my inner being, splitting me into two characters who have not stopped battling since that day.

That was the last time I saw her. Two days later, one of her comrades in the Party knocked on the door of my room. Horrified and panting, he said, "You need to get out of Damascus tonight. They have arrested Ruwaida and they are looking for you."

"You know that I have nothing to do with any of her activities," I replied.

"I know, but they don't know that. They're even arresting people on the charge of reading the Party's newspaper, so you can imagine what they'll do with you when they find out you're the closest friend of someone who's on the paper's editorial board!

"Here, this is an ID of one of our friends that you can use to cross the border into Lebanon. Do you know how lucky you are to have applied for a visa to the UK to study for that English course? You can actually use it now to get into the UK. My advice is that you leave out of Lebanon, not from here. Ruwaida was expecting this to happen. A couple of days ago she asked me to give this to you." He handed me $3,000 and left quickly.

In the less than twelve hours since her arrest, my entire life in Damascus collapsed. A few days later, I found myself in London, thrown out and fleeing, and enrolled in a second-level English course.

7

Anees

"Mr. Rajeh sends his apologies. He had to leave Damascus for an urgent matter," said the trainee working in Rajeh Al-Agha's office, "Here are the house keys. I think you have the directions to the house, and the inheritance papers are ready. All we need from you is to appoint a lawyer to finish the procedures. If you give us the power of attorney, we can complete it on your behalf. Please review the terms of the contract and check on the house. Your appointment is scheduled for the day after tomorrow."

"How long will the sale of the house take?"

"Between one week to ten days maximum. Everything should be finalized by then."

He grabbed the papers and the key and left Rajeh's office at 29 May Street and took a taxi to Al-Jisr Al-Abyad. On the way, he called the lawyer, Samia Saeed, and asked if she had time to meet him at the house. She said she would be there in two hours.

He arrived at the house, but no flock of memories swarmed him, no old feelings resurfaced. After having been away for so many years, a thick layer of protective fat seemed to have coated his mind and heart, and a sour taste of indifference permeated his senses.

He entered through a low tin gate and walked three meters down a long narrow passage decorated with *muqarnas*. The walkway could only fit one person. To his right was a large courtyard more than one hundred square meters in circumference, open to the sky, with a dried-up fountain in its center surrounded by a few citron and orange trees. A bare grape vine remained amid an emptiness drenched in sorrow.

He walked to the center of the courtyard, his eyes scanning around the place. There were more than thirteen closed rooms distributed over two floors and the area was open to light at any time of day. Faint glimpses of memories flashed in his head as he carefully began to open each door one by one.

He opened the door of the *liwan*,[6] turned the light on, and stood there with an astonished expression, as if seeing the place for the first time. Vintage luxury permeated the place. The reverent antiques and the splendor of the architecture were stunning. There was a large mirror in the center as well as a few leather and soft velvet sofas placed together harmoniously, and an entire wall lined elegantly with old photos in brass frames. Some of the photos were of public figures, leaders, and politicians from more than a century ago—past presidents and dignitaries all photographed during their visits to the house. It was obvious that the uncle had insisted that a photo be taken of every visitor to the house, and each one be appended with a name, date, and occasion. The photos of fourteen presidents who had visited the house were proudly on display, but there was not even a single photo of Hafez Al-Assad or his son on the wall.

He continued to tour the house and entered his uncle's office. In it was a massive library clad in black. A skull was placed on a small table, along with some writing materials including an inkwell, a quill, and blotter paper. On the table was also a cup of water, a piece of bread, and dishes of salt, sulfur, and mercury. Strange slogans hung on the wall and seemed to be speaking to him: "If you have entered this place out of curiosity, kindly leave. If you are afraid, stop and do not continue. If you decide to continue, you will be freed from your elements and will emerge from the depth of hell and into the light."

---

6   A *liwan* is an architectural feature found in traditional Arabic and Islamic architecture. It is a rectangular-shaped space that is usually open on one side and has an elevated platform or dais on the other side. The open side often faces a courtyard or an exterior space, and the elevated platform serves as a reception area or a private sitting room.

A cold chill raced up his spine and he wanted to flee, but curiosity, mixed with fear, and an overwhelming desire to continue, prompted him to stay. He opened a drawer and contemplated the carefully laminated folders. He flicked through the pages of one and found an ID card for his uncle: *Name: Badr Al-Deen Al-Aghawani. Profession: Merchant and lawyer. Date of Affiliation with Freemasonry Fraternity: 1939. Place of Residence: Damascus, Al-Jisr Al-Abyad. Entered Apprentice: 1939; Fellow Craft: 1935; Master Mason: 1955.*

Lulled by the charm of the place, he was suddenly awakened by the sound of the doorbell. He hurried to the gate and opened it.

"I was about to leave," she said, with an angry face and burning eyes.

He was apologetic but felt something blossom in him. *She entered like a storm with two feet made of clouds, her voice the sound of the wind*, he thought, and wished he could write down the thought before he lost it. He repeated it to himself so he would not forget. He recalled how he used to write such things during his youth, during a time that he had a love relationship with words.

She entered as a storm with two feet made of clouds, her voice the sound of wind. He closed the gate and followed her through the narrow passage, whispering to himself, *This woman is made of the wind.*

She stood next to the dry fountain, and after a few indifferent glances at her surroundings, she began to speak. "You are Issa and Layl's friend?"

"Yes," he replied, nodding his head with his eyes fixed on her, his lips pursed like a child.

"You want to sell the house?"

"Yes," he said, with the same childish look, a smile hiding behind his lips.

"Do you know who will be buying it?"

He shook his head, swaying right and left, as if he were listening to *Qudud Halabiya* from Aleppo, indicating that he did not yet meet the buyer.

"Do you know what this house represents and what it's worth?"

He stopped moving his head and shrugged, a look of curiosity on his face.

She circled the fountain and walked toward the rooms, her eyes glowing with fondness and awe. "This wall is from the remains of the Temple of Adad and dates back to 3000 BCE," she said. "Under the room where the food was once stored are Aramaic Greek inscriptions that say, 'He who owns Damascus rules the world.' This house was the only space to practice freedom of speech in this country for the past fifty years. Anyone who entered was safe. Even Hafez Al-Assad who suffocated his people everywhere else allowed politics to be spoken about here. This house has preserved the memory of Syrians and the memory of Damascus. Each chamber in it has its story, every room its history, and even minute details have significance. And here you are, ready to sell it without having the slightest idea who the buyer is or what the house means!"

With a faint smile, Anees shook his head, feeling his impatience rise with the churning of this woman made of the wind.

"Look at you, happy to sell it! Who in the world sells himself? Or is it that you no longer care since you are now British and only concerned with yourself?"

He stood frozen; his cynical smile disappeared. The place seemed to have become devoid of air, as if this woman made of the wind were an asphalt truck that had emptied its load on him. He replied defensively in English, holding back but ready to attack. "Excuse me!" Then, continuing in Arabic, "I'm sorry, I will not allow you to speak to me like this."

"I am sorry," she said, in a milder tone. "I am anxious and angry at the idea of selling the house."

He simply looked at her with an understanding expression, but also one that demanded an explanation. She explained that the house was priceless, but that now they want to turn it into a hotel or a restaurant. She said it was being sold to new masters who had nothing but contempt for Damascus, and that she, alongside a group of activists, were trying to register the house with UNESCO's World Heritage List and turn it into a museum to preserve a Syrian memory that was on the verge of extinction.

Dr. Anees was not convinced by her story. He rejected conspiracy theories and found it hard to accept that there was an ambiguous group of evil people who were systematically lurking and plotting to obliterate people, confiscate their history, and eradicate cities and humans. He always mocked his friends as they analyzed and spoke of mysterious systematic forces aiming to target history and religion. He believed that Arabs did not need others to conspire against them, for they conspired enough against themselves. He agreed that there was a power struggle, but he was just as convinced that Arabs brought disasters onto themselves.

He did not wish to relate his perspective to the angry woman. He was not interested in what she had to say about the historical value of the house or preserving it as a Syrian memory; nor did he care about the regime's desire to destroy Damascus and take revenge on it. All that really mattered to him was the monetary value of the house, which is why he was so taken aback when Samia declared, "The value of the house is equivalent to more than six million dollars, and its historical value is priceless." He then realized that he was being subjected to fraud and theft.

He asked Samia to join him for a cup of coffee so they could discuss things further. They made their way to a nearby journalist club. He was set on being direct and pragmatic.

"What exactly am I expected to do, dear?"

"All we are asking of you, Doctor, is that you make it known that you wish to turn Huddud's House into a museum, and we will mobilize all our efforts to make sure that we prevent it from harm. I have a dossier that was prepared by academics, specialists, researchers, and archaeologists that affirms the value of the house. Everything has been translated into English, French, and Italian. We're only missing a few evaluations from some notable experts and then everything should be good to go."

"I respect everything that you've shared, but the matter is much simpler for me. I want to sell the house for the best price. I don't mind trying to work together to find a buyer who is interested in both the monetary and the moral value of the house. I will be grateful if we can finalize the deal in a few weeks, and because you and I share trusted friends, I am happy to add to your personal fee one percent of the value of the house or whatever deal we get. What do you think?"

Vigorously, Samia stamped out her cigarette. She stood, put on her jacket, lifted her purse, and said, in a flat tone, "It's obvious that there is a misunderstanding here. I am not a real estate agent, nor am I here to strike deals. Anyway, what you need to keep in mind is that we will resist the sale of this house with everything we have. At least we tried. Your wishes won't be granted so easily. Have you been following what's happening in Tunisia and Egypt? We are no less than Egyptians or Tunisians."

Before he could respond to her surprisingly cold reaction, she said, "Good luck, Doctor, and thanks for the coffee."

She departed, leaving behind a void of silence and a thin thread of smoke from her cigarette, which was not fully extinguished in the ashtray.

8
Fidel

Three strange months passed, and I felt increasingly isolated. Each day, I memorized twenty new vocabulary words. I stayed with an English family and kept to my room, silent most of the time, unable to get close to anyone. Being away from home was eating me alive. I just didn't fit in and could not bear the thought of living here for the rest of my life. I was waiting for some miracle to take place, for something to happen.

From within the folds of the despair that enveloped my life, it was no longer possible for Fidel to be present. He was losing hope and backing away. In his place appeared Fadl, who took over the helm and led me to the London Muslim Mosque, where I met Sheikh Ghassan Al-Ayyash.

We talked after prayer. I confessed to him the story of Fadl and Fidel and about the pain I felt from being away from my country. I also confided in him about my struggle between faith and renunciation. The smile that appeared on the sheikh's face was unforgettable.

"You can count on me as your big brother," he said. "You are different, Fadl. Don't despair or give up on God's mercy. God will help you find a way out, and today I will call a brother who is a great lawyer and who will also help you. His name is Abdullah Al-Muhajer. I also suggest that you begin the process of submitting your papers as a refugee in this country."

"God bless you, Sheikh. But are you saying I should find a foothold in this country and just forget about my own country?"

"Yes. You must get your British passport because that's your right. Forget about what happened back in your country. You only have one choice and that is to start from scratch. But don't ever forget that you are Muslim, and that the nation of Islam needs you."

I turned myself in to the home office in Croydon, which in turn referred me to a refugee camp in Birmingham. I stayed there until my second interview. In London, Abdullah, the lawyer, helped me a great deal. However, Sheikh Ghassan informed me that he was under surveillance and could not do much until I obtained my residency papers. In spite of this, he secured a job for me at an Islamic butcher shop with one of the brothers. The halal meat sold there did not meet safety regulations, and the shop soon closed. The few pounds that I had were running out, and so was time.

I lived thanks to Sheikh Ghassan's charitable organization, my only source of security in London until he suddenly had to travel to Afghanistan. My fragile new world collapsed. We lost touch, and I really missed him. He was like a spiritual father to many of the Muslim youths in London. He was charmingly eloquent and persuasive, and his English was better than that of most English people.

At the height of my depression and loneliness, I sat on a bench at Willesden Park between two rows of chestnut, oak, and maple trees. The city felt gigantic and merciless. My hunger was worsening my feelings of subjugation, and I was under the threat of being evicted from my rotten room if I didn't come up with the rent in two days. Just then, a woman passed by in her wheelchair. She was in her fifties, and her hair was a mixture of brown and silver. A squirrel darted into her path and stopped to stare at me as the woman swerved her chair to the side to avoid a fallen branch. The rear wheel went over it, causing one of her purse straps to loosen. A small box of tissues, a nail clipper, and a wallet fell out, but she was too busy trying to regain the balance of her chair to notice.

I stared at what lay on the ground and then looked around. The nearest pedestrians were far enough away not to have noticed what had taken place. I waited for a bit, my heart racing, then made my way over to the scene and began picking up the fallen items. I then returned to the bench, where I opened the wallet. It was stuffed with twenty-pound bills.

My heart continued to pound. The bundle of money would sustain me for two months, without hunger or fear. I didn't care for anything in the wallet except for the money. My plan was to take the rest of what was in it to the closest police station. The plan seemed executable. and so I left the tissue box and nail clipper on the bench and placed the wallet in my pocket.

As I began to walk away, I caught sight of that sly squirrel. He stared at me with tenacity. His narrow eyes glared at me piercingly with what felt like deep reproach. I was terrified. Instead of quickening my pace, I went straight to the bench. I retrieved the box of tissues and the nail clipper and caught up with the woman in her squeaking wheelchair, calling, "Madame. Madame. I beg your pardon."

She stopped. I went to her. She looked up at me inquisitively with kind, cloudless eyes.

"You dropped these things," I said, handing her the wallet. She thanked me graciously.

"No need to thank me. Please do take more care in the future."

"Helen Doller," she said, extending her hand.

I couldn't turn her down. My guilt for almost having stolen her money helped me set aside the religious tenet that shaking a woman's hand would invalidate my ablution. As I hadn't yet performed my ablution and had just finished an intense week of prayers, I shook her hand and introduced myself. "Fadl Abdullah."

"Mr. Fadl, forgive me for the question, but may I ask where you are from?"

"From Syria, Madame. Syria."

"An amazing continent. I have never visited. My admiration to you, Sir, and to Sierra Leone. Africa is a great continent."

There was no point in correcting her faulty knowledge of geography. I needed to get away as quickly as possible. An inner voice was reprimanding me: "You're going to be thrown into the street, you idiot. Let's see how Sierra Leone will do you any good." Fidel's voice was loud and clear.

The lady rolled away in her wheelchair. I went back and picked the branch up off the ground and ran at that despicable squirrel, which was devouring an acorn and still giving me the eye. I cursed him and swung the branch at him, crying, "You had to show up, you animal—didn't you?"

It scampered away and climbed up a tall tree.

I left the park, headed for the nearest station. I took the bus to Edgware Road and then to Liverpool, only to find, for the second time, a letter of rejection at the lawyer's office denying my case.

"This means that there is no longer any hope that the Home Office will sponsor you or place you in a refugee camp," explained the lawyer, "The court and the Home Office are simply not convinced that your life is in danger. They think you're taking advantage of the system by having entered the country on a student visa and now applying for refugee status. They also think that had your life truly been in jeopardy, you would have applied for refugee status at the airport and not waited until your visa expired."

"Is there anything else I can do?" I asked desperately.

"We will appeal the decision and take the case to the Supreme Court. But you will need to provide some sort of evidence to the court, like a photo of you and Ruwaida, since you are not affiliated with any party and have not carried out any political acts, etcetera."

I could not bear to hear anymore.

From the upper deck of the bus, my mind wandered off to nowhere. I got off at Kilburn, where I lived. I felt what was left of the money in my pocket: a pound and a few pence. I stood in front of a second-hand store, took out my Parker pen, a gift I kept as memory from a woman who was now detained, and sold it for five pounds.

I bought one meat pie with fries and devoured it at Kingsbury Cemetery. As I arrived at my rented studio, I found a final notice indicating that I needed to pay my rent within a week or be subject to forced eviction.

The next morning, I felt a desperate desire to throw myself onto the train tracks. It was a frighteningly tempting idea, one that led me to avoid trains for a long time. Each time I entered a train station, something beckoned me to throw myself under its wheels.

Once again on a bench between two rows of chestnut, oak and maple trees in Willesden Park, I sat alone, a deserted man left prey to his loneliness and to the lethal cries of the tracks. With contempt, I watched that same squirrel.

"Good morning," a voice suddenly called, pulling me out of my loneliness. It was the woman in the wheelchair, who was smiling at me kindly. I turned around to look for the squirrel, but it was nowhere in sight.

9

Issa

"Hello?"

"Yes, hello."

"Is May available?"

"This is she."

"I am Issa."

"Issa! How are you? Welcome back. When did you get out?"

"Yesterday actually."

"What's happening with you?"

"I'm fine, thank God. I miss you. How are you?"

"I'm OK."

Silence prevailed for a few moments. He remembered her voice, neutral with a hoarse rattle that seemed to have been broken. It was not the same as the one that had intoxicated him a couple of years earlier, when he had met her at the military hospital, the voice he had played back in his mind and inhaled for months on end to the point where it became his talisman.

Back then, he was handcuffed, guarded by two armed men, waiting for permission to have an endoscopy for his ulcerated stomach; he was standing at the base of the valley of his solitude when a warm whisper brushed by him.

"How are you? Stay strong."

As he fathomed what he had just heard, he felt as if a storm had pulled him out of his misery and into utter bliss. These were words that became tattooed on his memory. He couldn't quite believe that these words had just come from an actual woman, a woman made of flesh and blood, who just happened to walk by.

Turning his head almost cost him his medical appointment, one for which he had submitted twenty requests, pleading in unbearable pain just so they would examine him. And still, turn his head he did, seeing that behind him stood a handcuffed woman with a charming and radiant smile, her concerned eyes telling him to beware.

One of the guards slapped him, shouting, "Keep your head down, you animal."

The slap confirmed that there was indeed a woman behind him who had just whispered to him. He wasn't dreaming or imagining. *I saw a woman, I saw a woman*, he began to repeat to himself.

As one of the two cars had broken down, they were crammed into a van—him in the front seat next to a man with an automatic machine gun, her in the seat behind his, next to a huge assistant officer resting a machine gun on his thigh. The assistant officer began to crack open sunflower seeds and the shells flew in all directions.

Issa's eyes met hers in the rearview mirror. He inquisitively gestured with his head and raised an eyebrow. She responded with two blinks and a wink indicating that she had been under arrest for two and a half years. With a raised brow and head tilt, she bounced the question back at him. He blinked three times and closed his right eye once.

Their gesture-only conversation continued under the nose of the two guards, amid the noise of cracking seeds. For the next twenty days, and time and time again, he replayed that conversation made up of a few words and gestures. He recounted it to prisoners in his dormitory for hours on end. There was not a detail that he left out. She had stormed into his soul and caused him to forget the pain of his endoscopy. It had been a long time since any of the men had come across a woman of flesh and blood.

On this night, it was his turn to sleep on the roof of the bathroom located in the corner of the dormitory; this was a strategy that the prisoners had devised to relieve the overcrowdedness of the nights where every man had forty square centimeters in which they could sleep. He stood on the roof of the bathroom and looked through a narrow window where he could peek at the women's dormitory. From behind the bars, he waved at a girl standing at the window across from him. Once she noticed him, she began bringing one detainee after another over to the window. He shook his head and gestured that none of them were the woman he was looking for.

She was the fifth one the girl brought over. As soon as he saw her, he pointed to her, and she recognized him. They stayed up all night and until dawn, gesturing to one another, sending scattered messages, drawing words, and telling tall tales in a barren space that was subject to being raided at any moment.

Day after day, their conversation evolved into their own language. They could compose full conversations with symbols that only they could decipher, discussions that lasted until the morning hours and all the clamor of jailers, officers, and the arrival of new detainees. For six months, his cellmates gave him the space to stay at the top of the roof during the nights and to sleep in until the afternoon. In the morning, they would gather around him as he wove his tales. The signs turned into pulsating words and the codes into stories about what took place in the women's dormitories, including their visits and raids. He poured a flood of emotion into his stories and stoked in the men a burning desire to be embraced.

The conversations continued until that one morning when they found him awake, his eyes congested. They barraged him with questions.

"The day after tomorrow she will be released," he said, his head bowed and his eyes fixed on a piece of paper he had torn from a cigarette pack, on which he had written her phone number.

"But that's great! Hopefully you will be next."

"I know I should be happy for her, but..." he broke into tears. They had never seen him cry like that before. Some of his mates also cried, and they agreed he should no longer sleep on the roof of the bathroom.

Life in the dormitory returned to its normal state, and so did their language lessons and the awaiting of visits. The days were unvaryingly monotonous, except for her voice and whispers. "How are you? Stay strong"—these words never seemed to get stale; they were always as fresh as if she had just whispered them.

He was released after four years, six months, and eleven days, without a charge or a trial. A year after having been tortured and interrogated, it was documented in his record that he was a reader for *Al-Raya Al-Hamra'*, a newspaper for the League of Communist Action.

He was overwhelmed by the noise of life outside of prison but also loaded with passion for life, in particular for May on the other side of the telephone line.

"Please don't call this number again," she said, which yanked him out of his jostling memories. Remembering that she was on the other line, he waved his hand, drew letters in the air, and said, "Inshallah."

"God be with you. Goodbye."

Hearing the beeping sound of the dead phone line, he suddenly lost the strength to hold the phone. He felt a sense of numbness creep into his soul like the hollowness in an empty clay urn.

When he finished telling his story to Anees, who had listened raptly, his friend was incredulous. "You actually lived this story, Issa?"

"Every detail of it. But it's as simple as this—it is not possible for any love that is born in prison to survive. Today, the country itself is detained and hence all its people are struggling emotionally."

Issa lived alone, on the third and last floor of a building at a main street crossing in Dweil'ah. The apartment consisted of two rooms and a large balcony that overlooked Damascus in three different directions. From one of its corners, one could see what was left of a Ghouta that was now filled with slums; from another corner, an erect church, meek and white amid the gloomy dark houses; and from the third corner, Mount Qasioun, perched like a giant breast on the chest of the city.

In an apartment that Anees had known for a quarter of a century, the two friends sat and reflected on what the days had done to them.

Issa's friends took care of the apartment throughout his imprisonment and paid his rent. When he was released, they took turns staying with him, while he bid them farewell as they left the country one after another. He married twice, but his wives did not wish to stay married to him. Everything around him in the country was broken and changed, even as his home remained as it once was, with walls stained with words written by friends who had stopped by before heading out to a fragmented diaspora. They were words that embodied memories of the absent; they were words that narrated the people's dreams while in Damascus, before being swallowed up by life's defeats. They represented a time when his friends left the country for far quainter reasons, such as fleeing military service or dreaming of a life that was less salty.

Issa's home was filled floor to ceiling with books and paintings, welcoming visitors into a combustible mihrab. Memories were stacked on the shelves, brimming with letters. Issa moved through his kingdom like a monk among flocks of book covers. He spoke like a majestic king before an army of paper. He asked everyone who visited his apartment to leave traces of themselves on its walls, a passing sentence with the date of passage.

He pointed to a sentence that Dr. Anees had written more than a quarter of a century back, lines that were immutable: "Dear Issa. I had assumed that you were like everyone else until I entered your home and found a homeland of people—Anees Al-Aghawani."

He shed the tears of a lifetime, throwing himself onto the chests of his friends, who embraced him as he sobbed uncontrollably.

"Is there anything we can fix in this country, Issa?" asked Anees, feeling flooded with nostalgia. Issa was the only person who could possibly explain to him what had become of Damascus in his absence, and so he began to tell tales about his country, filling in the voids of his absence and connecting the fragments. Then he spoke about the terrifying dark place that summed up the whole story: the ward of no return.

"If you want to know the truth about any country, go to its psychiatric hospital. It's the place where all the sicknesses and diseases lie, and you'll understand what has caused them over the years," said Issa.

"Back at the end of the nineties, I contacted my friend, a psychiatrist who worked at Ibn Sina Psychiatric Hospital and told him I was interested in writing about psychiatry hospitals. I asked if he could arrange a visit for me. The visit to the hospital ended up being on the same day of my release from prison, and I didn't think that there was anything more extreme than what I had just experienced. In prison, I naively believed in the power and agency of literature and in the safe space that existed between book covers. I saw it as an escape from a reality that I did not wish to be in.

The doctor arranged a visit for us during one of his on-call nights. He said he could show us the dormitories as well as the residents. I went along with a movie producer and a fellow detainee. We arrived at the hospital and waited for the doctor, who was examining a few patients. Once he was finished, he led us to the one of the men's wards and the only women's ward. We found ourselves in the company of a man named Abu Ali, who seemed to be the strangest of all the detainees. This was in a unit where prisoners were assessed before being sent to prison. Abu Ali had set up a prison inside of his unit where he punished patients who violated the laws and regulations that he introduced.

A former military officer, Abu Ali had disappeared in the war in Lebanon and returned to face charges of desertion from the army. He was obsessed with cleanliness and order. While in Tadmur, the jailers came to realize that he had lost his memory and his mind, and so they referred him to Ibn Sina Psychiatric Hospital, where he would remain for the rest of his life. He had an amazing ability to organize the affairs of the place and was the only inmate who free to come and go as he pleased. Because he had no life outside of prison, the ward was his safe and familiar place.

We recorded what we could of our impressions, the good and the sad, and left with a harvest of thoughts and feelings, one that would become completely forgotten after discovering the truth that lay in the ward next door. In a halting whisper, the on-call doctor told us of the dormitory of no return, as he referred to it, and warned us never to mention what we were about to see.

We left the lit-up hospital and walked for a few minutes until we came to a building that was under construction. At the entrance, a pale yellow light shone from a single bulb, illuminating a metal door with no sign of life behind it. A voice came from inside, asking what was the matter. The doctor told him to open the door and tidy up the place. He then turned to us and gave us strict orders: 'Walk behind me, and if I tell you to leave, then calmly back out of the room.' It seemed a bit dramatic, but we listened, obeyed, and waited.

The door creaked as he opened it, and then we were hit with a wave of putrid odors: the stench of human infection, rotten food, and feces. Then, a scene from hell opened before us: silhouettes of bodies dispersing in different directions in a purgatory of torment. On one side was what looked like a dark kitchen, from which two people emerged completely naked. Someone else emerged, dressed in rags and crawling on all fours, and as we approached, he stood up and gave us a look that I will not forget for as long as I live. His body was discolored and pigmented by vitiligo and his penis had been cut off.

Using a cable, the guard pushed them all away to keep them from following us. We walked from the dormitory's entrance to its foyer, a rectangular space of about twenty square meters. In the space were beds without mattresses, covered with thick sheets of canvas. Atop them were forty or more tormented people, most of them naked. Some moved away from us, others came closer.

In the center stood a stern-faced man wrapped in a blanket, holding a shoe in his hand. Unbelievably, he looked like Batman. When a guard approached him and told him to back away, the man began to fail at him with the shoe, repeating, 'Fuck you all, you sons of bitches,' over and over—the same words he used throughout our visit.

As we later learned, this was Dr. Ayman, a dentist who had once been humiliated by an officer of the regime. When the man came to his clinic to have his wisdom teeth extracted, Dr. Ayman used his drill to pierce the officer's jaw and then left the clinic shouting, 'Fuck you all, you sons of bitches!' Soon after, the Mukhabarat detained him for two years. Then they brought him to this place. This was supposedly the story, but as the doctor told us, there were no verification documents for those who stayed at the no return ward, except for Sami the Bastard.

Sami was less than twenty years old, and he was always naked. He grew up at the hospital and was then transferred to the no return dormitory after becoming a teenager. He possessed the longest penis likely known in history. He carried it between his thighs like the trunk of an elephant. He did not speak, but grunted in tones that were closer to those from primitive times. 'Hey, Bastard Sami, how's it going?' asked the doctor. Sami jumped up and down and let out incomprehensible noises; he looked like he was addressing the world with his trunk.

One of the clothed men approached us, scattering the crowd. He pointed at us, and asked angrily, 'Doctor, who are those people?'

Calmly, the doctor explained that we were visitors from a care center who had come to check on patients.

'Are you lying to us, doctor? Are these people here to get a look at us?'

'No, not at all. And after all, you are about to be transferred out of here in a few days, as soon as the procedures are done.'

As we tried to absorb his unexpected reaction, the doctor instructed us to leave. My friend and I began to back out, slowly and cautiously, as we had been instructed, and soon we were back in the dormitory.

The doctor tried to calm the escalating commotion as a guard pushed back against the swarm of patients advancing at him as a single mass. The distance to the exit door seemed endless. We thought we would never make it out alive.

'Whoever wants medicine, line up to the right,' shouted the doctor. Meanwhile, the guard waved his cable as he backed away, dragging us out with him and quickly locking the door behind him.

The guard's whip dispersed the bodies through pain while the loud clamor continued with the shouting of the Batman dentist, the grunting of the Sami the Bastard, and the hysterical sounds of a human mass triggered and agitated.

We stood there, paralyzed by the horror of what we were witnessing. The noise began to die down, leaving only the voice of the guard with the stinging cable: 'You motherfuckers. Fuck my luck that has brought me here.'

Then a silence enveloped the place and was sporadically disrupted by the rattles of Sami the Bastard. In the room of the doctor on call, I tore up what I had written in my notebook, more aware than ever that this was the truth about my country. I was speechless. The doctor explained that each of the patients who stayed at the no return ward required half of the hospital's budget for proper treatment. He also said that every two months a truck with a water tank came and sprayed them down to clean them, in addition to several other measures.

I interrupted the doctor with a gnawing question, as I couldn't understand how my friend had been cursed with having to serve in this hell for two years. 'Do you have a heart or a conscience? If you did, you would have poisoned them all. For God's sake, just kill them. How can you be a physician in such a place?'

'When winter comes, it usually harvests three-quarters of them.'

As I reflected on all that I had seen, I wondered about how Sami the Bastard had survived the winters until 1997, and whether or not he was alive today."

As he came to a finish, Issa said, "Anees, you've been so distant that you can no longer see the country as we have seen it. Forgive Samia and forgive me if we did not meet your expectations."

"I feel like I have come to a country that I know nothing about, Issa," said Anees, his face devoid of color or expression. "And I shouldn't stay here any more than is necessary."

10

Helen

"I had a feeling that you would be here. I brought you coffee," said Helen.

"Very kind of you, Madame," I said, sipping the coffee she handed me at serene Willesden Park. I shared bits and pieces of my life with her, and she told me about the passing of her kind husband, Edward, and that she lived on her own in a neighborhood close by. She said she had suffered from cancer in the spine for several years, and pulled a photo out of her wallet of the two of them in an embrace. Unhesitant, I asked if I could keep the photo until the next day. I walked alongside her until we left the park. I returned to my room and drew the photo with charcoal and lead, using all of my skill and ability.

The next day, when I showed her what I had drawn, she couldn't hold back the emotions. She thanked me tearfully and reached out with a hug of gratitude. She then asked if I could help her shop for a few groceries at a nearby Tesco supermarket.

Sometime later, with my arms full of grocery bags, we arrived at her house at 21 Garden Avenue. It was from the Georgian era and was spacious with classical decor. Upon entering, I immediately spotted photos of Edward on the walls, adorned as they were with matte gold embossed red wallpaper. There was a large collection of Chinese and Indian antiques in the living room. The curtains were red and thick, and the house was suffused with an ambience of loneliness and abandonment. It was a big home, and tidier than one might expect for a lady in a wheelchair.

"You are the first person to enter this house since the passing of Edward five years ago."

"I am honored, Madame, and it is my pleasure."

Following her instructions, I carried the bags into the kitchen and began to empty them and place their contents onto her shelves. It was impossible for her to reach anything up high on her own—I had to stand on tiptoe so I could get to the upper ones—so she must have had help to do so.

Contemplating the situation as I emptied the last bag, I heard her voice clad in a tone of masculinity and devoid of the sadness in which it was earlier drenched, "I think you have a question for me, don't you?"

I turned around and my jaw dropped. With eyes agape, I stared foolishly as I beheld the incomprehensible. For there was Mrs. Helen, up on two healthy legs and walking slowly towards me, leaving behind an empty wheelchair and a thousand question marks.

"He was my friend, lover, and husband," she said. "We did not have children. Instead, we sailed together across the Mediterranean and to the Red Sea, and from there to the Indian Ocean and the Arab Gulf. We sailed for three years, saw the world, and witnessed sunsets and sunrises. When our sea journeys ended, Edward devoted his time to writing while I concentrated on teaching. We were like conjoined twins, inseparable. When the physicians diagnosed him with cancer, I visited a church for the first time in my life. While there, I did not pray for God to heal him, since his cancer was end-stage. Rather, I prayed that I would also be diagnosed with cancer. A week before his death, he went completely downhill. He did not want to see any of our friends. The once perfect man became easily angered. His spiritual pain became greater than his physical pain.

Crying like a child, he confessed to me, 'I know I should not say this to you, but I am a very jealous person, and I know that after I die, no matter how sad you will be, you are bound to forget me.' Then, weltering in destruction, he added, 'Of course, you will have another relationship. I beg you to not be with anyone I know. I hurt badly at the thought of imagining you with another person, walking the same streets and visiting the same gardens that we visited together. I know that this is selfish of me and that I should not be saying this, but the idea of dying and leaving you behind is torturing me. I don't care what happens to me after death and I don't regret anything in life. But I hurt badly at the thought of imagining you without me in this life.'

"I knew that our lives together had taken us to great depths and had become rooted in one ground. I knew that he loved me and that I loved him, but I did not realize that this man of steel had reached such a level of madness and pain. For an entire week, I did not leave his side for one moment. I swore to him that I would not leave the house on my two feet ever again. I swore this to him more than a thousand times, trying to calm his ravings and delirium. A few seconds before he passed away, as he took his last breath, I kissed him with my mouth open so that I could breathe his spirit into my body. I did not cry on that day, nor did I call anyone. Instead, I held him throughout the night and fell asleep next to his corpse. The next day, as he had prearranged, we buried him quietly at Kilburn's cemetery. As for me, I've kept my promise to him and have not left the house without being in his wheelchair," she explained, pointing to the chair that sat in the corner in solemnity. "I have lost touch with all our friends and anyone with whom we shared a memory. They also made no effort to keep in touch or arrange to meet with me. Five years, three months, and two days have passed since his death, and I have not broken my promise. As I told you, you are the first guest who has entered this house in years."

Her confession carried with it the scent of a memory mixed with pain; I remained silent, feeling emptiness and dispassion. I truly could not comprehend such people.

I felt the urge to leave immediately. I was angry and felt deceived. I was reminded of how I felt like a nobody, everyone suspicious of me. I contemplated the fact that my greatest wish was to receive resident status and feel like a human being with the very basics of human rights. I thought about how, as a Syrian, I was exiled and split into two people living in the same body, where each part was constantly struggling to win over the other; how I was someone without a compass, direction, existence, identity, family, money, or children; how in this instance, I had reached out to help a person in need, only to find out that she had voluntarily held herself hostage and imprisoned herself, purely out of self-importance and conceit.

I didn't know what to do. How could I remain in her company with such strong feelings of wrath towards her? Finally, in a blunt tone, I said, "Helen. Helen."

She gazed at me through her unclouded eyes. Instead of angrily announcing that I was leaving immediately, I held open my arms and said, "Come and let me give you a hug."

Without hesitation, she embraced me. Gently wrapping my arms around her, I said, playing with her hair, "You'll be OK. It's going to be OK." She burst into tears.

I felt an odd sense of reverse motherhood and was overcome by a sudden explosion of empathy. I did not recognize the person in me who was now embracing her, but this felt like a moment of reconciliation between Fadl and Fidel. I no longer heard their conflicting voices within me, only the remnants of a vague rustle, as if I had become one with a tree whose trunk was this female body.

My life took a complete turn that lovely summer. Helen agreed to sign marriage papers with me to help with my immigration case. My papers were changed from a refugee application to a case requesting resident status for a spouse. Our relationship took new depths, and I moved in with her. We lived like spouses in every way, but we did not have a physical relationship. We remembered Edward together and visited his grave. I devoted much time to painting a great mural of him.

To no one's surprise, the Department of Immigration was very suspicious of us, but we were quite prepared for the interview.

"What if they ask about the number of times we sleep together in a week?"

We stared at one another, frozen in time amid a thousand passing thoughts we did not wish to utter. After a silence that lasted a few seconds but felt like ages, she turned and went to the kitchen, saying in a choked voice, "Just say at the end of every week."

11

Anees

"The offer price may sound less than market price, but believe me, this is the best you can get," Rajeh Al-Agha told Dr. Anees, and continued in a cautionary tone, "At any given moment the property can be flagged by the Directorate-General of Antiquities, and if that happens you will walk away with nothing."

"I'll need a few days to get things organized," said Dr. Anees, rising to his feet, ready to leave the lawyer's office.

"As you wish. My advice to you: the quicker, the better."

Dr. Anees left and headed off to meet Issa, who met him with an alarming expression of dread on his face.

"They arrested Samia," he anxiously told Anees.

Anees was shocked by the news, and they sat to discuss the details. Issa told him that he and Samia had taken part in a protest at the Ministry of Interior in solidarity with the families of opinion detainees. He explained that there were about a hundred people in total, both men and women.

"We weren't crying out for anything, just standing with the families in show of silent support. All of a sudden, the security forces attacked us with cables and pistol butts, punching and kicking us. We dispersed quickly, but they got hold of Samia, dragged her by the hair in the street for at least twenty meters, and took her away. Someone filmed the incident."

Issa passed his phone to Anees. Anees watched the video in horror, his hands shaking. He recognized Samia being dragged along the ground, kicked and punched, and pushed onto a detention bus.

"Oh, God," said Anees, barely able to speak. "What can we do?" he asked.

"I don't know, but your friend Abbas may be able to help."

Immediately, he called Abbas. His voice drenched in anxiety, he said, "My dear Abbas. I need you urgently."

"Are you OK? What's happening, Anees?"

"I can't tell you on the phone. I need to see you."

"OK, where are you?"

"At Havana Café."

"I can't leave quite yet, but I will send someone to bring you to me."

Thirty minutes later, he was picked up in a black Mercedes and taken via the Mezzeh highway to one of the security buildings. They walked to the office of Colonel Abbas Jawhar, passing through corridors with faded light and cold walls. Abbas approached Anees welcomingly. He invited him to sit on a cozy couch in the middle of the room.

"What would you like to drink?"

"Whatever you want."

"I still remember that you take your coffee black."

Through the intercom, he ordered two coffees without sugar, and they engaged in a spirited conversation about the past and how they had followed different paths in life.

"I can understand everything except for the fact that the gentle Dr. Abbas, the poet, became an officer with the Mukabarat."

"All there is to it is that life has a way of putting you in a place where you find yourself surrounded by strange choices. After graduating, I had to serve in the army, and unlike many others, I suddenly found in prison what I was missing. It was that sort of rigorousness and discipline. So instead of leaving the army service after two years, I thought that I might actually be in the right place. Change in Syria is not possible from the outside, and the fact is that the regime is the future of the country. Reform has to take place from within. I assure you that things are headed in the right direction. The county is rich and has great potential, and at the same time, it is full of problems. But it is not possible to change any of the basic rules of the country. If only the opposition could understand that the regime does not mind their presence and realizes their importance, but unfortunately they are naive, lacking vision, and unable to understand the reality of things."

"Abbas, out of curiosity, could you explain to me what reality is and what it is that the opposition should understand?"

"In short, for change to happen, the opposition needs to first be loyal to Bashar Al-Assad and what he represents. They cannot pressure him to be the way they are. The regime is harsh and strict when it comes to demanding loyalty, and without it they can become very violent. The opposition is playing with a country that is made up of gunpowder, and the regime will not acquiesce on requiring compliance, nor will it take risks. If they lose control of even the smallest detail, no one can predict what they will do next."

"So that's why they arrested Samia Saeed outside of the Ministry of Interior?"

Abbas laughed coldly. "You've only been in the country for two days and you're already playing with fire."

"No, not at all. It's just that I met this woman and she is helping me with an issue about the house."

"Anees, stay away from this woman. Actually, stay away from this entire group of people. They are disconnected from reality."

"But they didn't do anything. How is it OK for her to be dragged by the hair through the street simply for standing peacefully in front of a government ministry?"

"Anees, my dear. You've been away for a long time. Sure, I can understand how it may look from your perspective, but things are actually far more complex. If it were strictly a matter of protest and about caring for the people, that would be one thing. But one must also look at the way they got involved and their timing. You've seen how far things have gone in Tunisia, Egypt, and Libya. This protest was an invitation to import that same momentum and desire for change into our country. But Syria will never be Egypt or Tunisia."

"Personally, it doesn't matter to me, and I don't want to get into what's right and wrong and how the country should be run. You know me better than that. I'm only here to ask for your help with regard to this woman."

"Anything for you. You are an old friend, and you are genuine. I assure you that she will be well-treated and will be back in her home by tomorrow." He wholeheartedly thanked Abbas and started to leave.

"The driver will take you wherever you want, but before you go, I just want to advise you to complete the sale of the house and then leave as soon as possible."

Abbas's serious tone piqued Anees's curiosity. "You know about the house?"

"All of Damascus knows, Anees, and those who are interested in the house should not be rejected. I'm sure you know what I mean. Just finish things up and leave. We'll be in touch."

Issa was silent when Anees told him what had happened, and Anees had no choice but to try to understand. He was beginning to feel worried about being in a country that seemed to be wrapped in the gauze of mummies and soaked with the stench of diseases. He took his phone from his pocket and called to make an appointment to sign the sale papers for the house.

The lawyer, Rajeh Al-Agha, was happy to hear that the doctor was beginning to see the light, and said to him, "In three days, all of the papers will be ready." Praising the doctor's decision, he continued, "Do you want the money in Syrian cash or in pounds? For a small commission, our office can give you a great offer without having to worry about paying British taxes."

"No, please transfer the money to my bank account in the UK, with a notarized and translated contract. I am not interested in evading taxes."

He heard a hint of sarcasm through the phone. "I salute you doctor. There are only a few people left like you and you are all certainly worthy of respect. So, this will then require a little more time. A week from today and I will have everything ready for you."

There was something suffocating about the city. Faces looked as if they were made of wax. Whispers were getting louder, and eyes were widened with confusion and obscure questions. *Change was impossible in Damascus*, Anees thought to himself. *What happened in Tunisia, Egypt, Yemen, and Libya could never be repeated in Syria. This was the inconceivable.*

People flooded the streets, panting, besieged by the silence of anticipation. The city was a dormant volcano. People spoke under their breaths in cafés. There was fear of security outbursts. Meanwhile, the government was digging its claws into the city, like a predator with a wounded animal, waiting to snap its neck and tear it apart at any given moment. The predator had inflicted a thick wound on the body of Damascus, leaving her exhausted from his bite. He left her in his den, weak and bleeding and within reach of his fangs. He made her serve him in order to stay alive, forced her to feed him her children and pieces of her body. He sucked her rivers dry and she could find no escape from him, and he did not trust her. She tried to convince him that she thought he was indeed the master of the forest, pretending that she was a wounded deer gazing at the grass. But her eyes kept watch of everything taking place around her.

Anees was also observing. He heard snippets of talk from his friends in Damascus, some of which lingered in his memory. He agreed with some general opinions but could not bring himself to speak out.

He informed Hannah via Skype that things were taking a little longer than expected. She seemed cold but understanding. She also looked good; it was obvious that they both needed this break.

He was the first to arrive on the evening his old friends agreed to meet at Adel and Layl's home in Mashrou' Dummar. He did not pay heed to the heavy silence behind Adel's carefully drawn-on smile as Layl greeted him, gushing with kindness. Her face was round, with a glowing tan, and her smile was beautiful, revealing a perfect row of teeth. Her hair was not dyed. She was petite, and her friendliness brought back old times. Anees had witnessed her heartbreak when her fiancé, Samih, had abandoned her. He recalled how he had once walked by her side in the alleys of Bab Tuma, taking her to the goldsmith's shop and telling her, "You need to sell the ring, now."

She had pulled the ring off her finger, like someone pulling out her heart, and offered it to the jeweler with trembling hands. Anees then forced her to buy a pair of shoes with what she received for the ring and said, "Now you can move forward." She was wholeheartedly grateful for his support, and ever since that day, she passed forward his advice to friends who were also abandoned in their relationships, urging them to simply buy a new pair of shoes and move on.

Decorated with delicacies, the table was set to accommodate eight people. Dr. Hani arrived, wearing an elegant suit, his mustache placed slightly high on his upper lip, accompanied by his elegant and pretentious wife. Then Abbas arrived with his wife, her presence heavy as she wedged herself next to Hani's wife, who happened to be one of her acquaintances. Then came Issa with a bouquet of roses.

They soon began to revisit memories of their past, freeing themselves from the pressures of the moment, exchanging smiles, hugs, and jokes as if they were all still in school. Nothing could top the feeling of being with old friends. Layl pulled out a photo album of their days together at the university and they passed it around, resharing memories.

"All of our memories happen to be in Layl's possession," Issa joked. "Here's a photo of us when we were still good guys." He passed it to Adel, who was politely humoring him, while Hani and Abbas's wives showed little interest in the photos, dropping sarcastic comments instead.

Amid this warm atmosphere with windows open to the past, the doorbell rang and a storm barged through the door. Like a hut made of reeds in the blowing wind, Anees's heart was dashed as he saw her enter.

Samia's presence divided everyone into opposing teams, as if this scene was a dry run for what awaited all Syrians. Issa was completely on Samia's side and fully supported what she had done. Layl also supported her for her humane stand but, at the same time, blamed her for getting herself into such situations. As for Hani, Abbas, and their wives, they would not stop condemning her.

"You are provoking the security forces, who are already in a state of tension," said Abbas.

Adel and Anees declined to take a clear stand on the situation, doing their best to keep their distance from everyone. The evening ended with the depature of the disapproving group, who had rejected Samia and her escalation of the discussion to a level of confrontation and defiance.

On his way out, Abbas said calmly, "You all need to grow up and understand the nature of the country and regime. You are playing with fire.

I'm going to say it to you plainly: Bashar Al-Assad's regime will collapse only under one circumstance—when Syria ceases to exist. If it were about individuals and their faults, we would have all stood by you, but if the goal is to replace the system, then believe me when I tell you that you don't know who you're messing with."

"They treated us like animals. I was slapped more than a hundred times. I was dragged by my hair through the street, and you're talking to me about individuals and their faults?"

Adel followed the group that left the house in a desperate attempt to appease them. He wanted to make it clear to them that he did not approve of Samia's actions and that he agreed with them heart and soul.

At the car, Hani told him sternly, "If you disapprove of what this woman has done, then do something about it."

They drove off, leaving him vaguely bewildered. Adel, who was rarely angry, directed his outrage at Layl. He had warned her not to invite Samia to the gathering, fearing exactly what had just happened.

Layl felt divided between the people she loved. In vain, she wished that she could protect their fragile world and take care of what had brought them together.

The visit came to an end as Adel returned addressing Samia, "You need to respect my home and guests. And if you're going to insist on having these sorts of opinions, then I personally do not welcome you here."

They all left in silence, despite Layl's attempts to heal the rift.

"This is the way things are now," said Issa, in apology to Anees. "We're no longer the same people you once knew."

Samia drove on without a word, her facial expressions warning of an imminent explosion. She tried to change the mood, asking "Where would you like for me to take you guys?"

"To Alshahbandar Square. The night is still young. I know of a quaint restaurant, if you're up for it."

"I personally don't want to," Samia interrupted crankily.

"Then why not first take Issa where he needs to be, and then perhaps you can take me to Huddud's House," Anees said. "We can have a cup of coffee together and you'll have a chance to calm your nerves a little."

Anees was genuine in his invitation and Samia accepted without hesitation. The house filled her with an energy that tempered her impatience and calmed her anxious soul. Upon arriving, they had to find diesel fuel to light the warming oven in the attic, where she was able to get a view of Damascus, a city that was falling asleep on that cold night at the end of January. Laced with frost and anger, the space filled up with the delicious aroma of Damascene coffee.

As they sipped the coffee, their conversation took off without any direction. They talked about everything—their lives, Damascus, London, the obscure future, the sourness of fear, the bitterness of living—and Samia's cigarettes never stopped burning. They talked a little about politics and a lot about life. She told him about her divorce, activism, and arrest, and insisted that Damascus needed to change. A sense of familiarity began to kindle between these two souls, a man and a woman who had matured too early in life but were also now given a new opportunity to see themselves in new ways. Anees made two pots of coffee, and at midnight Samia ordered takeout. They ate the shawarma sandwiches with gusto. The doctor's uptightness melted away; he no longer felt the need to behave with the same coldness or exaggerated seriousness as he had to put on each time he opened a rib cage or mended a sick heart.

The attic glowed with warmth, and in a night that overflowed with confessions, the words turned silent, replaced with locked looks. In the silence of the moment, their eyes glowed. They were in dire need for embraces and touches, that feeling of needing to bring one's lips closer to a friend's face. Their kiss led to a moment that was awaited in their depths, and their night ended in one another's embrace, their bodies naked next to a stove that continued to warm them. They had been cold for so long.

He woke up to find that she was gone and had left a short note behind: "I never dreamt of a day in which I could enjoy all this warmth. As I return to the cold, I will always remember this great house and its ability to grant me security in this imprisoned city. This house that you wish to sell is the only safe place left in an occupied Damascus. If you end up selling the house, please don't call me. I don't want to hate you."

He reread the letter several times, took a cigarette from the pack she left behind, lit it, and began to organize and prioritize his tasks. Before all else, he needed to return to the hotel and make the call he kept putting off.

He told Hannah over Skype that he needed more time. She admitted that she was very worried about him and asked him if there was anything else that he wanted to share with her aside from the house.

"I don't have a reply now, but yes, there is something else."

After a short silence, she collected herself and calmly asked, "Is there another woman?"

"Yes, but I can't speak now."

"One more question and I'll leave you in peace. Is this revenge for that thing that happened with me years ago, in the US?"

There was a long stretch of silence as he also tried to understand if he had internally justified what had happened with Samia. He had indeed suppressed his pain and was severely wounded at the time. Back then, he controlled his pain with strength and reason, and continuously tried to erase it from his memory, believing that he had successfully overcome it.

The truth of the matter was that something about Hannah's question satisfied him, or at least restored some of his balance. Did he have a hidden desire to punish her for what she had done? Did he really want to know the details of what had happened with her and another man, a man whose name he refused to ask her to specify, to avoid even more pain? Was it even possible to overcome something like this, no matter how strong people believed themselves to be?

Rather than giving her a satisfactory answer, he added her question to a whole flock of deferred questions. He had nothing to say but, "I honestly don't know if it's about revenge. But what I do know is that I need more time to stay here."

Despite his sense of confusion after the call, he knew deep down in his soul that he needed to stay. He requested an extended leave from the hospital and wrote to his HR department and its head informing them of his need to stay and providing his place of residence and Syrian mobile number. He then packed his bags and left the hotel, heading to the house where he decided to stay until he resolved what was yet to be completed.

12
Fidel

We announced our marriage, and with Helen's help and care, I overcame all of my language barriers. I was accepted into a college of arts in London. Together, we reread Shakespeare, Milton, Lewis Carroll, and Charles Dickens, whom she loved. Helen taught me two things that I will never forget in my life—that reading is not an added or marginal task, and that any day that passes by in peace, without pain, and with a little bit of joy, knowledge, and experience, is a good day.

I quickly found my interest in advertising and the arts, and in my second year, I was ranked among the most gifted and passionate students. Helen became the dearest and most important woman in my life, and I was able to overcome my desire for sex by forgetting about it, or by pretending to forget about it.

I did not want to cause her any kind of pain. I was grateful for the Fadl in me who helped me maintain self-control. I exercised every morning, worked on elevating my spirituality, and immersed myself in work. But the question remained—was it possible for a human being to live without sex?

I made new friends—Scott, Elena, Jane, Robert and Lara—and I was slowly integrating into London life. I did not share anything personal about myself with them. Even though I mastered a Londoner's accent, some words I still used would occasionally expose my foreignness, but this did not arouse any suspicions. When they insisted on visiting me, Helen quickly took care of the situation and assured me, "Don't worry. To everyone else, I am like your mother, and no matter what, don't ever tell anyone about our marriage." And so, I was freed from embarrassment that I felt earlier among my college friends and told them that Helen had adopted and raised me. I claimed that Helen and Edward decided to adopt me twenty years ago and that they were the only family I had after the passing of my biological father and mother. I also told them that my origins traced back to Syria. I told them how my father, Edward, died of cancer of the spinal cord and that my mother had a breakdown and became paralyzed after his death, and was confined to a wheelchair. This was the story I told to strangers, but each time I told it, I would forget the details of previous versions or add something to it.

The truth of the matter is that none of my friends really cared about any of this. Their concern was to have fun at a dinner party, eat good food, drink lots of alcohol, and smoke some hashish.

Indeed, Helen welcomed them with great warmth. The house quickly transformed from a dark, dull space to one pulsating with life. Sometimes, all it takes for positive energy to find its way into our homes is to draw back the curtains and let the light in, stirring what was subject to routine and awakening it from its slumber.

The arrival of my college friends was accompanied by clamor, the opening of curtains, and the blasting of music. The noise, jokes, loud merriment, and resounding laughter that erupted after a few joints of hashish worried the neighbors, who knocked on the door to ask what was happening inside this usually dead house. More important to me however was the heavy feeling of desire and jealousy that began to knock on the walls of my heart and Helen's. That night, I shared with her a verse from our Arab heritage and culture: "Never has a man and a woman been together without Satan being a third among them."

I couldn't remember anything from the night. I woke up the next morning with her beside me on the couch. I was half naked, and a nearby vodka bottle was almost empty. I couldn't bring myself to ask her what had happened, nor did she speak about it after. The brand name of the vodka was Absolut, which in Arabic translates to no limitations, as was that night. Our marriage remained chaste except for that one dark night of which I remembered nothing.

"If I were to get married and be physical with another person, it would mean that the last seven years of my life had no meaning, and this would simply make no sense. I am bound to this wheelchair by choice, and any change would be a betrayal to a promise I made. There is nothing more dangerous for a woman than being without principles. A man can perhaps do so, but I could never. I am English, Fidel, and like England, I will not allow anything to divert me from my history—not my desire, not my lust, nor the fads of the youth these days," she elucidated.

"I am trying to understand you, Helen, but I believe that you are wasting your life just as England seems to squander the opportunities it possesses. How is it logical to voluntarily limit your abundant life within the confines of a wheelchair while you are still able to compete with the fiercest of marathon runners? Likewise, how is it possible for Great Britain to close itself off after having once been an empire on which the sun never set?" I said.

"You're not going to understand what it means to be English, Fidel. If what you say about me is true, I would have never given you the chance to become English. England needs you as an immigrant. Don't worry about what you have been told or how they treat you. What you do for England will be determined in this house. I will be frank and tell you that I do wish to marry you, to destroy this wheelchair, to strip myself of everything, including my clothes and my memory, and enter into a marital relationship with you in which I can exploit your youth while you exploit my nationality.

"It could be a relationship with mutual benefits, one that I control until you receive your citizenship in four or five years. But it would also be a relationship founded on doubt, where any act of giving would be subjected to accusations of hypocrisy. Sure, I want this. I find you gentle, young, handsome, and someone who can satisfy what remains of my femininity out of need and ignorance of the place you are in. I happen to be an intellectual woman in the twilight of her life who can actually gain a few years more of joy, but I wonder if I would continue to feel great when I face my reality. My promise to Edward was not only about him, but it also gave me a sense of worth and purpose and has served as a test for what I have learned. I don't want you to feel obliged to agree with me or flatter me. My actions with you were a blend of emotion and reason; they have satisfied me first and foremost, but they've also enriched you, and I believe they will have their effect on you. I have now been with you for almost two years. You are a promising and ethical young man, and you were quick to learn discipline. I've always seen a special flame in your eyes, but you also learned how to suppress your feelings. You're a true person, and you've worked on educating yourself and delved deeply into the language. You've become more confident in yourself as you strove for what you want. I know that you can and will accomplish what you want, but I also know that you're afraid of me and worried about me."

"Helen"

"Don't speak. Let me finish because we won't be talking about this again. Yesterday, when your friends came over, I was overcome by strange feelings—a desire to possess you, and I was jealous of your girlfriends, especially Lara. It's something that is bigger than me. I don't want to ever have to live through another night like yesterday. You must leave this house. I will not cause you any problems or end our marriage before you get your citizenship papers. We will rent the apartment across from us, in which you can be free and live independently. I have already instructed the lawyer to work on the lease and it should be ready in a week."

I approached her. She was at the window, sipping a cup of tea and gazing out at the street. I put my hand on her shoulder and turned her towards me. "I will not argue with what you have said, but perhaps I can tell you something important about me. Inside of me is a true believer. I love him. He has learned several things from Islam—chastity, benevolence, honesty, gratitude, and to believe in God's will. Because you are my wife, I will not betray you, even if I desired a thousand women. Being married only on paper does not change anything for me. I thank you from the bottom of my heart for your honesty. I cannot promise you anything. I am also undergoing a great test without many choices. But I want to ask you one question about that night, as I do not remember anything about it. Did anything physical happen between us?"

I will never forget the piercing look she gave me. "What happened was more important than sex," she whispered. "One day you will know what happened, but not now. If your memory chooses not to remember, there is no point in me telling you anything, except for one thing—on that day, you were not the Fidel I know. You were at once so very evil and yet pure as an angel.

"I should also tell you that Lara likes you, but my advice is to not put too much trust in her. She is a nice girl, but she has far more ambition than talent and may be willing to do anything to get what she wants."

Helen was right, I thought, not about Lara, for I found her to be kind, intelligent, and pleasant to be with, but about needing to leave her alone to peacefully choose her own path to solitude and also allow me the space to discover the things that I love. I was practically twenty-five years old and still a virgin. I may act like Fidel, but Fadl ruled me. I rarely drank, I didn't smoke hashish, I seldom joined rowdy parties with friends, and my relationships with women were nonexistent. Everyone knew that I did not exaggerate, lie, or express my opinion on public issues. I simply observed, smiled, and respected everyone who spoke as if I always agreed with what was being said. This made of me a good listener who everyone trusted and wished to speak with. With time, my friends began to call me Saint Fidel.

Time passed, but not a lot changed. College presented me with the opportunity to discover a vast culture in the world of colors and shapes and their influence on media and advertising. It was necessary for me to take additional courses to better understand this specialization. Meanwhile, the world was preparing for a digital revolution to which I was intensely drawn. Unlike many of my friends who were in the arts, I did not feel alienated from the computer and in fact felt a passion for everything related to this field. My life became continuous studying, and I spent my free time tirelessly working at the computer that Helen had given me as a gift. We maintained the ritual of eating a meal or two together every week, and I often cooked Middle Eastern dishes for her that she welcomed joyfully.

I eased Fadl's authority on me and dedicated some of my time to Lara. We went on walks and attended theatrical performances and exhibitions together. She carefully freed me from my virginity, and I freed her from her commitment to me.

My life felt full and I felt confident. I obtained my British passport and began preparing for a master's degree. Everything was bringing me closer to my freedom and independence. But then came that evening drenched in pain, when Helen told me that she had been diagnosed with bone cancer. That same damn cancer was back again.

I stayed by her side for six emotional months. During the last month, I did not leave her house, for she wished to die at home. The wheelchair was now a necessity. A week before her death, she asked that we visit Kilburn Cemetery. She chose to be in a grave next to Edward, picked out her headstone, and asked that I take detailed notes of what she wanted for the funeral. She gave me the addresses of a few old friends I would need to call and invite. Engraved on her headstone were the words, "Here rests Helen Simon. Born May 19, 1940 and died March 26, 2000. She is buried next to her beloved husband, Edward Smith. May she be eternally remembered."

At the house, Helen's friend, a lawyer named George, opened her will and addressed me. "This house is yours for two years, after which it will be donated to a charitable organization. In addition, ninety thousand pounds, after taxes, are yours. A key to her private safe is also yours. As for the rest of her properties and money, she bequeathed those to charities."

I left my apartment and moved into the big house. I felt a mixture of emotions, including contentment, gratitude, and a desire for solitude. I opened the safe with the key she left me. It contained her diaries—thirty-nine notebooks in all. I immediately searched for the last one, in which she would have documented her days with me, and naturally I looked for that one night with her that I had no recollection of.

'On this night, I witnessed a frightening struggle between Fadl and Fidel, between an angel and the devil, between desire and obligation. After the first two glasses of alcohol, Fidel's superego melted away and he felt a mad and lustful desire for me. He poured an endless flood of passion into me. He had a desire to possess, protect, and dominate me. He was violent and scary, undeterred and without control. I surrendered to him out of fear at first, and I almost called the police twice. But gradually, I realized that I was witnessing a rare moment of strength and weakness, an explosion that had erupted in a person once subjected to violence, cruelty, and lies. This kind man had accumulated an aggregate of pain and cruelty that not even mountains could carry. He had a frightening relationship with the image of a woman, a combination of sin and lust, mockery and contempt.

As I resignedly began to obey his demands, he ordered that I confess my sins, relationships, and betrayals. He was hallucinating and muttering all sorts of accusations. He accused me of belonging to a malevolent gender and told me that I could not be trusted. He said that it was only violence and scolding that worked when dealing with women.

He then asked, 'Why were you loyal to him while he was dead and not while he was alive?' I was shocked by his question. Indeed, my relationship with Edward was not perfect. I committed several mistakes and had admitted to most of them. That night, I knew that I was paying the price for my sins. I replied, 'I didn't have the courage to confess to my husband all that I had done. You're right, Fidel.'

'I am not Fidel. I am Edward, Helen. You will now have to confess everything.' The bottle of vodka was running low and our confessions were becoming more ferocious. We exchanged roles of judge and culprit, executioner and victim, confession and admission. I became his lover, mother, teacher, aunt, neighbor's daughter, and his beloved, whom he called a tree. And he became Edward, my father, the church priest, and my first love, who betrayed me. We exchanged confessions, judgements, punishment, and reward. We spoke the bare truth. We felt an unbridled lust and the clamor of pleasure, and exchanged many tears of pain and joy. He refused to have sex with me in the bedroom, so we slept together in the living room instead.

The next morning, as I was preparing to kick him out of my life, I found that he had no recollection of anything. It was indeed a true blessing that he could not remember. I kept a close eye on him afterwards and I came to believe that he truly did not recall that night, which in turn liberated me. Oh, how many women would dream of a night with a man who would not remember anything the next morning.

Nevertheless, I will tell him everything after I die. This is my decision. I know that one day he will read these words, and here I will say this to you Fidel: Thank you from the bottom of my heart.

As for your question about my loyalty to Edward after his death, the decisions I made had nothing to do with my husband. They were about me being a completely free woman, something that you may not understand now but that I hope you will one day.'

13

Anees

"I'm going to need more time."

"But everything is ready, Dr. Anees."

"I appreciate your work, Mr. Rajeh, but I'll be honest with you—I need to evaluate the house's contents carefully, and in particular, the manuscripts and documents. If the house must be sold after all, these items have historical value that can only be determined by experts, and this takes time."

"Honestly, Doctor, I think you're making a big mistake. The buyer will not be happy."

"I personally don't care about the buyer. I don't want to feel rushed into selling my house or feel forced by anyone to do so. So, tell the buyer that I will need a few weeks and we will finish the matter when I see fit."

Disgruntled, Anees started to leave, but the lawyer stopped him and said, "Doctor, please calm down."

"Listen, sir," Anees said, "I thank you for your efforts, but ever since I began speaking with you about the sale of the house, your words have carried a threatening undertone, and you have refused to reveal the buyer's name. This is simply unacceptable."

"You're right, Dr. Anees. But the minute I tell you the name of the buyer, and in case you refuse to sell, you would then have to confront him. And believe me Doctor, you've been out of the country for a long time, but this is not someone we can say no to. All I can do here is not to convey your refusal. I will tell him that you are planning to assess the furniture in the house. At the end of the day, the matter is in your hands, and I am only the messenger."

Anees walked out of the lawyer's office in a bad mood. He wanted to call Samia and tell her that he refused to sell the house, but his anxiety began to seep in once again. He walked towards Al-Kamaal Café, and as he expected, Issa was there. He sat to tell Issa about his predicament and ask for his advice.

"Alone, they will devour you without salt," Issa said. "You must protect yourself and let the case of the house go public. This would put them under pressure. Then, if you end up having to sell, they will not be able to destroy the house, change it, or dare to turn it into one of their investments."

"Would you turn up the volume?" shouted Issa to the waiter.

Issa's advice calmed Anees's gnawing anxiety. He reached for his cigarette pack, removed the plastic wrap and folded it several times into a triangle. He tucked the triangle between his cheek and gum, and used it to massage his gums rhythmically. Then, without warning, he got up announced that he was leaving.

He rushed out into the street, hailed a taxi, and asked the driver to take him to Al-Jisr Al-Abyad. He took his phone out of his pocket and called Samia. She replied in her sweet voice, stretching the first letters of *Aaaalo*.

"I need you with me. I will not sell the house. Come quickly."

Her silence felt ominous, like the ticking of a time bomb.

"I'm not sure it's a good idea to meet. What happened between us is over and I want to move on."

He took a deep breath, closed his eyes, and felt the salty taste of blood in his mouth as he bit away at the inside of his cheek. He thought about how he never once tasted blood despite having spent hundreds of hours cutting rib cages with saws and incising layers of skin, flesh and muscle with scalpels, always floating in blood. He broke the silence and said, "I don't want to pressure you, Samia, but I really want to see you again, with all my heart."

"Say it again," she said.

"With all my heart, mind, and body, I am longing to see you."

There was a rattle on the other end, a choking sound. "I've been waiting for two days to hear those words," she said. "Nothing fills that void for a woman who slept with a man she'd just met as does this noble sentence. I've been waiting to hear it. Thank you for saying it."

"Samia, are you crying?"

Her voice regained its confidence, "It's OK, Doctor. They're just a couple of tears that needed to be shed. What can I help you with?"

"I've decided to start a media campaign to make public the historical value of the house."

Her smile went through the phone and came out the other side, "I am coming immediately."

The house had thirteen rooms and four bathrooms distributed on two floors, with a total area of eight hundred square meters. The library consisted of one huge room stacked with manuscripts and two smaller rooms with high walls stacked with bound books.

In the first row was a guide for all the references, and Anees decided to start there. The table of contents indicated that there were one hundred and seventy thousand books and twelve thousand Arabic manuscripts in the collection. *Surely somewhere here we will be able to find a book that speaks to the history of this house,* he thought to himself. He scanned the shelves and quickly realized that the number of books mentioned in the table of contents was far greater than what was actually there.

He was surprised to see Samia enter the room with several guests. Professor Ma'moun Abd Al-Ghani was an archeologist and a historian with a notable career of over fifty years spent researching, excavating, and translating more than two thousand archaeological artifacts in Damascus. He knew the God Adad like he knew himself and had retraced his steps in search of him. Through this work, he confirmed that the northern city of Idlib derived its name from this mysterious god, where the origin of the name was Add-lib, the "add" referring to the name of the God Adad and "lib" meaning the center or the base, or in other words, the city of the God Adad.

The architect Raymond Khoury was another guest. He was an archivist of historical buildings in Damascus and one of the very few who understood that Damascene houses were in fact once cloned from ancient

Aramaic temples and as such possessed both polytheistic and monotheistic spiritual energy, which made them one of the most eccentric types of homes in the world. Issa was there too. They all knew the house well, but never had they been presented with such an exciting opportunity to enter every room and search through its contents.

Anees listened with curiosity and pride as these men explained to him the details of the place. He came to understand that his home was not only grand and ancient, but also a masterpiece of architecture laden with secrets.

Raymond led everyone into the living room, where the walls were painted with a layer of white lime paint. From his bag he took out what looked like a cotton swab, two boxes of concentrated solution, and a piece of cotton cloth. He walked to the wall, and with a pencil and a ruler, he sketched a square with an area of twenty square centimeters and divided it into squares, each taking up an area of one square centimeter. Carefully and skillfully, he began to remove the limescale layer with the cotton swab. The white paint began to fade away revealing a golden layer of sketches. Anees was astonished.

Meanwhile, Ma'moun was busy explaining the history of the house, "Huddud's House is not only one house. Rather, it is a combination of forty houses merged together." From a section of manuscripts, the historian reached for a thick book that smelled of age and began to read. "Every room in this house has a story and an era. The general character of the house is Mamluk and Ottoman. The genius architect Albanian Sinan, who built the most beautiful architecture in Istanbul as well as some of the most valuable structures in Damascus, added an external expansion of thirteen *muqarnases* stretched over thirteen feet from the door to the basement, in addition to thirteen bedrooms with thirteen windows on each side. There is also a chapter here that explains the presence of the thirteen steps that take us down to a lower hall and to thirteen underground tunnels. As a whole, the character of the house is considered to be Ottoman, but in reality it dates back much further."

From within the main room of the library, Dr. Ma'moun continued his assessment until he got to the last section of books. He inspected everything very carefully and began to empty the books off the shelves, tapping on the wall until he heard a change in the rhythm of the echoes. He then asked everyone to help him move part of the bookshelf. With a hammer, he knocked on the tiles until he found one that was not as stable as the others. Carefully, he pulled out the tile and found an iron handle behind it.

Breathless, they looked at one another in astonishment. Dr. Ma'moun grabbed the handle and pulled it slightly upward. The wall began to vibrate, and a hidden door opened into a hallway, from which pungent smells of putrefaction and thick particles of dust emanated. Everyone stood in awe, tongue-tied, their curiosity mixed with a gripping fear of the unknown.

Dr. Ma'moun opened the door fully, exposing an entranceway with a small staircase that led downwards, from where a cold stream of antiquated air blew.

"Let's go downstairs," said Issa excitedly.

"We will need masks and light," replied Professor Ma'moun.

Samia clung to Anees who in turn whispered hesitantly, "Don't you think we should inform the authorities?"

"The authorities?" Raymond shot back. "Where do you think we are? Britain? Don't even think about it. This will be their excuse to cordon off the house and hand it over to the Department of Antiquities. By the time they discover its content, half of everything will be stolen before it ever reaches a single museum. Let's not forget that we have Dr. Ma'moun with us, the most important archeologist and historian in the country. Let's document everything first and then you can tell whomever you want."

"Thank you for the praise, Dr. Raymond. Actually, we must first go downstairs, examine the place, and figure out where it leads. I wonder if Mr. Badr Al-Deen knew about this secret chamber. From its smell, I think the place was likely visited a few years ago."

In a storage room was a shelf stacked with lanterns and battery-powered lamps. They gathered the ones that were functional and decided that Issa and the professor should go down first.

They had to bend down in order to pass through the low door. They descended thirteen steps and reached a room with an unlocked grand wooden door. Once inside, they found themselves in a strange-shaped hall. The light revealed a conglomeration of equipment and flasks, and a large opening that looked like an oven. They proceeded toward a locked chest, emblazoned with decoration and miniatures indicating that it was once used for storing clothes in ancient Damascus.

Breaking the lock and opening the chest was no problem; to their surprise, they found a leather tablet on which a sword in a silver sheath rested. The professor drew the sword from its scabbard and passed a beam of light from his lantern onto its edge. The inscriptions were in Aramaic, a language he had mastered. He began to read, "This is the sword of the God Adad. Whomever carries it will not lose a battle." He was elated, and continued, "This house has always been known in Arabic as Huddud. And now that we have found this artifact, it explains how the Arabic names had indeed been derived from its Aramaic origin. I think we are actually standing in the temple of the God Adad himself."

The group carefully carried the tablets, manuscripts, and the sword, and left the room. Very cautiously, the professor placed the pieces on a clean table. With the tip of a small knife, he began to separate the tablets engraved on patches of deer and goat skin, and began to read them one by one, bent over and motionless. After finishing, he straightened up and said, "I believe that what we have here is one of the most important Damascene swords in existence, for if it is indeed what the tablets say it is, then it is more than three thousand years old and is in fact the sword of the God Huddud or Adad, and I mean the sword of his temple."

After a week of relentless work, the entire house had been inventoried. Samia organized a team of media professionals to launch an awareness campaign, which included four co-workers. These young men were enthusiastic, energetic, and well versed in modern media, and in less than two weeks, the story of Adad's House made it to Facebook, Twitter, and to a YouTube channel, and was the subject of articles in *Le Monde,* The *Guardian,* the *New York Times,* and several history and archeology magazines. An envoy from UNESCO was also scheduled to arrive to assess the house and add it to the esteemed World Heritage List.

"What we've done so far is good, but it isn't enough. We need a stronger push in this campaign," said Samia, putting on her clothes that were scattered around the bed.

Sami's blameful voice from their call the night before lingered as the son was trying to understand what his father was doing in Damascus and what was happening between his parents. "It's my right to know what's happening with you," his son had said. "You can't just leave everything behind without some sort of explanation."

The sight of her bare back as she was putting on her bra pulled him out of his stupor. She did not look forty. There was not one sign of sagginess on her body. Her satiny skin was a rich color of harvested wheat, her body lush and inviting like bread. He brought his hand close to his nose, her scent still on his fingers. He wanted to touch her again, but she had put her shirt on and a thick jacket. Her hair fell on her shoulders in a cascade of carob brown. She turned and saw him looking at her like a ravenous harvester, swept by the sickle of her smile. She leaned in closer and gave him a quick kiss; he quickly embraced her around her neck. He pulled her to him and drew her under a leopard-print blanket. She was laughingly resistant at first but quickly loosened up as he stripped off her clothes.

"I am going to be late. You're crazy. I'm going to be late!"

The gentle resistance waned and was transformed into frenzied sighs. She let out a trumpeting groan, surged, and rode him like a saddle on a horse, scurrying across vast steppes fueled by an inner *aah*, her hair flying at every moment as she thrashed on his ground. She galloped and he ran; she raced and he panted; she neighed and he roared; she thundered, he snickered, and they whinnied together, their pores secreting delicious sweat as they melted into one another. She swelled in his arms while his dripping phallus shrunk inside of her. Their world dimmed. In their embrace, they sank into that moment beyond the flesh.

Her whisper awakened him. "I once read that if a man and a woman could remain in a state of an embrace after pleasure, they would end up growing old together."

"Yes, I want to grow old with you."

Stretched above him, she turned his face so that she could look into his eyes; it was sweltering red, beaming like a full moon. It was in that moment that the unspoken word, dormant in his depths for decades, came to surface.

"I love you."

Her gaze, hazy as if coated with beeswax, was transformed into clouds that drizzled light tears that fell to the corner of her lips. He extended his tongue to taste them.

"I want a revolution for the sake of being able to, for once in my life, live a moment of truth like this one!" He quieted her with a kiss.

The ringing of her phone snatched her from his arms, "*Aaaalo* ... What are you saying?"

Her color suddenly changed and a smile formed on her face from ear to ear, "Where are you? I am coming right away." She was back to her stormy nature, geared up and in disbelief.

"There is a demonstration in Al-Hariqa, and the Minister of Interior is there. The people are shouting 'The Syrian people will not be humiliated.' Could this actually be happening! Could this be happening here? We're going out onto the streets; I am sure of it. I am confident. It is impossible for us to remain silent, impossible to tolerate, impossible to remain in this cemetery."

She was moving about and showering him with disjointed sentences that had only one word in common: impossible.

"Should I go with you?"

"No, no. You will distract me. I'll come back."

Frantic, she left as he called out to her, "Let me know that everything is OK." His words were met with the sound of the slammed door.

14
The Sword

She repeated her question to him, "Is there another woman?"

This time Anees answered confidently, "Yes."

"What do you want me to say to Sami?"

"Nothing, I will tell him."

Most difficult in these conversations were the last seconds of utter silence, where one knew that any word, whisper, or gesture could potentially cause irreversible damage.

Hannah responded in an attempt to avenge herself, but instead she made things easier for him, saying, "I do know exactly what you're going through, as I was in the same place a few years ago. My experience was extraordinarily wonderful, incomparable to what was between us. But it was temporary. Of course, it's your right, but if this whim ends, then we shall have been even. Good luck, Anees."

"To you, too."

He felt a heavy load lifted off his shoulders as he stared at the blue spot that replaced her image on the Skype window.

He went to the kitchen and made coffee. Leisurely, he sipped his coffee as he flipped through his uncle Badr Al-Deen's diaries. Issa and Dr. Raymond arrived on time, and they all went to the basement together.

"The results of the photo analyses have arrived," said Dr. Raymond. "The short sword is the Khopesh sword, a symbol of power and prestige. It was carried by Ramesses II and Tutankhamun. However, the one we have here is an imitation of Ulfberht swords used by the Vikings, which possess part of the secret to the ancient Damascene sword, but not all of it. The third is the Indian Khanda sword, and the fourth huge one is the Zweihander sword of the crusaders, which later was defeated by the short Damascene sword.

"The Syrian legend holds that the God Huddud, or Adad the God of storms, thunder, and rain, protected Damascus. He rode his chariot, wore his sword, and thrashed the clouds so that it rained in abundance in his kingdom, where Damascus lay in the center. It is also said that there was a time when danger intensified in Damascus, and so Adad rained down thunderbolts at Mount Qasioun with his thunder leaving behind nitrates of precious, divine steel. These nitrates were collected by priests who in turn documented the secrets of this supernatural blend and passed these secrets on to Damascene artisans, who used the steel to make the most famous sword in the world, the Damascene sword. They poured the elements into a melting pot, like the one we have here in front of us, which helped them separate the thick, malleable dough of pure steel into two strands. They then braided, hammered, and heated the strands with fire, and made them into a sword to be given to a knight on a bolting horse. The knight would then take the sword and raise it the air, kicking his horse to make it go as fast as possible to a different blacksmith, who would hammer and warm up the sword and give it back to the knight, who would take off with it again, wave it in the air to cool it, and return it to the original maker. The original maker would then warm it up again and cool it off, grinding it to its final shape. The end result was a sword that could cut through any metal on the face of earth with one stroke, and greater pliability than had ever been seen before. Through the ingenuity of the Damascene people, Damascene steel became a unique and corrosion-proof piece of death and beauty, one that defied time and did not tarnish or die, like the god who created it and the city that made it. The sword was then polished and engraved with words of supplication to Huddud like the prayers: 'Huddud, he who has carried your sword will not lose his war,' or 'O God of war, help us in unsheathing your sword against our enemies.' After the arrival of Islam to Damascus, Quranic verses were engraved onto the Damascene swords. It is said that no knight ever lost his life or battle if he carried the true sword of Adad in his hand.

"Later, when Tamerlane invaded Damascus, which had refrained from fighting back, he was amazed by the power of this sword, and so he took fifteen thousand of its craftsmen back to Samarkind with him. The descendants of the priests and the masters of trade who knew the secrets to making the swords remained in Damascus until the Ottoman Sultan Selim I entered the city and moved them to Istanbul. Only one master of trade remained from their lineage along with his brother, who would also leave Damascus to Samarkand and from there to India. The brothers were the last of their lineage, so the remaining priest wrote the secrets of sword-making in ancient Aramaic. Today half of that manuscript is here and the other half is in India, and this map indicates where it is located in India.

"As for the prophetic conclusion of the manuscript, it is stated that those who turned away from the sword had not fought with honor, and that justice in the world would only be restored when people once again used the Damascene sword to settle their matters. The prophecy also tells us that only the bearer of this sword will be able to regain the blessing of the God Adad and call upon him for help to take revenge on the wicked in the pursuit of justice."

As he finished his narration on the legendary side of the story, the professor added, "Personally, I think we should search for the remainder of the manuscript." Riveted, everyone was in a state of confusion at having believed the mythical tale.

The group agreed that the next task was for Dr. Anees to reach out to Fidel Abdullah, in the hope of persuading him to film a documentary about the house. Abdullah was agreeable, and they made a plan to meet.

After Dr. Anees finished his call with Fidel, Dr. Raymond said, "The Directorate of Antiquities and Museums commissioned me to evaluate the house, and so I have a committee coming next week. They seem to be getting impatient as they are the last to know."

Meanwhile, Dr. Anees was anxiously waiting for any news from Samia. A call came from an unregistered number. It was Dr. Sa'ad Al-Deen on the line.

"I need to see you for an important matter that cannot be postponed."

"Is everything OK? You're worrying me, Sa'ad."

"I can't talk on the phone. I'll wait for you at the hospital."

Anees entered Dr. Sa'ad's office with the sense of trust and security that one should have in an old friendship, but he left drenched in doubt.

"If you don't sell the house in a week, no one will be able to protect you. You're putting us in a very difficult position," Dr. Sa'ad began.

"Putting *you* in a difficult position—why? Who are 'you?'"

"That would be myself and your friend Abbas at the least. Everyone is running out of patience with you, especially after your relationship with this woman Samia. She is an untrustworthy woman."

"Untrustworthy? How is she untrustworthy, Sa'ad?"

"Samia has an external agenda, and she is working for suspicious organizations under the guise of human rights."

Dr. Sa'ad got up from behind his desk and walked over to sit next to Anees, "This is not my opinion. This is information from security sources who are well known to Abbas Jawaher. Your relationship with her is putting both of us in an uncomfortable position. You are our friend, Dr. Anees, and we have broken bread together. But when it comes to the interest of the country," here he continued in the manner that is used by braggarts who speak through their teeth with a tone of vanity and hypocrisy, "I am willing to abandon my son if he conspires against our homeland."

Changing this harsh tone into a softer, more pleasant one that was closer a plea, he said, "Look Anees, Abbas did not feel comfortable talking about all of this to you, and so we decided that I deliver the message instead—please do not call Fidel Abdullah again. He is here on a mission working for me, and I ask that you do not involve him in something that does not concern him."

Anees tried to swallow, but he could not. His mouth had gone completely dry from shock.

Satisfied with his sweeping victory, Sa'ad regained his tone of intimidation and offered a glass of water to his old friend. "The country is not as you see it or hear about it. The country is the regime. It is the regime itself. And the regime is no longer as you left it a quarter of a century ago. It has grown roots with Satan and has branches that reach to God. So, Anees, as a friend and someone dear to my heart, what I am about to offer you can save you before you stumble into serious trouble. We've tried to explain things to you indirectly, but you continued to make the wrong choices."

Anees reached for the glass of water and took a few sips that helped him regain his balance. He came to realize that he was standing completely defeated in front of a condescending and patronizing person whom he had assumed still carried remnants of affection for their old friendship. In a faint voice, he asked, "Could you please explain to me, Doctor, how things are run here?"

In an all-knowing tone, Sa'ad answered, "The regime here is not about the Mukhabarat, oppression, or a ruling family, as the naive see it. The regime is a complex network of interests. Its face is cruel and its hand aggressively strikes anyone who threatens its interests. And when we say interests, we are not only talking about money and power. These interests are about international and regional consensuses that serve as safety valves for the interests of the entire region. Today, the regime is leaning towards expanding the circles of benefit and decision-making. We are on our way from a state of coercion to a state of law, but no doubt, we will be facing corruption. Any fundamental transition is bound to be permeated with corruption. If you happen to think that we are a corrupt country, then it's a sign that we are on the right path. We enjoy a one-of-a-kind stability, and we are one of the safest countries in the world, with a solid economy that is independent of any bank in the world. For this reason, no one can control our decisions or sovereignty. Sure, we have many problems, including bureaucracy and corruption, and most of what is said about this phase of corruption that we are undergoing is true, but we have a genuine desire to remedy all of this with time. We only need some time, and we will get through it. I can guarantee you that Syria will be one of the G20. Look at what we have today—we are industrious, we are developing at the highest standards in the world, we have real safety, and the system's structure has expanded to include a wider circle turning a blind eye to many of the old restrictions. The problem is that some intellectuals want quick change, and this places everyone in danger. There is not one village or city in the country that the regime does not have influence over; I'm not talking about its security grip, as some think, but rather the more quiet grip of influence exerted by those chosen and fully protected by the regime, who have been charged with the task of securing the people's loyalty. Today *we* are the regime; whether I and others hate the ruling family or love it is irrelevant. I declare my loyalty to the regime because I want the country to be safe. I don't impose changes that come from those who are outside and do not understand the nature of the country or its system. If you want change, then you need to put your hand in the hand of the regime and work with them. What you give to them they will return to you multiplied."

Dr. Anees sat silent at first, but then he responded, "I don't want anything but my rights, without being pressured or oppressed. It is only natural that I demand the rights of those oppressed."

"Listen," Dr. Sa'ad said. "You have an opportunity and privileges that you are foolishly wasting, if I may say so. I am going to make you an offer that will change your life. Sell the house and buy shares in the third hospital that we will be working on, and you can come to live here. Your income in Syria will be more than what you make in Britain. Come and contribute to real change and modernization. You will be treated with respect and honor, and no one will come near you. You will be able to have whatever you personally desire. But to take the side of losers like Issa, Samia, and the group of intellectuals that you are hosting in your house is labeling you, when it comes to the security of the country, as a potential danger. We have been covering up for you by arguing that you are unaware of how things work here and that you are only here for a short visit and have unintentionally found yourself interfering with things that do not concern you."

"You're speaking as if you are a security officer or an authority, not as director of a hospital or a physician, and you are threatening your old friend and classmate as if you were part of a gang," Anees shot back in a stern voice. "You know what? Everything they say about you all is true. I have nothing to do with this place you belong to. However, this is the first time that I have a say in matters that concern in this country. I will not sell the house, Dr. Sa'ad, and I am willing to pay the price for this simple right of mine. Other than that, I am not concerned with anything you said, nor do I care."

Anees was well aware that his defiance was risky. Sa'ad's message was clear. As he left, his heart was racing, but his mouth was no longer dry.

Abbas was waiting in his car downstairs as he watched the friend from his youth walk out degraded. Sa'ad Al-Deen followed shortly after and headed to Abbas's car and sat next to him. After a few moments of silence, he uttered his final verdict: "He needs to be disciplined and put in his right place."

Holding the steering wheel and staring ahead, Abbas replied, "I should've talked to him."

"Are you out of your mind? Promotions for officers are coming up, and you have been excluded for the past three years. We finally were able to find a sheikh to teach you religion! You are under watchful eyes and every word you say could be held against you."

"Sa'ad, the last thing I expected in this life is that, in order for an officer in this country to get promoted, they would have to undergo superstitious religion courses taught by naive sheikhs."

"Careful, Abbas. Ninety percent of the country's officers did not have an opportunity to kiss the hands of sheikhs and receive their blessings."

"It's about the willingness of the ten percent of officers, including myself, to submit to humiliation."

"This is the way things are here. And as for your friend, you did your duty to him and more. You're only a few months away from becoming an honorable colonel. The future is wide open for you; surely you can put up with a few lessons."

"How am I to make sense of the fact that I will need to bring a rooster and a wine decanter to seek the purification and blessings from a sheikh whom I will have to call "master" so that he can teach me the names of fifty men from a secret lineage and inform me about commandments and texts that are closer to sorcery and fortune telling? How am I supposed to listen to some idiot who has not finished the sixth grade as he tells me about the great secret of Imam Ali and how he is not only the face of the moon, nor the true prince of the bees, nor the oppressed one whose mandate was stolen, but that he is God himself, and that the Imam's enemies will turn into animals, plants, or stones? Man, what century are we living in!"

"These superstitions do not harm anyone," Dr. Sa'ad said with a smile. "I think it's good that you are venting your anger with your friend, because if you were to say these things to the wrong person, your tongue might cost you the new star on your shoulder, or worse, get you transferred to the general army."

They sank into silence for a short while. If the matter were in Sa'ad's hands, he would have beaten this weak man to his satisfaction. The last thing he wanted was to turn into a fatherly adviser for the feeble. But he needed to be patient and to keep a record of all such conversations in case they came in handy one day.

15
Fidel

There was nothing left for me in Damascus but the graves of my mother, father, and my brother Fida'. My sisters got married and moved to other countries. We stayed in touch during public holidays, but our lukewarm conversations eventually waned into dispassionate silence.

In Damascus, everything I had done or lived was called into question. My battle was now to understand my fate, and I was determined that I would not allow it to take control of me yet again. I had always been liberated by someone else, not from within, as was the case today with you, Omran, when you opened the door for me to return to my country. Prior to this, my father, Uncle Mahmoud, Ruwaida, and Lara freed me, and perhaps what Lara did was the most liberating act yet, but one that continues to hold me captive in other ways until this day.

In the seven days that passed after Helen's death, I was immersed in her diaries, melting in regret. It was her good character that drew me to Helen, for it is character that matters most, not a woman's beauty or her body. By the same token, a lack of character can push you far away.

I continued to question how I let an entire year go by, next to her, without seeing her for who she was. I replayed every laugh, every meal, every stand she had taken. I thought back to everything she had given to me, limitlessly and unconditionally. What I had in Helen was a great woman who comes along once in a lifetime, and someone I neglected because of my naivety. She had expected me to be the miracle that would save her from the constraint of death, but I was neither fit nor experienced enough to do this.

I lived seven days of regret and tears with each sentence I read. I saw her anew through her words; how she resisted her desires and fought off her selfishness. And with every mention of a time I had hurt her without paying heed, and with every thought she wrote about me, she was transforming me into an angry mass saturated with loss.

I decided to go out and buy some groceries. I opened the door but was not able to move forward. I tried to step out, but I couldn't. Every step forward would mean the sharp pain of regret. So I walked backward, sat in her wheelchair, and quietly rolled out of the house, captive to the new chair.

By the third week, I was slipping deeper into Helen's world. I rested my head on her clothes as I went to sleep and wore them as I read her diaries. I lived in her letters and in her scent. I felt jealous of Edward and had arguments with her. I looked into the mirror and saw her. I was drowning in alcohol, surrendering my body to her so that she could breathe through it, and so that she would not leave.

Lara was my savior. She stormed into the house through the garden entrance after I had locked myself up in isolation. She found me wearing Helen's clothes, glued to her wheelchair, toasting her absence.

Seeing what had become of me, Lara was horrified, and she asked me to slowly stand up. I did. She walked me gently to the couch and drew back the curtains. The light was blinding, and her anger escalated as she began to see what I had been doing to myself.

I was unable to speak. I heard her call for an ambulance, demanding that they arrive quickly. She grabbed the bottles of alcohol and threw them in the trash. She hastily piled up the diaries, flipped through them quickly, placed them in a black bag, and dragged them to the junk room. She rushed back into the room and tried to destroy the wheelchair, then she charged at me and ripped off the nightgown I was wearing. When the ambulance arrived, they took me into the bathroom, where the stinging cold water left me unconscious until I woke up in the hospital.

With Lara's help, I was able to find my way out of the painful spiral of loss, and I moved into her apartment with her. Her abundant body freed me from the dead woman's stench. And in time, with the further help of a mental health center, I slowly overcame the grief.

My last visit to Helen's grave was pleasant. I took along a bouquet of tulips and one of her diaries, from which I made certain to rip out any pages that referenced me. I gave the diary to a publisher who agreed to publish it after I assured him that I would cover all the costs.

Lara said, "You've done all that you can. Let her go in peace." We decided that the time had come to leave London and travel the world.

We planned to participate in twenty-four festivals around the world. I bought camera equipment and we set off, grateful for Helen's generosity and for a life that allowed us the opportunity to dive in and document it with our senses and photos. The three-month trip turned into a year and a half. We traveled across continents, from the far reaches of the North Pole to the wilderness of Africa. We learned the samba at the carnival in Rio, delved into seasons of food and music at Mardi Gras in New Orleans, took our masks off at the Venice Carnival, played flutes and tambourines with the fisherman at the Dunkirk Carnival in France, and in Barbados, along the shores of the Caribbean, and during the sugarcane celebrations, we drank until we passed out.

We had long conversations about the Day of the Dead, celebrated by Mexicans with colorful shows and special costumes. We splashed one another with water in celebration of the Songkran, which marks the traditional Thai new year, and where an elephant was trained to spray water through its trunk at spectators. At the festival of Tomatina in Spain, Lara almost died from a tomato allergy after having overindulged in a tomato-throwing festival. We delved into the bustle of a sea of colors in India during the Holi festival. We climbed the highest illuminated and most exciting peaks in the Lantern Festival in Taiwan, where the skies were lit with an endless number of lanterns.

This is how we chose to experience the world—to witness people in festivals and capture photos of humans in their madness, arts, manifestations, colors, and celebrations of their senses, beliefs, and superstitions. Meanwhile, I was in the company of a partner who had a ravenous appetite for life and who was light in her heart and mind. I did not once tell her that I loved her, nor did she ever express that she wished to hear it, and so neither of us ever complained.

We spent two years traveling and discovering the world, not caring about what news channels had to say. I came to understand that to travel at the end of a lifetime was to miss out on life, while at the same time, to travel in one's prime as we did, lacks the wisdom to extract meaning.

When we discovered that what we had left in our bank account was barely enough to return to London, we had to accept the reality that our adventure had come to an end. Prior to the last festival we had planned to attend, I confessed to her that I did not love, nor was I someone who could love.

It was at the Thaipusam carnival that I discovered my relationship with pain and tolerance. Hindus pierced their bodies in public displays of pain. The more pain one endured, the more merits and blessings were bestowed. That is where I experienced that kind of pain that carries you beyond it and into a pleasure akin to the divine trial, the ecstasy of creation itself. Lara was united with me in pain; we exchanged roles as we both felt and caused pain. It was the first time in my life to experience such a moment of enlightenment as I watched her in pain, pleading more blessings and more pain, until she reached a state of ecstasy and begged for forgiveness and pardon. Our eyes were opened to human masochism, where men and women pierce their bodies with needles, step on embers of fire, and lash their bodies with whips. Masochism was to experience absolute pain in its purest form, where the greater the tolerance, the greater the liberation, until one reaches the brink of simultaneously screaming and smiling.

Play was mixed with seriousness, ecstasy with punishment, pleasure with fatigue, knowledge with uncertainty, pleas with rejection, conviction with doubt. Could it be possible that it was only through subjecting the body to extreme conditions that our hearts could be at peace, or that the outlandish and extreme could incite a sense of curiosity and shatter certainty? We returned to London completely broke and with a vague understanding of our inner truth.

We arrived at her flat in Camden, and after a few days of rest, we realized that we could no longer relive those great moments we lived in

India. All our attempts to stir our imaginations and to practice seduction with violence were futile. But at the same time, our bodies could no longer communicate within normal boundaries.

We worried that reality was bound to set in, and that our overbearing, questioning minds would no longer allow our bodies to simply be fulfilled. We lacked the maturity to transform what we had learned into an awareness that we could benefit from. Logical conclusions exposed our relationship to a frost that began to quickly take over.

Lara started going out under the pretense of looking for work, while I stayed home organizing the photos and videos of our journeys. Regret and fear seeped in, and they were as overwhelming as the many wrongs I had committed. I came see that I was not to be trusted with my body, and that I was cursed in this world and bound to be consumed in fire in the hereafter. Fadl, who had been absent, and whom I had suppressed amid my desires, lusts, curiosity, and travels, had now returned and began to infiltrate my conscience. He pushed me to go to the mosque in London as I crumbled under the vigorous force of guilt and fell back into that abyss of old fear.

Lara could not understand all of this. Silence occupied the space between us. We barely saw each other, and I began to sleep in the living room, making certain that I got up and left before she awakened.

One Friday night, she returned late with another man. They barely greeted me and went into the bedroom. I couldn't stay in the house and went out walking for the entire night, until dawn prayer at the London Mosque. I went inside and prayed with tears, pleas, and weeping.

In the morning I returned to the house and found my things waiting for me at the front door.

My life was endless series of attempts to heal from the bruises of fate. This time, I became displaced in the depth of the city and not on its surface. I began to ask myself explicitly about the meaning of life, about the meaning of my life.

After we finished the dawn prayer, the imam said to me, "This is the address for the Brotherhood Society. After the Friday prayer, there will be a meeting for all brothers coming from different parts of Britain to coordinate for the upcoming month of Ramadan. It will be good for you to get to know several good and active brothers."

Sheikh Shaheen was a close friend of Sheikh Ghassan, and over the months he helped me to get my life back. I felt indebted to him and to the Brotherhood Society. Most of the society's members were Muslim elites whose benevolent hand extended all over the world. Enlightened members spoke in every space, including universities, media institutions, and economic centers, and their Islamic centers provided classes on topics ranging from Arabic language to Islamic jurisprudence.

Sheikh Shaheen offered me a job as a full-time Arabic teacher, which helped me a great deal at that part of my life, while Fadl helped me avoid pains that were too great for me to confront. It was a turning point in my life towards God, one of repentance and which carried the delightful taste of faith. I learned that one feels a deep-seated sense of gratitude when your inner and outer being are in agreement; it is a sensation unlike any other pleasure, when life's boiling questions cease to exist and are replaced by a taste of eternal life, and when the believing mind finds satisfactory answers about equality, justice, and truth.

Many nonreligious people make the mistake of mocking believers, but the truth is that only those who have tasted, and who have scooped from, the sweetness of faith know its worth. It is something comparable to the ecstasy one feels at the first sniff of cocaine; it is to taste the delight of breaking out of the prisons of the mind, and to arrive at the inner kingdoms of the self, craving more of what allows you to remain under the spell of these worlds—worlds that offer successive waves of new ecstasies, bringing one's body to feel an excitement produced as one stumbles upon the answers.

Housed in the prisons of frigid minds, humanity produces an illusory language of control and influence. The greedy who are in power fear that the oppressed may come to discover the truth, and it is for that reason that their spiritual energy is sabotaged and transformed into arid and aggressive struggles drowned in accusations.

The paths to God have always been fraught with deception. It is not enough for one to only abide by the teachings; one must also have the will to embark on this arduous journey to find the right path. Religion brokers have made the path longer by erecting false road signs that lead to nowhere. You must find the true signs on your own.

At first, I had to cleanse myself of drugs and alcohol for forty consecutive days. I reread the Quran and never missed a prayer. Gradually, I restored that delicious relationship with heaven.

After a few months of working at the Brotherhood Center, Sheikh Shaheen approached me and informed me that it was time for me to get married. He nominated Mariam as a potential candidate. I met with Mariam a number of times; she regularly attended Arabic language classes. She was a girl beaming with liveliness, a nutritionist and a volunteer at the center. She was born in Birmingham to an Afghani Pashtun father and an English mother from Wakefield, and she stood out because of this. She wore the veil and was devout and proud of her Islamic heritage. It was an easy courtship, for I needed a woman who could nurture my reborn soul. Indeed, when your body is cleansed from alcohol, nicotine, and drugs, your soul is also cleansed, and then your mind is clear. We got married and rented a house in Maida Vale.

Life was tranquil, passing by routinely, free of surprises. Things were foreseeable and predictable, and from an inner sense of happiness sprung spiritual serenity. The clamor and temptation for the adventurous and the unknown ceased.

I was not fond of teaching, especially because most of the students were interested in asking questions about religion more than they wanted to learn Arabic. The religious curriculum taught in Europe in general, and in England in particular, relied on quantity and not quality, on the form and not the content, on ordaining the authority of so-called sheikhs and not on enlightenment, on hearing and counting good deeds toward the promise of paradise and not on integration, interaction, and working together with everyone in a society that accepts difference.

Technically, all licensed organizations present reasonable discourses, but religiosity is about the destruction of the ego and implanting new taboos and permissibles on which everything should be constructed and judged, and by which people are enslaved, exiling one another. The new entrants to Islam, after having been committed for a certain period of time, no longer stop to listen to sheikhs about moderation; they are the ones whose craving for knowledge and action are not satisfied except by extremist discourses.

As for third-generation immigrants, they are truly unable to integrate, not because they do not want to but because the existing system, despite its ingenuity, slogans, and power, only accepts them by way of formality, even though it was their fathers and grandfathers who built London's tunnel, bridges, and infrastructure. More than two million Muslims fought with the Allies in the First World War and just as many in the Second World War. But they remained on the margins. It was a resentful generation, fueled by a new and extreme Islam rooted in victimhood and seeking true equality for the oppressed, a generation that knew how to speak to their dignity and extraordinariness, a well-educated generation that understood technology and knew the secrets to modernization, but they continued to be rejected and accused. It was a generation that was rescued by Islam, ridding them of the gnawing feeling of being third- or fourth-class citizens.

Extremism in the West is a blatant example of how the social contract is eroded and swallowed up by savage capitalism, and it foretells a much more dangerous future that is yet to come. For this extremism can infiltrate one in every fifty thousand people to form a nucleus of those who will no longer accept being nobodies, and that the politics of the country will have to pay the price.

My marriage to Mariam was an attempt to belong to a group, driven by a desire to feel protected. At first, I was able to attain this feeling of security. But little by little, I began to feel a sense of shock, not about faith, as it was not something new for me, but with marriage itself and how a person unintentionally begins to tie himself down with so much weight that his gait becomes heavy and his desire slow, and where the dust of marriage begins to accumulate in life and routine begins to eat away at him, bite by bite.

When marriage fails to turn into a great friendship, then no doubt it will end in a great calamity. After a few months, everything was turning into a disaster—the teaching, the society, the marriage, and the new brothers. We belonged to two different worlds, not because we were of two different cultures, but because the culture of the country in which we lived failed to bring us together. Gradually, differences turned into disagreements, friendly feelings into criticism, and trust into jealousy and doubts.

I could no longer live with marriage, particularly when the feeling of suffocation and besiegement took root, in addition to Sharia laws and daily questions about the permissible and the forbidden. At the beginning I escaped home by keeping myself busy at work, hoping that the inevitable would be postponed or a miracle would take place and a solution found. My confessions to her about my life prior to meeting her was the most foolish act I committed. Instead of giving way to truth and trust, it was like giving her a reason to become anxious and terrified that my past life would be restored at the first opportunity that arose.

Instead of appreciating my honesty, the stories that I shared turned into condemnations. Her fear of losing me or that I would betray her put her in a constant state of alert. She became unbalanced as she constantly searched for any sign of betrayal, suspicious of the smallest things. She resented any mention of the past. Gradually, I learned to take caution, for indeed the fearful come to know how to build a defense against predation.

During a rare moment of calm, she said to me, "I am like your opposite riverbank. Love needs a riverbank, Fadl. You are my riverbank. The river of life passes between us, but we must build bridges between our riverbanks."

I replied, "What you are doing is stretching the riverbanks closer to one another and turning the river into a stream. What you want, Mariam, is to join the two riverbanks, but then, my wife, all the water will disappear. We must each stay on our side of the riverbank; when I long for you, I sail towards you, get wet in order to get to you. To build a bridge is to fix us in place. We must walk with the river's flow. Bridges are bars made by humans to roof the river of life, under the pretext of coming closer and crossing over. Love does not need a riverbank; instead the river should be turned into a sea, one with no need of boats but rather skilled divers, swimmers, risk-takers, and patient fishermen.

A few months of marriage passed where failed attempts were made to stay in the kingdom of happiness, and all precautions were taken in order to avoid pregnancy. She made me feel like someone who hated himself. Nothing is uglier than for the person you love to make you hate yourself under the pretext of loving you. Nothing is more ridiculous than a sick person pretending to appear healthy, a fool trying to appear knowledgeable, a lowly person trying to appear refined, and a married couple pretending to be happy.

Trying to hide who we really are is truly laughable. My wife, who desired to be committed and loving, wore masks and exercised her harmful control and ugly powers by causing me to feel permanently under suspicion and accused. Complying with her rules comforted her, but at the same time was destructive for me. Her jealousy evolved into a thousand ambushes. Her accusations, on the pretext of my dark past, were always at the ready, while she justified her actions in the name of love. My phone, my emails, my bills were all subject to scrutiny, reviews, questioning, investigation, and interrogation. Our home turned into hell itself, a place where I was tortured upon entering and fled from as an escapee.

I returned to my old habit of wandering aimlessly through the streets and contemplating the fleeting faces in a London that swarmed with all kinds of women and desires. I stared at blondes dressed in black. One of them approached me around Victoria Station. She was unstoppable, her smile cutting through the cold; I first felt her touch through the perfume she was wearing. The scent of African lemon rind and amber roots, mixed with a storm of orange and mint essence, swept my senses away and cleared my congested nose. By regaining the blessed sense of smell, I felt a sense of relief from the curse of being at home.

The anonymous perfumed woman passed by, glowing, her steps dancing to the rhythm of the musical sound of her breaths. I moved close to inhale what I could of her dazzling scent, in the hope that I might be bestowed the privilege of her black coat brushing against me or the fortune of bumping into her. But she gently avoided me and went on her way through the silent streets of London, which knew nothing about the art of listening, where people stuffed their ears with headphones listening to music that cannot be shared with anyone. There was no greater selfishness. They passed by with their bodies cloaked, ears shut, eyes indifferent, leaving behind mute cries.

With the return of my sense of smell, my sight and wisdom also returned, and so did Fidel, who began to awaken from a long slumber.

"You are a committed, religious woman. The Quran gives me the right to marry four. What if I marry another woman and I try to be fair?"

Burning with anger, twitching like she had been stung, she screamed, "I will call the police and send you to prison! The law here does not permit this right."

"Now you're suddenly concerned about respecting the law in an infidel Britain?"

The worst thing about religious people, not believers, is that they don't hold clear values and they manipulate everything to serve them.

"You are not to blame. You have nothing to do with it. I will bear the consequences of your breaking the fast." I told her this after I convinced her to make love during Ramadan before breaking the fast.

"But this is haram, Fadl."

"Rules are made for the wicked ones, but you are a good person, Mariam. I am your rightful husband. Forget about the teachings of the sheikhs. The righteous only need to keep an eye on their own conscience," I replied sarcastically.

It was then that she gave up and we parted ways. With this quiet divorce, I left teaching and joined a major advertising firm as a designer. Then I became a film director and later an executive producer for the Middle East region. I was assigned to work with a company that had a branch in Dubai, and with my travels to the United Arab Emirates, Fadl disappeared, sad and defeated yet again, while Fidel continued to move forward and prove himself, not only at work but also as one of the world's most important filmmakers.

16
Layl

"This man is a womanizer," Maysoon warned. "Be careful. He has a bad reputation in Dubai. I can see that he's hovering around you."

Hearing her friend's words of caution, Layl responded by putting up a thick barrier and taking all measures to protect herself. "Who are you talking about?"

"The slightly tall one, wearing the hazel jacket," she said, referring to Fidel.

Layl's faint smile put a stop to the torrent of gossip swarming in her ear, "Let him dare and make a mistake," she determinedly told Maysoon. "I will show him!"

Maysoon was a divorced woman and a screenwriter who found her way into middle- and upper-class circles in Damascus through her unparalleled ability to gossip and flatter. She was aware of every incoming and outgoing detail that took place among the elite families. She made it to the presidential palace on two different occasions where she received the patronage of the First Lady, Asma Al-Akhras, wife of Bashar Al-Assad, and took photos with her that she enlarged and hung on the walls of her living room. It is also notable that she upgraded her furniture every few months, although with an obvious lack of taste.

Although Layl was mildly curious to hear more, she had to choose between listening to her friend's gossip or answering his question.

"Dr. Layl?"

She turned to the sound of the voice that came from behind her. He stood in front of her full of charisma and with a mysterious smile, his savage and treacherous looks planting their way into her.

"I am Fidel Abdullah."

"Hello," she answered coldly, an overly stern look on her face.

"Would it be possible to meet over a cup of coffee tomorrow, at your convenience?"

"Of course not," she replied.

"*Of course not!*" he mimicked, and laughed loudly. A strange look came over his face, his wolf-like eyes becoming childlike and playful. "Very well then," he said. "But I was hoping that you would be part of the promotional film that we are making about the hospital."

"Everything you need will be sent to you via email," she said, in a calmer tone. "You can direct any questions you may have to our public relations and marketing officer, who will be following up with you and your company."

"But I thought you were the one who came up with the idea of tying the marketing aspect of the hospital to a breast cancer awareness campaign, or at least that's what I was told by Dr. Omran."

"It wasn't only me. Dr. Hiyam, who you met today, was the one who came up with the idea. As a gynecologist, I encouraged her to include an awareness campaign, which is also to say that my work has nothing to do with you, ever, ever." She backed away from him and repeated the word "ever" in an attempt to hide her smile, but he caught it as she turned away. He moved closer to her, leaned in, and inhaled her perfume.

"To have trusted doctors in the film will add real value to it. I'm sure the camera will love a face like yours. I'll be at the hospital tomorrow at eleven to finish up the interviews. Of course, I am interested in seeing Dr. Hiyam, but I'll also be happy to see you."

She pulled away gently to a safe distance from him and asked, "Who exactly are you?"

"The executive producer. I represent RST International and am originally from Syria. I've been commissioned to make an advertising film about the hospital chains owned by Dr. Omran. Today I found out that your hospital focuses on medical tourism in Syria and decided to come and see for myself. I believe that the low cost of medical treatment in Syria, combined with the high quality of the physicians and the services they provide, can help move the country forward." He added, "It will be a welcomed change from the ubiquitous Syrian dramas."

"What do dramas have to do with this?" she said with a laugh.

"Drama is the only industry that Syrians seem to be proud of. I think it's time that they allow for something else. And since investors have shown interest in the health sector, that should be given priority. There are more than a hundred thousand doctors who currently lack real opportunities to make a difference."

Maysoon's warning about Fidel dissipated as Layl listened to the kind of conversation this man had mastered, and she spent the remainder of her time at the evening gala with him. Before he left her to speak with Dr. Omran, who nodded at him from afar, he threw a barb at her that left her flustered, "By the way, don't wear Gucci anymore. The scent doesn't suit you."

As he walked away, she was in a state of sudden joy, her face locked in a tormented smile. She escaped to the bathroom and stared at her beautiful oval face in the mirror. She took a quick, spontaneous sniff of herself, and for the first time in years she found her perfume unpalatable.

It was as if she was suddenly seeing her face again after a long absence. There were light wrinkles under her eyes and other signs indicating that she would be turning forty in three months. She noticed a few silver hairs that needed touching up. There was luster in her eyes' dark brown irises, flickering each time her medium-length eyelashes glided over them. Her nose was pretty, her eyebrows natural looking, her chin delicate, her bottom lip slightly protruding with seductive plumpness. She unconsciously licked her lips as her eyes fell on them. She puffed out her small breasts, admired the tightness of her stomach, which she had worked very diligently to recover after giving birth twice. She once again saw herself as a desirable and beautiful woman, like in the days when she was a student in the college of medicine and made heads turn with her sheer gait and light presence. Her body and soul savored the admiration and flirtation of others as they fixed their eyes on the places she knew how to draw attention to without vulgarity.

Her father was formerly the chief justice of the supreme court, a professor at the faculty of law, and one of the most prominent legal figures in the country. Her mother was a pharmacist and a professor at the schools of medicine, dentistry, and nursing, and a woman known for her rigor and integrity. Layl had three sisters, one of whom was a dentist who resided in Beirut with her husband, a successful plastic surgeon. Her other sisters were also physicians, one an ophthalmologist and the other a hematologist; they moved to Canada and the US after getting married. Layl also had a brother, a physician who worked with Doctors Without Borders. Spending his time amid epidemics and wars, he brought pride to the good exemplary family even as he kept them in a state of worry and endless longing for him. Everything in her life had been calculated and clear, from the inevitability of studying medicine to marrying an oncologist several years her senior.

The only detour she had taken in her life was when she had fallen in love with a journalism graduate during her second year of university. For two years, the relationship kept her trembling and rejoicing until one day he visited her parent's home and asked for her hand in marriage. With seeming indifference, her father listened to him and declared, "I have raised my children with the understanding that they are free to choose their own futures and that I will always support them. In this family however, we don't marry for love. I don't mind that you are together, but it is as clear as ever to me that as a couple the two of you will not make it."

"Do you see religion as the problem, sir?" asked the poet-journalist in a defiant tone.

"No, my son, this condition doesn't apply in my household, and it makes no difference."

"Then why do you expect our relationship to fail?"

The father replied in a firm and loud voice, so that Layl could hear him clearly and not necessarily the poor, so-called intellectual sitting in front of him. "Listen, my son, Sameeh. Great love stories do not end in marriage, but rather death. All the stories of the great lovers end either in death or separation, and were it not for death or abandonment, we would never have heard about a single one of them."

"Allow me to disagree with you, sir. There are indeed success stories, and marriage without love is not possible." The naive but provocative journalist spoke in the idealistic tone of a university student, but the judge's coldness and logic made him feel stripped and raw in the face of life.

"Indeed, there are success stories," the judge agreed. "But logically you are at the beginning of the road, without a profession or clear future; you have not completed your compulsory military service and have not experienced life except through words. What is between the two of you today is simply a wave of emotions that will ultimately recede; that's all."

The father was aware, through his experience and wisdom, that if he exercised oppression and rejection, his infatuated daughter might bypass the family altogether and foolishly get married in secret.

With the dignity of the weak and the poor, the journalist, who had not yet written one piece of news, put on a fake smile. He then added a phrase that came across as disrespectful to the older, intelligent, and stern man, "Very well then, let's see who will win."

Their love, or rush of affection, lasted two years, during which she was introduced to an ideal world made up of exhausted but attractive Syrian leftist youths. Sameeh Al-Ghawrany introduced her to theater, cinema, and art. It was her first time to taste a man's body, and she was shocked by the amount of cohabitation that took place among her university colleagues, all of whom were doing it in absolute secret and took refuge in rented rooms and apartments, justifying their absences with the excuse of studying. They were a generation that was taking a leap forward in a society that was fixed and perpetually political.

Nevertheless, a permanent wall continued to remind her that she belonged to a different world. The gatherings held by Sameeh's friends were bustling with arak, intoxication, and talk of postponed revolutions. She was introduced to a new side of the regime, one that she knew nothing about, and came to discover the poverty in her country. She was unaware that her friends who were burning with liveliness and energy couldn't make ends meet or secure their daily bread. The two amazing years added great depth to her life. She read the books that Sameeh recommended as he tried to mitigate the effects of the bourgeoisie on her. She did love him; he was honorable, poor, and full of knowledge and ambition. She decided to give him her precious virginity without prior planning. But most painful for her was when he tried to break her away from the walnut shell, as he put it; he did not differentiate between her and her class. Fueled by alcoholism—a vice that she could not help rid him of—and successive disappointments, he would lose his temper and often destroy her in the process. And, instead of allowing her to help make a difference in his life, he pulled her into his chaotic world, unable to cope with the heaviness of the political reality.

After he graduated, he was unable to find employment anywhere. Security reports always pointed to the fact that he was an anarchist and the son of a former political detainee imprisoned for eleven years, and this constantly threw his loyalty to the party and the government into question. So he finally gave up and decided to flee the country as convoys of others before him had done in the seventies. His departure came at a time when she needed him the most, after he had subjected her to an abortion, unable to protect their fetus, just as he did not fight for their marriage or to keep their child. After leaving the operating room that day, their love had also been aborted. And upon arriving back at his place, he informed her that he was leaving the country.

Layl was surprised at how the sudden appearance of this new man brought back repressed memories and opened old wounds. She thought she had already crossed the waters of old anxieties and had landed safely onto the shores of routine and marriage. She was suddenly reminded of the failure of her relationship, as her stern father had predicted. The end of her relationship left a deep wound in her heart. She recalled how she wept and pleaded for him to stay, but with a stern voice, he ended things by saying, "Listen, dear, your father was right. All my friends have left the country. I am sick of goodbyes and tired of having to drive others to the airport every month. It's now my turn. There will never be reform or shit. Do you remember how I always told you that my heart is detained and that I would not be able to protect you in a country where the Mukhabarat and its men are everywhere? I've given up, Layl. Your father and Hafez

Al-Assad have won. I am leaving. I don't know what I'll do, but I do know that I have enough anger to crush this world. I'll return when we have a country in which we are able to love. Layl, the reason we love in this country is to make up for all of our disappointments and defeats, but love alone can't carry this load."

She pleaded with him, cried, tried to change his mind, but he showed her his visa to Abu Dhabi and his plane ticket. "Sameeh. I am begging you. Please calm down. For my sake. For the sake of what's between us."

"I can't stay any longer. We are completely defeated. Or actually, I am defeated; I no longer want to speak on behalf of everyone. After all, who is everyone? All of them put together do not exceed ten, forty, fifty, one hundred thousand people who I know, knew, or heard about—all of them are defeated. I have never known of anyone who has not been defeated in Damascus. All that I possess in Damascus is my love for you. But love dies when it is a compensation for disappointment. Running away from confrontation to living stories of love produces lies and detains people in massive prisons. Love cannot be in prison. Love needs freedom. Love cannot compensate for the loss of freedom. But freedom can compensate for the loss of love, Layl. I am going to search for my freedom, and perhaps there will come a day when I can love again. We are lying to ourselves, Layl, and I can't do it anymore. Set me free, and set yourself free."

Sameeh, the leftist and failed journalist, went off to the Arab Gulf, evading his mandatory military service and the entire country. He joined the thousands of young Syrian men and women and left the physician deeply wounded. She was only able to overcome the pain by accepting her reality and fully submitting to her father's laws. She always knew that he would collapse and leave. But she resented him for abandoning her on the day of her abortion, leaving her with her shame, pain, and loss.

Fidel Abdullah did not seem to be looking for love. Yet, when he spoke, he reminded her of the soul of her runaway lover. Both men had a similar look, intrusive courage, and a high intellect, but whereas Fidel was filled with confidence, Sameeh was crushed by defeat. Sameeh was pessimistic and critical of everything. He was never satisfied, and most important, he was incapable of doing anything.

She realized that she needed to put an end to her thoughts. It was useless to think about a past that had left no traces behind. She did not hear anything about Sameeh after he left, nor did she come across anything from him as a writer or journalist. Even his friends whom she had stumbled upon told her that he had disappeared without a trace and most likely left the UAE after several years and gone somewhere else, and that there was no news about him whatsoever.

It was obvious that Fidel would not give up. He was in her office at noon, carrying a yellow rose with stems of violet around it. He entered without permission and gave her the flowers.

"I stole it for you just now. I won't take too much of your time."

He moved to her until his face was buried in her hair. After inhaling her, he said, "Now, that's better. Chanel No. 5. That's your perfume."

Confidently, he took a seat, opened his mini-notebook, and said in a serious tone, "Time your watch for one thousand seconds, and after that you will find me outside your office. We need to get to work."

Her mind wandered as she tried to calculate the thousand seconds, and instead of kicking him out of her office, she said, "Very well. Let's see where this will take us."

She watched him as he worked. He was serious, well-versed. They spoke about their target audience and about medical tourism. He gave her space to flaunt her knowledge. She was grateful in her heart for a man who listened with respect and knew just the right time to interject a useful comment. Their work discussion ended in less than five productive minutes, but she did not want their conversation to end. She wanted to talk about herself, her experience, projects, and her goals and achievements as a physician, a mother, and a woman in the community.

He encouraged her by listening attentively, although the smile of satisfaction drawn on his face was at times provocative, as if he was mocking her, but at the same she knew that he was listening. As she criticized the country's corruption, nepotism, and banalities, he said something that stayed with her and continued to surface each time she listened to a news bulletin, a statement he uttered only a month and a half before the bloodbath erupted in the country: "Syria will not be liberated except with blood, and once the blood is spilled, it will not stop."

Fear brought her back to reality, and she said with great conviction, "Our hopes are hanging on President Bashar Al-Assad. May God help him. I met with him twice; he is a great person, knows the reality of the situation, but needs a little time."

Still maintaining his provocative smile, he responded, "Have you seen *The Godfather*?"

"Of course. A long time ago."

"Let me tell you something. Even if he were great, it's not about him. In a country like Syria, its security is constructed on the influence of the mafia and the godfather's ability to create new ethics. Don Vito Corleone was like Hafez Al-Assad as he prepared his eldest son for the leadership of the mafia, before the son was killed by other gangs. Corleone was forced to bring along his educated and intellectual university son, Michael, to take his place and to face the violence. The son turned out to be more criminal and bloodthirsty than his father, not because he wanted things this way, but because he felt in his heart that he did not deserve the position and was forced into it. Consequently, he wanted to prove himself by any means necessary and to outperform his father. For Bashar, this is all in addition to his inferiority complex and his jealousy of his murdered brother. Up to now, Bashar Al-Assad's performance has been reasonable and acceptable. However, if he is forced to resort to violence, he will not know when to stop, unlike the more restrained Don Corleone."

The conversation went too far, but this was the first time since Sameeh that she did not worry or fear mentioning the ruling family, nor did she have to calculate the safety lines in a country ruled by secret ghosts, lack of trust, and an instinctive fear at any mention or violation of any of the taboos.

"I think that the one thousand seconds have turned into three thousand and two hundred seconds."

"I am inviting you to dinner this evening at 8 PM at a piano bar in old Damascus. I stumbled upon it in Bab Sharqi. I will not take a no for an answer because tomorrow is Friday and I leave the day after."

"I am not that kind," she said, the sentence slipping from her mouth as she still felt the influence of Maysoon's warnings.

"Very well. Then this will be an opportunity for us to know what kind you are. As a matter of fact, according to the theory of the origin of species, every organism has the ability to achieve the appropriate mutation for evolution."

Feeling uptight, she laughed, "Darwin would be happy to hear you say this, Mr. Fidel. People like you only confirm the existence of Neanderthals."

Ignoring her comment, he said, "Wear the most beautiful dress you have. I will wait for you."

Her face took on an angry expression and her tongue became tied at this intrusion, which felt closer to audacity. Speechless, she was unable to respond or ward off his looks. She was pierced by his wolf-like eyes, which made her want to howl just as before when he left her to look for Dr. Hiyam.

She closed the door behind him and looked for a wall to lean on, feeling that she was about to explode from happiness and anger. She also felt a silly twinge of jealousy at the thought that he might approach her colleague, Dr. Hiyam, in the same manner and strike up the same sort of conversation.

17
The Uncle

"We're going to express solidarity and gather in front of the Libyan embassy. Do you want to join us?" asked Samia, who was listening to Anees describe what had taken place between him and Sa'ad Al-Deen, and how Fidel, the film director, declined his request to work on a film by claiming that he was too busy. He also informed her that the UNESCO delegation could not secure a visa to enter Syria, and that without their evaluation and firsthand inspection, the house could not be registered. She seemed indifferent, which left him feeling frustrated.

"Samia, you need to be a little less impulsive. The house is being watched and so are you."

"We would've never gotten here with such scare tactics," she responded, infuriated. "Today, they happen to be more scared than we are. And don't worry about the house. We will make sure that all its possessions are photographed and that its appraisal is completed."

"Come quickly," yelled Dr. Raymond from the library. He had just finished removing limescale from the first mural on the wall, depicting a scene that left Anees and Samia speechless. The God Adad was on his chariot lashing the clouds and sending thunderbolts with his sword. The mural was covered with gold water. They stood before it in awe.

The features of a house that had preserved the legacy of Damascus for four thousand years were revealing themselves. The house was rich and abundant, solid and unchanged. Its history was written with divine ink, its architecture constructed with the spirits of the three great religions, and its edges adorned with miniatures that revealed answers to history's queries. It was a house that served as a temple for Adad to rest in, and where his testament was inscribed in Aramaic: "Any ruler who does not rule with justice will bring upon himself the wrath of Huddud and his thunderbolts."

The house had existed in silence since the seventies, with a brief period of activity during the independence movement. It had been visited by every head of state and had been part of every honorable event in the country's history. This was the case until the Baath Party took over the country. Although the country was accused of being a hotbed of coups and political unrest, the fact is that prior to the Baath coup, not a single drop of blood was shed in the streets.

As the visitors cleared out of the house that evening, Anees stood alone at the library entrance, gazing at an entire wall covered with memoirs from everyone who had ever lived in the house, indexed and bound in chronological order.

At the end of one shelf was a huge volume that belonged to Anees's uncle; beside it was a large, blank notebook made of cotton. Dr. Anees's name was inscribed on the first page, an indication that every subsequent heir of the house was to write their own personal volume.

He returned to the previous volumes. Each of them began with an introduction of the inhabitant or resident of the house, with photos of the house and their specific date. The oldest photo dated back to 1836, or in other words, it was taken not long after the first photo in history, taken approximately ten years earlier by Joseph Niépce, from the window of his workroom in Le Gras, France.

The deeper Anees delved into the past, the more the text changed. Photos became drawings, and the Arabic was gradually replaced by other languages such as Syriac, Latin, and Aramaic. More than one hundred and twenty volumes, lined up together in consistent sequence, told the story of the house and the story of a city inextricably linked to the earliest memories of life and human history.

Anees felt a sense of awe and reverence at the great splendor in front of him. He stared down at his uncle's empty volume and contemplated what he would write in it. He randomly flipped through the pages, reading what his uncle had written, copied, and archived:

"The first women's demonstration in Damascus took place against the French occupation; it originated from Al-Aqsab Mosque in Saroujah. Eleven women were arrested and brought to trial, charged with rioting, disturbing public order, inciting a rebellion, and disobedience. The French prosecution, represented by Monsieur Morgan, presented the state's case and described Syrian men as cowards hiding in their homes, sending their women to protest in the streets. In response, Fakhri Al-Baroudi, the representative of Damascus in the Parliament, wrote a letter to Monsieur Morgan:

> 'You have insulted Syrians, and they will not rest until they avenge this injustice. I ask you to withdraw your insulting words and to apologize to my honorable people. Otherwise, I will invite you to a duel with a weapon of your choice.
>
> If you refuse to publicly apologize or decline the duel, you'll be considered a coward.'

The news spread across Damascus and caused a crisis among the French. Senior French leaders and those in charge of the Mandate's system met to discuss the issue, which had become the talk of Damascus. Monsieur Morgan decided to accept the duel, and everyone across Syria waited in anticipation of the outcome.

In the end, the French decided that killing the prosecutor would only bring shame to France, and that killing Al-Baroudi would fuel anger and unrest. They decided that the public prosecutor would have to apologize. And so it was that a forced public apology was made, and the women were released from detention.

Syrians ridiculed the event for a long time. The news reached the diaspora, and the editor of *Al-Bayan*, a newspaper based in New York, wrote a lasting sentiment about the incident, 'A knight against a knight, two to a knight, a thousand to a knight, and France against Fakhri Al-Baroudi.'"

Dr. Anees wondered how he had not heard the story before nor taught anything about Al-Baroudi. He placed the massive book on his lap and opened it to a random page. He found a photo of a stamp with the name Taj Al-Din Al-Hasani, Prime Minister of Syria during the Mandate era. He continued to read:

"During the occupation, Taj Al-Din Al-Hasani accepted the position as the head of the government. In so doing, demonstrations ensued that denounced him and the Mandate, and he became the subject of general mockery, particularly in student demonstrations at the University of Damascus and the Faculty of Law in particular. One young man, carried on the shoulders of demonstrators, chanted the following slogan:

'I am Taj Al-Din. Love me,' and the crowd responded, 'Shit on you. Shit on you.'

'I can't hear you! I can't hear you!' the young man shouted, and all would reply, 'Shit on you. Shit on you.'

Taj Al-Din Al-Hassani did not try to disperse or suppress the demonstrations, but vowed, 'By God, I'm going to make you lick my behind.'

And sure enough, true to his word, he later ordered that his full-length image be printed on stamps most often used by the students and mandated that every student applying to the university affix one of these stamps and lick its back."

Dr. Anees flipped through the pages, devouring its content and soon stopped at the amazing story of the Fares Al-Khoury. Al-Khoury, a Christian, represented Syria at the United Nations prior to its independence and later became its prime minister as well as its minister of religious endowments. Anees looked up at the photo of the large man hanging on the wall; Fares Al-Khoury had also visited the house and met with his uncle Badr Al-Deen:

"At a Security Council meeting where Syria had requested that the French Mandate be lifted, Fares Beyk Al-Khoury, the Syrian representative in the Council at the time, sat in the seat of the French representative. When the French representative arrived and found Fares Al-Khoury in the seat assigned to him, he was angry. He asked the Council President to order Fares Al-Khoury to vacate the French seat and sit in the seat assigned to Syria. To this, Fares Al-Khoury replied: I sat in your seat for a few minutes, and you could not bear it; but what about us? You who have been perched on our chests for twenty-five years!"

The book was filled with newspaper and magazine clippings, and the stories were deeply moving for Anees. He had never known this feeling before, one that filled him with pride for ancestors past and for the place where he had grown up. He realized he had never truly known himself or the truth of his identity. He had always heard Damascenes express a kind of pride, but he never really understood what it meant to be Damascene. But today, he fully understood what it meant for Damascus to be occupied by someone spiteful who erased its history, strangled its present in order to dominate it, and who, out of fear, forced future generations to choose between survival or annihilation.

Hours passed while he pored over the archived stories, enthralled by the photos of personalities and news events, all with references to the sources in the library. Dr. Anees was most astonished when he read some of the historical information that his uncle had documented along with photographs.

- The toothbrush arrived in the city of Damascus to replace the miswak in 1914, a few months prior to World War I, and by 1930, 60 percent of Damascenes owned their own toothbrush.
- Damascene women first wore high-heeled shoes in the summer of 1924, when the city's merchants introduced this product to the Hamidiyah markets, inspired by Paris.
- The Great Ummayad Mosque was the first building to have electricity in the city of Damascus, in February 1907.
- The first ballet school in the Arab world was founded in Damascus in 1951, in the home of the notable Muzaffar Al-Bakri, who was married to the Greek artist Anna Francolli; she was fascinated

by ballet dancing and so she decided to introduce this art to Damascus.

He began to understand the significance of this house and what it represented, and also to comprehend what Samia had tried to convey with all of her energy. At that very moment, he felt an overwhelming longing for his son Sami and wished he was with him. He called Sami and they talked for two hours as he spoke with passion about Huddud's House. When Sami said he wanted to join him, Dr. Anees said, "Don't be late. Come as soon as you can."

He wanted very much to share this time of great expectations and unfolding truths with his son. It was as if a strong hand was scraping off the limescale that veiled the city, revealing to the entire world what lay behind the high walls of silence. He ended the call and went to the door, where he encountered her radiant face, dancing eyes, and lush mouth. "I've been trying to call you for the past hour but your phone was busy," she said. "We did it, Anees. We did it and shouted our second chant in less than two weeks."

She took out her phone and showed him a video of a group of young men and women lighting candles and shouting at the top of their lungs, "He who kills his people is a traitor!"

18
Fidel and Layl

She ended her day quickly and returned home in a grumpy mood, feeling exposed. How could strangers tell that she felt so empty? The last time she had slept with her husband was months ago. Routine, monotony, and endless responsibilities allowed the mite of boredom to burrow its way into their lives and cause their relationship to fall into decay. After that one disappointing evening, they fell into another spiral of silent conflict. Something was dying in their relationship, and now she was afraid of this sudden surge of emptiness she had begun to feel.

For the entire day at the hospital, she could not shake off the imbalance she felt after Fidel swept over her world. She felt restless, unable to focus in the exam room, checking on her patients hastily. She caught glimpses of him as wandered through the wards carrying his notebook. Each time their eyes met, something in her burst into a sudden blaze. On ten different occasions, she went into the bathroom, opened her purse, and took out her bottle of perfume. She fidgeted and sighed, struggling within herself. Feeling the need to get away, she dashed to her car and took off. After sending a text message to the director of the department telling him that an urgent matter had come up and that she had to leave, she pulled over to the side of the road and took deep breaths.

She needed to calm down, to collect herself. She began recalling all of the beautiful moments she had shared with Adel, rearranging the assortment of precious images that she had leaned on all these years.

Her husband was a successful physician and a thoughtful man. She never heard him utter a single curse. All of her girlfriends envied her. He was a distinguished gentleman. He had an excellent relationship with their two children. He did not speak much and was guarded, but wore a permanent smile. He was strong, his body healthy, his gut small. Even the early stages of baldness looked good on him. He was very observant, to the point of near obsession with the smallest details.

The day she met her husband, after having been invited to their home by her father, he had just completed his PhD in France and was appointed as an assistant professor at the college, enjoying the respect of everyone. He was direct, methodical, open minded, and he knew what he wanted.

After having lunch together at the luxurious Versailles restaurant and then a cup of coffee at the Cham Hotel café, he confessed to her that he was looking for a wife, someone who understood the nature of his job and who was not a virgin.

She laughed at the idea. "And why the condition that she not be a virgin?"

He was brief and succinct. "I'm talking about not being a virgin both mentally and physically. I want a partner in life, not an immature girl. I don't have time for that."

A month later they were married. Everything was conveniently arranged. With great understanding, he helped her become independent and fully supported her in everything she did. They continued to work, their family grew, and no one ever heard of any quarrels between them. He worked at a private hospital and hoped to one day build a hospital of his own.

Today, she discovered what was missing. For the past two years, their disagreements, as trivial as they were, were becoming more common. Each time, he would escape to the village for a few days until things returned to normal.

Where did things go wrong? she wondered. *I have an excellent family, a large house, a chalet in Latakia, two luxurious cars, good relationships with well-known families in Damascus, a pleasant and orderly life, a vacation in a new country every year, and everything appears healthy and well from the outside. Where did things go wrong? And how could the presence of a fleeting stranger leave her this shaken up? Why could she not stop thinking about him? Why did she have such a strong desire to see him? Why did her secret love, which she thought was long buried, surface once again?*

She was angry, unable to concentrate, and feeling unbalanced. She needed her husband, her security and source of confidence, that kind man filled with empathy, beauty, and elegance.

She called him. "Adel. What time will you be home?"

"I'm going to be late today."

"Adel. I need you. I miss you."

"I do too, my love. But, as you know, today is a long day—we have our monthly meeting for the Society of Oncology and we need to make urgent decisions."

"Adel, pass by the house. I am begging you. I need you."

"Now you're starting to worry me."

"Nothing is wrong. I just miss you. When was the last time we slept together?"

"There are people around me, Layl. It's not a good time for this sort of talk, he whispered, laughingly."

"When is a good time? Come home! Let's go out tonight and wander the streets of Damascus looking for some trouble."

"Wander around? What's happening with you? We're too old for this. Just kidding. I'll stop by before I leave for the meeting."

"OK, as you wish."

She turned to the children. "What time are you going to your uncle's house?"

Excited, they answered in unison, "You mean we can go?"

"Yes. Call him and ask him to pick you up at five."

In disbelief, the two children jumped joyously like monkeys.

"Can we sleep there?"

"Yes, you may. You'll come back tomorrow night."

"Tomorrow is Friday and we're going to Bloudan. Since you're already letting us go, please let's stay until Saturday."

She laughed from her heart at their noisiness and beauty. She felt an immense love for them, Adel, and the world, overflowing within her. But Fidel's scent returned to seize her senses, and once the children left, she surrendered to him.

She entered the bathroom, immersed her body in the hot bath after applying the mud she had brought from the Dead Sea. She lit two candles, poured a glass of wine, and sipped it slowly. Adel will come and save her. She would not go to dinner with the cheap scoundrel, Don Juan. He was no more handsome than Adel, nor more intelligent or prestigious. Adel was a true man, working on establishing values upon which to build a better society, while this one was a player and a vagrant without principles or morals. Otherwise, why would he hit on a married woman? *Where are the noblemen during these times?*

Layl was angry with herself for letting a stranger invade her thoughts to such an extent. She should have been sterner with him. But it was not too late. She was grateful for the blessing of a good marriage and a beautiful family. Completely naked, in the state that He created her, she asked for God's forgiveness. "Dear God, forgive me."

She shed a few tears, and she felt better. She then vowed to do everything in her power to renew the treasures of love she once had with Adel. After her bath, she coated herself with deliciously scented moisturizing cream and put on light makeup. From her closet she pulled out a racy dress that she bought in Istanbul—short, black, sexy, and quite snug; it was practically glued to her thin body. She spritzed herself several times with Chanel No. 5 and put on a silk scarf tinged with bright green and black. She let down her black wavy hair and put on fishnet stockings and high heels. Overflowing with femininity, she wanted to be seen, praised, and appreciated for her worth that evening.

After setting a lovely table of delicious mezze, she dimmed the lights and lit candles in every corner, so that the scent of vanilla and burnt jasmine filled the space. She selected a Lara Fabian CD—she was Adel's favorite singer, and Layl had often been told that she resembled her. As the music played, she sat and waited, sipping a glass of chardonnay that was over twenty years old. She couldn't imagine a more perfect night to open the bottle.

Everything was ready, pristine, and alluring. When her husband let himself in, he was greeted by the sound of Lara Fabian's voice. A pale smile was drawn on his face as he walked through the corridor and into the living room to find a table filled with joy, amazing mezzes, and bedecked with seductively aromatic candles. At the table also sat Layl, striking in a black lace dress with a green shawl embroidered with gold and black threads. A glass of wine in her hand, her loving and beautiful eyes danced, and her smile cut through the dimly lit space.

He placed his briefcase on the cabinet next to the wall, walked towards her smiling, gently kissed her lips, and sat next to her. He reached for a glass that was also waiting for him, raised it, and said, "Cheers."

Reading his quizzical expression, she added quickly, "The children are at their uncle's house until the day after tomorrow."

He was about to speak, but she stopped him with her lips. She kissed him from the depth of her soul, and then suddenly she stopped and asked him to drink his glass in one go. She wrapped her arms around his neck and pulled him to her so they could dance. He placed his arms around her waist, and they stared at one another in wonder. She lay her head on his shoulder and whispered, "I love you."

He drew her closer. They stood, their bodies against one another's, lightly, seductively. His erection brushed against her. She exhaled in his right ear; his hands were feeling her bare back, removing the perfumed and dizzying shawl, and loosening the straps of her dress off her shoulders. Her shiny black dress fell to the floor, revealing a tantalizing body in Calvin Klein sexy bra and panties. His mind, busy with details, hindered him from realizing the intensity of her desire. He unhooked her bra, and her breasts, their nipples protruding, spilled out before him.

He did not know where to begin. His indecisiveness led him to rush and pull down her underwear made of silk, lace and cotton and with a red butterfly perched on the thong that cut through her strong buttocks. Still kissing her, he carried her to the bed, put her down gently, straddled her, and quickly, with her help, freed himself from his clothes. He pulled out his swollen, hard penis and pushed it forcefully between her thighs. Her pores opened, her soul in full anticipation. She broke into flames, her body twisting. But, within a few seconds, he lost control of himself. She tried to catch up to him, to pull him closer, keep him inside of her, to take refuge in him. But he wilted, depriving her of a beautiful and much needed climax. If only he could have held out for a few more seconds.

She relented quietly. He pulled out of her, wet, light, and vestigial. Once his panting subsided, he came closer to her, kissed her lips and forehead, and went to wash off. She remained astride, staring at her sad reflection in the mirror of the dresser. When he returned, he began to put on his clothes. She made no attempt to move or change her position. He said he would try not to get home too late and that tomorrow they would celebrate. By way of apology, he said he had no choice but to leave. She smiled at him kindly, without resentment, and whispered, as if surrendering to her fate, "Don't worry. I'm glad you came home."

He was ready to leave. He put on his shoes, picked up the briefcase he'd thrown on the cabinet, and left, as Lara Fabian sang "Je suis malade" and his naked wife sat upright in their bed, a warm liquid trickling down her thighs.

The arrival of a new message flashed silently on her mobile. She had no idea how much time had passed. She quickly rinsed off and tried to collect her scattered self. There were four messages, all consecutive: "Where are you? / Don't be late / I am waiting for you / My night will be hell if you don't come."

Her response was succinct: "On my way. Wait there."

It was half past eight. Once again wearing the clothes she'd left scattered across the living room, she pinched her cheeks, applied more Chanel to her neck and behind her ears, combed her hair with nervous strokes, and stared at herself into the mirror. Buried anger, deep resentment, and a burning sadness glowed in her brown eyes. She faked a smile, took a deep breath, and went out. Instead of taking her car, she hailed a taxi.

"Bab Sharqi, the piano bar."

"Can I drop you off near it, Madame? The car cannot enter that street."

Bab Sharqi was an elegant Arab house that had been transformed into a fine-dining restaurant. It exemplified the booming transformation taking place in Damascus. Fidel reserved a table in the crowded courtyard.

Once he saw her, he rose to greet her with great respect. He wore an elegant suit with a striped, red tie over a white shirt infused with blue. His cologne was intense. There was a hint of tears in his burning eyes, which looked more like the eyes of a deer than those of a wolf. Many of the twenty-something men in the room took note of her. She looked regal, exuding elegance and nobility. She was surprised when he suddenly assured her that he understood her position.

"I know how difficult it must've been for you to come. You are safe with me. Tonight is about celebrating you and thanking you for your presence. And you should also keep in mind that you are free and you can leave anytime, without any justification. Your trust, and the fact that you came tonight, is enough for me."

She knew he was lying, but she lacked the energy or the desire to stop his torrent of words, dripping with subtle flirtation. She wished that he would stop talking and order a strong drink for her. She wanted to feel lighter, get intoxicated, let go of everything, and have him then fuck her, forcefully, without any introductions or justifications. She needed him to extinguish the flaming passion that continued to burn within her. She did not care for his praise or random trivial compliments. She was angry, full of self-pity, and experiencing an acute degree of pain, loss, and vulnerability.

Somehow, as if he understood that it must have been one of the worst nights of her life, he began to pull her out of her hell.

"Today, you will consume one of the strangest dishes in the world," he said.

He asked the waiter to explain to her that they were about to cook a banana in cognac right before her eyes. The waiter did so, in a mixture of French, English, and Arabic, and when he left to bring the equipment, Fidel mimicked his delivery in a way that made her laugh heartily. He continued with the show, his gentle sarcasm lightened her soul and helped her forget her misery. Her face came alive, and her shy smile was liberated. He looked into her eyes and said, "This is the best evening ever, being in an amazing bar nearby the Jewish quarter in 'Damascus, the Resilient'[7] and in the company of a woman from Damascus. 'This is Damascus, you sons of bitches!'"

---

7   One of the nicknames given to Damascus by the Baath Party.

She burst out laughing, feeling light. Holding her glass of cognac, she said, "Don't associate Damascus with obscenities."

"I wasn't the one who said this."

"I know, it was Muzaffar Al-Nawab."

"No, the poem is not by Muzaffar. It was written by a Syrian."

"No, I am sure it was Muzaffar Al-Nawab. He's Iraqi."

"I know the Syrian author personally. He lives in Dubai and wrote this poem in 2005. He writes under the pseudonym Abu Adad."[8]

"Everyone thinks that it's Muzaffar Al-Nawab."

"At the end of the day, it doesn't matter who wrote it. What's important is that it is dedicated to Damascus."

"You know what? I feel like hearing it."

He pulled out his cellphone and looked up the poem. He then began to recite it to her:

> "She is Damascus, a woman with seven wonders, five names, and ten titles; she is an abode for a thousand saints, a school for twenty prophets, and an inspiration for fifteen gods.
>
> She is Damascus, the more ancient and the more orphaned, the beginning of dreams and their ends, the starting point for conquests and their convoys, the moseying of poems, and every poet's trap.
>
> From her balcony appeared Hisham wooing a passing Umayyad cloud after having finished irrigating her Ghouta with blood. And it was from Damascus that the Falcon of Quraysh flew dreamily until he faced his death in the Pyrenees Mountains.
>
> This is Damascus. She has tolerated everyone—the pimps and the dreamers, the petty and the revolutionaries, passers-by and residents, those addicted to biting her, those who chewed her nails, the losers, the convicts, the innocent, and the lustful.

---

8   "This is Damascus, You Sons of Bitches" is a poem written by Fadi Azzam, also the author of *Huddud's House*; some continue to misattribute the poem to Muzaffar Al-Nawwab, an Iraqi poet.

They fed off her breasts until her Barada dried up, and so she offered her blood, trees, and shade. And when her Ghouta was consumed, she offered Mount Qasioun, her beloved mole, while they drooled, raided, assaulted, and invited all kinds of bastards to take their share from her innocence.

But this was Damascus, and each time they sucked her marrow, her youth was renewed."[9]

Layl interrupted him with a wave of her hand. "Stop here. Repeat that last sentence."

"Each time they sucked her marrow, her youth was renewed."

"Say it again."

"Each time they sucked her marrow, her youth was renewed."

"I also need for the marrow to be sucked out of me so that my desire for life is renewed."

When he finished reading the piece, they fell into a deep silence, a feeling of numbness filling the space between them. Finally, he broke the silence. "Excuse me, the bill please."

They left the restaurant and walked through the alleys of Damascus, indifferent to the gentle but chilly breeze. He held her hand. She did not object. He pulled her closer. She did not object. It was an amazing feeling of lightness, exaltation, and sublimity, as if cognac was a key to locked doors.

The narrow streets were rich in beauty and safety and intimacy, inviting one to run or fly, and awakening the senses to taste, delight, and desire. They touched the walls, carved their initials into the stones, and drank water from *sebils*.[10]

"You know, this is the first time I've done something like this."

9   The full text is translated into English at the website of *ArabLit* & *ArabLit Quarterly* (arablit.org). The original piece, "This is Damascus, You Sons of Bitches," is by Fadi Azzam and translated by Ghada Alatrash.

10   Sebils are small kiosks in Islamic architectural tradition where water is freely dispensed to the public by an attendant. Today, the term is also used to refer to unmanned fountains with a tap for drinking water.

"If you stay with me, I promise you that you will do a thousand things for the first time."

"Fidel, you're always like this with women, right?"

"Almost."

"How am I different from the others?"

"You're not, for the most part."

Upset by his sudden frankness, she jerked her hand away from his. He took it back and held it, "This time I am the one who is different, Layl. Ever since the day before yesterday, I have been different."

"Explain this to me."

"It's like I have been carried away by a tender Damascene breeze. It's hard to explain. In this city, everything is different."

"I don't know many other cities aside from this one. Usually, I feel that she is weary and old. But today, there's something different about her."

"Damascus is mysterious, astonishing, and generous, particularly when she's in a good mood." He then took the pose of an actor, and in a theatrical mock-serious tone, he said, "He who has not been scorched with her fire will never know her burn."

Together, they strolled one street after another. Under the scant light, between the slanted arches, amid the whispers of history, they walked with their arms around one another's waists, celebrating the birth of something new, something inexplicable, something that they could no longer control.

They were oblivious to the fact that they were being followed. Abbas Jawhar had tasked a group of men to keep them under careful observation, and they trailed after the couple like a heavy, unseen shadow, monitoring their every move and capturing those movements on film.

Fidel had parked his car at Bab Tuma Square.

The night no longer felt cold, as if winter was a robe that could be cast off when in the company of the one your soul desires. Instead of heading back to her house, they drove to Mount Qasioun. He stopped the car on the side of the road, and they stepped out to view Damascus from above. A breeze greeted them as he wrapped his arm around her. She rested her head on his chest. They were charmed by Damascus, charged by its dazzling energy to celebrate. It was as if she was getting to know her city, and seeing it, for the first time.

She whispered into his neck, "My city and I have been waiting for you for a long time."

"You and your city are the most beautiful things that have happened to me in the past five thousand years."

She laughed. "And you and my city are the most beautiful things that have happened to me in the past five days."

"A day with you is indeed like a thousand years."[11]

She wished she could be alone with him without disrupting the mood, the amazement of feeling alive. The beauty of Damascus seen from above emits a feeling of tranquility. It was a city that had its wings stretched out like a butterfly yet was unable to fly. She could hear the city's loud whispers, mixed with feelings of fear and mystery, beauty and pain; she felt the city as if it were her. Her moans broke through the stifled silence, glimmering from her flickering innerness. She wished she could throw herself upon him, breathe in his scent, invade him like a swarm of locusts, and attach herself to him like a birthmark.

They went into one of the cafeterias, and he ordered a bottle of red wine. They drank with great gusto. Her speech started to slur after the second glass.

"You're drunk, and maybe now I can take advantage of you," he said teasingly.

"Take advantage of me all you like."

He only had a few sips and laughed heartily at her drunken slurring. She doted on his brown bright eyes, his light beard, his strong nose, and his long fingers. She switched her gaze between this dazzling man and Damascus; the two were blended into one another. She felt a rising sense of dizziness and lightness, and an irresistible desire to kiss those lips.

They returned to the car. He caressed the roots of her hair with the tips of his fingers. He moved his face close to hers, his breath touching it.

---

11   This line is a reference to Surah Al-Hajj, Ayat 47: "... But a day with your Lord is indeed like a thousand years by your counting."

His scent was lush and delicious. He smelled her cheeks, imprinted whispered kisses on her forehead, eyebrows, eyes, and lips. They sank into a kiss that knew no boundaries. In the midst of the glory of the delightful touches and the wit of the seductive fusion of their bodies, she felt herself slowly transforming from a barren desert to a land being rained upon by clouds of pleasure. Her body sprouted, moaned, twisted, and lolled between his sweet hands.

She let go of herself, as if resurrected, returning from a cave, and emerging from a spring. Each time he approached her, she swayed again, feeling moistened with dew.

"I am yours. I am yours," she said.

"Don't ever be anyone's, except for your own self."

"In this moment, I want to be yours. Don't start lecturing me. And besides, I'm drunk so I have an excuse."

A bright light flashed quickly next to their parked car, awakening the bats of fear and opening the doors of anxiety. He calmed her down and embraced her. She felt his scent nesting its way into her being, and she longed to drink from its springs. His quenching kiss brought her fortresses to collapse, and she cried tears that had been imprisoned for years. But it was a kiss that was also illuminated by the lights of passing cars.

He drove the car smoothly and lightly to the rustling rhythm of silence. He arrived in her neighborhood, stopped the car, his fingers sailing over her body, and he kissed her again. She exploded into tears that tasted like the sea while he whispered to her, "You will be fine. Everything is going to be OK."

She had become a patient standing before a physician who could heal her with just his whispers. She was drowning and he was her savior. For years, she was an expert in reassurance, knowledgeable about human pain, the one who spent a decade and a half repeating to her patients and their loved ones, "You will be fine. Everything is going to be OK."

Although she uttered these words daily, she did not realize how much positive energy they carried. She was now harvesting what she had once planted in this life. Today, she had found someone who could whisper to her, alleviate her pain, someone from the unknown, who was trying to undo one of her earrings.

In a less reassuring tone, he said, "You have to go now."

She was floating on a raft of unimaginable comfort, feeling a sense of safety kneaded with gratification. He had not taken advantage of her vulnerability and they did not make love in the car, although she felt a slight sense of disappointment as she had dreamed of having sex with a man in a car ever since she was a teenager—ever since she'd watched *Titanic*. *But then again,* she thought, *perhaps making love to someone in a car could lead to death by drowning.*

Her head had cleared as he undid her earring. "I'm going to take this with me," he said.

"Take the other one too."

"No—one with me and one with you. This way we'll stay connected."

"Will I see you again before you leave?"

"I've finished everything. But I'll be back soon."

"I don't want to say goodbye."

"Neither do I."

"Good night."

She closed the car door before she could hear his response, stepping out of his car and into the reality that awaited her. Without looking back, she adjusted her steps and regained confidence in her gait as she began to think up an excuse for her absence. She made it home by 2:30 AM, with the ground swaying and spinning unsteadily. She let herself in with her key. No excuses had come to mind.

She decided, *If he asks, I will tell him everything. I will not lie to him.*

Adel had not yet returned home. She sighed contentedly.

At least his absence would give her a little more time to take in this incredible feeling; tomorrow she would sort things out.

Without wiping off what was left of her makeup, she got in bed and sank into a deep sleep.

19

The Guard of the Booth

*The detailed events described in this chapter are based on stories told
by Syrians who lived through them.*

The house turned into a hive of activity, its doors wide open to youths, activists, and intellectuals. It was the site of dialogue sessions on the events in Egypt, Tunisia, and Libya—and as March began, the relationship between Anees and Samia was at its peak.

Upon Sami's arrival, the father and son found themselves standing together face to face with the astonishing discovery of their roots. Touring the house of his ancestors and coming to better understand its meaning, Sami remarked with sarcasm, "In Britain, they boast about Georgian and Victorian houses while it seems that my grandfather was using a basin engraved with the God Baal to make raw *kibbeh nayeh*."[12] His father replied regretfully, "What's the point of having ancestors at the forefront when their grandchildren are at the bottom of every list?" In response to his father's pessimism, Sami replied grouchily, "Dad! Don't start now!"

The father and son wandered through Damascus, revisiting the streets that Anees had once walked when he was in school and university. Sami was happy to see his father in high spirits, filled with pride and nostalgia.

Nothing could compare to the happiness of a father sharing memories with a son who had surpassed him in height. Damascus felt more

---

12   A popular Arab dish famous in Syria and Lebanon. Its main ingredients are burghul and
     ground lamb.

intimate in the company of his dear son, and as he shared its stories and explained its history to him, it was a thousand times more beautiful. Anees was claiming this history back so he could pass it down to his heir. He was trying to make up for all the years when he had nothing to say about it, for the times when Sami was a child and he would speak to the boy about London, impassively and dispassionately, of its landmarks and history, stuffing his head with information that had been packaged and stockpiled from scattered books. He did not want to do the same thing with Damascus. Instead he wanted Sami to touch the soul of the city, to open doors that had been closed to him and to tap into the city's roots. Anees wanted to find a way to apologize to his son for not having nourished his roots in the soil of his homeland.

Sami was not only discovering the city and its wonders, he was also discovering a spirit in his father that he would never have imagined him to have. As they passed the Citadel of Damascus, near Souq Al-Hamidiyyah,[13] the noon calls to prayer resounded in a dome of melodious and intertwined sounds. The clamor of a crowded city, clouded with fatigue, faded away as heartfelt calls to prayers were heard. And so they entered the small Mosque of Abi Al-Dardaa, which was built into a wall and lit by bright green lights. They prayed together and left with hearts filled with indescribable feelings. As they continued lightly on their walk, it was as if they were following the rustle of their wandering souls in the bustling city.

The son's curiosity for the city was insatiable, and the father's overflowing joy unsparingly opened its gates one after another. In Al-Buzuriyah Souq,[14] fragrant with delicious aromas of spices that invade the senses, Sami said to his father in English, "Now I know why you're stuck here. Thank you for inviting me. Had I not come, it would have been impossible to understand you."

Grateful for a Damascus that opened gateways he would've never expected to cross with this young man, Anees replied, "I am seriously considering settling here and opening my own private clinic."

---

13   Souq Al-Hamidiyyah is the largest central souq (market) in Syria. Located next to the Citadel in the old walled city of Damascus, it is covered by a 10-meter-tall metal arch.
14   Al-Buzuriyah Souq is a souq located in Damascus known for its spice vendors.

They arrived at Jabri House[15] and ordered food when Sami asked the anticipated question, "Did you agree to divorce?"

"Yes."

"Do you have a good relationship with Ms. Samia?"

"I think so."

"Can I do anything to help you and Mother?"

"No. It's over."

"I finally have answers. Thank you, Father."

Within just a few days, Sami met a group of acquaintances who eagerly invited him to join them and introduced him to the city's neighborhoods, suburbs, and stretches. They took him to Maqam Al-Arba'in, where it is said that Cain killed Abel, and where according to legend, the mountain gasped in shock and horror and a cavern formed, resembling a human mouth with a protruding rock shaped like a tongue. The site has since become a shrine, and the mountain is said to still drip water, as if crying over history's first homicide.

Sami's new friends were amazed at how this young Englishman refrained from drinking alcohol, never smoked, and turned a blind eye to the seductive charms of Damascene women. Each time he saw the flushed faces of the veiled Damascene women, eyes glimmering with pure beauty, he would whisper in Arabic, in glorification and praise of God's creation, "*Masha'Allah. Subhan Allah.*"

At Huddud's House, Sami attended several information sessions, the first of which was presented by a professor of economics who explained the government's so-called social market economy, which he blamed for the three million unemployed farmers forced to abandon their lands and resettle in urban poverty zones. If things remained as they were, he said, an explosion was inevitable and imminent. In the second session, a group of Sufi jazz youths from the new generation, obsessed with different styles of music, filled the house with wonderful songs.

The third session consisted of a recorded lecture on the ancient gods of Damascus, with an emphasis on the god of thunderbolts and rain,

---

15 Bait Jabri (in Arabic, the house of Jabri), is one of the oldest Damascene homes. Built in 1737, it has been converted into a restaurant.

Huddud or Adad, the protector of Damascus. Dr. Raymond explained that Damascus was the oldest capital and oldest inhabited city in the world, and that it is mentioned in most of the manuscripts of the ancient civilizations, including Egyptian ones that date back to the fifteenth century BCE as well as Aramaic, Assyrian, Akkadian, Babylonian, and Phoenician documents, among others.

Huddud's House was shaking off the dust of history and regaining its soul. Its walls looked younger and its rooms warmer. Camera crews flocked in and documented its details and almost brought it to speak. Meanwhile, Sami was immersed in reading his uncle's diaries.

During this same time, in Daraa, a city not too far from the house, four teens were playing, the oldest of whom was no more than sixteen years old. They bought red spray paint and, passing time, they sprayed several phrases on walls. They were feeling mischievous and wanted to leave a mark while expressing their confused emotions. They drew red hearts and sprayed their names and their initials in the spirit of naughtiness and childish innocence. In a fleeting moment of teenage foolishness, one of them sprayed an unintentional phrase in poor handwriting on a wall that was filled with other scribbles: "It's your turn, doctor."[16]

When the spray paint ran out, one of the four would-be rebels used a piece of metal to etch another phrase he had heard on television as news poured in from Tunisia and Egypt: "The people want to bring down the regime." The same boy would later admit that, when he wrote it, he did not understand the meaning of the phrase, and that he was just killing time with his friends who had dropped out of school and spent their time working small jobs or wandering aimlessly around town.

For several days, people passed by the two phrases without taking notice of them, until the day when a different group of kids, who had nothing to do with the spray paint, came to play in front of a military parking lot near a guard's booth.

---

16   "Doctor" refers to Bashar Al-Assad, the current president of Syria, who graduated with a medical degree from the University of Damascus and sought postgraduate studies in London, specializing in ophthalmology.

The bored guard, for whom time passed slowly, sat as lifeless as a leper. Hoping to outsmart the slow and cold passing of time during his shift, he placed a tea kettle on an electrical heater and read last week's *Al-Baath* newspaper. He felt sleepy and dozed off, but he awakened in a panic when the kids' soccer ball smacked into the wall of his booth. Enraged, he picked up the ball, grabbed a knife that he usually used to open food cans, and slit a hole through it. He threw it back at them, with an ominous warning. "This time, I've flattened your ball. Next time, I will skin each one of you."

The children quickly retreated but they were angry at the loss of their precious ball. They lit a bonfire in a nearby barren field, cursing guards and booths. Having let loose their anger, they were ready to leave, but one member of the group picked up one of the remaining embers in a tin can and walked towards the haughty guard. He was in a pleasant mood, not for having caused fear in the hearts of the children but because the event broke the monotony of his day, and he had decided to reward himself with a tenth cup of tea.

The boy threw the burning ember at the booth and ran away. It landed directly on the guard's hand, burning it, and causing the guard to take a few steps back in panic. In the process, he tipped over the tea kettle, spilling its contents onto a heater, which then burst into flames and short-circuited. He tried to extinguish the fire by kicking the heater out of the booth, but it fell back on him and his pants caught on fire. Terrified, he ran out and tried to save himself, his rifle empty of bullets. He managed to put out the fire on his pants but stood helpless as his booth went up in flames. His hands and feet were burned, his eyebrows singed off. Shocked at what they had done, the kids ran away as fast as they could, the heels of their feet touching their bottoms.

The guard called his immediate supervisor, who came rushing along with a Mukhabarat patrol. An arrogant officer got out of the car and, after a brief interrogation with the guard, ordered him taken away—not to a hospital but to a prison, and commanded that his hair be shaved as a preliminary punishment.

The supervisor lit a cigarette and stared foolishly at the burnt booth. He turned to the wall sprayed with the scribblers' names, and he caught a glimpse of the phrase that had been sprayed in that moment of reckless-ness and laughter, "It's your turn, doctor."

In true Sherlock Holmes fashion, the supervisor examined the rest of the scribbles and put the pieces of a conspiracy together, concluding, with his genius, that those who wrote the phrases must've been the same ones who set fire to the booth. He then quickly summoned the school principal and demanded "a list of every son of a bitch whose name is on that wall."

Within a few hours, the principal had consulted with the school's teachers, administrators, and janitors and prepared an inventory listing every student whose name appeared on the wall. The list was then sent to the Mukhabarat who mobilized all its members to roam the city with their cars, raiding homes to arrest children! It didn't matter that some of the names had been written years ago by students who were now in their twenties; all were arrested and taken to detention. In a matter of days, dozens were imprisoned. A torture party was prepared for them, and eventually about twenty kids between the ages of twelve and sixteen remained in custody.

One of the Baathist fathers who provided services for the security forces for years extracted confessions from his own son, who had not even been included in the initial list of detainees. When he discovered that the boy was indeed one of the kids playing ball next to the guard's booth, he handed him right over to security forces and told them, "Teach him a lesson so that he never does this again."

The security branch was steeped in corruption, often harvesting profits from Customs Enforcement and deceitfully confiscating lands at undervalued prices, stripping more than a thousand farmers of their properties. To divert attention from his corruption and appear loyal to the regime, the branch manager submitted a false report claiming the existence of organized networks that were working to stir discord, and that he had crushed the conspiracy by catching the first of these groups. He turned the teens over to the Sweida Branch, which, upon reading the accompanying report, deemed the matter to be far beyond its authority and transferred the detainees to the main security branch in Damascus.

While all of this was going on, a group of young civilian activists who belonged to what remained of the leftist parties were following the events in Tunisia, Egypt, Libya, and Yemen on the internet. They wanted to take to the streets and bring down the corrupt governor of their province, with the ultimate goal of being able to participate politically.

Some of these youths were partisan, and some were simply enthusiastic activists. Most of them never wanted to overthrow the regime but simply sought to assert their presence within the scene. The activists numbered no more than one hundred and fifty, most of whom had not even heard of the mass arrests of the teenagers, their eyes fixed to the internet.

In Stockholm, Sweden, a child was born to a father who was part of the Muslim Brotherhood and a mother who had no power but to obey the father's orders. Now in his early twenties, the young man sat in his cold room trying to create a web page similar to the "We Are Khaled Saeed" page,[17] which had served as a compass for the people's movement in Cairo.

The first headline he posted, titled "The Syrian Revolution Against the Baath Party," called for demonstrations. It resulted in a lot of noise but little action. He then changed the name of the web page to "The Syrian Revolution Against Alawites," which was met with disgust and dismay at its sectarian implications—no one took to the streets. He then tried out a phrase that struck him as very naive but eventually found great acceptance, particularly within Islamic groups who had been exiled from the country for decades: "The Revolution Against Bashar Al-Assad." It called for demonstrations on March 15, 2011, and dozens of youths responded to it. As a result, the second documented demonstration took place in Damascus, with other undocumented demonstrations to follow in Banyas, Douma, and Homs. Each demonstration was spontaneous and chaotic without any central organization. They were simply acts of light defiance and attempts to feel out the pulse of the beast.

On that historic Tuesday, March 15, 2011, the youths in Daraa attempted to hold a demonstration. But their handwritten banners remained hidden under their clothing as throngs of security officers greatly

---

17   Khaled Mohamed Saeed (1982–2010) was an Egyptian man who was brutally killed while in police custody on June 6, 2010. He helped incite the Egyptian Revolution of 2011.

outnumbered them and made it impossible for them to gather in any public space: universities, schools, or public squares. The one place where they could assemble was at a mosque during the Friday prayer. Most of the young men were not mosque-goers, although they were brought up in Muslim environments and understood Muslim rituals and its moral value to people. So they divided into groups and dispersed across three large mosques. Security forces learned of the possibility that something was brewing that would take place at the mosques. The families of the detained teens desperately sought answers, but received only a shockingly callous response from a security branch officer: "Forget about your children. Go make other children." Indeed, a rumor circulated among locals that this same response came from the head of the political security branch, who happened to be the maternal cousin of the president and was known for his short fuse and stupidity.

At Hamza bin Al-Abbas Mosque, worshippers lined up in rows, including young men dreaming of a demonstration, relatives of the detained, who were hearing horror stories about children being tortured, the helpless poor whose lands were stolen, and a crowd of worshipers who believed in the slogan "A just ruler is better than plentiful rain."

Adhering to the guidelines he had received from the political security branch, the imam finished his Friday sermon. As he made his concluding remarks, the worshipers dispersed and began to leave the mosque. Just then, one of the men dared to raise his voice and shouted, "*Allahu Akbar!*[18] Freedom."

Most of those present immediately rushed out in terror, while others slowed their footsteps, summoning an exceptional courage to overcome a fifty-year legacy of oppression and fear and to echo the contagious chants. The outcry was enough to liberate and spread the voices of the people. Shoulder to shoulder, they departed as one, bewildered in a space that had become unintentionally theirs.

They emerged feeling the pulse of the day, growing braver with every step. Young men were excited to voice more chants, and one of them

---

18   "Allahu Akbar" is Arabic for "God is [the] greatest," and is the opening phrase in the Islamic call to prayers.

shouted, "The people want to bring down the governor. We want our children out of prisons. God, Syria, freedom, and nothing more." It was an uprising against a fifty-year legacy of accumulated injustice and pain. The crowds walked along under the gaze of the shocked and retreating security men, and were joined by demonstrators from other mosques. People lined up on both sides of the streets, watching and documenting how a spark had ignited and spread slowly to confront despotism, corruption, anger, and arrogance. It was as if time and place had met in an explosive collision.

In the governor's office, a security committee made up of Baathists and heads of Mukhabarat branches had been summoned for an urgent meeting but they were unable to come up with any containment plan except for one that they (and others like them) had mastered throughout history. The plan was simple: crush, with an iron fist, those peasants who dared stand up against their masters. But instead of thinking things through calmly, their hatred poured like a flood of gasoline on a single spark, a spark that could have been extinguished with a water bucket of understanding and respect.

In the streets, fear mixed with courage, and oppression mixed with the air of change. Yet the fact of the matter was that the subsequent downpour of hateful bullets could have never succeeded in forcing people back into the quagmire of their lives. And so it happened that the first martyr fell, heralding the arrival of a new era for the country and its people: it was the beginning of a bloodbath era.

Inside the house, a group of those who had witnessed the first days of the revolution took refuge. Samia brought them to hide them from the eyes of security. Sami and Anees listened as they described what had taken place and relayed the news of the army's siege of the city—a city that had declared its anger.

20
Layl

Adel let her sleep while he prepared breakfast and a cup of Nescafé with milk for her. Instead of turning on the news as he always did, he put on an album by Fayrouz. The lyrics of the song seemed a continuation of the night before:

> *"They were saying that he hugged me tightly twice*
> *and that my hand did not turn him away nor did he turn away"*

Adel tried to kiss her. She felt trapped between two worlds. She did not want yesterday to end but, at the same time, she had to get up and face the day with its weight and facts. Trying to woo her, he whispered to her, interrupting her dreams. With his every touch, it felt like he was piling another row of stones upon a wall of rejection. Blinded by his sudden arousal and driven by guilt from the night before, he did not notice that she was trying to stop him and continued to push himself on her. She finally surrendered to him and shut her eyes as Adel pushed himself inside her and ejaculated soon after. When she opened her eyes, his face was far away, his expression distant, his mouth agape and still emitting muffled groans. Then he collapsed on top of her.

That morning marked the beginning of their psychological divorce. He no longer meant to her what he once did. She tried to push him away.

"Get up. I've prepared breakfast for you," he whispered.

"I'll be right there," she replied.

She desperately needed a few minutes. The last thing she needed was more heaviness. The alcohol churned in her head, and a feeling of weakness and guilt permeated her body. She dragged herself to the bathroom and locked the door, turning the key twice. Swollen and smudged with leftover makeup, her face was a morning disaster. She turned away from the mirror, splashed quick handfuls of water on her face, stripped off her clothes, and stood under the hot water, rubbing her head with vigor, pulling on strands of hair at the roots and rubbing her scalp with soap and shampoo. She scrubbed her body until it started turning red, feeling a desperate desire to be liberated from everything, from her own skin and body, and from her desires. She cried a river as she came face to face for the first time with such inner disappointment and hopelessness. She stopped crying, still barely able to breathe, and switched the hot water to cold. The shock of the cold water helped put a stop to her quickly deteriorating psychological state and helped her regain her equilibrium. As she dried herself off, she decided that she was going to go and tell Adel everything.

He was trying to be lighthearted, but every gesture he made sat heavy on her heart. His jokes were unbearable. He looked miserable and devoid of life.

"I'm sorry about yesterday and today as well."

She picked up her cup of coffee and calmly took a sip before responding in a barely audible voice, "No worries."

"I wouldn't have stayed out so late last night if Dr. Badee' hadn't insisted on inviting us to Mount Qasioun to view Damascus from above. Can you believe that was my first time going up there?"

Raising her eyes slowly to see if he was hinting at something, she felt as if a burning metal rod had pierced her head.

"I wish you could've seen how many people were going at it in their cars," he said. "It was like the whole mountain was shaking." He then added a phrase that she had never heard him use. "Open prostitution. I have no idea how the criminal police haven't gotten involved."

Gathering all her energy, putting on a stern face, and feeling ready to confront and confess, she responded, "Adel, what exactly are you trying to say?"

"Nothing at all. I was about to say that we should try and go together to Qasioun one day soon, but the place is too exposed."

"No, let's not go up there. Let's stay down here, it's darker."

He laughed and moved closer to her. "Are you still upset with me? I swear I had no choice but to leave, and I promise you that today we will be bride and groom again. Besides, when I came back, you were in a deep sleep. I know I let you down yesterday and I want to make it up to you."

"Make what up? Please, Adel! Have you checked on the children?"

"Make up for the fact that I left you alone yesterday."

She puffed her cheeks and let out a sigh to indicate that she did not want to talk about it. In response, he changed the topic. "I haven't called my brother's house yet. I assumed that they would be sleeping."

"What are your plans for the day?" she asked.

"The guys invited me to Yafour—my entire class. We're going to be meeting with Dr. Sa'ad. Honestly, yesterday he hinted at the possibility of a partnership with him, you and me. I didn't give him any feedback, but I think it would be great for us, and that way we won't have to work for people anymore and can start on our own project."

She was no longer listening, though; instead, she drifted off into the details of yesterday. It was a relief that his visit to the mountain was only a frightening coincidence. She thought about the prospect of being caught by Adel and his friends while immersed in that deep kiss with Fidel in the car. *How tragic that would have been*, she thought to herself, her heart laughing in fear, misery, and pleasure. It was a strange and terrifying feeling.

"Layl, what's the matter? You don't seem OK."

"It's nothing. I just miss the kids. We're not used to them having sleepovers."

"So, what do you think?"

"About what?"

"I swear you didn't hear a thing. Enough already! I made a mistake and I've been begging for forgiveness. Do you want us to plan something for today, or should I go out with the guys to Yafour?"

"I can't. Samia is coming."

She lied and wished he would just go and leave her alone. "But you should go. I mean, it doesn't make sense for your entire class to go and you stay here. It's not every day that you're going to meet up like this. We'll have plenty of time to do something later."

"Thank you," he said. "That's just what I'm thinking. I'll go and get ready."

"Perfect."

She took her coffee to the kitchen sink, looked out the window, and let out a sigh of relief for the chance to be alone. She desperately needed to sit with herself in quiet contemplation so she could make sense of what was happening—all the signs, interactions, and conversations invading her effervescent inner being—it was a feeling she had not known before. Hearing the door slam behind him, she let out a big sigh and hurried to check her phone. There was a message from him; her heart raced.

"My doctor. I did not shower. I wanted your scent to stay with me for as long as possible. Your voice is still lingering like your perfume on my clothes. I knew that Damascus would be generous to me, but I would never have expected it to be this bountiful. I will think of you a great deal and I will always remember how we got lost in the streets of Damascus yesterday. We will meet again."

She reread the letter again and again. She typed out a response, erased it, typed and erased, her hands trembling and her mouth dry. Something was pulling her like an irresistible magnet. *What's happening? Where did reason and self-control go? Where am I?* she wondered. It felt like she was floating on a thin raft in a world that was not big enough for this flood. Caught within her dubiety of feelings, she responded, "I loved getting lost with you."

She bit her lip, closed her eyes, held the mobile close to her chest, and then dialed—not his number as she desired, but that of the only friend to whom she could confess what had happened.

"Samia, I desperately need you."

"What's wrong?"

"I need you. Leave everything and come."

"Is everything OK? What's happening?"

"I can't speak on the phone. I need you. It's life or death."

"My God! That serious? OK, OK. Do you want me to bring anything with me?"

"No, no. Nothing. Don't be late. Or actually, bring me a pack of cigarettes."

"Cigarettes? Are things that bad? I'll be there as soon as I can."

Confessing felt good, but also scary. Layl was desperate for advice and terrified of the possibility of a scandal. Cups of coffee were poured one after the other and cigarettes were continuously lit as she confided with her friend about her burnt heart. Samia was astonished at her friend's shocking revelation, and she embraced her, whispering, "Follow your heart. Nothing is going to stop you. Just beware that the price may be very high." Layl poured tears on her friend's shoulder—tears of heartache and hope.

"Why does love have to come at the wrong time? Why do we get married without love? Why do we have children without love? For God's sake, Samia, what is love?"

Samia calmed her friend down. After thoughtful consideration, they decided to keep the matter a secret and allow for time to take care of things; after all, her beloved was far away and did not pose an immediate danger. In fact, it was not about him, but rather the new feelings of passion and empowerment that were born within her.

"I will be better and stronger. I refuse to let go of this feeling, but at the same time, I will not allow it to sweep me away. I want to fall in love without being shackled or possessed. If he can accept this, I will be the happiest woman in the world. I will live on the dream of seeing him again, but I will strive hard not to meet him."

"Are you crazy?"

"No, I am not, Samia. I think I know what I need to do. No one has studied love nor does anyone understand it. And although love happens to be one of the greatest human experiences, to date no one really knows its cause or effect. It's a mystery how it comes to be, and a mystery how it ends. Neither songs can say it nor can words tell it. It changes our ways of being and our lives. It strips us of our illusions and brings us to discover new things about ourselves. Most of the time, we don't know how to celebrate it, name it, welcome it, or bid it farewell. They say that love is blind, but the moment love ends, all flaws rise to the surface in plain sight."

"My God, listen to you! Is it possible that all of this has all happened to you within one week? I can't believe what I'm hearing. Do you remember the days when you would persecute us for talking about couples being in love or for telling a love story? Or the times we asked you to listen to a love song, and you would pout and sulk, and lecture us about how silly and small-minded we were, as if there was no such thing as love?"

"You're taking complete advantage of the situation! Well, the answer is no ma'am. I just needed for someone to light the fuse, to stimulate my mind, heart, and soul and to remind me that I am alive and that I exist after years of having forgotten who I am. We're all so good at wasting our lives waiting or justifying disappointment. Love is that slap that exposes all truths at once."

"You know, Layl. This talk scares me. Maybe because I also can't admit it to myself. I know it and I ignore it. But something similar happened to me a few days ago, and it's like you're speaking on my behalf. I'm sure I haven't felt what you're feeling, but I can completely understand what you mean."

"Seriously? And you've been silent all this time! You have to tell me everything."

"I can't get into the details, but I will tell you one thing—when we're thinking about measuring our feelings, we should consider how far these feelings are motivating us to move forward and giving us incentives. Love in its essence is getting to know all that is great—God, faith, a homeland. With love, things become more meaningful. But a married person who stumbles on love is choosing a dangerous path and opening themselves up to the charge of infidelity."

"Betrayal is a word that was invented by men to settle scores with their male counterparts," said Layl. "The day women figured out this secret, they used it as a means to teach men a lesson in humility. But my case is different. I needed someone to come and show me who I was, to help me come to a decision with Adel, and to put an end to things with courage. I need to stay strong; and the most important thing is that Fidel will finish his work and leave in two days. Now, let's make some lunch. I haven't eaten much since yesterday, just falafel and a flaming banana," she laughed from her heart at the thought of it. She continued, "Now it's your turn to talk just as I did, Samia. You're not going to get out of it."

"I'm sorry, but I won't be able to eat with you. I need to go before your respectable husband returns. As you know, since the last time I was here, he can't stand me. Secondly, my dear, I just got a message saying that my man is waiting for me," she said, snatching up her bag and slipping away from Layl's resistance, both women laughing.

"You think you're escaping, but sooner or later, you're going to talk!"

21
Adel

It seems as if a god of fate is always looking to expose true love, while at the same time keeping affairs hidden.

He had forgotten his personal computer at work, so he opened her laptop to send an urgent email. Her password was automatically saved and the screen opened to her emails. A quick glance showed him that she had one unread email. His curiosity led him to the trash folder. Several deleted messages were there, but she had not emptied the trash bin yet. He forwarded each of them to his own email, shut the laptop, and left for his office. He printed everything out and was shocked at what he saw. He became a boiling cauldron of anger and defeat. On the way home, he did his best get back on an even keel and reclaim his wisdom and self-control.

Her heart dropped to her feet as he stormed into the bedroom, panting, and demanded to know, "Who is Fidel Abdullah?"

She continued ironing, pressing a little harder on the spray nozzle. She was expecting it sooner or later. She continued to work while he stood there holding the printed messages, confronting her with them. He was disheveled, his face ghostly, with foam at the corners of his mouth. She let out one word: "Finally."

"Finally, what?"

She unplugged the iron, put the ironing board back in its position, folded the shirt neatly, and placed it in the dresser.

He felt denuded, humiliated, and paralyzed. Her calmness provoked him. Breathing in fiercely, he demanded, "I want to know everything.

Everything. Do you understand? Everything!" He let out a sharp scream and threw everything he was carrying inside him at her.

Feeling as though she was covered with a layer of frost, she did not turn to him. She had always known this moment would come. He came toward her and grabbed her violently by her shoulders so she faced him. "Look at me!" he shouted. "Look me in the eye!"

She did as commanded, and when she did she felt slightly reassured at the sight of his eyes, which were those of a helpless and disappointed man, too weak to commit any foolish acts.

"I want to know everything. Everything, I said! Do you understand?"

"Yes. As you wish. Calm down and everything will be as you want."

"How? How?"

He raised his hand as if to slap her, but he couldn't. She remained silent and calm, still not looking him in the eye.

"I feel like I'm suffocating. I'm going to try and settle myself down. I'll be in the living room. We need to talk calmly and rationally before the children return."

"Layl, you've destroyed us," he whispered, his tone shifting to one of reproach. But then, his anger flared up again and he started shouting. "Get your story straight, Layl. You're going to tell me everything. Do you hear me? Everything," and he slammed the door. Before she could catch her breath, he came back inside and said, "Give me your phone."

She pointed to it on the nightstand next to the bed.

He began to search through it, but when he found nothing incriminating, he threw it against the wall, shattering it into pieces. Layl showed no signs of fear and was even amused by the wisdom that had inspired her to purchase another phone for calling Fidel.

Adel left, slamming the door again.

She pulled the secret mobile out of the pocket of her black coat hanging in the wardrobe, and sent him a message: "He knows. I don't know how he found out. I will call you as soon as I have a chance. Do not call me, no matter what."

After adjusting its settings and deleting everything that was saved on it, she powered the device down and returned it to its hiding place. She took in a calming breath, tied her hair in a ponytail, and assumed a look of sadness, for nothing could provoke a grieving, disappointed husband like a nonchalant face. Then she left the room to meet him. He was waiting for her in the living room. She took a seat across from him, resisting the urge to smoke a cigarette. He grabbed the pack of cigarettes and offered her one. She took it.

"Am I the reason? Where did I fall short with you?" he asked.

She reminded him of the night she called him for help and tried to turn to him, recounting every minute detail. She reminded him that the topic of separation had been on the table for three years and had preceded all of this. He began to relax a little, and the tension eased in his face. She said she had no prior intentions when things started, but that one thing had led to another.

"Do you love him?"

"Adel. It was just a matter of venting. We met one evening in a restaurant, and I returned home."

"Do you love him?" he repeated, more insistently.

Feeling completely persuasive, she offered him a half-truth and was amazed at her ability to fabricate with such confidence.

"But the messages say that you kissed one another."

"I was drunk, scared, and also mad at you. It was a revengeful kiss." Here, she took over the conversation and toppled him. "I never desired a man like I desired you on that day. I wanted no one except for you and did not dream of any other man but you. Please believe me, Adel. I am begging you. You are my love, my king, the jewel in my crown, and the father of my children. I've been with you for fifteen years, unscathed like a gold coin. I've been with you through the bitter and the sweet. I have not been with any other man but you. He took advantage of me." It pained her to say this; she knew perfectly well that Fidel did not take advantage of her, but she had no choice but to exploit the history of men's cowardice.

"He kissed me in the car. I said your name. He backed off, apologized, and drove me home. You and I had not been doing too well. I found an escape with a man who lives far away and who I could not see. I was being childish; it's a bit of teenageness that women in their forties go through.

154

Forty is a scary thing, Adel. Men should be aware of this; it requires consciousness and cleverness. We women need twice the attention, like teenage girls. I swear on our children's lives that no man has touched my body except you. Forgive me and do what you need to do to feel better. I needed this shakeup."

"I will feel better if you tell me the truth. Do you love him, Layl?"

"Yes, my feelings are strong."

"And what about me?"

"No matter what I say to you, you will not be convinced Adel, but time will tell."

Without warning, he hugged her tightly, and with an overwhelming desire that he had never felt, he kissed her and asked, "Did he kiss you here?"

She didn't reply.

"Did he kiss you on your neck?"

Before she could speak, he began to kiss her in a way he had never done before. He tore her clothes with his teeth and hands, laid her on the sofa, stripped what remained off her body, and fucked her very hard, with incessant, violent, assaultive, and possessive thrusts. This gave her great pleasure and she burned for him to hurt her more, to slap her, scratch her, bruise her, and punch her. "Hit me," she whispered fiercely.

He slapped her. Her eyes welled up and she felt an exhilarating chill run through her body.

"Again."

He began to slap her with both hands, as if he had been longing to do so the whole time he was fucking her. He spat in her face. It felt like another person, someone she did not know, had taken over her body. She let out a loud groan and reached out with both hands to grab both her husband's buttocks and dug her nails in. She prodded him more, begged him to insult her, to be more violent, to ride her, to dominate her, to be her master. She was uttering phrases that were strange to her, vulgar phrases she never expected to know. It was as if another woman suddenly possessed her body—someone who loved violence, revered it, and found pleasure only in it.

As he ejaculated, he spat on her face with force. She opened her mouth, saying, "Fill me." He howled on top of her, and in that moment, they reached a great climactic explosion. Then silence fell over them.

She could no longer guess his intentions. Everything fell into a vicious cycle of suspicion. He monitored everything that was coming or going. It took him days to collect himself. He cried twice; the first time tore her heart apart and she felt guilty. The second time, she felt pity for him. Both times, she hugged him and gave him her body, after which he relaxed and slept. He demanded an apology and he received one. He asked to promise that she would stop texting Fidel and she agreed. Then the list of awful suspicions and endless insults began again. She could no longer argue with him about anything or even watch TV with him. Any dialogue, no matter how simple, ended with a reminder of her betrayal.

It seems that when a marriage fails, the couple either turns into an overbearing octopus or a guarded porcupine. Divorce becomes a solution in the same way that marriage was. The only difference between the two is that people ask about the cause of a divorce as they look for a scandal to satisfy their curiosity, but no one asks why a couple wanted to commit to each other in the first place.

Gradually, Adel's irritability and pain subsided, with only subtle traces remaining in occasional looks he gave her. He returned one day after work and said, "Tomorrow, we're going to go and spend the evening at Dr. Sa'ad Al-Deen's villa."

"But I can't."

"Oh, so now you can't make it? Well, it's not up to you. This is a formal event, and you have to be there. The papers for a partnership are almost ready. I'll be an investing partner and I will need some money from you."

"Money? How much money?"

"A million dollars?"

"I don't have that kind of money and you know it."

"You're going to have to sell your share in the hospital, sell your gold dowry, and also sell the apartment in Al-Tijara. I'm not asking you to agree or for your opinion. I'm telling you this is what's going to happen."

"But Adel, Dr. Sa'ad's does not have a good reputation—in fact, it stinks!"

"Look who's talking! As if your reputation smells good! What would people say about your reputation if they knew?"

She realized that his punishment had just begun—with implied threats, stripping away her elements of power, and taking full financial control of her—and all just a precursor to the inevitable destruction. He had arranged everything in the preceding weeks. He took advantage of his power of attorney, transferring ownership of the house and the car to himself and leaving very little in her personal bank account.

That evening at Dr. Sa'ad's villa was an opulent affair. He had hired two singers to sing in the garden, and there were many stars from TV there, along with artists, nouveau riche businessmen, military officers, and Mukhabarat agents, all clad in Armani suits and glittering Rolex watches on their wrists. These were elites brimming with cash and swagger, actors and directors, everyone glamorous and festive against a backdrop of serious deal making.

The television stars took turns entertaining the audience with jokes and musical performances. Layl found the whole scene cheap and vulgar. She wanted to lean over and whisper a snarky comment into Adel's ear, but she stopped herself, knowing how he would react. He would give her a mocking smile and mimic her words scoffingly: "Oh is that so? Cheap and vulgar you say?"

Ushered in by a waiter, the guests moved into the VIP room. The place was refined and well curated, which Layl attributed to Dr. Sa'ad Al-Deen's wife, Wafa 'Ammari. She drank only fruit juice, wore a kind smile, and did her best to avoid the attempts of her husband to immerse her in the swamp of disdain and ridicule that she faced with everything she said or did. At the table, Dr. Sa'ad Al-Deen could not stop glaring at her or throwing out tactless comments.

"Dr. Adel, our partnership depends on Dr. Layl's blessing. I would very much like to have her with us."

"Of course! As a matter of fact, it was because of Layl that I was encouraged to join hands with you."

As he prepared to stand, Dr. Sa'ad Al-Deen extended his hand to Layl, saying, "With your permission, I will steal Dr. Layl from you for a five-minute urgent consultation."

With her eyes, she pleaded with her husband to intervene, but instead his eyes had a look of encouragement, while his tongue uttered the first thing that came to him: "Don't worry, my love. You're in safe hands with Dr. Sa'ad Al-Deen."

She extended her hand to join his thick-fingered grip. Guiding her away, he said, "Just like Syrian petroleum," and laughed uproariously.

One of the guests took it upon himself to explain why this bad joke had become popular. "One of the caricature-like members of Parliament once asked, 'Where is the revenue from Syrian petroleum? Does it even make it into the budget?' To which the Speaker of the People's Assembly rebuked him sarcastically, 'Don't worry, and don't ask. The petroleum is in safe hands.'"

It goes without saying that everyone understood that the revenue went straight into the budget of the presidential palace and the ruling family and their cronies. All eyes turned to Adel with looks of pity and abasement, for Dr. Sa'ad Al-Deen's sexual adventures with women were widely known. It was said that he was like a graveyard that does not turn away a dead person. Shortly after, she pulled her hand away from his grip and asked, "What's going on, Doctor?

"I have a model of the hospital in my office. I want to you to see it."

"I'm sorry, but I don't think this is an appropriate time or place to speak about work. And what you're doing right now is uncomfortably awkward for me, my husband, your wife, and all of the guests."

He laughed, devouring her with a provocative look. "As for my wife, I don't think so. As for your husband, sure. For the guests, I don't care. I wanted to tell you that I am interested in you for two reasons—first, because your professional reputation is world-class, and second because I am attracted to you, Doctor."

"Thanks. But forgive me, Doctor, it's a known fact that you are attracted to every woman."

"No, no. Sure, I might not spare any woman I come across, but there is something different about you, and I think we should discover it together."

"Dr. Sa'ad. Thank you, but neither my mental state or life allows for this, nor is it my nature or my way to accept this sort of thing. Please. With all due respect, I am asking that you not put me in an uncomfortable position. I am quite happy with my work, home, children, and husband. And if you will, I am counting on your ethics not to involve me with any work between you and Adel."

He looked at her coldly, dripping with contempt. "I will not pressure anyone, Doctor, but let me be clear with you: I don't care to be a partner with your husband for different reasons, most important of which is that your husband comes from a family that is prohibited from entering our private space."

"I don't understand you, Doctor."

"Your husband's uncles are from the Muslim Brotherhood from Hama, Doctor, and this happens to be taboo. They are not allowed into any of the circles of national sovereign investments. I, and those with me, are interested in partnering with you. Your family is well-known. It's not personal; it's practical. This is the way the system in this country works. Moreover, you have a good record in this domain. As for the second reason—well, it's personal. Dr. Adel is a good physician, but I want brilliant doctors, and I personally have no interest in him being part of the medical staff. Sama Al-Sham Hospital—Damascus Sky Hospital—is going to be a medical and scientific gem in the Middle East. And to be even clearer, the average requirement is much more than what Adel has to offer, but it is very close to what you have. Besides, the surgeon who owns fifty-one percent of this hospital happens to be the most important surgeon in Syria."

"Who?"

"I thought you'd be smarter than that, Doctor.[19] Who is the surgeon whose wounds have no cure?"

Feeling clouded in confusion, she was desperate for a cigarette and to escape the cold gaze sweeping over her lips, chin, and neck. She had to end the moment at any cost.

---

19   A reference to Bashar Al-Assad

"Inshallah, Doctor. I'll think about it and get back to you."

"Unfortunately, there is not much time. If you choose to join the team, this is the address for my apartment in Abu Rummaneh. Tomorrow after 6 PM, come and we can discuss the details." He placed his personal card in her hand. She took it and said in a steady voice, "If you'll excuse me." She walked a few steps, faked a smile, and returned to the table. Adel was immersed in a spirited conversation. She sat next to him and waited until he was finished. She then whispered, "We need to go."

"Not now."

Feeling great anxiety, she waited patiently, trying to seek refuge in him. She wished he could protect her and help her find a way out of this calamity and away from the entire evening. She concluded that there was no misery in the world that was equal to a woman feeling as exposed as she did.

22
Anees

As Anees witnessed his son passionately embracing the movement that had begun to spread across Syria, the joy he felt because of Sami's presence turned into anxiety. He knew that the silence of the authorities was only temporary; they were simply in a state of shock and busy with having to improvise uncertain and conflicting decisions in the face of an uprising that was beginning to shake the solid ground on which the country's existence depended.

"Sami, I know how excited you are, but I want you to go back to London."

"Why? Father, this is the first time that I've ever felt a sense of belonging to this place and to its people. And you want me to leave? I've made friends in prison. I now have a cause, and you're asking me to abandon these brave people now?" He voiced these objections mixing his classical Arabic with English.

"The situation is headed to the extreme, Sami. I know this place and its people better than you. The country is splitting into two sides, and each is as stubborn as the other, harder than flint. Neither side is going to give up."

"It doesn't matter. I'm not leaving. You can leave if you're scared, but I won't go. If you didn't want me here, you wouldn't have been as keen to obtain a Syrian passport for me and to keep it renewed. Each time I asked about Syria, you aroused curiosity. It's too late now to tell me that this place does not concern me."

In the grand house, Sami and three of his friends were busy on their mobile devices; Layl was wailing next to Samia, who was trying to calm her down while keeping up with what was happening in the country. Meanwhile, Dr. Anees was waiting for Issa, who came with an urgent message from Abbas Jawhar: "Tell your friends that this is the last thing I will be helping them with—the house will be raided tonight."

Anees called everyone and conveyed the message to them, and Issa insisted it was a real warning and that they should take it seriously.

"I beg of you to leave immediately," Anees told Sami, this time unbendingly.

Seeing the anger and fear in his father's eyes, Sami promised his father that he would leave as soon as possible, realizing that the matter was much more than a romantic dream that had begun to caress his soul.

The young men and Sami moved to another place, while someone waited for Samia to take her to the countryside of Damascus. Dr. Anees insisted on staying in the house, and Layl called a relative who secured a place for her to sleep until things cleared up.

The house was indeed raided after midnight. Dr. Anees was summoned for investigation and detained for several hours in the Air Force Intelligence branch. The investigating officer tried to explain to him that things were no longer about the legitimate demands of the people, but about infiltrators who intended sabotage. By the end of the interrogation, they decided that there was no evidence of any suspicious activities, but, as a precautionary measure, they still put his name on the no-fly list.

After a few days, Sami reluctantly left Syria. His father promised that he would wrap things up and follow him soon after. Anees also gave him the power of attorney to follow up on his resignation process and obtain compensation for his work at Chelsea Hospital.

This was the best path forward for Anees. He needed to focus on what was at hand, and he asked Sami to send him some money. He also gave his son a handwritten letter in which he explained to Hannah that it was not about a woman as much as a new reality that he had to face, and he apologized for all the disturbance he had caused in the recent months.

He felt great relief once Sami left and after having ended his ethical and practical commitments in London. He met with a prominent lawyer and hired him to remove his name from the ban list on the borders. His mission had been accomplished, and he no longer felt a need to stay there, especially after the disappearance of Samia and his failed attempts to reach her.

A state of chaos had descended upon the country, with excessive violence, improvised decisions, and a failure to recognize the truth of what was happening. The country was slipping, little by little, into a bloody unknown.

A sense of hope kept Anees close to Issa, who was euphoric over the revolution. He pondered the young people, in their twenties and around the same age as Sami, as they held their secret meetings. The courage of this new generation of youth, who had rid themselves of a dark legacy that had haunted his generation and others before it, inspired him. They had found a talisman against barrenness, fear, and death, penning a brave new epic in more than fifteen hundred protests, in a country where one could be thrown in prison on the false charge of conspiring to weaken patriotic sentiment or for simply telling a joke about the regime.

"The country is menstruating," proclaimed Issa. "The blood is confirmation of the fact that our country is no longer barren and is now able to give life."

"But the situation should not remain like this for long, Issa. For how long will the people continue to protest and be killed? They are getting killed even as they are burying their dead! The regime will not stop the killing. The moment they stop, the streets will be filled with millions of people. They have no option but to arm themselves, and they are releasing Islamic jihadist leaders from prisons and throwing peaceful activists in jail."

Issa was too enthusiastic about the revolution to be swayed by Dr. Anees's evaluations, and responded, "This is what I've waited for my entire life, and this is how it should be. Anees, one of my friends, who was in prison with me, wears his wedding suit every Friday, sprays on cologne, and despite his old age goes and joins people in different places of protest. And each time he comes back, he tells me, 'I can't believe that I lived to see this day.'"

"But you're only hearing what you want to hear, and you do not differentiate between your personal mission to seek revenge and humiliate those who humiliated you and those who will actually pay the price."

Someone else among the group added, "This country will not be healed except by blood. What do you expect will happen if the revolution stops tomorrow? The regime has no plan for reform because every step towards reform means its collapse. And besides, they are vengeful, for how dare the slaves defy them! The brutality of the regime today will pale in comparison to what lies ahead if the revolution stops now."

Listening to the conversations taking place around him, Anees found them mature and correct in theory but filled with logical fallacies. What was happening was unprecedented—it was different from other movements and revolutions in history. The closest to the Syrian revolution was the Spartacus revolution, for slaves do not usually revolt, but when they do announce their anger, there is no turning back.

"There is no turning back, but I'm not sure there is a way forward."

"The only solution is for that criminal Assad to leave."

"And if he refuses?"

"We will continue."

"You mean *they* will continue, Issa. What you're doing is nothing but indulging in personal revenge without a workable plan."

"You were in London, Doctor, and did not live what we lived, nor do you know what we know," Issa shouted angrily, realizing that he might end up losing his friend if the conversation continued in this manner. "You shouldn't just sit there and criticize, Anees. Give us a solution."

"Only God knows the solution."

It was a place where the valves suddenly opened, and everyone spoke at once. Fifty years of silence suddenly exploded.

23
Layl

"I am in trouble, Adel," she began, once they got into the car after leaving Dr. Sa'ad's villa. He did not respond and drove in silence, his expression cold as stone. She did not say another word. For half an hour, amid the heavy silence, her mind wandered, musing on trivial questions. She turned her head away from him and looked out onto the desert road from Yafour to Damascus, lit with pale lights. She waited, her face clouded with anguish, her body incapacitated, her head drained.

She heard him whispering icily, "You're the one who put us in this position. Dr. Sa'ad was the one who alerted me to your photos and messages. Do not ask me how."

Her world began to spin, and she felt nauseated.

"What do you mean he was the one who alerted you? How can you give him permission? What's happening? So, you actually know what he wants from me?" she cried, exploding at him, the questions involuntarily coming out of her mouth, her hands wrestling with the air and her body straining against the seatbelt. He raised a stiff hand and slapped her hard with the back of it.

"Shut up. This is all because of you, all because of you."

The shock, the pain, and the blow left her speechless. She raised her head, trying to stop the blood trickling out of her nose and the tears.

That night, he slept in the living room for the first time while she lay awake the entire night, with eyes wide open. Hearing the dawn call to prayer as it echoed throughout the sleeping city, she left her bed and opened the door. He was sitting in the dark, smoking, with the TV on but muted. His face looked ghostly in the reflected light, infused with disappointment. Feeling pity for him, she approached him quietly, put her hand on his shoulder, and whispered, "Nothing will be solved this way. We need to talk."

He jerked her hand away and gestured for her to sit.

"Dr. Sa'ad wants to meet me at his apartment in Abu Rummaneh, and he does not want you as a partner."

"Did he say why?"

"It's ridiculous. He said that you aren't from the honorable sect,[20] and that your uncles have a long history with the Muslim Brotherhood."[21]

"Not a problem. You can just go in as a partner and give me a general power of attorney."

"And what about going to his apartment?"

"That's your decision."

"No way. Even if it gave me ownership of the entire hospital, I will not go. Adel, you need to protect me."

"And I need to protect my children and their future. I'm sure you will come up with a solution." It seemed futile to continue with this sort of debate, for it was clear that Adel had made up his mind. She returned to her bedroom, resisting the urge to call Fidel. She felt reassured by the thought of having coffee later in the morning with the only man in the world who could truly protect her: her father.

She took a cold shower that awakened every cell in her body. She helped get the children ready for school and prepared breakfast for them. Adel withdrew to the bedroom, and she left, headed to Al-Muhajireen neighborhood.

Her father and mother had just woken up, and she hugged them affectionately. Her childhood home was her place of refuge. She ignored her mother's questions about the bruise on her face, and contemplated

---

20   The honorable sect is the Alawite sect of the ruling party.
21   In the eighties, the Muslim Brotherhood clashed with the regime, particularly in Hama, and they were defeated by the regime. Some died in prisons and others went into exile. Any affiliation with this party was grounds for execution.

the photos of her siblings that filled the vitrines in the living room. She reflected on a lifetime that seemed to have passed in the blink of an eye.

Once she was alone with her father, after her mother left them on the balcony to prepare breakfast, Layl rushed to tell him what had happened, but only gave a partial account. She did not tell him about Fidel or her husband's reaction, just of the trouble she was in.

He bowed his head quietly, unresponsive. His silence was intermittently interrupted by the sound of her mother's incessant chatter from the kitchen. Layl was on the verge of exploding when her father whispered, "Tell your husband and let him handle it."

"Father, Adel is blinded by his excitement about the partnership with those people."

"Layl, Adel called and told me about everything going on between the two of you."

"What did he tell you?"

"He told me about your emails, and frankly, I can't bring myself to look him in the eye."

"Father, don't believe him. I haven't done anything. I apologized to Adel, and I am willing to spend the rest of my life atoning for this accidental mistake. But my problem is bigger than this, father. You know these kinds of people in power in the regime better than I do. Please give me advice. I have no one to turn to but you."

"My advice to you is to protect yourself in every possible way. What you're calling an accidental mistake is the reason that Adel refuses to help you."

He left and went into his office. He returned with an envelope, threw it in front of her, and made his way to the balcony to stare into the unknown. Inside the envelope she found photos of her with Fidel in the streets of Damascus and at Qasioun, and one of them kissing in the car. She quickly stuffed the photos back in the envelope and realized that her father and husband were both being blackmailed, and so was she. The issue was much bigger than she had thought, bigger than her father, husband, or herself; she had no choice but to surrender everything to them. She shoved the envelope into her bag and headed to the door. Her mother tried to stop her, but Layl could not come up with words to respond and ran away in tears.

In her car, she looked through the photos again, taking snapshots of each one with her phone and sending them to the bastard who was to blame in the first place. Before she got to the last photo, her mobile rang. She answered angrily, "This is all your fault. God damn you."

In an earnestly worried voice, he replied from the other end, "Calm down and tell me what happened."

As she regained her composure, she told him everything. At once, he said in a definitive tone, "First of all, you will not go to this bastard's apartment. Second, everything will be solved. I will not abandon you. I am the one who got you into all of this, and I will not leave you to deal with this alone."

She finally felt a sense of safety. The person who had turned her life upside down was the same person providing her with the only reliable feeling of strength and security. She desperately wanted to believe him, his voice filled with assurance in the midst of such uncertainty. She felt a shiver of gratitude, joy, energy, and longing.

Not knowing how the words escaped her mouth, she told him, "I love you."

But he had already hung up.

Layl did not go to meet with Dr. Sa'ad. She didn't pick up the phone, even though it never stopped ringing. She didn't go to work at the hospital, and she didn't return home. Instead, she went out walking in Damascus, with quiet confidence, in silence and pain. She crossed Al-Hamidiyyah market to the Umayyad Mosque. She covered her hair with a headscarf and entered the spacious square of the mosque.

Grasping the iron bars of the shrine of John the Baptist, she broke into tearful prayers. She cried as hard as she could, feeling as though piles of rocks were being taken off her chest. She leaned back against the shrine's fencing, gazing at the stained glass windows through which the light filtered in. If only she could forget about all of her worries of the world and be left alone with the spirit of this man called Fidel.

This must be what love is; it strengthens; it gives meaning to everything;

it fortifies. Love can only be confessed in one of the houses of God, she thought. She was grateful to be in the right place and whispered, "Oh Lord, help me."

She didn't know how much time had passed, but the sound of the call to prayer and the commotion of the people lining up to pray awakened her. She was surprised to see women lined up in the same place. It was the only mosque in the country where men and women prayed together, next to the shrine of John the Baptist, the remnants of the walls of the temple of the Gods Baal and Adad, and the remains of a Jewish synagogue. The mosque was visited by Druze, Alawite, and Ismaili communities, all seeking the blessings of the Khidr shrine; it was a place in which Christians came longing for the spirit of John and tourists to see traces of Rome and the pagan gods before monotheism.

The Umayyad Mosque possessed an awe-inspiring energy that emanated from its heart and poured out into the city of Damascus and flooded the entire country.

Amid all this incredible harmony, the place suddenly exploded in shouts. She could not make sense of what was happening as she heard the first shout coming from the outer courtyard of the mosque. The voices were raging, rising, and calling out, "Peaceful. Peaceful. Peaceful."

Many came out from inside the mosque and stood at doorsteps. The imam was trying to bring them back in, calling them to prayer, "Line up for prayer. Line up for prayer. May God have mercy on us and you." But the crowd that had gathered was taking the shape of a demonstration, chanting, "In blood and spirit, we shall redeem you, O Daraa."

Another outcry shook the shrines of Abd Al-Malik ibn Marwan and Salah Al-Din Al-Ayyubi, and more than a thousand philosophers, thinkers and historical leaders who lay under the soil of Damascus: "God. Syria. Freedom. Only. God. Syria. Freedom. Only."

For a moment, she considered what was happening an answer to her prayers. Her lips trembled as she looked at the faces, some crying out and filled with beauty and anger. For the first time, she saw her people with clarity, vigor, strength, and defiance. She was afraid and happy, amazed and in disbelief. The youths entered the mosque during that great Friday, chanting, "*Allahu Akbar.*" Then the place erupted in unison: "Freedom, freedom, freedom." It was a word that came out stained in blood, raspy, born from the womb of darkness. The imam stopped inviting people to line up for prayer, while hordes of security forces entered the place and began randomly beating people. The chanting youths were pulled out one after the other, while throngs clamored to flee from the doors.

Layl carried her shoes under one arm and crept out with the crowds onto the street. She stood in front of the "Khabbeeni"[22] café, as it was called during Ottoman times. It is said that when the Ottomans were looking to enlist young men for military service during the Seferberlik[23] war, the sergeant, wearing a long, felt fabric hat, would go into the markets and search for them. To warn one another of his presence, people would shout, "*Abaya,*[24] *abaya,*" and the young people would know to run into the coffee shop (their only place of refuge) and plead with the shop owners to "Khabbeeni."

Layl saw a group of youth running towards the same café, but instead of helping them hide, the owner shouted to the security officers, "Look, they are here! They are here!"

She ran to the first market in Al-Hamidiyyah and bought a container of Bakdash[25] ice cream, and caught her breath in the crowded shop. She then continued to the main street and, miraculously, found a taxi to take her home.

Frightened, the boys rushed to greet her. "Where were you, Mama? We were worried about you."

"I was at the Umayyad Mosque."

"Since when do you go to mosques?" Adel snapped.

"I saw a demonstration that came out from the heart of the mosque. It was unbelievable."

---

22 *Khabbeeni* means "Hide me" in conversational Arabic.
23 Seferberlik involved the mobilization by the late Ottoman Empire during the Second Balkan War of 1913 and World War II, during which Lebanese, Palestinian, Syrian, and Kurdish men were enlisted to fight on its behalf.
24 *Abaya* is Arabic for cloak, or a loose outer garment worn by women and men in the Arab and or Muslim world.
25 Bakdash is a landmark ice cream parlor in Al-Hamidiyyah market established in 1895.

"Oh really. That's all we need now. A bunch of thugs wanting to destroy the country while you go and watch them."

"They're not thugs. They are the children of our homeland. We must not keep silent about what's happening in Daraa. People want freedom."

"Freedom? People? What's happened to you? Are we talking freedom as in your kind of freedom—to prostitute? Or do you mean freedom for armed gangs?" he added, laboring to keep his voice down so the children, who were busy with their ice cream, would not hear him.

He took a deep breath, trying to swallow the contempt he felt towards her and maintain his composure, "Look, Layl. You have nothing to do with the conspiracy taking place in the country. Stay away. I apologize. I was hoping that you were trying to find a solution to our problem instead of wasting your time."

"Our problem? So, now you're saying this is our problem and not only mine?"

"I am with you, Layl. We have to get past this. Tomorrow night we'll be with friends, and we can join hands and finally relax. I've invited them to dinner. It's all arranged."

"Invited who?"

"A friend of mine and his wife who are here on a vacation from Canada."

"Your friends don't have names?"

"Of course they do. Raja and Ilham. I've known them since my university days in Paris."

She let out a deep sigh of relief; he was finally behaving normally. She replied with enthusiasm, "Very well. I'll take care of dinner."

"The children asked if they could go to Al-Zabadani and I agreed. It's really important that everything goes smoothly."

"I'll try my best."

Is it possible that God is this responsive? she thought, as she stared at herself in the mirror smilingly. But her sarcasm quickly made her uncomfortable and she begged to be forgiven. The chants liberated her; they empowered her. She wanted to keep this overwhelming sense of defiance as a talisman and never let it go.

Adel returned to the door and said, "By the way, Ilham is very chic. I want you to look very fashionable when they come."

She glimpsed his reflection in the mirror and saw he was not looking at her. She tried to read what was behind his murky expression and soft voice, but she couldn't arrive at anything except for the feeling that this man had become a stranger, and that it was only a matter of time before she shouted her anger in his face.

She whispered smilingly, "I will."

He shot her a look of contempt and left with his usual door slam. The voices of the boys arose from their room, singing and playing along with their electric guitar to a loud rock song, but not even Carlos Santana's endless piercing guitar solos could mess up her mood. So deep was her sense of peace and serenity.

That morning, she went to her appointment at the salon. She needed urgent care as her relationship with her body was not in its best state. She never neglected herself, but neither did she overdo the self-care.

It was a full ritual at the hands of Mrs. Falak Al-Halabi—four hours of plucking, scrubbing, and cleaning. She always finished with a satisfied gleam in her eyes. The beautician had the skill to turn the long hours into a pleasant engagement as she told stories and gossiped about the velvet class[26] and their endless adventures.

In discovering the beauty of oneself, a woman naturally desires for the world to admire her, but all Layl wanted was to be seen by one specific person. She sent him a photo that she had taken with Falak, with a message: "I miss you." The same sentence that she often sent to others now carried a heightened meaning with him.

Before long, she heard his voice on the other side of the line, and she was filled with joy. She told him about the dinner planned for the evening and updated him on what had been taking place. A space of pure affection was born between them; it was a space of delightful whispering and longing; a space of a gentleness that caressed their hearts and where a fire flowed through her veins and lit up her face. When she hung up with him, her internal and hidden whispers rose to surface: *Yes, I love him.*

---

26   The velvet class refers to the ruling class in Syria.

She returned to the house and ordered dinner from the finest restaurants in the city. She chose what to wear and hired two women to help her tidy up the house and prepare the table for dinner. She took out the crystal plates and silver spoons. The scent of sweet candles filled the place, and the sound of soft music permeated the air. Adel arrived to find her glowing and radiating, overflowing with femininity and in a cheerful mood.

He seemed shocked. The scene exceeded his expectations. Instead of praising her, an acute sense of irritation gripped him, and the two women rushed out quickly after he paid them and asked them to leave immediately.

She suppressed her anger. Despite the way he had just treated those two poor women, she did not want to get into any kind of argument with him as she knew that it would cost her hearing a few upsetting phrases and get herself worked up.

She went to her room and busied herself with anything she could find. She heard him talking on the phone. A few minutes later she heard the doorbell ring and came out to answer the door; she had a kind smile drawn on her face, her body raised ten centimeters off the ground by the high heals she was wearing. She opened the door and the smile froze on her face. She felt as if the high heels she was wearing had perforated the sole of her shoes and pierced her feet to the bone.

Confused, she looked behind her, hoping to find her husband so that he could help her understand what was happening, but he was nowhere to be seen. She wanted to slam the door in the face of the guest but could not bring herself to.

He asked, "Are you going to keep me waiting at the door?"

"No, of course not. Welcome Dr. Sa'ad."

He took her hand, brought it to his lips, and planted a kiss that made her hair stand on end. She pulled her hand away and said, "Come in," as she tried to hide her shock. Adel greeted him welcomingly. She couldn't believe her eyes. Dr. Sa'ad was the guest.

She went and hid in her room, shattered with anger and defeat. She took her mobile phone and sent a quick message before hiding the phone under the pillow. Adel entered with a predatory face, hatred shooting from his eyes, "You're going to get up now and sit with him. And he will not leave this house before you sign the papers. Do you understand?"

She understood that he had orchestrated all of this. He had considered all of her reactions, besieged her from all sides and left her no alternatives. She had no choice but to surrender resignedly. She drew a smile on her face and she went into the living room with exaggerated charm. She asked, "Dr. Sa'ad, why did you not bring your Madame with you?"

"She is on her way. She is just running a little late."

In the kitchen, she closed her eyes and repeated the voices from which she drew strength—his voice reassuring her that he would stand by her side, and the voices of those who chanted in the courtyard of the Umayyad Mosque.

She regained confidence in herself and went back to the strange men. There was not a subject she did not discuss. She chatted about everything, brought both the guest and her husband to laugh together, and invited them to the table. As she served them salad, Adel brought a bottle of arak, poured a glass for each of them, and raised a toast, "To Sama Al-Sham Hospital."

She humored them with a sip. Dr. Sa'ad's triumphant looks gnawed at her, while Adel tried to help avoid any direct clashes between them. Dr. Sa'ad went on and on about the hospital and its auxiliary research centers, and about his future plans to establish medical cadres. The phone rang, and Adel answered it in a voice that was louder than necessary and disrupted their conversation, "Are you sure it can't be postponed? OK, fine, I'll be there in fifteen minutes."

He hung up, announcing, "It's an emergency. I have to go but I won't be late."

He grabbed his jacket and said, "Dr. Sa'ad. I hope you know that this is like your home. I will be gone for one hour. As you know, an ER patient can't be postponed. If you'll excuse me." Dr. Sa'ad calmly welcomed Adel's departure.

Deep down, she was not as shocked as she would have imagined herself to be, for her husband was now no longer a man. She digested the plot twist calmly, acted sad to see him leave, stood up to help him get ready, walked him to the door, and before he left, she whispered to him,

"Have some shame, that is, if you have any dignity left in you."

"Look who's talking about dignity. You are one to lecture me about shame. Sign the papers. Do you understand?" He slammed the door.

She returned to the table, her face radiant with defiance. "Listen Sa'ad, I swear even if you were the only man left on this earth, I would not let you touch a hair on my head."

He gulped what was left in his glass and stood up, saying, "You are very hardheaded and your head needs to be cracked. Anyway. Here are the papers. They are all ready."

She took them calmly, and without reading a word, she tore them in half while looking into his eyes, "Get out of my house."

His face turned savage as he coolly approached her. He slapped her forcefully. She fell to the ground, and before she could collect herself, he pounced on her with all his might, straddling her, his hand gagging her mouth. He was spewing a stream of filthy insults. The sudden ringing of the doorbell stopped him. He covered her mouth and reached for a table knife. Holding it to her neck, he said, "Look here, your worth is a stab of a knife."

The doorbell continued to ring persistently. He lifted her off the ground and said, "Get up and open the door, and no matter who it is, you're going to kick them out, or else your pimp and children will cease to exist."

She obediently nodded her head, her eyes wide open in horror and disbelief. He slowly freed her mouth and went back to sit quietly on his chair while she went to the door to find her friend Nawwar.

"I got your message and rushed right over. What's wrong?"

She grabbed her hand and stepped outside, "Get me out of here, I am begging you."

Dr. Sa'ad stood alone in the living room, grabbed his phone and dialed Adel's number. Furious, he said to him, "My advice is that you find another country for you and your family to live in."

24
Samia

Anees was torn. On the one hand, he had witnessed the bravest of his country's young people, many his son's age, die one after another in their insistence on delving deeper. On the other, brutal machines were blindly crushing anyone who stood in their way. What he had seen, heard, and lived in recent weeks amounted to decades he had lived and experienced.

He longed for his beloved, who had suddenly disappeared and was now hidden in a besieged area. He also hoped to get out of a place whose shadows weighed heavier on him with each passing day. His only consolation was the prospect of seeing her, even once more, and the thought of persuading her to leave with him and work abroad.

Although roads to the countryside were cut off, she put his heart to rest when she texted him from time to time and assured him that she was safe, in an area that was under the protection of soldiers who had defected from the army and were protecting the demonstrations that filled TV screens.

Now he lived his life one day at a time, devoid of expectations, where each day was a face-off between death and life, rumors and truth, mind and heart, fear and courage. The people living in this geographic spot on the globe faced questions of epic proportions; ordinary people were thrust into situations that required godly powers to navigate. Questions arose, like, how does one defect from the regime? And once one has defected and been accepted by the other team, what does one do?

The days were filled with gloom, crowned with more deaths—they were baffling, horrific, and they rushed by. He couldn't believe that it had been almost a year since he had arrived. He spent his time either volunteering in the hospitals, immersing himself in the world of his uncle's books, or joining private circles with his friends to keep up with what was taking place.

He received a message from her, waited for a few days, and then risked everything to go and see her. A group of youths smuggled him into the besieged area, where he passed through a horrific *barzakh*.[27] No one could believe that it took half a day to travel a distance of a few kilometers.

He arrived at a barricaded apartment where walls had been built for complete isolation. Equipped with satellite internet, it had been transformed into a center for documentation and coordination between all involved in the resistance.

Samia received him warmly, although she was surrounded by several of her colleagues. Her eyes embraced him as they shook hands. She did not want to attract the attention of her co-workers as she was respected by everyone, in particular the religious ones among them.

"Sister Samia, you didn't introduce us to your husband."

She fumbled over the implied question and took a quick look around at their curious eyes, all of them wondering about the man she had asked them to take such a risk on. She responded quickly, "Everyone, I would like to introduce you to Dr. Anees. We were actually married recently, but we've had to hide the fact due to circumstances."

The reserved looks faded away. His heart was pounding with joy at the lie she had just told. He thanked those who had helped bring him there and offered assurances that he would no longer be a distraction and that they could resume their work.

"Madame Samia, why don't you take the doctor to rest, and let us take over from here."

They left with one of the young men from the office and walked to her nearby residence. On the way, Anees asked her, "Seriously, what are you doing here?"

---

27 *Barzakh* in Arabic is the stage between this world and the hereafter, purgatory.

"What do you think? How is it OK that we are not all here? These children who are having to face death become like one's own children, Anees. My presence with them is very important."

"It's clear, Samia, that everyone is being dragged towards hatred."

"Hatred and anger are necessary for action. We know that he is playing the sectarian card. But look at us, for example. I am Alawite, and half of the young people here come from different Syrian backgrounds. When it comes to the revolution, we all work alongside one another."

"Samia, the problem is not with ordinary people—it is the extremists and people with agendas. Their battle is not a battle for freedom. It is one waged under the pretext of defending religion, but ultimately, it is taking people out of the lion's den[28] and putting them in even narrower cages."

"That's why we are here. Until now, things have been bearable. But the more people are killed, the more extremism there will be."

As she spoke, she was glowing, becoming more beautiful, ascending. He interrupted her and reached for her hand. She looked at him as if she had just noticed his presence. Their eyes met and became interwoven, two smiles emanated from two hearts full of affection for one another. Instead of telling her what he was worrying about in that moment, he whispered, "I am proud to know you."

The house they arrived at served as both an office and a living space. She felt as if she'd been crowned with a laurel of affection. She needed to take refuge in this man's chest. She went closer and embraced him.

There was something uniquely special about being in each other's embrace, as it was an embrace of love in times of war. Nature intervened in fiery ways to counter violence, and desires were enraged. Nothing compared to love in times of war. The ferocity of passion is unleashed, reason ceases, reservations subside, and people's judgements no longer matter. The most beautiful things that have happened to the human soul, an outpouring of creativity, have taken place in times of war. This is what Dr. Anees concluded as he spent time with Samia, in an area that pulsated with life, freed from the regime and its control.

---

28   The lion's den is a reference to Al-Assad's rule, where Assad in Arabic means lion.

The circumstances brought out the best in people. Together they were coming up with new teaching methods, establishing media channels to convey facts, living altruistically and sharing their burdens. The movement had taken on a life of its own, coordinated and supervised by new committees made up of university youth, believers and atheists, rich and poor, men and women, all protected by the rifles of a few defected soldiers, as well as some of their friends who had joined in. It was a mass of life ignited by the place and by a continuously renewed faith in victory.

Samia cried after every ardent demonstration. She whispered to Anees, "Imagine, these are the same people who were once accused of being insignificant, and did not dare to even tell a political joke. Look at what they've become. Can you imagine what these people will be capable of doing once the country is liberated?"

"What is the story behind this threat, Samia?" Anees worriedly asked after she casually relayed the news and played it down.

"Don't worry. It's just a silly piece of paper that we found at the door of the center."

"What does it say?"

"It's just a childish threat written in bad handwriting: 'You will be punished, you spies.'"

"Childish threat, you say? And what are you doing about it?"

Irritated, not wanting to awaken her fears, she replied, "Anees, I told you not to worry. We have security teams coordinating with the Free Army.[29] We've informed them of the threat, and have received immense support from the people. Anyway, I want to go to the field hospital with you and figure out how you can help us."

Within hours, Anees was working with a team of doctors to assess the hospital's medical equipment, medicine, and supplies. He made a list of the most important things they needed. The director of the center, a reputable doctor who worked with a team of more than twenty physicians and nurses, said, "The situation will worsen. Things are still under control

---

29 Formed in 2011, the Free Syrian Army comprised soldiers and officers who defected from the Syrian Armed force, refusing to partake in the deadly crackdown on protesters by Bashar Al-Assad's security apparatus.

as of now. Some of the wounded who were admitted into government hospitals were either killed in cold blood or immediately taken to detention centers. When it comes to the regime, we can't trust anything and must rely only on ourselves." He handed Samia a piece of paper, saying, "This is the list of medicines we need."

"We will try to secure it as soon as possible," she replied.

They returned to her room, where one of the young men was nervously waiting for her. "What's wrong Mus'ab?"

"At the mosque in the neighboring town today, there was a call to cleanse Al-Ghouta this upcoming Friday and rid it of the filthy seculars, Alawites, and spies. Rumors have spread that most of the instigators are released prisoners who were once convicted of crimes like child rape and armed robbery. Sheikhs with large sums of money are making the calls, and Friday upon Friday, they are gaining more and more support."

"Can we talk to someone from their leadership?"

"Actually, today they assaulted Hassan and Jamal, and they mentioned your name."

"What did they say?"

Mus'ab looked at Dr. Anees and hesitantly said, "I am very sorry, Madame Samia, but they are saying that you and the doctor are not legally married and in an illegitimate relationship. They said that they know people in the Vital Statistics Office with access to your records, and that your marital status is divorced. Here is a copy of it."

Calmly, she took the paper from him. "We left our marriage contract at home due to circumstances," she said. "We have a legitimate contract prepared by a sheikh. We didn't have time to go to court and register it. In any case, tomorrow the doctor is going to leave and work on securing medical supplies, and when he returns he will bring the marriage contract with him. Don't worry."

He bid her farewell with a cold smile and left. This warning expedited the departure of Dr. Anees, who would be gone until one of the young men could help him arrange a forged marriage contract.

"Samia. I don't feel good about this. Come with me, and you can serve the revolution away from here."

Irritated, she replied in a tone that brought memories of the woman made of the wind, the day they first met. "This is nonsense—it's just an excuse to escape. I've heard it from many others. Revolutions are only served on the ground. I'm not leaving this place except to go to my grave."

"And what about us, Samia?"

"I am with you and yours, and you are my heartbeat. Come back and stay, and we will be together."

As he bid her farewell on that evening so drenched in anticipation, he could not have known that he would never return to this place, or that it would soon be subject to a deadly gas attack and turned into an enormous open graveyard of lifeless bodies—all as cameras stood by as silent witnesses to several massacres, one being enough to condemn the entire world.

"Take this mobile with you. When you reach the demarcation line, you will be taken on foot through private roads, and then a car will transport you to a private house. There, you can contact organizations to secure the needed supplies, some of which will be available in the country, and some will need to be smuggled in. You will have a whole team there to help, so you won't have to worry. Anything can be brought in these days—the borders are complete chaos. You should prepare to move in a few days, and when you do, send me a message every hour using the number that's stored on your phone and let me know how things are, even an empty message. If anything goes wrong, send me any letter or word, and I will know that you have been arrested."

As soon as he entered Damascus, security forces surrounded the car. He was violently dragged to the investigation branch, but he still managed to write one full sentence and send it to her: "I love you."

25
Adel

In less than a month, the country was heading towards the unknown and news bulletins were splattered with blood. Layl watched as her life fell apart in front of her. Adel lost all he had invested and was fired from his job. Soon, without warning, she too was fired.

Without employment, she was forced to leave Huddud's House and move in with her parents, draped in shame and pain. Under the shunning eyes of society, her father sank into a crushing silence. Calls from her sisters conveyed a mixture of reproach and blame for what she had put herself and the family through. The most difficult part was having to explain to her two sons, Mayar and Nawwar, what had taken place. Their father gave them permission to stay with their uncle in Al-Zabadani, away from the eye of the storm. No one answered her calls anymore, and the family became outcasts, living between waves of fear and the salinity of reality.

As for the country, it was shocked at the shattering of silence and torn between a stubborn resolve to take revenge against an unyielding regime that had nothing to offer but violence, and the urgency of others to secure its permanence. The deeper things penetrated the people's blood, the more inflamed the uprising became.

Layl retreated to a neutral zone, like many Syrians. She trembled in fear of the violent regime that had begun to classify noncompliant people as the enemy; at the same time, she was terrified of an acutely polarized opposition movement characterized by unifying national slogans and vague desires to Islamicize and turn things religious, where those who did not go along with it would also be classified as enemies.

Adel suffered a stroke that almost killed him. She was late in receiving the news. One of their old friends, Dr. Hani, volunteered to perform an urgent operation in defiance of the ban that had been imposed on the family by Dr. Sa'ad and his partners. The surgery saved Adel's life, but he was left a heap of a man facing a long recovery period and terribly high follow-up treatment costs.

She arrived at the small hospital, thanked Dr. Hani graciously, and decided to go to Adel. She felt fury, anger, and wished that he was dead, but as soon as she saw the pale faces of the children grieving their father, her only concern was that he survive for their sake. She buried her resentment deep in her heart and activated her ability to forgive, and so the anger dissipated, replaced by a feeling of cold pity. His condition improved quickly, and the boys' laughter returned. The family's solidarity was strongest amid such a calamity.

She did not give up. She applied for work in a medical complex and prepared to open a private clinic even as a war was being waged against her. The director of the medical center came to her, ashamed, and said, "Dr. Layl. I must let you know that you can no longer work with us. It has nothing to do with your professionalism or skills. It's much bigger than me, and I am sure that you understand me. All I can say is, may God help you."

"Don't worry, Doctor. Thank you for everything."

Dr. Hani added, "I will keep your name as a home doctor, meaning one who makes house calls. And this is the number of my brother. He has a good relationship with those upstairs. I'm sure you know what I mean," he said with a wink and continued, "Try to get in touch with him and explain the situation. Just tell him that you were referred to him by Dr. Hani and he will take care of the rest."

"Thanks Dr. Hani. You've done more than enough," she replied with heartfelt sadness, trying to appear calm and collected while seething with rage and disappointment.

A few days later, she called Dr. Hani's brother. After introducing herself, he said in a sharp tone, "I am sorry, sister Layl, I can't help you with anything. Please do not call this number again."

Her attempts to seek help from her college friends in Aleppo and Latakia also failed. In their eyes, she empathized with the revolution by virtue of her friendship with the activist Samia Saeed and for having spent a few days at Dr. Anees's house after she left home. Of all her friends, only Nawwar welcomed her lovingly and gave her the keys to a private clinic she owned in Jaramana, offering to let her live or work there if she needed.

Then, an ominous phone call came her way: "If you dare open your mouth about Dr. Sa'ad Al-Deen, it will be the end of you and your children, you infiltrator, you traitor. You need to thank God that things are not worse for you. You no longer have a place in Syria, and not even in Lebanon. Our advice is that you shut your mouth and leave the country. It would be better for you."

She did not say a word. She understood the threatening message for what it was and accepted her defeat calmly. She secluded herself to take care of Adel, who was regaining consciousness. He watched as she moved around him, took care of him, changed his diaper, bathed him, and gave him emotional support. At first, he was silently bitter, his looks sour. But gradually, his two sunken eyes cleared each time he saw her by his side taking care of him. Tearfully, he whispered to her, "Layl, forgive me."

She looked at him coolly. Continuing to arrange a flower bouquet, she replied, "It's not the right time to talk about this."

"I need to tell you that you are a noble person, and it was the moment that I couldn't protect you that brought me here."

Her anger began to surface. "Adel, what needs to happen is for you to get better quickly because we need you. What's important is that we protect the children. You need to recover your health as soon as possible. We need for you to come back to us."

"Do you still love me?"

"The children may come at any moment. Please change the subject."

"Layl, just tell me, is there any hope that you might love me again?"

"Adel, I am begging you, let's not talk about this. Concentrate on your health. I am here next to you and with you and the children. I will say it again, we need you."

Like any defeated person overwhelmed by feelings of guilt and dis-appointment and crushed by sickness, he began to cry tears of bitterness and weakness. "I swear I would die, I would die, Layl, if you leave me. Give me a chance," he begged. "I know that you are here because of the children and that deep down you despise me. No matter what I do, you will always despise me."

Unable to hold in her anger anymore, she headed to the door and yelled, "For God's sake, stop. Enough! Stop."

She slammed the door behind her, saying, "God damn you, fucker," and left him to drown in his bitterness and disappointment. He suddenly had a great urge to urinate, and indeed, before he got to the bathroom he wet himself.

She finally answered the phone, "Layl, I've heard about everything that's happened."

"Fidel, please leave me in peace."

"I will not leave you. I am the reason for everything that is happening to you, and I will not leave you."

"You have already left me alone with a pack of wolves," she said, her tone full of reproach. "Nothing happened to you, and I was the one to pay the price, alone. I know I deserve all of this and more. You are safe and secure in your job, relationships, women, and cities. The only thing that's changed for you is that you have an additional woman—a broken one."

"Layl!" he yelled, shutting down her torrent of anger. She had never heard his voice sound this raw, commanding, and strong. She felt a sudden tremor, and a delicious desire to obey. She whispered subserviently, "What?"

"Listen to me. You need to come to Dubai. I've secured a guaranteed interview for you to work at a large private hospital. In principle, the director of the hospital does not have any issues with this. But you have to come. There are procedures required for the interview and for obtaining the needed equivalency of your degree. Leave Damascus as soon as you can. Can you be here at the beginning of next month? I will send you a visa and a plane ticket, and take care of your accommodations as well."

Hearing this, her anger melted like a lump of salt under an abundant stream of water. "Wait, last month I received an invitation to participate in a medical conference in Dubai. They think I am still employed. They said that they would take care of everything. Let me check on the date and if the invitation is still valid, and I'll let you know."

"Let me know today. You need to leave the country—you, the children, and Adel."

"Adel is in bad shape and needs to continue treatment."

"Don't worry. Leave all this to me. Just focus and come. I am waiting for you, Layl."

"God. I don't know how to thank you. I will just say God damn you for knowing how to reignite hope in me."

"I don't want a thank-you. Just do as I say. That's all."

He hung up. She stared at the screen of her phone for a moment and then rushed to her emails.

Introduction to Chapter 26

A part of this chapter depicts what takes place inside a Syrian security branch. It is fictional in part, while informed by twenty verified and intersecting testimonials, in addition to authenticated testimonies from a group of survivors who provided their accounts to international human rights organizations including Amnesty International and Human Rights Watch.

In the first Arabic edition, the testimony of a physician who shared part of his experience on Facebook was included in this next chapter. However, in the second Arabic edition on which this translation is based, the physician's account was omitted. The omission does not constitute any significant change in the narrative or outcomes of events.

My gratitude and appreciation are extended to the following individuals, including Mr. Mahmoud Darwish, Mr. Ilyas Idilbi, author Dara Al-Abdullah, Dr. Diaa Sarrour, artist Najah Albukai, activist Irman Khatib, as well as to a large group of pseudonymous individuals whose testimonies were published by credible international reports.

I hope that the reader finds an opportunity to review what has been documented by international organizations on what takes place inside Syrian prison and dungeons, or, what Amnesty International has described as "human slaughterhouses."

26
Anees

When he arrived at the security branch, they placed him in a large prison dormitory that had once been used as a shooting range. Odd machines were scattered everywhere, and the walls were plastered with wood, cork, and rubber to block the trainees' bullets.

The dormitory seemed to be located two levels underground, or so he thought until he began to discover that things were more complicated than they had first appeared. He later learned of a secret floor (or more than one) in which several long-forgotten prisoners had been held for years. To the left of the entrance was a hall known as the Welcome Party, and to the right was a row of prison cells.

Approximately three hundred prisoners were detained in the former shooting range. Prisoners took turns sleeping in upright positions for their first six days and were collectively beaten with whips by the guards. Unable to escape the barrage of whips, they curled into fetal positions to protect their heads like a terrified herd facing a pack of famished wolves. Anees was tortured significantly less than the other prisoners, almost as if the guards were intentionally ignoring his presence. For the first week, he tried to hold himself together. It was nearly impossible to fall asleep amid the moaning of those with open wounds and broken ribs. One night, he was summoned by a guard. The guard led him to a room at the end of the dark corridor, where the investigator gestured for him to take a seat.

"As you've probably guessed, we've received orders that no one is to lay a hand on you. Consider this five-star treatment. But the time has come to talk."

"And what exactly do you want from me?"

"You need to give us Samia."

"But I don't know where she is."

"Surely you can get to her. We know that she's in Ghouta. It should be simple. Tonight, you will take a shower and sleep in a clean room. Then tomorrow morning you will find a way to communicate with her. You have three days. If you hand her over to us you'll be free to go, untouched, and allowed to return to London. And if you don't? You will regret the day your mother gave birth to you."

"And how will you guarantee that I'll actually leave this place after handing her to you?" he asked, trying to sound confident. The investigator exploded in his face, shouting to the guard, "Take this animal to dormitory six. It's obvious that being good to him is a waste of time."

"I would like to speak with the British Embassy."

"Embassy, you said? You filthy, dirty agent. Do you think this is Scotland Yard? You asshole. You dog. Take him and let him talk to the Ambassador."

It was his first step into hell and its inhabitants. He was taken to the torture room. They stripped him naked, tied his hands together, and drew him up to the ceiling with a pulley like a lump of hanging flesh. His feet did not touch the ground. The officer called in three guards and said, "All of you. Listen to me very well. This is an enemy of our homeland, a traitor, and an agent working for British Intelligence. We caught him planting explosives in the market. I want the three of you to show me which of you loves our President the most. Whoever hits him for the longest time, without his hands growing tired, will be the winner. The one who stops first will be denied his employee-leave. And, the one who lasts the longest will have two nights off. Are you ready? One. Two. Three."

The three contestants started beating him savagely, with no mercy. They were set on destroying the piece of meat hanging in front of them. After a few minutes, he lost all sensation. The cables fell on his body, leaving marks on his back, stomach, buttocks, and legs. Each time he passed out, they woke him up with a spurt of cold water.

He looked at the three of them. They were exhausted, and finally one of them collapsed panting.

The officer untied him. He fell to the ground like a piece of meat. One of the jailers dragged him to his feet, following orders to "Take this pig away."

They threw him into an already crowded cell. He developed a fever and was delusional, confused about the time and place. He imagined that he was in his home in London heading towards the plush sofa that overlooked a garden highlighted with shades of enchanting green. He tried to reach the couch but was unable. All he wanted was to rest and contemplate the beautiful view. But something always got in his way, hindered him as if he were walking in a sticky muddy cesspit. Soon he came to see that he was actually trampling upon the bodies lined up inside the overcrowded cell. As two men struggled to hold him down, every step he took opened someone's wound in a blinding darkness and unleashed shrieks from the wounded and the broken. He was completely disoriented, but it still took great effort to keep him pinned to the floor. One of the prisoners began to recite Quranic verses in his ears, in steady rhythmic whispers, and he was gradually brought back to reality. He had become part of a mass of carnage, sharing a similar fate, pains, and stenches, and faint glimmers of hope.

He was amazed to find God so close after he had built walls of steel to prevent the idea of God from ever coming near him. The pain that was pulsating in every pore of his paralyzed body brought him to regain full consciousness. The pain was his sign of being alive. He felt a warm fluid streaming between his thighs and was overcome with a feeling of intense pity for himself.

As he was having these revelations amongst the emasculated, helpless and numb bodies around him, a man stood up on the opposite corner and yelled, "Where is God! Where is He? Fuck you all. God damn you all." He then tried to run but stumbled on the piled bodies, urinating on himself. Fearing that the jailer might hear him and punish the entire group, the prisoners tried to hold the man down and cover his mouth.

Someone nearby whispered, "Another one has lost it."

The next morning, a sheikh was dragged away from the "extermination chamber" to the "numbers chamber" where he would most likely end up tortured to death, with a number stuck to his forehead, another photo to add to the archive. Finally, his body would be transferred to a mass grave in an unknown location.

The pungent stench and nauseating sight was reverse torture for the guard. As the jailer opened the door, he was covered his nose with a rag and tried to avoid touching anyone. The bodies would be taken out daily, three or four at a time and placed on a blanket. The corpses looked like heaps of human flesh covered with abscesses and sores. The prisoners turned their heads to the wall as they moved the bodies. Once a number had been placed on the forehead of each corpse, prisoners dragged the bodies to the basement and piled them in a storage space; a funeral cargo truck would later transport them to a burial site. Ironically, this process provided the prisoners with their only chance to leave the dormitory and possibly find something along the way that might prove useful later.

Dr. Anees was transferred to an underground dormitory. A door to the lower floor was pushed open and he was dragged down the stairs. One of the officers, who was short-tempered and intent on getting Anees inside as quickly as possible, slammed the door shut with his baton. Anything to get away from those on the other side, who had been forgotten in a horrifying darkness where time was stuck and meaning absent. A door was opened—they pushed him inside and quickly closed it, their feet racing to leave. He was alone, lying at the closed door, suspended in a meaningless, gelatinous void.

Underneath a pale-yellow lightbulb covered with a layer of soot from the prisoners' rotten breaths, he caught glimpses of four ghost-like figures covered in tattered rags, each one curled up in a corner of the room. They looked frightened, staring blankly at the newcomer as if he had arrived from another planet or the Stone Age. Three of them had hair that hung down onto their beards, their bodies dried with the fermentation of time and decay. One of them had a scalp that was ravaged by alopecia, which left him with only a few strands of hair to dangle over his sunken face. His big nose and ears made him look like an extraterrestrial.

"Hello." The stray word came out of Anees's mouth, wandered around the place, and returned to him without being detected by anyone. There was only the sound of breathing in all the four corners. He stepped forward. The room was no larger than three square meters, but in contrast to what was happening above them, it seemed as if he were in a vast ocean.

Exhausted, he took three steps backward, turned around, and leaned his back against the wall; his body slid to the floor. A few hours later, he woke up and found himself in the same curled-up position as his co-prisoners, his hands wrapped around his knees. He stared at the door trying to avoid the sight of the half-naked creatures whose rhythmic humming signaled their acceptance of the new guest. Soon the room was silent, disrupted only by raspy breaths.

The first day in the dormitory passed; then the first week; then a month went by with no interruptions except for when the door opened once a day, and a tray of food was placed on the floor with four loaves of bread and a bowl of broth. One of the inhabitants, who looked like a ghost crawling on his hands and knees, took his loaf of bread, returned to his designated corner and began to slowly chew his food. The other men followed and left Anees his portion. Following the same procedure, Dr. Anees fetched his portion of the food. He moved slowly and was careful not to disrupt the order of the place or cause any commotion that might provoke someone from the upper floor to have him transferred back.

The days passed monotonously. Aside from the daily meal, the only interruption to the austere routine was the defecation that took place in a hole next to the door, followed by the creaking of the water faucet. Each drop of water was a nerve-wracking reminder of the passing of time. Nothing was more brutal and terrifying for a prisoner than being reminded of time.

One day, to the rhythm of water dripping from the faucet nozzle, a rusted voice came from the right corner of the room as if from another world and asked him a single question, "Has Saddam Hussein left Kuwait yet?"

Anees only wished that he could see Sami. He realized that their names shared the same root: Sami and Samia. He contemplated how in life so many obvious signs often go unnoticed. He longed for his home in Willesden. He missed his work. He thought of his cold and steadfast London, a place that he never really cared for but was now the only place in the world he wished to be.

At dawn, before the dawn prayer, he was summoned by the guard. The guard's voice was calm, free of insults. Walking with great difficulty, he entered the interrogation room located at the end of the hallway. The investigator composedly asked him to sit and ordered a cup of tea for him, a bottle of water, and a plate of fruit, with a few apples, oranges, and bananas.

He couldn't believe his eyes, for this humble meal looked to him like a heavenly feast. Hesitantly, he studied the face of the officer. He looked familiar. It wasn't long before things became clear.

"The last thing I would have ever expected was to see you here!" said the officer, who then reminded Dr. Anees that they had met years ago in London when he performed an open-heart surgery on his wife.

"I remember you," Dr. Anees replied coldly, suspecting that he was being set up.

He didn't care to hear the officer's praise, nor did he hope for any potential promises this officer might make in light of his rank as a physician. Satisfying his immense hunger was his sole focus in that moment. Expecting the worst, he was afraid to reach for anything. He worried a trap was being set for him. The officer quickly dispelled these doubts, saying, "I will leave you alone for ten minutes. Get comfortable and we will talk when I return."

He was left with such unexpected bliss, and when the officer returned, Anees's feast-engorged stomach was audibly expressing its gratitude.

"Dr. Anees. As of tomorrow, you will be moved to another location. This is no place for you. I don't even want you to return to your dormitory tonight."

Anees suddenly felt an urge to say goodbye to those he would be leaving behind in this living hell. In that moment, it was difficult to imagine being without them. He kept his thoughts to himself, afraid of this true desire, and decided to focus on the lifeline that shined down upon him from the abyss of oblivion.

"You will be taken to a better place," the ambivalent officer officiously continued. "I don't have any details, but I do know that some people in power are pulling for you."

He knew not to argue or ask any questions, to listen quietly, not to build hopes, and to expect the worst.

"First, you will need to recover, and soon all will be well."

With the little energy he had left, he collected himself and asked hesitantly, "Will I be released?"

Signs of displeasure appeared on the officer's face. "No Doctor," he said. "Your crime is significant and the standard punishment is for you to rot to death here. The only thing I can do for you is to spare you from dying here or at least from dying now. You will shower tonight, and tomorrow you will be seen by the prison's physician. After a few days, you will be transferred from here. This is the most I can do for you."

"Where will I be transferred?"

"To a much better place. But if you do something stupid, which I don't think you will, then you will return to this place. And if this happens, then I can assure you that neither I nor anyone else will be able to do anything for you."

Here, Dr. Anees played the one card he had left. "Listen. I remember you clearly, when I left the surgery room and informed you that your wife's surgery was successful. I remember your tears, gratitude, and appreciation. I remember that you told me that I could ask you for anything. Today, the only thing I am asking for is that you tell me where I will be transferred to."

The officer paced around the room several times and answered in a different tone, one that betrayed his weakness and fear. "You will be in a place that I know nothing about except that it is a thousand times better than this place. Ever since I found out that you were here, I have been thinking of a way to get you out. Perhaps you are not going to like where you will be, and you may object. But at least I will have cleared my conscience.

"Look, Doctor. We are no longer one people. We are now at war. You are either the killer or the killed. I need to free myself from the guilt of not helping you so that I can concentrate on my work again. Since I discovered that you were here, I haven't been able to focus on anything. Although I have been trained to separate work from my personal life, your presence here hurts me. Each time I go home and see my wife and children, I feel a sense of gratitude towards you. Where you will be going is not exactly the perfect place, and I know very little about it. But I've done the impossible to have you transferred there. I cannot do anything else. This will make us even, Doc." He rang the bell and the guard came.

"Take the doctor to my room, and let him take a shower and give him new clothes."

Filled with loathing and disgust, the guard led him to the room and said, "You are all motherfuckers." He slammed the door and left.

It was his first night in weeks to sleep in a bed with clean clothes on. It felt unreal. He did not know what to do with the space. Despite its small size, the room seemed vast. He felt lost and didn't know how to sit. The bed morphed into a mattress with spiky nails digging into his pores. It was another kind of torture, a ravaging torture, for he couldn't bear to think of those who were lying only a few meters below him in their cells. He left the bed and curled up into a corner that was the size of one and a half floor tiles. Only then was he able to fall asleep.

27
Fidel

A month after the call, Layl arrived in Dubai. She dropped her bags off on the fifth floor of the Hyatt Regency, freshened up and called him.

"Hello."

"Where are you?" he asked coldly.

"Where am I?" she said, overcome by a strong feeling of disappointment. "At the Hyatt Regency."

"Twenty minutes and I will be there. Bring your passport."

In dismay, she had imagined that he would react in a more celebratory way upon hearing her voice. She consoled herself with the thought that he was coming, at least, and that he must have been busy or unable to speak.

She was fully ready. A hot bath skinned Damascus off her. She sprayed on a few spritzes of Chanel No. 5 and carefully examined the finest details of her face; despite the pain and worries, it remained flawless. She opened her purse and added two more sprays behind her ears, anointing herself with the scent he loved most.

She was calm as she went down to meet him. Before long she received a message: "Come outside immediately."

She laughed at his commanding in his tone, feeling overjoyed. She had a deep desire to hand her life to a man who was good at giving orders.

She stepped out through the revolving door and found his car waiting for her with the passenger seat door open. She got in. He was wearing his earphones and continued with his phone call. As she closed the door, he leaned over and kissed her on both cheeks. As he smelled her perfume, he buried his nose in her hair and neck and kissed her on the shoulder. He then looked at her with his mischievous eyes and smiled widely. He straightened up and returned to his driving position, continuing with his phone conversation, "It's your fault. No, I can't come, and I can't see you today either. I already told you that my friend from Damascus is coming and, yes, I will be with her."

She could hear the angry woman's loud voice on the other end of the line. Irritated, he put an end to the conversation. "It's none of your business. I will call you when I have time. Bye."

Aggravated, he placed the phone back in its cradle, removed his earphones, and turned to her. "Welcome, welcome! Thank God you arrived safely," he shouted, celebrating her arrival. Reservedly, she smiled and swallowed the shock. But something was choking her heart.

He drove through Sheikh Zayed Highway, reaching out every few minutes to touch her hand and uttering, "You're finally here."

Then their conversation began. She started to recount what had happened in bits and pieces, and told him the things that she couldn't say on the phone. He gently interrupted her as he took a turn towards Jumeirah.

"Let's first go to the hospital so you can meet the director."

"But I'm not prepared."

"You're not expected to prepare anything. He only wants to see you and talk. He'll let you know what you'll need to do, how you can quickly get the equivalency of your degree. You will need to give him your passport right away so he can get started with your residency and work permit."

He looked at her affectionately, his light spirit flooding hers. "Everything has been taken care of. All you have to do is relax."

She felt cocooned with safety, surrendering herself to a man who she did not really know and had no choice but to trust. This was something she had never experienced before. Her soul, full of anticipation, was flooded with joy, her body felt shivers of overwhelming pleasure at the thought of being in the presence of the man of her life.

The meeting was quick, as everything was arranged in advance. The director of the hospital welcomed them with exaggerated enthusiasm, and everything was smooth and straightforward. They finished their cups of coffee and left after she handed her passport to the director and signed the contract. He informed her that her American Board certificate was likely to exempt her from having to work on an equivalency. He also assured her that the salary was lucrative and the benefits excellent. He then added, "What matters is that Mr. Fidel is happy. All else is secondary."

In the car, she asked him, "How did this all happen?"

"The company is responsible for the hospital's ads. I offered them a special discount. Anyway, don't worry about it. Now tell me, where should we eat?"

"What are my options?"

"We can have seafood at a restaurant near the water, steak in a Latin restaurant, or *labneh*[30] and *za'tar*[31] at my house."

She laughed. "You know what—I'm allergic to fish and I don't get along well with steak or meat."

"OK then, I will make you the best *labneh* and *za'tar* sandwich, and I'll also throw in a cup of tea. Enjoy this bliss!"

He took off driving, madly zigzagging between cars. The phone rang; the name and photo of the caller flashed on the screen.

"Excuse me," he said, and put her on speaker before she began to speak.

"Hello Ilhamo," he said.

"Where are you?"

"I am out with a friend who has freshly arrived from Damascus."

"Can I see you?"

"Is there anything important?"

"What do you mean? Seeing you in and of itself is important."

His piercing laughter put Layl in low spirits again. She couldn't bear to hear this sort of ill-mannered and rude flirtation. She rolled down the window and stretched out her hand, colliding with the moist air. He ended his conversation and turned to her, "What's wrong?"

"Nothing."

---

30 *Labneh* is a strained yogurt served as a dip with olive oil and pita bread.
31 *Za'tar* is a blend of savory dried herbs, including thyme, oregano, sumac, and toasted sesame seeds, and is often mixed with olive oil.

"Tell me what's wrong?"

"At least respect my presence."

"Respecting your presence is about being truthful to you and being my true self, just as I am."

"I thought that what we have between us was something special. Now I'm discovering that you speak to all women the same way."

"I'm not going to respond to this. I don't think that you've asked me about anything that I haven't replied to truthfully and without lies. I am clearly a single man. My relationship with you is special, but you should also know about me so that there is no confusion. I have many friends in my life who are women and they have nothing to do with my relationship with you. If you can accept me like this, I will be very happy. If you can't, I will respect your decision. But what's most important is that I don't lie to you or to myself or to anyone."

"That's your right. But I assumed that there was something special between us."

"Special in what way?"

"Well, that's what I thought, and you're right, I didn't ask you. But I certainly did not expect that all the love that I have been receiving from you was simply a normal part of your daily routine and not something unique you felt just for me."

"You are not like any other woman. Your place and your presence is special, but this is how I live. Before we get to the house, you need to decide. You can come with me or I will take you back to your place."

"You're unbelievable." She was overcome with anger and felt a desire to slap him. The words shot out of her mouth, anger mixed with screaming and tears. "You're acting as if you are innocent, free, and democratic. Do you think that a woman in my place should have to withstand your existential tests? You are a despicable person, an opportunist, low and worthless. I don't want anything from you. Stop the car. I said stop the car!" she screamed. "Let me out here.

"It's not your fault. I want nothing from you. You are like all other men. You're no different than Sa'ad and Adel. You're no better than they are. Actually, they are at least frank about the fact that they are lowly. But you are a wolf in sheep's clothing. Let me out of here. Let me out."

He was frozen, pale like a wax figure. He let her get it all out, and he continued to drive, but calmly. He dared not look at her as she curled up in her seat, weeping bitterly. She stopped crying for a moment as they entered the parking garage of his building. But as he took her to his chest, her burning tears flooded anew, leaving a wet spot on his shirt before they headed inside.

On the left was a modern kitchen that opened onto a large living room, with a dining room that seated six, and a balcony that overlooked man-made lakes. Framed posters of films and plays from around the world hung on the walls. There was a painting of Charlie Chaplin, several cameras of all kinds lined up on the shelf, red sofas with thick curtains of the same color, a home theater with a giant screen, and all the technology imaginable. There was a large bookshelf with bound books, most of which were illustrated encyclopedias. She was stepping into an entire movie-making world, swept away by an atmosphere full of movement, excitement, and mystery.

Joyfully, he walked her through the apartment. To the left was a room with a bookshelf that reached the ceiling, two Apple computers, and a digital editing machine.

"It's Final Cut Pro, he explained. "It's classy, elegant, and exciting. It has its own mood as it stops working when it feels like it, but it's still better than Avid, which lacks spirit. It has a 16-terabyte storage in which I keep all the films and ads that I love. It's my nutrient in my days of hunger."

She had no idea what he was talking about, but the way he spoke and how he gave things feelings and humanized them made everything interesting. He was a man full of knowledge, and unlike many people, he knew too much. Pointing to the guest bedroom on the right, which also had a private bathroom, he said, "I'll make the sandwiches. Consider this room yours. There are clean towels and sheets in the closet and other things you may need."

She thanked him as he closed the door behind him. She did indeed need a break and some privacy, and she was grateful for a man who knew enough to give a woman some privacy, so she might savor the surprises at her own pace.

In his apartment overlooking Jumeirah Lakes Towers, from a balcony fertile with plants and rooms crowded with high-tech equipment, in an evening suffused with desire, she silenced all conversation, words, and blame. Half an hour later, she came out of the bathroom and sat on a beige single-seat sofa in his living room and contemplated the paintings on the walls as the voice of Amália Rodrigues sending forth her groans to fado music filled the place. The one that caught her attention depicted three bald women, their bodies stretched in an empty room. He brought her a glass of white wine and she said, "This painting is very moving."

"It is by Roya Issa. It's a stunning painting—she turns nightmares into images. In her paintings, she dispenses with women's hair, because no one wants to put a hijab on a bald woman. They embody the cancer that exists in the outer world, one that is treated with chemotherapy."

"I never thought of it that way," she said, looking at him with wonder.

He pointed to an engraving, "This is the work of Yasser Safi, a great engraver. His piece bears prophecies about a savage creature that will come to devour color and leave the place in black and white. And Abdurrazaq Shablout paints reality with the most minute details possible."

"Don't tell me that this is a painting and not a photograph."

"Yes it is."

"No way!" she shouted like a child and got up to examine the image closely. As she touched it, it slipped from the nail on which it was hanging. She tried to prevent it from falling by holding it against the wall. Acting on impulse, he reached out with his arm to help support the painting, his body pressed against hers, both holding their breaths. Slowly they lowered the painting to the ground. She turned, their lips met, and it was as if all the intensity of desire, color, passion, and longing were encapsulated in one moment. The kiss that she had been dreaming of for months had finally arrived, without warning. Soon they were naked on the sofa, their clothes scattered all over the living room.

This is then how passion is extinguished in less than fifteen minutes, she thought to herself. Not even one single word of love was exchanged.

It was just a burning desire that passed through them at the speed of light. *Was it possible that what just happened was the summary of an entire story?* He lay on his back, his eyes closed, with his semen drying on her stomach. She stared again at Roya's painting and felt as if she resembled the bald women. Desire was still raging in her body; she had reached the brink of a quick climax, but when he chose to pull out before ejaculating, he left her stuck in a *barzakh* of pleasure.

She went to the bathroom and showered. In the mirror, she saw herself without hair, completely bald. Funereal music, likely Bach, was coming from the living room. She was thankful that she no longer heard Amália's voice. She was not fond of the choice he made. Amália reminded her of all her wounds at once, but the music that she was now hearing reminded her of God's torment. As the second movement of the symphony began, she finished getting dressed. She asked for God's help.

Do I love him? she hesitantly asked herself. *How can a man like him be loved? God only knows how many women he sleeps with every week.*

Do you love him? she heard an internal voice ask, in a tone like organ music.

The answer came to her like the sound made by a hand passing over the keys of a piano for the first time, its notes mixing with the thrill of wonder.

When there is doubt, then it must not be love. What is important is that now you are safe. In order to lessen your disappointment, seek to please your body for as long as you are with him.

Yes, today I am considered unfaithful. I am a married woman willing to sleep with a single and strange man. So let this be a day of pleasure and I will sort the rest out later.

Her forty-year-old body needed a thousand climaxes; seething with life, it needed to be quenched. She decided to help him regain his energy, passion, and erection, for at least there was a possibility of love. She preferred this man over all other men in the world, despite all his flaws. She yearned to go with him to the extreme of what their bodies could compose of music, and to live betrayal to its fullest.

28
Anees

Anees was transferred to a military hospital, and in less than a month he began to regain his health. Then came an order to transfer him to the Cultural Center. He was blindfolded and placed in a blacked-out van with his hands cuffed. The drive took almost ninety minutes. As the noises faded away, he assumed that they were outside of Damascus.

Still blindfolded, he was led inside. The whispers were free of insults and the vulgar language that he was used to hearing at the branch and even in the hospital. The guard guided him as they went down the stairs. He counted more than thirty steps before he was ordered to stop. He heard the guard speak with another person and say, "This is the doctor."

They continued to walk for a few moments. A door was opened and he was let in. His hands were untied and the blindfold removed. As his eyes adjusted to the light, he gradually took in his surroundings. He was standing in a very clean room—with a neatly made bed, a wardrobe, a small table with a chair, a small stove, and a few glasses, cups, and plates. Without a word, the guard left and shut the door, locking it from the outside.

For days, all he did was receive food and wait. The only interruption was the guard delivering food three times a day, which also signaled the time of day and whether it was morning or evening. The temperature was moderate, which told him that it was spring or on the cusp of summer. Things remained the same until the day an elegant man in a white suit and wearing expensive cologne came to see him.

In a tone mixed with empathy and malice, the man said, "I hope you are comfortable in this room. You can call me Director."

"All is well."

"Surely you must have some questions. In short, it's time to get to work."

"What kind of work?"

"Here we have people who donate their hearts. Your task is simply to perform heart transplants with a medical team. I have heard that you worked in London and that you are an excellent surgeon."

"Are you saying I'll be performing heart transplant surgery here?"

"No, only extracting hearts here. Transplants will be done in another place."

"And who are the donors?" he asked, hoping to extinguish the doubts that had begun to race in his head.

"That's none of your business. There may be some additional requests, like livers, corneas, or kidneys. I think you're skilled enough and nothing we will ask of you is beyond your capabilities. For now, the surgery that you are most skilled in will suffice. I need you ready to begin today."

"You haven't answered me. Who are the donors?"

"I advise you to not ask too many questions, Doctor. Just carefully do as you are asked and prepare yourself for the operating room. If you need anything specific, just write it down and we will secure it for you."

Before long, he entered a reasonably equipped operating room, sterilized himself, and began to inspect the surgical tools. He had a team of three assistants. As he looked into their eyes watching him from behind their surgical masks, he could see that they were deeply worried. The first patient was under full anesthesia with good vital signs, but the naked body lying in front of him showed signs of extreme emaciation. He was a young man, no more than thirty years of age. Anees stood frozen.

What I am about to perform is an execution of a living human being, he thought to himself. He stepped back and turned towards the door. The guard stood in his way and sent a text to his supervisor, who arrived within a few moments.

"Listen to me, Doctor," the man said angrily. "This is not how things are usually done here. I have a few friends who care about you and I am treating you well for their sake. You don't have choices here. Your job is only to follow orders. I am going to overlook your behavior because it is obvious that you didn't have a clear understanding of how we do things. But we have no room for any more delays. We don't have time. You either do as you're told or I'll send you back where you came from. I don't like to threaten or intimidate anyone, and I never force anyone to work with me."

It seemed to Anees that he only had one option, for the alternative was to return to the dormitory—the inferno. *Here at least I could begin to look for a way out. There, I am bound to rot and die at any moment.*

"No matter how hard I try, I cannot kill another human being."

"No one is asking you to kill anyone. We're only asking you to do what you do best. Just take out the heart and make sure it's healthy and then you can leave the operating room. You have two minutes. Please don't waste time. I really don't want to have to send you back to the branch. None of the people I work with will listen to you or discuss anything with you. Sure, I am patient and understanding, but honestly I have no time to sit and try to convince you."

Shifting to a friendly manner, he added, "All I can do for you is to play music that's suitable for your artistic work. What do you think about Wagner? Or do you prefer Strauss? Please don't say Mozart because I will be upset with you."

He was in utter shock. He blinked his eyes again and again, hoping that he was having a nightmare from which he would soon awaken.

"In two minutes, you can leave the room and the guard will take you to the surgery room. Two and a half minutes and you will be heading to the branch. I think you are wiser than to test my patience."

The Director left him stranded in what seemed like a spiderweb, trapped in a sticky, prickly net made of spit. It was clear that he was serious with his threats. Anees was unwilling to gamble or risk his life; he needed to survive no matter the cost. He pulled himself out of his web of anxiety, opened the door, and said to the guard, "Take me to the operating room."

Feeling completely numb, he began to operate accompanied by Wagner. He contemplated how Wagner continues to reopen a human wound where many people around the world continue to associate his music with the Holocaust as it once resounded in Nazi concentration camps. He remembered having read something about this.

The energy of the operating room strips one of emotions. The music celebrated greatness and glory, and it was to Wagner's militaristic beats that he began to slice open the skin, revealing the rib cage, and with swiftness and precision to cut the arteries and extract the pulsating red mass. He placed it in the hands of one of the assistants, who placed it in a cooler, closed it tightly, and carried it out of the room.

Sluggishly, Anees went to the bathroom and vomited his guts out. He could not believe he had done it so easily. He had just killed a human being.

29
SMELL

She made her way around the apartment with more confidence once she decided that this was her moment and that she would live it as it should be lived, without fear or regret, free as if she had just been born, with no tomorrow.

She entered his office. There were dozens of old cameras, photos, posters, scraps of paper and sketches of unfinished advertisements.

"Even at home you work on advertising!"

"Yes, you can say that. For me, advertising is not only a job, it's a way of understanding life. Many people underestimate advertising but it's actually the secret to understanding contemporary life. Whoever controls advertising owns both the producer and consumer."

"I'm immune to ads."

"No sane person is immune. Only the insane and the love-struck are immune."

"I don't watch ads and I change the channels during commercial breaks. I don't look at or listen to sales ads, and I don't look at images or read what's on them—not even out of curiosity."

"Reality is much more dangerous. Producers of goods don't only advertise through the media. The minute you choose your clothes, music, friends, work, or faith, you should know that you are being subjected to the age of advertising, that you've begun to consume, and that there are those who wait to collect payment for what you desire."

"You are complicating the issue. This is normal."

"Sure, it's normal. Look at God himself—he has been turned into a commodity. Faith is a commodity. War in the name of God is a commodity. Everything has become a product, and people like me orchestrate and promote these products for those who pay the most. Before we know it, we will be selling the scent of heaven, and I'm sure we'll find customers ready to buy it.

"Smell is a mysterious sense," he continued. "It's said that Plato launched a crackdown on perfumes because only prostitutes wore them. Consequently, he associated the senses of hearing and seeing with the elites, and he came to despise smell and touch. He considered those who enjoyed smelling and touching to be commoners.

"Think about the vastness of the world of smells—there are scents like acetone, volatile benzene, and chloroform. Then there is a group that includes smells like lemon, apple blossom, strawberry, lavender, and laurel. And another group that includes scents like the vanillas, lilies, jasmines, and most wild fresh flowers. Then there are scents of berries, musk, onion, and garlic. There is the smell of coffee, of burnt bread, the smoke of pipes and cigars, and the smells of goat cheese and blue cheese, smell of sweat, urine, the smell of belladonna, and the smell of peppers, tobacco, and coriander—toxic and thick. There is the repulsive smell of decaying meat and predatory flowers, smells that attract insects with their stench. And it is from this kingdom of smells that the process of choosing and favoring takes place to cater to the contemporary modern person. Our target groups are those in the artistic and creative sectors, elites with refined tastes, and those who can appreciate the value of these products."

"I see all of those things as a luxury," said Layl. "And I'm not entirely sure that you can fool people with these sorts of things."

"Don't worry," he said. "In a world where people are convinced that Pif Paf[32] is a necessity for crushing, destroying, and killing repulsive creatures, you can also sell a product that induces love. There is a Dutch company that will begin selling this product in sex shops as well as in pharmacies. I'm currently working on an ad for a pillow that I haven't finished yet:

---

32   Pif Paf is a popular brand of insecticide analogous to Raid in the US.

Dear valued customers who appreciate the gift of nature,

Sex is a process in which two bodies are united under the banner of love. What is as important is the moment after climax, a moment free of regret and hope, free of the past and the future, but also one that is often destroyed by words and questions; a moment in which the pores of the soul begin to breathe. It is a moment in which scents and aromas are distilled, and turn into floods of lather, foam, sweat, and drizzle leading to that post-sex moment of serenity. Our pillow helps you to breathe in, scoop from, sink in, and prolong the climax of happiness."

Seeing how stunned she was at his exotic idea excited him to elaborate further. "These pillows are stuffed with a mixture of ostrich and peacock feathers as well as other soft materials. They also contain small, aromatic vesicles of perfume designed by erotic-scent experts from around the world. As your head rests on the pillow, the texture of silk is rejuvenating. The vesicles, arranged on top of each other, begin to gradually burst and release pure wild fragrances, the essence of pine and spruce trees. The aromas, breathed in slowly, infiltrate the blood and travel into the deepest extremes of our inner worlds, shaking, rearranging, and reviving them." After a pause, he added, "The slogan of the campaign is Kama Dunya: Plunging into depths not yet tread."

She laughed at his exaggeration and over-embellishment. "Is it possible that there is actually a product with such characteristics?"

"Naturally. The companies that I work with do not pay me just to promote products or for successful ads. They also pay me because I provide them with ideas for new products, which they end up selling to manufacturing companies and giving me exclusive rights to advertise, and so on."

"Do they ask you for goods based on market studies?"

"Not at all. There are no studies or any of the nonsense that you hear about. I work based solely on the principle that every desire is a commodity."

"Even love?"

"Love. It is a mighty term. No, it's not a commodity, but it needs to be distinguished from passion, affection, infatuation, and all their attributes. Did you know that there are eighteen different synonyms for love in Arabic, and that they all happen to be derived from love and all its phases, stages, and qualities? They all fall under the wing of love. My dear friend, infatuation should not be confused with love; infatuation is a desire, but love is not. The opposite of love is not hate but indifference. Everything you desire can turn into its opposite."

She wanted to return to the subject of women and to understand how this cold, arrogant person saw women. She said, "You also happen to make a cheap commodity out of women in advertising."

He laughed heartily. "The truth is that men are the cheap commodity. We use women to get men to pay as the majority of the world's wealth is in the hands of men. Every commodity needs marketing, and marketing needs advertising, and every ad that does not stimulate the desire is a failure."

"OK, I will go along with you. But tell me, is love a desire, and is it predisposed to advertising?"

"Infatuation is. But because infatuation is a quality and part of love, then perhaps by understanding the part, we can better understand the whole. Let's look at infatuation for example—when you meet someone at one moment in time, you think it is a special moment simply because you are in it. Infatuation is not attached to the past but is also not liberated from it. It remains hostage to it. It's like the idea of postponing today's work until tomorrow and living in the moment. Infatuation cannot be without a declaration—people declare their infatuation. The moment it is announced, declared, and made known, the instinct of possession is activated. Then it becomes about wanting to possess what's been declared, and woe to whoever comes near my share. My dear, don't take advertising lightly. It is what decides your worth in the market of life."

She moved closer to him as he concluded the conversation. "It's true that love only begins when we stop being infatuated with one another." He fell silent, while the rhythm of his breath changed and her face came closer to his.

She thought to herself, *I will move to this place where people are busy talking about things other than revolution and regime, doom and madness, revenge and pleas. Here, I will arrange my life as it should be. I will finalize the divorce with Adel, I will secure a place for my children that is free of worry, and I will concentrate on my work, regain my strength, and open my own clinic. In normal cities, life is straightforward, simple, and free of complications. Everything is direct; people can take ownership of their affairs, work hard, and achieve stability.*

He asked, "What are you daydreaming about?"

"What I've gotten from you, my share, is a kiss in Damascus and photos that exposed me and destroyed me in the market of life," she replied.

30
Layl

It was after nine in the morning when she opened her eyes. He was curled up next to her, playing with her hair, showering her with light kisses. A few moments later, they were lost into each other's bodies once again, feeling fully quenched, quivering. He rolled over on his back, lit a cigarette, and closed his eyes. As the cigarette withered between his lips, he plunged into a world of his own. She contemplated everything that had happened, feeling an overwhelming sense of satisfaction.

She studied his face. His eyes were closed and he showed no expression; a cigarette protruded from between his lips.

"What's wrong?" Layl asked, as she admired his long locks of hair glistening with sweat.

Dubai's sun streamed through the windows. The distant sound of traffic returned to her ears. She was filled with the delicious after-sex smell, and her heart regained its regular rhythm. Naked, she stretched her body next to his. She gazed at the cigarette in his mouth and the chiseled contours of his body; he was like a gift from the universe, one she had not expected to receive after all that she had been through.

He looked peaceful, like a serene lake shimmering under the rays of a whispering sun. The smell of sweat mixed with perfumes mingled with the cigarette smoke casting a shadow over his face. He was immersed in tranquility, his mind in faraway depths. She wished she could be the smoke that entered his lungs and circulated in his blood and veins, so that she could arrive at his mind and see where he was in that moment, what he saw and where he wandered.

In that moment of harmony, she suddenly felt panic at the thought of losing him. The soothing yet fragile world that was beginning to entwine them frightened her, and she asked again, "What's wrong?"

He responded with an annoyed gesture for her to keep silent. He put his cigarette out on the edge of the bed frame and threw the butt into the wastebasket. His nudity was enticing. He rested his arms at his sides and took a deep breath, sinking into distant worlds. An overwhelming sense of loss came over her. She wanted him to return to her, and she feared what might happen. She ran her hand over his forehead, her questions piercing his kingdom of silence.

"What's wrong?" she asked again.

He opened his eyes, bright, tinged with innocence and beauty and the color of radiant honey. His lips curled into an unreadable smile, and he whispered in English, "Shut up."

She was shocked. "What did you say? No, you shut up!"

Still smiling, he sat up at the edge of the bed, grumbling, and then stood up and went to the bathroom. From behind, he looked like an old warrior. Even the slight sagging at his waist was attractive to her. Peeking his head out from behind the bathroom wall, the lower part of his body hidden, he said to her as she lay naked, "This time I'll forgive you. But next time, just leave me alone for a little bit. I like to take a nap after the storm so that the noises inside my head can slowly be subdued. No talking, whispering, moving, questioning, or washing up. Let everything calm down little by little."

"Aha. Good to know."

"Also, as for your genius question 'What's wrong?'—not even Freud can answer it. So, please, just don't ask me again. The worst two questions in life are 'What's wrong' and 'Where were you?'"

"You're something else! You just can't help it. Sure, will do."

She felt a mix of anger, helplessness, and joy. *How dare he speak to me like this? What is this unjustified arrogance?* She attributed his attitude to the many concessions she had made, to her clandestine presence, and to the feelings of guilt that began to fester in her heart. From the bathroom, his voice interrupted the feelings of self-rebuke that were beginning to form inside her: "Make us some coffee."

With rising anger, she stretched out her tongue and began to mock his facial expressions and the way he talked, as if to ask, *Who do you think I am, your maid?*

"I can see you," he shouted from inside the bathroom, although of course he could not.

What if it's true, she thought to herself. Stifling her laughter, she checked for surveillance cameras and replied, "At your service!"

She could hear him singing in the bathroom as she stood admiring herself in the bedroom mirror, amazed at the way her face was glowing, no longer pale, her soul satisfied. She noticed a small box in front of the mirror and opened it carefully. As she caught a glimpse of what was inside, she gained the courage to open it fully.

Suddenly, she felt an infuriating desire to dump out its contents and search for what he had taken from her in Damascus. The box was full of earrings. They were all single pieces. She began looking for her butterfly earring and eventually was able to find it. She returned the contents to the box and shut it, shocked and appalled to realize that he had collected an earring from every woman he had slept with.

All of these? She reopened the box, talking to herself, astonished at the sheer number and variety of earrings. *Son of a bitch! More than three hundred women!* She closed the box again, whispering, "May you never be fulfilled!"

She quickly composed herself and went to the kitchen. She put the pot of coffee on the stove and contemplated the reasons behind her irritation. Did she expect things to be otherwise? The truth was she did expect it, but hoped that she wouldn't have to discover it on their first day. No matter how certain a woman is about the baseness of her partner, she still hopes for a grand story, particularly in the beginning. But after the physical contact, she simply wished to satisfy a curiosity that ate at her. She longed for him gratify her femininity and assure her that she was unique among other women. She knew it didn't really matter, but she burned to hear his opinion of her. She longed to ask him, "How did you find me?" But she quickly dismissed the idea for she knew that this man, guarded behind a thousand masks, would turn her question into a sarcastic lecture.

The sight of his mobile in the kitchen disrupted her mood of dissatisfaction. She immediately opened it and read some of the messages he had received, mostly from women. Throughout the night, with his phone on silent mode, intimate messages had been pouring in. She felt her blood boil and was overcome with fierce jealousy, along with a touch of self-loathing for having looked at his phone. She wasn't sure whether her mix of feelings stemmed from peeping at his phone or because she had surrendered herself to him so easily.

She put the phone back in its place and busied herself while waiting for him to finish showering. When she felt something running between her legs, she hurried to her purse and was irritated to not find a sanitary pad. This was a surprise. She was very regular with her period and had not experienced the usual pre-menstrual symptoms like fatigue, breast tenderness, or mood swings.

Just then, her phone rang. How could she have forgotten to put it on silent? Seeing her husband's name made her tremble; it was flashing on the screen of the phone as if he could actually see her. Her stomach turned and she felt nauseated. A sizzling sound came from the kitchen. The coffee that she had forgotten about was boiling over. She hurried to the stove, feeling helpless and confused, not knowing what to do. All the noises came at once—his raspy voice from the bathroom, her husband's persistent phone calls, and the sound of spilling coffee. All of this was in addition to the unexpected menstruation.

She froze for a moment, feeling intense fear, confusion, and resentment. She willed herself to regain control. First she dealt with the phone and put it on silent. Then she turned off the stove, put the coffee pot in the sink, grabbed a handful of tissues and tucked them between her thighs, and grabbed a few more to wipe up the spilt coffee. She then dressed quickly and left.

His raspy voice seemed to follow her until she got to the elevator, then it slowly faded away. She got into a taxi. "Hyatt Regency Hotel, please." She sent a message to her husband: "Will call you in an hour. I'm at the conference hall."

Immediately, he replied, "OK. I was worried about you. It's nothing urgent. I am missing you. It is raining in Damascus today, and I miss you."

His message fueled her anger. *Now you are romantic, my ass!* She couldn't utter the words. She turned her face away, full of resentment and anger. She covered her eyes with thick sunglasses as she couldn't hold back the tears. She felt as if she was shedding stones of pain and let out sobs of relief. She thought to herself, *How wonderful it is that women are able to cry as they desire.* Before arriving at the hotel, she turned her phone on and checked it for the hundredth time. He had not called, nor did he send any messages. *Did he not notice her absence,* she wondered. *I wonder how he reacted when he came out of the bathroom and didn't find me.*

She was grumbling to herself now. *How could he not check on me? Damn him, how insensitive of him. Fine. I am also not going to call. We'll see who is more stubborn.*

She was about to throw the phone in her purse, but instead, she wrote to him, "Thank you for the scents in an incredible dream. Sorry I didn't have coffee with you."

She waited a bit. He did not reply. She felt worse and left the taxi without even waiting for the driver to give her back change for the one hundred dirhams. She went up to her room and found a box of sanitary pads in her luggage. After a short rest, she stood under a steaming hot shower and felt her back burning. She looked in the mirror next to the tub and saw the marks he left on her—bruises, scratches, and blue spots. For reasons she could not explain, the burning pain also sent pulsations of joy. She ran the tips of her fingers over the scratches, dried off, and readied herself for the conference hall.

There was a new message from him. She opened it smilingly, filled with expectation. Her smile slowly faded away as she read his words: "This time you got away with it. The next time you do this to me, you will pay. This will not go unpunished. Get yourself ready for it."

At the conference, she kept herself focused by giving it all her energy. She continued to check her phone every five minutes only to feel the same sense of emptiness and find a few romantic messages from her husband, which she no longer even bothered to open.

She made up her mind about Fidel. She was going to be strict and kind with him, for they had reached their end. She was going to wish him a wonderful life, thank him for his help, and end the next chapter before it began. It had been a whim, and it was over; she was not going to go on. But as soon as she smelled any perfume, she thought of him; and each time her mind wandered off, the memories took her back to his chest.

His carelessness and his silly message filled her with anger. *Who does he think he is to punish me? Why is he using this language with me?* At the same time, deep inside she felt a strong desire to be punished by him. She remained steadfast and did not try to speak or communicate with him. Her mood plunged as the end of her stay at the hotel drew closer.

She was unsure whether to extend her stay, at least until she received a serious offer from the hospital. Nor was she certain, with things ending in the worst way possible, that she wasn't being punished.

Her state of confusion didn't last long. A representative from the hospital called to inform her that her residency papers were ready and that she could start with the procedures immediately; she was also informed that they would temporarily move her to a hotel until her paperwork was completed and would thereafter rent her an apartment. The representative asked that she pass by his office to sign a few papers.

Now she had a reason to call Fidel, while still pretending to be angry. She grabbed the phone, dialed his number, and took a deep breath. After three rings, she heard his voice, acute and intrusive. He didn't even give her the chance to utter a word, "If you don't remember the address, I will send it to you. Be at my place at nine."

She attempted to speak, but he had hung up already.

"Damn you! You animal!" She didn't usually curse, but right then she felt like she could crush him, slap him, kick him. *I am going to go and put an end to this and let him know his worth. Who does he think he is?*

Her anger waned as she made up her mind to end this absurd chapter, restore her dignity, and bring him to face his true self. She planned to demand an apology from him, as he was after all the cause of all the sorrow she was feeling. She was not going to accept anything less than an honest, true apology that was good enough for her.

She rang the doorbell at exactly nine o'clock. By ten after nine, they were both naked, exchanging kisses, slaps, and insults.

31

The Storm

Layl lived two months of a wild storm where her life plunged from rock bottom to even deeper depths.

Love ravages, destroys, and digs deep. It is impossible to understand or explain. Suddenly, the world around you vanishes. You are no longer able to focus with anyone or anything, unless they have something to do with your beloved. It's all-consuming; the mind works at its maximum capacity and your emotions operate at a thousand horsepower.

Within three weeks, she was a consultant in a large hospital working four days a week, with a good salary and accommodations. She rented a spacious house for her family at Emirates Hills, about a ten-minute drive from Fidel's house. She got her driver's license, bought a navy blue four wheel-drive, and registered at three different sports clubs, including one for cricket and another for golf, not because she cared for those sports but because he played them.

She devoted her time and self to him, and began to eliminate the other women in his life, one after the other. She classified them into different groups and befriended some of them. She utilized every power a woman possesses to protect her man. *They can have all the other men in the world, but just let me have him,* she reckoned. With a calm vengeance, she threatened, *I will destroy and crush anyone on earth who comes near him.*

As for how to deal with him, she continued to implement a strategy that she had devised—*treating him like an enemy and loving him with all her being; although enemies are not to be trusted, they should be studied and dissected; one should make peace and strike deals with them.*

In short, she arrived at a dangerous conclusion: if a woman cannot tolerate that her male partner sleeps with someone else, she must convince him that when he is with her, he is the manliest male known to history. He should be allowed to express his anger without reservation. Equally important, if he has had multiple relationships, he will likely want to talk about his adventures. Here, a woman should confront the man and tell him, without holding back, about her own romantic adventures, conveying the idea that she is no less than he is and is in fact superior him. She should bait a nice and innocent story with burning jealousy and embellish it with sentiments like, 'He was great at kissing,' or hint that she discovered desire at the hands of a remarkable lover.

And so she told him that her husband had "deluxe merchandise" but that he did not know how to use it nor understood its value. This hint was enough to open the gates to a hellish interrogation. The more jealous he became, the more she would throw one of his basic moves back at him.

Hearing him talk for hours about his past without exploding required a high degree of emotional control. All the while, she had to avoid his frenzied, revenge-seeking mistresses. Indeed, loving a man like Fidel meant having to crawl on a road of embers, and to be prepared that a landmine could blow up at any time. It meant living in a constant state of exhaustion, terror, and dread, alternating with feelings of peace and unimaginable pleasure.

She took care of him. She had the keys to his house, came to know his secrets, and read his writings and emails. She classified his mistresses, monitored his mood; she examined and dissected him, knew that she was dealing with an excessively sensitive being with heightened senses, composed of two opposite personalities that could not meet. He was a nihilist, destructive with sadistic tendencies, but also a devout religious believer, an ascetic person with a passion for Sufism. With one of his personalities, she had to take care of her body and prepare for him what he had not tasted before. For the other personality, she had to fortify herself with yoga, Reiki, and fasting, and trying to keep up with him.

She knew how to harness his imagination and was a saint when he needed her to act as a prostitute, for only ignorant women seduced men's bodies without also engaging their imaginations; as for men, they were perpetually ignorant when it came to this equation.

As the days passed, she found that she did not know herself as well as she thought she did. He shook up the very basics of her own understanding of herself. She came to understand that great love requires a revealing of the truth and essence of the self. And all her discoveries would not have happened had it not been for what had taken place in Syria. The new reality caused people to stop observing one another. Things had become a choice between survival and annihilation, and as a consequence there was an explosion of desires.

At times, as she witnessed the pain in her country, she felt ashamed of her affection for Fidel. The more bleeding that took place there, the more she indulged in this madness that did not resemble her.

Terrible violence causes instincts to explode. Sex was not a question here, but it was part of the answer. The body spoke its own language to the fullest, while the mind and morals shied away from engaging with this language. Layl knew she could only put an end to this emotional torture by ending their relationship, and that meant going with him to an extreme end. This needed to happen before her family arrived. She believed that the beginning of the end would be when she would hear him say, "The frenzy is now over—let's get back to our lives." Each of them was waiting for the other to say this and accused the other of looking for reasons to end their relationship.

At Jebel Ali Club's magnificent sandy beach, they swam to a wooden buoy. They had sex in the water. She held on to a metal ladder while he gripped her. It was a salty penetration; they were fighting to stay joined despite the resistance of the water, ignoring the whistle of the lifeguard and a blazing sun that scorched them with its blazing rays. They returned to the shore. The combination of alcohol and sun intoxicated their passion-filled bodies. He continued to sit and watch the majestic sunset and contemplated an overflowing love that exceeded rational boundaries. It was a sinful love, and sin yields great passion.

After the sun had set and the crowded beach began to thin out, he picked up a large towel and led her by her hand. Between two long lounge chairs he flattened the towel and laid her down. They slept next to one another, tranquil under an endless sky lit with stars, whispering softly as they were afraid of a raid by the resort's security. It was in that moment that he breathed to her, "I love you." That moment marked her return to reality; she now felt equal to him and ready to take initiative. They fell asleep in that nocturnal space while the waves played their eternal melody.

In the morning, once they were both awake, she asked him, "When do you want me to send the visa to Adel and the children?" He didn't answer. "You do know that I will stop seeing you after they come," she said, although she wasn't certain she was ready for his answer. She hoped that he would object, but she feared his silence more than his words. And so she waited feeling as if the night had been swarmed with a pack of voracious wolves devouring her anticipating flesh.

He slapped her with the back of his hand, and before she could fathom what had happened, he flipped her over on her stomach, spread her legs apart, and mounted her, penetrating her from behind. Panting with vengeance, he cursed, scratched, and spanked her with great force until he emptied himself into her. He then pulled out and went into the waves, hiding in the darkness, shouting and cursing, immersing himself in a coal-black sea. She lay on her stomach, feeling shocked. Although she was crying in disbelief, there was also a sensation of pleasure that she did not want to admit. Her tears relieved some of the pressure of the moment and eased some of the pain she was feeling, not in her heart but in her ass.

Three weeks later, Adel and the children arrived. She had made the decision to bring them. Their visas were ready and all she had to do was purchase their airplane tickets.

When she called to tell him, he replied coldly, "I hope they arrive safely" and hung up. She had to prepare herself for the post-Fidel stage. Indeed, when a woman makes such a decision, she becomes stronger than she could imagine. But those who do not realize the worth of this strength within them end up giving up. She was not going to give up—she contemplated whether she was being subjected to masculine extortion, and if her relationship with him reflected her true desire.

Gradually, she came to discover that he drew strength from her weakness. He was in control because she had given him the opportunity to manipulate her. But in Fidel, she had found the satisfaction of taking revenge on Adel. Questions continued to surface and were met with floods of uncertain answers; she despised herself, trying to hold steady while stuck in a gray zone.

She decided that she was going to do everything in her power to get rid of him and to keep herself extremely busy with her family coming from Damascus. She continued the medical treatment for Adel, without any feelings of guilt; for when a woman discovers her husband is willing to sell her in exchange for power and money, she can sleep with the entire world but still consider him too lowly to go near.

Once her family arrived, she dedicated her energy to entertaining her two children, compensating for her period of absence. To pass the time, she accepted being part of a normal, stable, and boring social life, a disappointing phase that was free from the storm of love.

The news from Damascus was not only a cause for concern but also terror. She began to meet the wealthy elite who had fled Syria, purchased houses, and moved their money to Dubai. High-end neighborhoods filled up with wealthy Syrians. She also arrived at an understanding that she did not disclose until years later—that those loyal to Damascus's dictator were wealthy, phony, lowly opportunists. It was true that several of those who supported the revolution were also opportunists and vengeful, but she never met anyone with morals or a noble character who defended the Syrian regime. These people glorified killing, accused the poor and revolutionaries of being scum, and called them animals. At one point, she could no longer bear the situation. In a gathering, she made the mistake of uttering a few unfiltered sentences.

"The people who you have always despised are revolting against you," she said. "In life as in medicine, if you can't come up with the right diagnosis, you won't be able to treat anything. If you don't understand that this is a revolution, then it will crush you and your regime." At first, people were silent. But soon they condemned her and called her a traitor. She was threatened by an agent of the Mukhabarat, who insulted her in the presence of Adel. She returned his insult and left. Ever since speaking out, she no longer joined these people when they met for coffee or lunch and expressed their hypocritical nostalgia and longing for a beautiful homeland.

The worst of what happened during the third month of Fidel's absence was that Adel, who had become nothing but a shadow of a stolen soul, attempted to act like a normal husband, especially in bed. For Layl, nothing felt more despicable than feeling guilty for sleeping with her husband. It was a three-dimensional feeling of contempt—towards herself, her husband, and her lover. In the end, she often blamed Adel for everything. Although, in fairness, any betrayal within a marriage, whether in the past or in the future, was the responsibility of all parties involved.

Her life took on a new rhythm. She paid a high price for her dead feelings towards Adel, who swayed the children to side with him. It was great torture for her to know that he had told them the story, but only from his perspective. After his sickness, he became skilled in emotional blackmail. Her harsh stance towards the families and friends of her children meant they were forced to endure outright ridicule and subtle jabs about her in front of other Syrian children. She could no longer bear to leave the house.

Attending yoga classes three times a week helped her. She tried to find a friend from another world, one that was far away from hers, and she was finally rescued. Ayyoush was a divorced woman, once married to a wealthy man, who had worked hard to rebuild her life, landing a prestigious job in Abu Dhabi. Layl would visit with her in Dubai at the end of every week and they had a good time together. She needed this enchanting simplicity in life. She also needed to tell someone about Fidel so that she could join in solidarity all other forsaken women in their great grievance.

32
The Chef

With the arrival of new physicians came several new rooms on the floor, and Anees's meetings with the Director became less frequent. From snippets of conversation between the guards that he'd overheard, he gathered that they were in a very large building outside of Damascus, near the eastern mountains.

Anees entered an elegant room that was in stark contrast with the rest of the place. He stuck a red rose in the buttonhole of his suit jacket, and with radiant skin, doused himself in cologne. He held a deck of cards that he shuffled skillfully. Gathering all his strength, he spoke boldly. "I would like to present you with a deal."

"I am listening."

"You've no doubt heard that I own Huddud's House. It's a grand house and I have not yet agreed to sell it. How about I leave this place in exchange for the house?"

"Your house is worthless now, and what I make here in a month is worth more than its value."

"You're not just a businessman. You're different because you appreciate art and have a particular take on it. You would be getting a small, priceless museum. After the war ends, the value of the house will increase a hundredfold."

"Your departure from here to any place other than the grave or one of the discipline branches would mean my death the next day. You are flagged by security, Doctor, and we are keeping a close eye on you. There is no way to get you out of here. They check on you every week, sometimes three times a week. Your presence here is my responsibility. Do you understand what I'm saying?"

"I am sure that, with your genius, you can figure out a way to grant me a pardon."

Something snapped inside him, and he blew up and started hissing like a snake, "Now you're mocking me! Do you think you're better than me? Don't you dare use this trashy, coaxing language with me."

"I am not trying to coax you or puff you up. You are my lifeline. I have no one else but you. Sure, in the beginning, things were difficult. But today I'm actually able to find some satisfaction in what I am doing. You were right when you told me that I would be in a bad mood on the days that I don't work."

The Director gave Anees a piercing look, trying to see if he was being sincere. He must have felt convinced; he calmed down, and his blue eyes returned to their clear, malevolent state. "Ah, I'm happy that you're finally speaking with such depth. I have a question for you. Have you ever gambled?"

"Pardon?"

"Have you ever gone gambling? You know, games of chance?"

"Yes, I've been a few times with friends for fun."

"Do you consider yourself a lucky person?"

"However I think of myself no longer matters because my presence here makes me one of the unluckiest people on the face of the earth."

The Director laughed, his pale face turning a little crimson. He asked, "Seven and a half, blackjack, or poker?"

Anees shuffled the playing cards in his mind trying to come up with an answer. He knew the names of some of the games but did not remember the details of any of them. He answered, "I think I know but I don't remember."

"Let's make a bet then. If you win, I will try and consider your offer, and if you lose, you will forget about it."

Anees shuffled the cards and dealt them. He had two queens and asked for a third. Luck was on his side. The fourth card was a nine, and the fifth was another queen. As they revealed their cards, the Director eyed Anees's hand admiringly, saying, "The worst kind of luck is good luck that comes at the wrong time. Regardless, I will try to figure out something that will help you, Doctor."

The Director switched from cards to playing *Basra*,[33] and with the change of game, the mood of the conversation also changed. "We have an opportunity in our hands that may never be repeated in history," he said. "What they call evil, I call reality. You and I, Doctor, have arrived at a stage that not many people reach. We are in the middle of a great enlightenment. God creates and we determine endings and give life to others. What the weak are unable to stomach, we live, breathe, and touch. We open the human body and contemplate the miracle of creation."

As they continued to play, the Director seemed happy chattering while Anees listened. He was a lonely, isolated creature who longed for participation and conversation. He found in his captive a mirror through which he could hear his own voice without feeling afraid. He spoke fluent English with a British accent, and fragments of expressions he used hinted that he had once been there. Anees reckoned that he must have studied medicine for a few years, or that he may have actually been a doctor. He was nearing his fifties and had come from one of the wealthy families close to the regime. Anees continued to listen, desperately trying to find any glimmer of hope he could grab onto as they exchanged cards.

The Director continued, "Do you really think people like us can go back to living with the trivialities of life and in that hell of emptiness they call simplicity and quietude? Do you think that after having discovered all this we would be able to live amongst others or be like others? We belong here. There is no other place in the world that can tolerate us or that we can tolerate.

"Stay here, Doctor. The outside is a sick place, fraudulent and frightening. People's struggles and their emotions, their selfishness and banalities do not come close to the feeling of touching a spleen saturated with beauty, majesty, and the pulsating taste of life. He who has not devoured a human liver does not understand the meaning of taste." He

---

33 *Basra* is a popular card game, similar to the Western game casino.

indulged himself, referencing *The Silence of the Lambs* and adding that he considered Hannibal Lecter to be one of the greatest film characters of all time.

Anees broke in smoothly as he drew a new card and tossed another. "Hear me out, your excellency, the Director. At the beginning of my stay here, I may have listened to you out of flattery and fear. But I now acknowledge that I have come to better understand you. I am not saying that I agree with you or fully accept your logic. Yet even more dangerous—I am no longer angry with you, nor do I condemn you."

The Director raised his glass, "We can now toast the beginning of our friendship, Doctor. Here's to your health. You deserve to be heard because you are now starting to be realistic, and I was counting on this all along."

Anees's chance had finally come. Trying to speak in the least emotional way possible, his words came out bare. "You knew what you wanted, and that's why what happened to me did not happen to you. I need to see my son at least one more time, and I also need to see Samia again because the memory of her weakens me."

Irritated, the Director snapped, "You see, this is a sign of weakness, one that will keep you from reaching perfection, Dr. Anees."

"Even your friend Hannibal Lecter needed Clarice," interjected Anees.

"The difference between us and the great lineage of saints—Fritz Haarmann, Ed Gein, Joachim Kroll, and Albert Fish—is that they were living in times of peace and so their miracles were cast as horrifying crimes. Yet what the rich do to the poor is a thousand times more brutal, and is all done in disguise. They destroy hundreds of hearts each day, burn tons of livers, devour nature, and accumulate fat on their bodies. Are these not also crimes? They hold honest people like us accountable but accuse this great and true lineage of the most horrible traits, and continue to punish them not for the sake of society and morals but because it is only those people who expose the lies on this earth."

"I need to leave, boss, so I can put into practice what I have learned here. I need to test my new faith."

"I'll think about it, but I can't promise you anything."

He laid down his cards down with signs of victory showing on his face. As he stood ready to leave, he cast a devious look at Anees. "From today forward, don't call me Director. Call me, your excellency, the Chef. I am certain that one day we will both taste eternity together," he said, and departed.

Feeling overcome with defeat, Anees held back a curse in fear of the eye that watched him through the camera in the corner. Trying to maintain an expression of cold indifference, he sat reshuffling the cards and trying to predict his future with a fortune-telling game. When dinnertime came, his meal arrived with a note and a fine bottle of wine: "Try this four-course meal and let me know what you think. I reserved the most precious piece out for you—the pituitary gland—cooked in olive oil with a dressing of lemon, coriander, and garlic. The heart was taken from an exquisite virgin, the liver from a boxer, and I will leave you to guess what the fourth piece is. I need you to join me in the feast. We will talk later about making an exception for you to leave. Enjoy for now."

It seemed like a disgusting joke, the perverse antics of an insane person. He sat motionless in front of the fragrant dish, tilting his head to the corner of the room where the camera was directed at him. He poured a glass of wine, held his knife and fork, cut a large piece of the skillfully cooked brain, put it in his mouth, and chewed it slowly, savoring the exquisite taste. He raised his glass of wine to the camera, then leaned forward to finish a meal that became more flavorsome with every bite. He no longer cared whether what he tasted was human or just a sick joke by a cold-hearted, bloodthirsty killer.

33

Taher

Adel came to see Layl as merely a bank card and nothing more. The coldness between them transformed their relationship into one that was cordial, devoid of drama, and polite in its outward appearance.

She did not give up in the face of her children's biased emotions. She received their complaints with a smile, overwhelmed them with kindness, and met their rejection with more devotion. Within a few months, she managed to establish a balanced relationship with them. Her main concern was to rid herself of the side effects of the complex amorous entanglement that had almost destroyed her. Meditating and seeking spiritual peace helped relieve her pain and restore her concentration. The strange thing was that she could not transfer her abundance of emotions to anyone else in his absence; she only felt them for him.

She returned to being the Layl who was always kind and devoid of desires. *Where do desires come from and where do they go when they vanish?* The effort to understand love and the hold it can impart only led her to feel more uncertainty, for love is not a means to an end. It is everything; to feel its pleasure is to experience the delights of paradise and to feel its pain is to be in the fire of hell. Her passion was like the suffering of the caravans of Sufis[34], the great lovers who chose to give

---

34 Sufism is a mystical and spiritual dimension of Islam, focused on developing a close and personal relationship with the divine, seeking inner transformation, and striving for a state of enlightenment. Sufis often use allegorical language and metaphors to describe their experiences and teachings. They may use terms like "suffering" to refer to the challenges and trials one encounters on the spiritual path, as growth and transformation often require overcoming personal struggles and ego.

up everything for the sake of their beloved.

Her psychiatrist, Dr. Taher, explained that the treatment would first require her to acknowledge the illness and her desire for recovery, because one of the pitfalls of love is that one learns to live with the condition and even enjoy it. He told her that the desire to be tormented by love has been sanctioned throughout history, where separation has been glorified, abandonment relished, and rejection indulged in. He said one need only to listen to Arabic songs to understand the topography of emotional pain and how sentiments can be transformed into chronic, masochistic inflammations. Dr. Taher's approach led her to his clinic, and after several sessions she began to regain control and escape the vortex of destruction.

She soon found herself in a new world, in which there was an amalgamation between the tremendous spiritual energy she felt and her religious beliefs. She fasted dutifully during Ramadan and prayed to tame the self and its desires—all of which made her feel better, and her thoughts about him started to wane.

Following the proverb "Immersing oneself in work protects from poverty, emptiness, and vice," she decided to work five days a week instead of four. This led to an increase in her income and a great improvement in the family's standard of living.

As for Fidel, she considered him a passerby in her life, a secret of hers that did not hold any future promise, and consigned him to an oblique *barzakh* between reality and imagination, between survival and annihilation, between marriage and love.

She no longer considered going to places where she might run into him and avoided passing by his home. She would not allow herself to burn at his indifference or imagine him sleeping with other women, anointing them with his oil of eternal misery.

"I will be honest with you," remarked Dr. Taher, "I am more concerned about a potential relapse than the condition itself. Your mind wants to sort out something that is not susceptible to order, and to make sense of something that does not conform to reason. You are now in a truce with this storm and have found ways to build a strong wall against it. I fear that this structure will not survive a second wave of the tsunami. You are one of the few who are aware of what you are going through and wrestling with. But I will tell you this—whoever rejects the truth of love ends up rejecting love for truth."

He continued, "What you are doing now is concealing the truth and not treating it. Your suffering is an indicator of the fact that you have not overcome the situation. To date, this stormy emotional condition, call it as you will, has not been taken as seriously as it should be. Its energy has touched something in your depths and penetrated the dark chambers within you. It has led you to behave in ways that you are unable to admit or explain. To reveal the truth of what you've lived would create turmoil. Also, because what you experienced, and I insist that it remains in its infancy, was suddenly born in you without having had any experience in dealing with these kinds of intense emotions, it will take a long time to heal from it."

"Are you saying that there is no cure and that I'm prone to relapse?"

"What I am saying is that you are overreacting about having to overcome things. Love helps time pass by, and time helps love pass by. In short, don't be too hard on yourself in case you regress or relapse. I also want you to know that you're welcome on this couch anytime, and that you will not be judged here."

"You're right, Doctor, when you fall in love, and that love begins to die, it can turn into a corpse inside of you that refuses to be buried. Do you think that he loved me, or that he still loves me, Doctor? Honestly, my curiosity about this question is driving me insane."

Dr. Taher was silent for a moment, then he said sternly, "That's not what's important, Dr. Layl. Throughout history, humans have attempted to understand or define their emotions. Someone, a playwright or a poet, once summed up how men generally think about women. He said, 'What wins over a man's heart is not her beauty, charm, or how naughty she is in bed, but her nobleness. And what hurts a woman more than being cut off is when a man does not see her nobleness."

As she left the clinic and went to meet Ayyoush, Dr. Taher's words did not worry her at all. She was convinced that with every passing day she was moving further away from her former submissive state, when she felt robbed of her very self.

Ayyoush oozed seductiveness in her form-fitting *abaya*. Her bangs covered her dark-skinned forehead, and her wide, kohl-lined eyes shot fatal looks. Her lips were passed down from a long line of Dhofar's[35] dark-complected women. She was tall and plump, with heavy rounded breasts. Ayyoush was Iraqi-Omani and held Emirati citizenship. She studied business administration in London and now had a high-paying government job. She knew how to live and maneuver her reality.

As an Emirati she lived according to what society and power expected of her, and as a daughter of life she also chose to live according to her desires. She was married and divorced twice, and the mother of a son and daughter. In Abu Dhabi, she behaved in line with what was decreed and prescribed, wore the *shaylah*[36] and a modest *abaya*, and always made sure to place a veil on her face in public.

She drove the latest model of Mercedes and had a driver to go with it. On weekends and holidays, she used her BMW X6 or her Lexus to drive to Dubai for the weekend with her girlfriends.

During their nights out at one of the upscale tango, salsa, or free dancing clubs, they stripped off their *abayas* and *shaylahs*, and stirred up wild storms. They returned to being free women who did not belong to anyone. Their adventures did not involve alcohol, not for religious reasons but because they did not enjoy it. They were also not looking to find deep or sexual relationships. Most of the time, their outings would simply end up with a dozen young men driven crazy by the anonymous seductiveness and sexiness of these captivating women. Filled with energy, seeking nothing more than a good time, when they gathered, there was not a man they could not bend to their will and turn into a laughingstock.

Layl first met Ayyoush at the hospital through one of her friends. Ayyoush took the weight off Layl's heart. While in her company, Layl felt the security that comes in the presence of other women, and what it means to be both strong and malleable. Ayyoush was in her mid-thirties, armed with a solid understanding of her lived reality.

---

35   Dhofar is a governorate in the Sultanate of Oman.
36   *Shaylah* is the name for the headcover in the Arab Gulf worn by some Muslim women.

One night they got together at Bazarati, a club in Dubai. Ayyoush, full of life, asked, "What's wrong, Layl, my love?"

"You know, I really love your accent—Iraqi mixed with the Gulf accent."

"And your accent is also seductive—Damascenian! What's worrying you?"

"Nothing really. It's just that I met with a psychiatrist and I'm thinking about what he said."

"Forget about these doctors and their nonsense."

"It really is nonsense. It's like psychoanalysis wants us to think that men are nothing more than wild, sexual animals."

Ayyoush laughed. "God! Why is it that all the ones I meet end up being gentle pets?"

In fifteen minutes, Layl was in tears laughing with Ayyoush, lightened by her spirit. She was a force of nature, and her presence was captivating. She could make fun of herself and others, maintain balance, and draw clear boundaries. She was financially independent and managed to survive suffocating categorizations in a society that was both highly conservative and open-minded at the same time.

Ayyoush made it clear that she was free to travel to any country in the world, whenever she wanted, and to do as she wished anytime she wanted. She did not depend on anyone, and as long as she was productive, she felt empowered. She did not allow anyone or anything to hold her back or imprison her, neither emotions nor a husband. In her view, the era of slavery for women had passed.

"Don't you think that Arab revolutions will also reach the Arab Gulf?" Layl asked her.

"We don't want it to. I will stand against it. Revolutions will bring the Islamists to us. Here, we have a reasonable social contract with our rulers. It's not the ideal situation, but it's especially wonderful for women. Look at the state institutions today, for example—they are filled with women. Our problems have to do with tribal systems and not with the government, or at least this is the case here in the Emirates."

The arrival of two of Ayyoush's friends ended their serious

conversation. Sitting with these Arab women, Layl felt a great sense of strength, satisfaction, and the freedom to see life, not from a hole in a door of a prison cell, but from the highest climbable peak on a hill, basking in the clarity of sight.

In this beautiful moment of revelation and ultimate delight, she was suddenly overcome with a strange feeling of dizziness, the sensation of falling from a great height. Suddenly, she couldn't breathe or stand. She grabbed Ayyoush's hand and said, "Get me out of here."

At the other end of the place, Fidel Abdullah was holding a bottle of beer and looking out onto the sea. No sooner had she caught a glimpse of him than she was on the verge of collapse.

"Don't run away from the truth. Confront it," rang Dr. Taher's words.

After all the torment it had taken her to ensure a minimum level of security for her family, to break the ice with her children, to get to a point where Adel's health improved enough for him to return to work, and to achieve a general feeling of stability and success at her own work—after all of this, everything collapsed in one glance.

"Dr. Taher. Advise me."

"Professionally, I can't do that. I can't tell you to do this or that. But what I can tell you is to not run away from facing the truth. I don't want to prescribe Prozac for you, or any antidepressants. Layl, you're a physician and you know that you don't need medicine. What you need is inner strength."

After hesitating a thousand times, she sent him a couple of words, "I want to see you." She stayed attached to her phone, floating on clouds of anticipation.

A few minutes later, he replied, "You know where to find me."

"I want to see you in a public place," she responded.

"Pentagon Hotel, at the bar. Meet me at 6."

For the first five minutes, she could only stare at his face, unable to speak. Something was broken in him. His beard had grown long, as if hiding immense pain behind it. He whispered gently, "Tell me, Ms. Layl. How can I help you?"

"Just listen," she answered, before drowning him in all the recent details. She was unloading; it was like complaining to a father and blaming a lover.

He listened attentively, did not stir until she finished. Her tone changed as she confessed, "I love you, for God's sake, and I need you to help me."

"Layl, ever since you walked into my life, something in me started to change. Ever since you came to Dubai, my whole existence has been in turmoil. Layl, I don't know how to talk about love, and I don't even know if I have it in me to love. What I do know is that there is one thing that can resolve this whole story. Marry me." He said it firmly, with confidence and without any hesitation.

If she had ever lived a moment of ultimate satisfaction, of genuine happiness, this was that moment.

"If I marry you, you will destroy me."

"Possibly. I don't know. The only thing that I do know today is that I am trying to make up for the worst mistake of my life—working with these criminals and covering up the truth of what's happening in Syria."

She did not want the conversation to turn political. She wanted to stay in the moment, to hold onto it, and cling to its sincerity and the sense of security it provided. But he continued to talk about the latest developments in the most complex catastrophe in recent history.

"I was not neutral or even loyal to the regime. I took part in the massacre. We were bribed by senior journalists and took part in a coordinated and organized effort to create another narrative. With the power of media relations, we pushed away all the main facts and distracted the world with irrelevant details.

"The change that took place within me did not happen because of an awakening of conscience, but in that moment I deeply felt you in my life. I didn't realize it until during this period of separation and absence. Layl, they say that we don't have a choice when it comes to those we are born amongst or even live with. The choices we make have to do with the people we think we can't live without. Today, I am weak and feeble. This time, neither Fadl nor God were able to help me. I have lost Fidel as well and I'm not sure how to get him back. Marry me so that we can rid ourselves of this illusion. I don't know if I love you, and I don't know about this mysterious thing that people talk about, or whether it's real or only a phantom that people imagine and call love. Layl, you've hurt me as much as I've hurt you. You liberated me to the same degree I held you in bondage. We will only be able to attain our salvation by removing the obstacle and barrier, or if one of us disappears, and if this is the case, then it will definitely need to be me."

"Take me to you," she said.

His house was no more than five minutes away by car from the hotel. Both of them drove their own car. The five minutes felt like five thousand years to her.

Nothing could come close to the moment she immersed herself in the frenzy of his body. She surrendered like a lover, knowing now that nothing would keep her from a relapse. It wasn't only a relapse, but a destruction, a fierce war, a continuous bombardment, a bloodletting where no sooner had the wound healed than it ruptured again.

Face the truth of things. Stop building on a shaky foundation. Wherever truth happens to be, go to it and look it in the eye. Only then will you will be able to choose what you want, heal yourself, or discover that you are not suffering from anything more than your own truth. Dr. Taher's words fueled her desire to break the adhesion of these two opposing worlds.

She dropped the boys off at their friend's house. They did not speak to her the whole way, and they were sitting in the back seat because neither of them wanted to sit next to her. As they got out of the car, Mayar said, "If you don't mind, can Dad pick us up later?" Before she could reply, he slammed the door and walked away.

She was on the verge of exploding, but somehow she remained calm; she took a deep breath and went back home, where she prepared coffee and joined Adel in front of the TV. On the news they were talking about the waves of displacement, the bombardment of the cities, and the daily bloodshed that had not ceased for four years.

She poured the coffee and served him a cup. She then picked up the remote, muted the TV, and said, "Adel, I need to talk to you."

He silently stared at the coffee cup. She repeated the sentence, "I would like to talk to you about something."

"Coffee. You made us coffee, Layl?"

"Yes, and without sugar. You know that you and I haven't had coffee together for a very long time."

"Did you forget that I am not allowed to drink coffee?"

She remembered and quickly carried the cups to the kitchen, emptied them, and put them under the faucet, while the blackness flowed out and filled the sink. She increased the flow of water, and noticed how the grounds dissolved after floating in small swirls until the color of water cleared. She shut the tap and headed back into the living room. Adel was sitting with his fingers interlaced, slightly bent forward, his eyes fixed on the spot where the cup had been.

"Adel," she said, in an even tone, "I want a divorce."

Without changing his position, he looked up at her and said, "Finally, you said it. Does this mean you're back with the producer?"

"This has nothing to do with anyone except us."

"I'll make it easy for you. There isn't an issue with Mayar—he is now sixteen. Nawwar is the one suffering, and we need to minimize the impact on him."

"This is how it is then. You're turning my children against me. This explains their hatred towards me."

"On the contrary. I'm not even defending myself. All I am doing is preparing them."

"Adel, what have you told my children about me?"

"It wasn't me, Layl. Your behavior is what told them. Everyone is talking about you and knows your story."

"Who is everyone? The insignificant *Shabiha*[37]?"

"They used to be your friends back home. These people also have opinions. They are not ignorant nor *Shabiha*. Anyway, the children found out from their friends. I've been trying to rectify things the entire time."

The grinding resurfaced in her heart; she could no longer bear it. "And so now you're the courageous victim suffering because of the prostitute

---

37   *Shabiha* is a term used primarily in the context of the Syrian conflict. It refers to pro-government militias or paramilitary groups that have been accused of carrying out brutal actions, including human rights abuses, during the Syrian civil war.

that you've had to put up with for the sake of the children? Now you're the gallant and noble one, while no one knows that you were actually a pim— "

"Enough. Shut your mouth," he bellowed like a wounded bull. As he stood up, he said, "Layl, don't make mistakes. I have no intention of mistreating you. Do as you wish, and after five months you will receive your divorce papers from me."

"Why five months?"

"That's all I have to offer."

He turned around and left. Though crumbling in despair, she still searched her mind to figure out what game he was playing. In five months, Nawwar would turn fourteen and past the age of protective care.

She went to the bedroom her boys shared, opened their closet, and breathed in their scents as if they had been apart for years. On the wall were photos of them with their father, none of her with them. There was no trace of her existence. She had been entirely cut out of their lives.

She got in her car and began driving aimlessly. Two hours later, she pulled into the parking lot of his house. She felt her feet walking her to his apartment, to the only place she belonged and the place in which she also burned. At the door of the elevator, everything descended while her fate was ascending.

34

Anees

Most amazing about humans is their ability to adapt and get used to things. What hurt Anees is that his desire to live grew more ferocious with time, and not even once did he consider suicide, clinging tightly onto life even with death so close. A black hole was growing inside him, like a dark vacuum sucking away all his feelings, sensations, and dreams.

Today, he had calmly carried out three operations. Most disturbing was that he had started choosing to listen to the music of Mounir Bashir while working, and enjoyed eating two ice cream cones afterward.

He returned to his room to find an internal telephone that would only receive calls. Within a few minutes, it rang. He picked up the receiver and heard the voice of the Director-Chef on the other end of the line: "Get ready for dinner tonight. I have good news."

"Is there hope for release?"

"I don't want to play games with you, Dr. Anees. Yes, there is a strong possibility for release. We will discuss it over dinner."

Anees shuddered with fear. As his thoughts of release began to graze the outside world, they were accompanied by a torrent of guilt and horror. How could he reconcile with what he had done and start over again?

The features of Samia's face had blurred in his mind, while Sami's remained fresh in every detail. Hannah's face remained cold. Here, Anees came to realize that ever since she betrayed him years ago, Hannah had been withering inside of him until she just faded away.

One of the toughest things about being in prison is that it brings to surface, and fully exposes, that which was buried in the depths where pain resides. He was burning on the slow fire of anticipation, while bubbles of toxic memories continued to surface.

The phone rang again. When he answered, a deep voice commanded, "In the closet are two suits that I personally chose for you. Get ready. We are about to meet some guests and I want you dressed to the nines. Be ready in two hours."

The Armani suit was navy, matched with a light blue shirt that paired perfectly with a Francesco Smalto red-striped tie and handkerchief of the same color, much like the one the Chef had in his jacket. The guard accompanied him through a narrow passageway to the top of the stairs. He arrived at a luxurious lounge where a table was decorated with exquisitely arranged candles.

Standing tall, eyes glittering, a smile on his thin lips, the Director-Chef was glowing. Half serious, half joking, Dr. Anees rushed to ask, "It looks like we will be celebrating. Bring on the good news!"

Looking straight at him, the Chef said *yes* with his mouth, but his eyes said *I wish*. "Let's have a glass first."

He poured two glasses of white wine. Anees took a large sip without even waiting to clink his glass and said, "I am a vegetarian today. I don't want any more meat, please."

"Remember Doctor, I didn't force you to do anything. If you are afraid of the complications of human meat, let me assure you that it's been eaten throughout history and continues to be."

"Are you saying that you actually served me ..." Anees could not bring himself to say the word.

A nauseating smile appeared on the Chef's face as he continued his disturbing performance. "All you hear about the perils of eating human flesh is nothing more than mythical or ethical warnings. The effects on a person who consumes a meal of cooked human flesh are no different from someone who eats any other animal meat. Eating human flesh was once a traditional tribute to the dead and an attempt to adopt some of the dead person's qualities. Some of the qualities of the consumed animal are also passed down to those who eat it."

"You really pique my curiosity. So what do you do besides organ transplants in this center?" Anees said, knowing he had to interrupt him or else be forced to listen to this historical narrative about cannibalism and its various types for hours.

"My dear Anees. The incredibly genius minds that can drive the world forward are besieged by banalities and regulations, and they are in desperate need of experiments that can only be done in completely free cultural centers like this."

He pulled a small vial out of his pocket that looked like an eye dropper with bright white powder inside, "I advise you to first try this so that you can relax a little."

He drew a line of cocaine on the glass table and snorted it all at once.

"If you've never tried it before, wet your finger and rub some on your upper gum. It's actually better this way."

Anees hesitated for a moment and then pressed his finger on the powder and rubbed it on his gums. He knew that cocaine needs three minutes for the effects to reach the brain when sniffed, seconds when injected directly through the bloodstream, and about seven minutes when absorbed via the gums. By the end of his second glass of wine, his heartbeats accelerated, and he felt continuous waves of mental clarity and fantastic euphoria.

If a person's higher self is constructed piece by piece over eighteen years through advice, values, education, and experiences that help to form a bloated, social, protective sense of self, then a single sniff of cocaine and a glass of wine are enough to dissolve everything within a few minutes. Throughout the period of elation, his mind opened up to new worlds, feeling an unprecedented physical energy free from fatigue and exhaustion.

The Chef took Anees on a tour of the center, a place where facts intertwined with delusions emanating from within the terrifying crypt chambers.

"Here, in the laboratories, we perform great work for humanity," the Chef explained. "We receive requests from prestigious academies and from competing scientists obsessed with winning the Nobel Prize and all the rewards that come with it. In the suicide-bomber rooms, the minds of men who were captured before they blew themselves up are being analyzed. These men cost us very little, as they are already sentenced to death by those who sent them and by those who receive them.

"In the gambling dormitory where humans are exposed to absolute truths, one comes to understand the finest of human behavior. Here people play Russian roulette every day and learn the value of time and luck. There are thirteen people, and at every party, a lottery is drawn where six survive and the other six leave us. The thirteenth person is exempt from playing for three consecutive rounds of play. The overseeing professor asks us to put one bullet in six guns for each party. Sometimes, we don't put in any bullets, and other times we fill all the guns. Cameras record everything, and gamblers from all over the world join us via Skype. We provide the best possible service to satisfy our customers, for we have what no one else has: power, knowledge, and the desire to serve the truth."

His mouth agape, Anees took in the serene dormitory and its inhabitants, relaxed in their beds. Each of them stared at their cards. They played alone trying to learn the secrets of luck or perhaps just to pass time, time that did not move except with the muzzle of the gun.

Anees became increasingly disturbed, and the Chef's words sounded muffled, disjointed, and stammered. The Chef told him, "All of them were suffering from different diseases. Do you know that the adrenaline that pumps in their bodies helps some of them heal? Before we send them to your table, Doctor, many others express interest in them, including psychologists, terrorism experts, sociologists, biologists, and neuroscientists. Each requests their specific tests and samples, and we provide them with the desired results. As you see, our services are unparalleled and invaluable, and our customers cannot find such quality merchandise anywhere else in the world."

He carried on, "It was only a few years ago that the United States government apologized to Guatemala for the experiments they conducted infecting prisoners and soldiers with syphilis, in collaboration with their regime. Had it not been for these experiments, syphilis would be as common as the flu today, Doctor. Think about the surgical experiments that were performed on slaves that made you the excellent surgeon you are today. If it weren't for these things you call 'evil,' people would still be dying from ruptured appendixes today. Unit 731 in the Imperial Japanese Army conducted experiments on thousands of Koreans and Chinese. Without these experiments, we would still be dying from common bacteria. Do you think that humanity could have rid itself of typhoid, measles, and tuberculosis without paying a price? The price was the experiments conducted on humans, not on rats or mice, that have even found advocates for their rights in the ridiculous West."

He kept on, "War is a necessity. Without it, humanity would have been consumed by the trivialities of peace. Stupid cultural centers only produce more stupidity and boredom and kill the imagination. This is the truth of things, Doctor."

They continued with the tour. "These are the visual arts and theater departments. We bring some clients here on private planes. Preparing for these shows takes time. Right now we're preparing the fourth show with ticket prices reaching up to a quarter of a million dollars for an audience member and a half million for participants."

"Theater and clients? Are you serious? How can you always find the raw materials for all of this? Don't these people have families, friends, and organizations monitoring their disappearances, or at least lawyers? How do you maintain the secrecy of this place?"

"Sometimes our enemies provide us with more than what we get from our security branches. Personally, I don't like dealing with the Mukhabarat—they are completely archaic, stupid and totally corrupt. Their leaders lack imagination and intelligence. They give us headaches, and so we deal with them with extreme caution. They are all amateurs, not power brokers. For this reason, we have people who carefully analyze the files we receive, as was the case with you. On the other hand, we have organizations interested in innovation and development, and these people provide us with abundant resources and diverse genes. Everyone we have here is technically deceased, but instead of turning them into anonymous numbered corpses handed to us by Mukhabarat branches, we give them the honor of contributing to progress and civilization by turning them into something important and useful. And lest you say that I am heartless, we offer them a chance to fulfill their wishes in their final days, wishes that they would have never even dreamt of in a thousand years."

The Chef entered the fortified media room with his personal fingerprint and a secret code. The space was expansive, furnished with rugs and filled with candles and flowers. A Buddha statue was placed at the center. The presence of Buddha in this living slaughterhouse seemed surreal and absurd. They sat in the editing room, and he opened a cabinet with hundreds of archived DVDs and videotapes.

"This is my private room," said the Chef, "As you can see, I create the scenarios here. God prolongs life while I draw glorious endings. I'm sure you are wondering about Buddha. He guided me here and brought me to this position of clarity, raising me to the highest of Atma levels where I discovered the ultimate meaning of creation."

He played a video that had been shot in the same theater that Anees had seen earlier. As scenes appeared on the screen, the rush from the coke faded away and was replaced by a severely dry throat. The screen was filled with images of naked, disfigured, hanging, gagged bodies that twisted under the gaze of customers from all over the world united by their desire to quench the mysterious black holes inside of them.

These scenes took place in the same abyss that he had fallen into. He felt nauseated and he stood up signaling to the Chef that he had had enough, disrupting the obvious pleasure he derived from the viewing.

As they returned to the dinner table, Anees found new guests waiting for him. The Chef welcomed them and introduced Anees to one of them, saying, "This is the doctor, the owner of the house, and this is Mr. Karamani, who is interested in buying your house."

Mr. Karamani spoke broken Arabic with a Persian accent. Praising the house that he seemed to know very well, he got right to the point. "How many people know about the existence of the secret chamber in the house?"

Looking at the Chef inquiringly, Anees asked, "Did the gentleman visit the house?"

"Of course, my dear. Mr. Karamani is currently one of the biggest investors in the country, and he and his company will play a major role in rebuilding the country after the crisis is over."

"The crisis! What a nice word to describe the current state of the country." The sarcasm that slipped out of Anees's mouth put the men gathered around the luxurious table in a state of alert. Anees had to act quickly before he ruined his meager chance of survival. "Professor, I mean, Mr. Karamani, yes, a few people do know about the secret chamber and what it contains."

"We want their details—names, addresses, and everything they know about the house. Also the names of anyone you've contacted or consulted about the chamber."

Karamani's companion had a rocky face covered with a crust of hatred and contempt, and his eyes pierced Anees violently, as if he was on the verge of pouncing on him and tearing him apart with his teeth.

As he tried to remember the names of the people Samia brought to the house, the Chef handed him a large notebook and a pen. "Write down everything you know and don't leave out anything, no matter how insignificant it may seem. I will now take our guest on a tour of the center."

He then took out the vial from his pocket and put it next to the notebook while looking at him with pity and sympathy. As he left with the group, he said, "You may need a drop for your eyes. Remember, don't neglect any details. It's not easy to get the attention of Mr. Karamani."

Anees poured out a light line onto a knife and brought it close to his nose. He took a sniff and was energized; now he could recall every person who had entered Huddud's House and all of its great heritage and secret vaults. He wrote ten pages, although he deliberately made no mention of the blueprints of the house or his uncle's memoirs. The only thing on his mind was the vision of escaping from this endless, horrific hell.

35
Al-Hallaj

*Note from the author: Content Warning—This chapter describes a
meeting between Fidel and Layl and contains dialogue written in a
language derived from the Islamic Sufi lexicon. It contains scenes
that may be uncomfortable or disturbing to some. Not reading the
chapter does not take away from the plot of the story. However,
reading it will deepen the reader's understanding of the novel.*

*Al-Hallaj, also known as Mansur al-Hallaj, was a Persian Sufi
mystic and poet who lived from 858 to 922 CE. He is considered
one of the most controversial figures in Islamic mysticism due to his
unconventional teachings and practices, which often
challenged traditional Islamic orthodoxy.*

Fidel arranged their photos together and chose to play Giuseppe Tratini's
"Devil's Trill" as soft background music. He created a film inspired by
their world, one that reflected his unique mood and overflowed with
eccentricity. Their photos were a series of cascading flow, and his words
began to appear on the screen.

He seated her like a queen, after loosening her hair so that it fell on
her shoulders. He covered her naked body with a sheer white, silk scarf.
He turned off the lights and turned on the projector. The words emerged
accompanied by his recorded over and slowly began to appear before her:

"Layl. Seductive you are, like water gushing onto the sands of thirst.
Seductive you are in the salty fragrances of memories stored in your senses,

in your taste and smell. Astonishing you are in your persistence on creating life amidst the ampleness of death, on rising up from the depths of pits."

"Layl. All descriptions would seem inadequate in depicting you. If only you knew how I see you and with what eyes I perceive you."

"A single letter of the alphabet from you is enough to fill my heart with joy and turn the rest of the world into an ashtray for the remains of your tobacco."

"In the stillness of this morning that carries your fragrance, I hear the rhythm of your mood swaying to the winds blowing from your inner depths. I taste the olives and figs in your breasts, my tongue overflows with the syrup of your body."

"How do I explain your presence in my life? A storm. More than a storm. An explosion. A delirium?"

His hands caressed her hair, explored the softness of her shoulders, the vastness of her back.

She disintegrated into fragments in a dark space that lit up and blackened with every note of the Devil's Trill. She radiated and dimmed with every touch, was liberated and subjugated with every breath.

She handed him her reins, while he steered the moment to the rhythm of the bow's strokes on the violin. She found no escape but to surrender to his fire, wishing the flames would consume her. She was sentenced to him, to his mood, presence, absence, madness, sorrow, doubts, charisma, joy, and his ability to create life out of anything. He was a man who did not live in the moment but tore through time, extracting its beauty, majesty, music, and the wild frenzy of desire.

Her soul was shaken in anticipation, her body bruised from the previous time she was with him. He fed her crumbs of sweet emotions, quenching her heart's thirst drop by drop.

Suddenly, his kind face transformed into that of a stray wolf, and he pounced on her. He examined his marks from the last time, the blue bruises around her breasts and on her back, marks on her neck, and streaks of fingernails on her body.

He drowned in bitter tears and kneeled, asking forgiveness. "Forgive me. I am begging you to forgive me. Did I hurt you, my love, my soul?"

He continued to break down in tears, until she made the same mistake again and granted him forgiveness. She knew that if she did not forgive him, he would drown in the consuming fires of sadness. But she also knew that if she did forgive him, he would repeat the same cycle. There was no escape from the viciousness of it all.

As she began to soothe his broken heart, he regained his ferocity. He put one hand around her neck and the other on her head. He harnessed her head by pulling her hair, twisting it again and again in a dizzying serpentine spiral, almost ripping it from her skull.

He then stretched her out and took off his clothes. Taking his time, he finished his cigarette and approached her. No sooner had she thought he had calmed down than he descended upon her again.

She cried out as she felt the stinging sensations. Her blind desire mixed with pain boiling from the springs of her soul. She shed tears and sweat. Her moans became a melody of Maqam Saba.[38]

She kneeled down, her lips found his knees and climbed upward. He was erect, majestic. She rose, like a humble believer yearning to see his face. Her longing to be with him was a rugged terrain, like a Sufi's journey from sin to purification.

On the screen, a phrase appeared, "The path to truth begins only with self-annihilation." Arriving at the truth is to annihilate one's supposed pride, to rid oneself of delusive dignity, to let go of what one knows of illusions, to remove the burden of the mind from the spirit to crawl, pray, repent, and seek forgiveness.

Her body trembled. She wanted to reach a climax, her streams turned into rivers with colliding waves.

He knew that she did not belong to him, but was a soul entrusted to him by her Creator and Beloved. The path to God was through him, his presence was the guide, and it was through him that the doors were opened.

---

38 Maqam Saba is a musical mode or scale used in Middle Eastern music, including Arab, Turkish, and Persian music traditions. It is considered one of the main *maqamat* (plural of *maqam*) in the Arabic musical system. The scale has a unique tonal quality that is often described as melancholic or mournful.

Her heart blazed in thirst, her mind emptied of everything except the desire to reach him. She saw him from below, from under his blessed phallus, yearning for him in her inflamed emptiness. He penetrated her, filled her, rubbed her to satisfaction, and quenched her thirst. Truth be told, there was no truth but through him.

"The butterfly circles around the lamp until dawn," and Layl circled around his brilliant erection, tasting, smelling, seeing, touching, and listening to the pulse of desire, blood, and semen flowing in its veins. She engulfed it in her mouth and extinguished its fire with her saliva. After unveiling the veil and a journey of hardship, he let out a cry and commanded her, "Take it. It's yours."

She whispered, "Your wish is my command."

She had been rewarded for her patience and finally achieved and savored what she had long awaited. She devoured it, tasted and drank from it. From beneath, she looked him in the eyes. He unleashed barbaric groans. His face reflected the despair of a Sufi who had reached the threshold of acceptance and mercy.

She regained her strength, grabbed his center of power, taking control over him. He surrendered to the reverence of her devotion. He roared and moaned. His time had come to crumble in her hands.

He shouted at her, "I am you!"[39]

She echoed, "I am you."

And so, he thundered, thrashed, grinded, crushed, plowed, pounded, stabbed, and ripped in the lurking place of her desire. He then subsided like a wounded animal at its death, collapsed like a dam destroyed by the flood, trembled like a naked creature in the snow, curled up like a fetus, and moaned like a child.

She came closer to him, embraced him to her chest, stroked his hair, and consoled him in his loneliness. He was transformed from helper to the one seeking help.

---

39   This phrase is for Al-Hallaj "أَنا أَنتَ بِلا شَكٍّ فَسُبحانُكَ سُبحاني" translated as "I am you without a doubt, so glory to you, glory to me." It represents a form of spiritual expression in Arabic, often used to convey the idea of the interconnectedness of all things and the oneness of the universe.

On the screen appeared words that filled her heart with pure affection: "I seek your forgiveness. Forgive me. Of all those I have known from pre-eternity to eternity, you will always be the one who possesses this soul of mine, awakening in me the spirit of sin."

The roles became reversed, and she lived with the exhilaration of the power that he typically possessed, and he felt the splendor of the weakness that resided in her.

In the battle between humans and the divine, humans always lose. But what astonishes the Almighty is the courage possessed by a weak and fragile human being who can vanish with a single blow.

In this abysmal universe, the most pleasurable feat of the Creator is to witness this insignificant creature, called man, continue to endure, and He is amazed with how this lowly person can possess an imagination that surpasses His own imagination, continuing to resist so that hope remains alive.

She listened to his deliriums as he shriveled in his lifelessness, curled up in the womb of his solitude, covered with a layer of light. She did not ward off the desire to embrace him. She did not feel any trace of anger towards him, and forgave him again. His head on her wrist, he delved into deep sleep.

She left him in his solitude and went home to a world that rejected her, barely noticing her presence. In the bathtub, she inspected the marks on her body and felt the scratches on her neck, chest, and thighs. She curled up in the warm water and cried until she had emptied the overflow from within. She cursed him hatefully, swore that she would not return to him, wished for his death and disappearance, that she could kill him a thousand times and liberate herself from him.

For several days she did not hear from him, then came the familiar message: "Where are you? Come. I am waiting for you."

36

Karamani

Nothing brings you closer to collapsing during confinement like holding onto a false hope of getting out.

A month passed without the phone ringing, nor did any message come from the Chef. The routine devoured his days. For Anees, time was measured in the stream of anesthetized bodies that he left with empty chests and bellies in this human slaughterhouse. The silence and stoic looks of the guards remained unchanged. In addition to requesting food, whiskey, and tobacco, he asked for the precious powder. It arrived every few days and became one more thing that held him prisoner.

While he was living a moment of exultation, swimming in a sea of Native American music, listening to their chants and the celebratory beats of their ceremonial drums, the persistent ringing of the telephone awakened him. He was barely able to reach it in time.

"I have been granted permission to get you out of here," said the Chef. "Get yourself ready. Mr. Karamani will come for your signature and fingerprints so that we can proceed with the sale of the house."

The news sent his mind soaring to the seventh heaven. An intense euphoria spread throughout his body and surged through his veins, giving him an erection. Under the showerhead's stream, for the first time since he had been detained, he milked the pleasure, wrenching the desire for Samia's dark hued skin from his memory.

The papers were spread on a table in front of him in the presence of Mr. Karamani and his companion, whose face looked familiar despite

Anees's foggy vision. As he heard the man welcome him, the name of the speaker flashed in the doctor's head like a sharp blade. It was the voice of the lawyer Rajeh Al-Agha, who had transformed his life into what it had become.

He felt a swarm of locusts sweep over his body. His face began to age and become furrowed. He felt like the remains of a creature, a skeleton, a living dish on one of the Chef's tables being devoured by a pack of hyenas. His throat dried up, his mouth cracked, and his words shriveled.

Anees stared at the lawyer as if looking fate itself in the eye. The lawyer's face was devoid of color, his eyes glazed, and he tried to avoid Anees's gaze, as if to say, "Didn't I tell you?"

The Chef intervened by pouring a glass of water and asked the three men—Karamani, his companion with the predatory-looking face, and Rajeh Al-Agha—to sit. Holding a camera on the edge of the table, the Chef prompted them to get started. Rajeh began by reading the agreement: "The subject is the sale of property, on today's date of Monday, February 12, 2012. We are in the presence of both Mr. Anees Jalal Al-Aghawani, referred to hereafter as the first party, and Mr. Ali Hassan Karamani, referred to hereafter as the second party."

Anees felt that something was off. "Excuse me," he broke in. "About the date—you mean the year 2014."

"Doctor," the Chef interjected, "please do not interrupt. Save your questions for later."

Right then, Anees understood that backdating the document this way was an attempt to suggest that he had no longer existed since that date. The lawyer reread the document in front of the camera and began anew. When he finished reading it, he brought the papers to Anees, who signed them, pressed his left thumb print against an ink pad, and left his mark on every page, putting an end to a deal that had cost him more than he could ever be compensated for. As he completed the remaining procedures, they continued to film him. He was then presented with a check in the amount of 300 million Syrian pounds. They sealed the deal with a handshake and forced smiles, and the filming stopped. The lawyer gathered up the papers and returned the check to Al-Karamani, who tore it up, pulled out a large bag from under the table, and handed it to the Chef. He then took his copy of the contract and left the table, followed by the lawyer. The Chef pulled the lawyer to the side and called the guard to take care of him. As he waited at the door, the lawyer took a last glance at Anees, his eyes filled with pity. A guard then handed him a blindfold to cover his eyes and dragged him away.

The Chef approached Anees with a bottle of wine and said, "Listen, this was very difficult for me, and I usually don't get involved in all this nonsense. But this was the best I could do for you. You will leave this place, but unfortunately, you won't be free. Ever since you told me earlier that your two wishes were either to see your son or Samia, I have been working hard at trying to get the best offer for you within a reality that you know nothing about. On the outside, you are wanted everywhere. Your wife and son contacted every possible organization and intermediary appealing for help, and they put your name on all the search lists. But your name troubles our leadership, and as you can imagine it would be very risky for them if you were released. I presented them with all kinds of guarantees, showing them all the videos that documented your involvement and management in the organ sale operations and tried to assure them that it would be impossible for you to utter a single word. I told them that you would be ready to repeat any story they would suggest with regard to your absence—that you were kidnapped by terrorist gangs and later released, and that you would be willing to participate in media interviews with international organizations and the global press. But we were ordered to not let you out of here alive or take any risks with you. The truth that you have come to know about his place is a guarantee of your death, Doctor. All of my attempts to let you out were met with an absolute rejection.

"However," he added in a reasonable tone, "I've managed to get an offer that you may find appealing. Samia was kidnapped and is being held captive by a terrorist organization in Ghouta, along with her group. We will hand you over to this group in exchange for her release. You'll be saving her life, but you won't have any hope of getting out yourself."

"Perhaps if they were with the revolution, there may be hope for me?" said Anees.

"I think you've become disconnected from reality, Doctor. Two years ago, Samia and those who worked with her were the most important sources for documenting the troubling truths of both the regime and the rebels. She was summoned by armed groups for what she was told were a few questions, but instead her headquarters was raided, and she was taken to another faction, which in turn sold her to yet another faction, until she ended up with the so-called ISIS."

"ISIS?" shouted Anees.

"Yes, Doctor. In this wonderful country, you will witness comedy, tragedy, surrealism, and realism all at once. It's become a place where imagination is embodied and reality imagined."

Anees bowed his head in silence. He had no desire or curiosity to know fragmented and incomplete pieces of information. Trying to appear kind, the Chef whispered in Anees's ear like a father to his son, "Today, you will have a television in your room, and you will be able to see what is happening with your own eyes. Your days here are numbered. Samia will be released, and you will be handed over to ISIS."

"Will I be able to see her?"

"I'm sorry, Doctor, but if you see her, she won't come out alive. Anyone who has access to you after you've been our guest here can no longer live. The leadership has no tolerance for gambling or trusting in people's promises. Samia will be released in exchange for you, but she will never know that you did this for her. It will be a silent sacrifice on your part, that is of course if you care about her to that extent."

"And what will ISIS do to me?"

"They will demand the release of their leaders detained in Guantánamo or Jordan, or maybe in places where the British government has influence. The British government will be blackmailed with you despite the fact that you are not considered a full English citizen. But ISIS will take advantage of the noise that your disappearance has caused and will put pressure on the official bodies in England who have adopted your case."

"And how will you guarantee that I won't tell ISIS about what happened here?"

"Doctor, you'll discover on your own that they will not listen to anything that you have to say and that you will simply be changing the language, not the reality of the place. I will miss you very much. I wish we could have stayed together. You are the only man I was able to speak with freely, and I will make sure that your last days in my company will be comfortable."

This chapter of Anees's life was coming to an end, with only a few pages left to write. The guard accompanied him back to his room, and a final question crossed his mind. He turned to the Chef, who remained seated and sipped from his glass. Hesitantly, the question came out.

"What about the lawyer? He knows everything. Do you trust him more than me?"

The Chef gave him the same cold look he always gave when he heard something he did not like. "Good night, Doctor," he whispered.

In his room, with a television finally there, he learned that 2014 was coming to an end. Three years had passed. *They will have a video that supposedly proves that I sold the house from the beginning, received a huge amount, and disappeared.* Obsessed, he followed world news, switching from one station to another and he came to better understand the Chef's reference to ISIS—siege, factions, kidnapping, forced disappearance, displacement, and destruction. It was as if all the demons of the world were unleashed on this hellish land called Syria.

Ten days of obsessively following the news were enough to bring him up to date and compensate for the years of abduction. And with the deal that the Chef had proposed, he had an excuse to refuse performing any new surgeries. Meanwhile, he continued to request and receive his daily needs, and was indifferent about anything else.

After a long period of silence, the phone rang. Gently, the Chef asked Anees to perform one last operation. Anees thought it would be futile to reject or defy him at this point, so he agreed, for whoever drinks a sea of blood will not choke on one more cup.

So the Wagnerian music echoed in the operating room and a team awaited him, ready to commit the crime. The body was shrouded, not connected to monitors, and the face was covered. It was a limp corpse, still warm.

He worked faster than usual. As he removed all the body parts on the request list, he reached the final item, which was for the corneas. He went closer to the covered face and lifted the sheet. His fingers froze with the scalpel in his hands. Despite all that he had been through, the Chef was still capable of surprising him.

Here was the answer to the naive question he had asked earlier, after signing the contract. The lawyer's face was gaping, a bluish red mark on his neck indicating that he had been strangled to death.

Anees needed God very badly. He needed His presence and at the same time he was afraid of it. How would he be judged? How could Anees stand before Him? Would he be able to ask him why he had committed this terrible revenge? He had been living a secure existence, with an abundance of peace. What was he doing here? What had he done to deserve being subjected to this bitter test? Could this crazy butcher have been right after all?

37
Adel

"Good morning, Doctor."

"Good morning. I am ready for the first patient."

She hung the stethoscope around her neck, examined the child clinically, and looked at his lab results. "All he needs is some potassium," she said.

The child was dehydrated after a bout of diarrhea. Layl asked for a syringe and withdrew liquid from a vial she was holding. The nurse muttered, "Doctor, that is potassium."

"I know it's potassium," answered Layl, annoyed.

She continued to fill the syringe and prepared it for an injection. Suddenly, the nurse's voice interrupted a vision she was having of Fidel standing in front of her, laughing wildly and rambling, "I am Alexander the Great, and you are the land I shall conquer."

She poked the baby's leg with the needle and injected the liquid into the vein. The nurse screamed and pounced on Layl's hand, crying, "It's potassium, Doctor. Potassium!"

Layl quickly realized what had happened. A few millimeters of liquid had entered the vein. She pulled out the needle as if she had been stung, picked up the child, and rushed to the intensive care room. She called for Dr. Tariq and Dr. Nazem.

"What's going on?" asked Dr. Nazem.

"I injected potassium into his vein."

"What are you saying?" Shocked, the doctor took the baby from her.

The nurse followed them, prepared the intensive care room, and began the resuscitation process. The baby was saved, the matter was hushed up, and Layl was given an indefinite leave.

The baby's parents had no idea that had it not been for the nurse, their son would have been dead—for even a first-year medical student knows that potassium should not be given intravenously. Layl needed to snap out of it and get a hold of herself.

"We enjoy beginnings and give them our all. In the beginning, we give relationships all we have, but we do not know how to end them. We get caught in a *barzakh*, unable to retreat and without the strength and motivation to continue. We run away, lie, change, read silly self-help books, seek salvation through horoscopes, or search for someone with whom we can share our grief, all to no avail. We then turn the matter over to the One above, rely on false hopes, and spiral into a void that leaves its marks on our bodies." Layl was talking to herself and to Dr. Nazim all at once, asking questions without arriving at satisfactory answers. "Ever since he told me that he was going back to Damascus, I don't know whether I am sad or if I've gone crazy."

Fidel had to return. His long journey had called him back to the place everyone was trying to escape. But before he went, he had to close this painful chapter, to bring peace to this woman whom he could never satisfy.

He came to a conclusion about love that helped him—insofar as it was possible for Fidel to speak of love. *Love is to let go, not to possess; to release your beloved of your captivity, cages, and selfishness. She did this, but I did not.*

Amid the fever of anxiety, of thinking and questioning, the last person he expected to knock on his door was Adel. A thousand thoughts passed through his head as he opened the door and stared at a face he had only known through photos, a disheveled face filled with anger, hatred, and pain.

"I am sorry to bother you. I am Adel, Layl's husband, and I would like to have a few words with you."

"Sure, come in," he said, feeling a mix of surprise and fear. He stepped aside and made way for him to enter, but Adel stayed nailed to his spot.

"My matter is simple," he said. "I am here to do what no husband in the world would do. I have come to the house of my wife's lover, to beg him to leave her in peace. I am asking you, man to man, that you leave us in peace. I am not here because I love my wife. I am here for the sake of her children. If you have any decency left in you, stay away. No civilized man with a shred of ethics would have a relationship with a married woman, no matter the reason. Only the lowly do that. I am begging you, Mr. Fidel, spare us your evil and leave us in peace."

He let it all out in one breath, and without waiting for an answer, he turned away and left.

A few minutes later, Fidel had made up his mind about two things. The first was that he would never tell her about Adel's visit, and the second was that it was time to set this noble woman free to live her life, for she had done nothing wrong except for loving the wrong man at the wrong time.

"I am going to report about some real stories and come back. It will be my first documentary. I'm tired of making ads, and I feel guilty because I contributed, in one way or another, to this death. Perhaps this film will liberate me. I will have the honor of confessing my mistake and trying to fix it."

She was broken, in pain, scattered, barely able to form a single sentence. "Promise me you will come back," she wrote.

Reluctantly, he made a promise, but his trip to Syria was like jumping from the twentieth floor and hoping that there would be a net to catch him.

"Can they detain you?"

"No, they sent me an invitation—they think they will still benefit from my services."

"Promise me, swear on my life, that you won't go more than three days without sending me a message."

"I promise, Layl," he snapped, knowing he was lying.

"One more thing. I want to take you to the airport. Please don't refuse."

"OK. If that's what you want."

"When are you leaving?"

"Tomorrow morning at seven."

"I'll sleep at your place tonight and I drive you tomorrow."

"You can come to the house anytime. Don't lose the keys."

Trying to lighten the mood, he brought up her recent disaster at the hospital, "So you wanted to give the child potassium, Doctor?"

"It's all because of you," she replied with childlike innocence.

The conversation ended with the echo of his laughter, which warmed her heart. He hung up, swallowed the forced laugh, and headed into the airport to catch his flight to Beirut, and then to Damascus. This time he was not visiting his country to stand amid the ruins of memory. Instead, he would document the suffering of the earth's womb after four years of labor pains. Perhaps he would even witness a newborn come into this world.

38

Anees

A few hours before Anees was transferred from the cultural center, the Chef came to see him. He had done nothing to prepare himself to leave except for nourishing the false hope that a change in location might provide him with a better chance to escape or be released. Inside the vortex where a storm of silent and savage killing contaminated and cursed anyone who entered it, Anees was no longer able to stop; the black hole in his soul was only satisfied by more victims.

The Chef entered with a cold expression on his face. He had gotten things ready for Anees's departure. Casting a look around the place, he said, "As you know, I have no emotions. It's a detestable quality that messes up my day and puts me in a bad mood."

Sarcastically and indifferently, the Doctor responded, "You may not have emotions, but you certainly have moods."

The Chef smiled. "I will miss you, Doctor. In fact, the eighteen months that I've spent here with you have made my work more enjoyable. You will be leaving a void behind when you leave."

"Don't worry, you'll find a way. I'm sure you can find someone else to fill the void. You keep yourself busy here. You don't seem to be married or capable of being married, nor does it look like you have friends or family. Loneliness consumes you, and you don't trust anyone. But despite all that you have, you're waiting for your turn at the autopsy table, just like me."

The Chef let out a stiff laugh that was louder than necessary. "I'll take what you said as a compliment. You truly amaze me, Doctor. Your departure will be a loss. Do you know what's truly exciting in this life, Doctor?"

Anees shook his head indifferently as the Chef strutted with measured steps, speaking his words with precision and clarity. "Boredom is a rich source of great ideas, a womb that gives birth to truth in life. In addition, as Leopardi tells us, boredom springs out of a fundamental dissatisfaction with life, and no amount of worldly pleasures or achievements can fully satisfy the human desire for fulfillment and meaning. Look for example at the limitless expanse of space, its enormity and astonishing number of worlds, and you will find it insignificant next to the enormous capacity of the human soul. The human soul can encompass all these infinite numbers of planets and stars."

Anees let out a grumbly sigh. "You know, over the past few years, I had two experiences. One in the Mukhabarat prisons and the other here. There the pain was physical. Here, despite not having been subjected to physical torture, cruelty, or violence, I have been completely broken and have lost everything. Here, my spirit and my soul were destroyed. What I regret and what is most painful to me is that I was a coward and preferred to stay alive. I was afraid of being tortured. But instead, I feel torn apart from the inside. If I could go back in time, I would have refused your offer and chosen to return and die under torture."

The Chef came over and patted his shoulder. "I understand you Doctor, and I don't blame you. If I were in your place, I would have probably come to the same conclusion. But the difference between us is that I was better than you in making choices. Look at yourself. Nothing brought you here but your own decisions—first, your emotions and second your ego. Had you been a bit more clever, you would be at your home in London by now, planning your luxurious retirement after having made a fortune in your world tour. No one has wronged you, Doctor, and you have not been deceived. According to your file, you are one of the few who have been treated with respect. They were patient with you, and they relied on your intelligence. You couldn't understand because you are emotional and idealistic, but at the end of the day, emotional and idealistic people only produce follies."

For the first time, he felt a sense of parity with this warden. He no longer cared to convince him of anything, but at the same time, he didn't want to miss the opportunity to hear himself declare the truth of what he believed. "I sided with what satisfied my conscience, and I have no regrets. It was a just revolution, and a price had to be paid. I was hesitant at its beginnings, but after my experience here, I've become sure of its necessity."

Cynically, the Chef smirked, his smile laden with anger, and responded, "I knew you would say this."

He regained his composure and continued, "It's all about the angle from which you look at a situation. Let me clarify. Let's assume that it is a just revolution, a revolution for dignity and an attempt by the people to reclaim their rights. At the very least you should understand who you're rebelling against. The regime possesses a stockpile of power. Its violence is rooted in the country. To uproot the regime means to destroy the country. The regime knows that it is not going to rule in the same way as it did before, so it acts decisively and in terminal ways. It will make certain that the country is destroyed before it departs so that for the next one hundred years people wish that it had never departed. The regime will never accept for history to remember that its rule was ended by a revolution. It would be acceptable if it were said that it was destroyed by war or by a world war against it, but to say that it was brought down by protestors, only a fool would believe, and that includes you Doctor."

Now it was Anees's turn to assume a mocking smile and reply, "I knew you would say this."

In response, the Chef reverted to his standard justifications. "You will see what I mean. Today, the whole world has set aside its emotions and higher morals and is acting pragmatically. Just so you know, I personally prefer to be here. I have two Western citizenships and I can choose to live in any country in the world. But it is only here that I am truly myself. This place grants me depth and power. To hell with money, and yes to power and strength. In this place, there is a true reality, worlds away from lessons on the nonsense of development and coexistence, or the petty desires of humans, their slogans about equality, or the joke of democracy."

Listening to the Chef was like swallowing chips of glass. His confidence and rigid logic were hidden behind the fragility of hypocrisy. "Do you know that I am honoring you by listening to your nonsense and justifications solely for the purpose of entertainment and nothing else?" Seeing that he had successfully provoked him, Anees added, "You're a creature that does not even dare to have a name, and you will end up anonymous and worthless, nothing more than a despicable criminal."

The Chef walked towards the projector, took out a DVD from his pocket and inserted it into the machine. He used a remote to turn on the screen while continuing to talk. Samia appeared on the screen. He said, "You have finally expressed your feelings. I know you are trying to upset me before you leave, but you have to make a greater effort, Doctor. I came to tell you something other than this useless nonsense. Samia was released hours ago and is on her way home. She may be able to leave the country in a few days. I didn't have to tell you this, but I thought it would be good to provide a service to a friend who will be executed, either by beheading, burning, or drowning. She is now free because of you, and also because I have honored my promise to you, more than anyone you've ever met in your life."

Anees was glued to the screen, his eyes about to pop out of their sockets. Samia was wearing a hijab, her face pale as if it had not seen the sun in a long time. Her eyes shone despite her broken gait. She was alive, present, and able to make him tremble again.

Before leaving the room, the Chef turned back at him and said, "Doctor Anees, now you can die without feeling absolute injustice. At least your death will have not be futile. But like all the weak, you are ungrateful."

He did not close the door behind him. He left it open, and the guard walked in and asked Anees if he wanted to take anything with him. Anees asked the guard if he would wait for him outside for five minutes. He reluctantly agreed. Anees picked up the remote, pressed rewind, and then hit pause so the screen froze with a picture of her face. He contemplated it deeply, retrieving its physiognomy after having almost forgotten its features. Before the five minutes were up, he was ready to leave.

39
Layl

He tossed the passports at her feet. She looked into his eyes and it was clear that he had regained his confidence. The state of despair that had overtaken him for some time was no longer evident, and he appeared strong and composed.

"We've got two weeks before we travel."

"We're traveling?"

"Basically, I contacted the university I graduated from and secured contract work at its university hospital. I also submitted refugee papers for the family to the embassy. They took our passports and today returned them with visas. I think the time has come for us to leave this place, for the sake of our kids above all else. And this will also be our chance to either restore our relationship or end it properly. The important thing is that I can't stay like this anymore. The time has come, Layl, and it's in your hands now to start fresh in a new place and in a healthy way. You also need to leave this place. You need to take a break from work for a while, clear your mind and reconnect with the children. I have hope that we can get past all this craziness and maybe get closer to one another again. I didn't want to say anything before I was sure, but I'm asking you for a real chance. I don't want to force you to do anything."

What she could not forget is that she had gone to Fidel's apartment early that morning after tiring of waiting. With the set of keys he had left her, she entered his apartment and found it emptied of all of its contents. All that was left was a small box with five bundles of money and a short note:

> Layl, if I stay, I will either kill you or you will kill me. If I go, there will be hope for you to survive at least. Forgive me if you can, most exalted of all women, for all the pain that I have caused you. I had to escape because I knew that if I saw you this time, I would not be able to ever leave you. I will not call you, and you will not see me again. You can now be rid of me forever.
> *Signed by: Your curse ☺ Fidel/Fadl.*

She did not collapse as she would have expected. She read the letter again and again, and each time she arrived at the smiling face that he had drawn, her lips also tried to smile. She walked around the living room. The paintings had small stickers attached to them that said, "If you like them, take them."

She went to the bedroom and saw the box of earrings. She opened it to find another small note: "Ever since the day you got your earring back, the number did not increase. You can throw this box in the trash."

She continued to search the space, confident there was another note hidden somewhere, and examined every corner of the place. She was at the verge of giving up as she entered the bathroom, but there, written on the mirror with one of her lipsticks, was a line she knew from Ibn Arabi.[40] "'Love is a small death. The time has come for you to awaken.'"

She was not awakened, instead she felt like she was careening down a steep meandering road without brakes. She burst into tears, cursing him, damning him. Her pain was genuine, as if in losing him she was losing her own soul. She wailed and wept, feeling solace after an outpouring of tears and screaming.

Trying to fathom her loss, she returned home desperately needing to be held. When she walked through the door, Adel was there to greet her with open arms. She threw herself on his chest while he embraced her with fatherly tenderness and understanding. He asked no questions,

---

40 Ibn Arabi is a great Sufi and philosopher, known in the West as the teacher of the poet and mystic Rumi, who proclaimed that love was his religion.

and simply whispered "It's OK. You will be fine. You will be fine." He was the only human in the world capable of understanding and indicting her at the same time. He was her safety valve and also the trigger on her time bomb, the cause of the disaster in her life and the only one who could grant her salvation. She returned to him in surrender after she was defeated by love. He didn't act as most men would, rather he behaved as every woman wishes a man would—with chivalry and without asking questions, exploitation, or gloating over her grief.

In Fidel's absence, Dubai felt as if it was regressing to its pre-prosperous times, devoid of its splendor. The most difficult losses are the ones that are ungrievable and inconsolable. She could not talk about him or tell their story to anyone.

She would never forget when Adel told her, "I know how you feel, Layl, and I understand."

His empathy seemed more like revenge. It was about ridding himself of guilt. After he had survived death, something had changed, as if his life had fallen into the depths of an abyss, and when he emerged, he was soaked in darkness.

As for Fidel, he had thrown his cloak of farewell at her, leaving her with nothing but denial of exile and banishment. Abandonment is like a slaughter where the abandoned becomes like a bird fluttering and bleeding in the hands of a merciless butcher, caught between life and death.

For Layl, Adel's chest was like the tent for a hopeless refugee with an empty heart and a fragmented mind, grateful for any shred of security. Seeking refuge in Adel, with all the confusion that it embodied, was about accepting disappointment.

The children, it seemed, wanted to see her broken so that the walls of frost between them would also break. She found it inconceivable that those beings she had raised in her womb could be her butchers and her saviors at the same time. But with short bursts of understanding and care, she quickly improved, although she was greatly embarrassed that her children knew what happened. There was no greater embarrassment for a parent than for their kid to help them overcome a breakup with someone other than their father.

Nawwar was the closest to her, and as it happened, his first romantic relationship as a teenager coincided with all that she was going through. The love he felt blooming in his heart made him much more forgiving. He said to her, "Mom, I'm on your side—not just because you're my mother, but also because I know what it means to be in love. I'm on your side because you're suffering just like me."

This being who had consumed years of her life as she worked to meet all his needs had grown up and become someone she could lean on, even someone to protect her from collapsing. As for Mayar, he clung onto his father's pains.

But she had an impossible existential decision to make. She had to decide between emigrating to France with the family and having the possibility of a future, or remaining in Dubai with the ghosts of her memories. Pain was reality for her; Adel had made sure of that. She had never had control of her reality. She had lived life simply by reacting to other people's actions and wants. She had the option to remain silent, or swallow a thousand sleeping pills and sleep for eternity. She let out a scream that no one could hear but her. "Leave me alone! I don't want to travel, nor do I want to become a refugee." But what he heard was, "Give me time."

"Layl, we don't have time. I am going to pick up the children from school, and by the time we're back, I hope you'll have made a decision."

She desperately needed to hear Fidel's voice, to receive any sign from him. She wished she could ask him for help. She yearned for Samia, who had disappeared into the unknown. She tried to think of anyone who could tell her what to do and rescue her from the cleaver of having to make a choice. She felt completely alone, confused like a gray pawn in the middle squares of a chessboard.

Layl called her remaining contacts in Damascus. Talking with her mother, she only felt added pain as she was subjected to a torrent of warning and condemnation alerting her of the need to care for her husband and children. She tried to glean whether her father was still angry, but her mother insisted on changing the subject. It was a collective punishment from the family after the news had spread. Layl knew that, if not for the revolution and the people's preoccupation with the reports of shelling and daily calamities, she would be the talk of the town. As usual, after a few seconds of a conversation with her mother, she regretted having called her and looked for ways to end it.

Her desire to speak with someone in Damascus was rooted in her longing to be with Fidel in the place where he was. So she called Issa Darwish.

Like every broken Syrian within a cursed Syria, Issa sounded crushed—sarcastic and bitter. The children's noisy arrival and their excitement over their upcoming trip interrupted her call with Issa, who had described to her the wounds of the place and how its soil was being turned upside down, exposing the most beautiful and the ugliest of its features. He described how there were explosions of old resentments, pus oozing from hidden abscesses, wounds reopened, pains inflamed, wolves of instincts unleashed, and a brutality that had become a way of life. Continuing in his usual poetic style, he said, "In its final struggle, Damascus is taming death while being tamed by death, and no one knows who will emerge victorious."

He went on telling stories about people who had turned from extremism to its opposite, from faith to atheism, from seeking God to killing God. He told stories about rampant poverty, pervasive injustice, of strangers who roamed Damascus with weapons.

"Layl, Damascus never knew such pain in its history. Just yesterday they found a dead man in the street who had been there for three days. Can you imagine it? They finally noticed him because of the stench. There are stories about displaced people that would curl your hair—kidnapping, ransom demands, you name it. Did you know that a kilogram of squash costs a thousand liras? For someone whose entire salary is 10,000 liras, can you imagine that?"

"And what about you?" she said. "How are you?" It was the sort of question people ask when they really want to say, "I'm not OK."

"I am still holding on and resisting the urge to leave. Half of the men in this country have fled. It's crazy—there is a sharp decline of males in Damascus. For every ten women in the streets, you'll find one man. They've all either disappeared, fled, been imprisoned, died, or are serving in the army."

After telling countless familiar stories, he suddenly said something that made her tremble: "Layl, Samia has been liberated from the hands of her kidnappers."

With her heart racing and voice trembling, she asked for Samia's number. He gave it to her, and before ending the call he said, "It's a wonder how a person like Fidel Abdullah can turn into an extremist ISIS filmmaker producing films about murder and slaughter."

Hearing his name threw her off balance, but she was not surprised. She had a feeling that she would hear something about him after the agonizing months of abandonment. She turned pale and took in a breath that she didn't know how to exhale. It was impossible to bury her flaming love for him, the fire she felt in his presence and absence. To feel the ghost of his spirit and to hear his name was to be in the presence of fire, on the verge of collapse, her screams stifled. Her thirst for him was unquenchable.

She hurried to end the call and reminded Issa to send Samia's number and Fidel's videos by email. She hung up, suppressing an anxiety that began to boil inside her again.

She tried to keep things smooth, for the family faced a long list of tasks that needed to be completed within two weeks. They made a schedule of what needed to be done: submitting their resignations, selling the furniture and car, informing the children's school and requesting necessary documents, packing their things, and deciding what to keep and what to give away. The house suddenly became a Syrian home, destined to be abandoned and left behind, its occupants off to join the new Syrian diaspora.

She put on a face and pretended to accept the situation, but behind the facade her face was featureless as it tried to predict the future. She consulted horoscopes, hoped for any sign from the unknown, and dreamed of some miracle that would help her decide what to do. In the final days, it was like being grilled on the flames of time, burning no matter how she turned.

She bid farewell to her very few remaining friends and prepared the luggage. But perhaps subconsciously, she packed her things in separate bags. Two days before their scheduled date of departure, she received an email from Issa with Samia's number with videos that Fidel had produced about ISIS. It took all her strength to watch them.

Each video contained links to documentaries that spoke of the strength of ISIS, its men and its scouts. The videos were of good quality, and captivating in their description of how the organization carried out the executions of rebels, apostates, and infidels. The images unmistakably mirrored Fidel's signature style, but there was nothing to indicate that he was the one who had made them. Spotting Samia's number in the email, she decided that if she didn't call her right away, she never would.

Fearing that Samia would have changed with the passage of time, she hesitated a great deal before calling. She was afraid to hear a new broken voice or face another condemnation that she could no longer bear. Feeling uncertain and uneasy, she dialed the number and began to count the rings, hoping that no one would answer. A weary, skeptical, and cold voice came on the line. "Hello. Who is it?"

"Samia, it's me, Layl."

"Layl! Layl! Oh my God, I can't believe it."

"Yes."

Choked with their tears, their entire worlds thrown into disorder, Samia was the first to speak. Layl breathed a sigh of relief to hear Samia's voice. The conversation that followed was long, painful, tearful, and funny.

The voices of Damascus were like umbilical cords that kept the city's children tied to its womb. Samia's voice was both the umbilical cord and the womb of the city itself.

In an intentionally direct tone and without any prefaces, Samia said, "Layl, don't believe anything you've heard about Fidel. Don't believe it. Follow your heart. Layl, I am free because a selfless man sacrificed everything for my sake. In war, Layl, the mind is intuition, but the heart is rightness."

As the call began to reach its end, she saw clearly what she needed to do. In the face of flames of doubt, she had made up her mind to answer an irresistible and alluring call.

"I am returning to Damascus."

40
The Camera

If any other country was struck with a quarter of this destruction for a month, it would undoubtedly collapse and crumble into ruins. But here, on this spot of earth, death is defiantly rejected. For every death, a life is born.

Damascus was suffocated with checkpoints, dizzied by the smell of gunpowder, and deafened by the unceasing noise of shelling. Sleeping to the sounds of thundering planes and the ramming of cannons had become a daily reality for people. Falling asleep to the roaring of mortar shells and the ringing of bullets had become so much the norm that they joked about how much harder it would be to sleep once the shelling stopped.

And yet Damascus was the only place where Fidel could escape the pain of being separated from the woman who had become one with his soul, for the only escape from love was war.

The company covered his financial costs, but he lacked a trusted team, and access. After four years of war, Fidel simply sought a way to enter the red zones, record whatever testimonies he could, and quickly turn them into a documentary before fabricated narratives swallowed up the truth. This was his overarching goal, but the important question for him personally was about death, for he believed it was the starting point for all unanswered questions as one searches for meaning in this mysterious and strange experience called life.

Escaping love to go to war set their souls ablaze, but it was a way to make history, an individual's history, instead of waiting and sulking in a place of safety amid consumption and laziness.

He was assigned to work with a group of revolutionary youths. He asked them to search for human testimonies away from politics, ones that spoke of the transformation human beings experienced in times of war. He needed to understand Syrians who were able to carry weapons and kill other fellow Syrians who shared the same homeland—how were they able to justify their actions and live with themselves?

It was not easy to persuade people to speak openly about such matters, or for the warring factions to provide material that did not serve their agendas; and so it was agreed upon that both things could be accomplished simultaneously—to deliver reports to the international press that would serve the conflicting parties, and, behind the scenes, to give those who volunteered to tell their stories the stage to speak about themselves, to confess or to justify their actions and explain what drove them to kill their brothers or sisters.

The volunteers were asked to enter a dark room and speak. At the end of the session and before leaving, they were given the choice to reveal their identities if they wished. Things turned out better than he imagined. Everything had been very carefully coordinated. The team entered the besieged areas through tunnels that were known and guarded by both sides.

"Could it really be this simple?" Fidel asked Abu Miqdad, a young man in his late twenties.

"Yes. You see, there is a mutual understanding—if the one party were to destroy a rebel tunnel, the rebels would in turn destroy one of theirs. Everything is separated and connected at the same time. There are rules of engagement that everyone understands and abides by."

The leaders learned of Fidel's presence and arranged to meet with him the next day. To alleviate the sense of panic that overtook them, both Fidel and his cameraman went out to visit residents of the city. People talked about how they were able to identify different types of bombs, planes, and shells by the different sounds they made, which helped determine whether they should take refuge or could simply go about their daily business. They complained that random barrels were the most frustrating as they were arbitrarily thrown over residential areas, aiming to mess with people's minds and destroy buildings whose upper floors were now inhabited by casual snipers and watchmen instead of residents.

In spite of it all, life continued; marriages were celebrated, and children were born. Many of the children were exactly four years old, born to the revolution.

A physician who worked in a field hospital told them, "Although we lack most everything, we continue to perform major operations. The worst times are when planes shell crowds of people at once, in markets or in schools where the wounded arrive in masses."

Fidel did not know where to begin. How could he tell the story of this place? Death was a daily ritual, but so was life, a colossal struggle for survival. If he were asked for a suggestion to help the besieged endure, the answer would undoubtedly be that they relied on God and believed in Him. Although the definition of faith in this place greatly varied from person to person, it was the common ground on which all people agreed—not because they were afraid of dying, for those who died were able to find rest—but because death was a consolation for the future of the living; they believed that life was undoubtedly a divine test, and that by handing their troubles over to Him, they would be bestowed with patience.

Fidel knew these towns and villages inside out. He had grown up in one of them, although it was now impossible to reach his village. They were small towns with intimate neighborhoods where people knew one another. And because he was a son of the region, it was easy for him to gain people's confidence and to understand the complexities of the place in a way that an outsider would not.

Abu Miqdad warned him: "Do not discuss religion; simply swallow your thoughts. For religion is like a pill. It's useless to chew it."

With death as a daily reality in these besieged cities, all worries on the outside seemed absurd and banal. The experiences in this place were fit for philosophers, poets, and artists, to contemplate the essence of life.

Being under the protection of army commanders greatly facilitated Fidel's mission and allowed him ample freedom of movement. Within fifteen days, they were satisfied with the reports he sent to news agencies.

He contemplated Mount Qasioun and how distant, angry, and hostile it seemed. From its grounds only a few kilometers away, they fired heavy artillery shells that rained down on rebellious towns and turned them into rubble. But it was also beneath this rubble that an entire system of mines, tunnels and shelters was emerging. It operated daily and provided job opportunities for hundreds of skilled diggers.

Fidel established his headquarters under one of the homes, and it was from below that he began a journey that would soon lead him to the heart of the kingdom of horror. He positioned the camera in front of him and dimmed the background light. The volunteer's face was rough, like a rock, bearded and deeply furrowed, with every detail clearly lit. Fidel stepped back and had him stare into the camera. He whispered to the fighter who had a face that looked like it was made of TNT, "Whenever you're ready, you can talk about anything you want."

He concealed himself under the dark cloth to block out any light from the camera's screen. He put on his headphones and focused on the monitor. Silence prevailed. For the first minute, there was nothing but a man staring into emptiness. Then the words began to emerge, quavering, soaked with memory. He insisted on speaking classical Arabic in light of his profession as a teacher of Arabic.

"Imagine, sir, that your twenty-month-old daughter's feet are burned until they are charred. The place smells like grilled meat although you have not eaten in two days. Your reflexes make you salivate but since your hands are tied behind your back, you cannot even wipe the drool running down the right corner of your mouth. A thick hand forces you to turn your face to the side. You close your eyes so that you don't have to see two men taking turns raping your wife, one of whom you happen to know well from the neighboring village. He was once a nice man, poor like yourself. Many times you sat with him and complained about life. The thick hand slaps your face and forces your eyelids open. You see a tattoo of the immortal Commander in Chief carved on his bicep. You try to distract yourself in any way possible, thinking of a way to die but to no avail because the grunts of your bleeding thirteen-year-old son demand your attention as he sits in the corner having been stabbed seven times but not yet been fully silenced. His hand moves slightly and points at you with his inquisitive and horror-stricken eyes, pleading for you to do something or to simply be able to touch you. You blame yourself for not having done enough for him and regret not having touched him enough throughout the years, but instead demanding respect and maintaining delusions of manliness and fatherhood. You hope that soon you will awaken to discover that this is all a passing nightmare. You dream of fleeing with them into the woods, back to the farthest point in time, before man stood on two legs, to the stone ages, to the sea, and to drown them if possible. Before you can begin to think about screaming, crying, or complaining to the sky, a mutilated mumble comes out of your baby's mouth and addresses you: *baba*. You turn your face, your son's hand has fallen, your wife jolts in shock, no one says anything. The noise subsides. They leave you alive and they leave. Imagine what would be 'on your mind' if you had to post a thought on Facebook at that moment. Would it really matter to you how the world would classify you—terrorist, sectarian, Islamist, shitty? A world that has abandoned you. Your only remaining family member is your rifle, the only thing you can rely on. Your only wish becomes to attain justice, so that you can die with less pain, justice that no one can grant you but your rifle."

He fell silent; it was the silence of a man staring at the phantom of nothingness in the camera, a silence that spoke to an entire universe.

Fidel could not pull his head out from under the black cloth. He did not have the courage to look into the man's eyes. It was as if language had dissolved, giving way to herds of unsheathed feelings that tore into his chest and sank their venomous fangs into him, dripping with poison and malevolence.

He saw the absurdity of his work—of documenting a truth for an indifferent, demonic world. But he had to bury his feelings, calm down, and keep listening.

"I've never carried a weapon in my life." This is how the next young man began. He was pale-faced, but his paleness was not reflected in his colorful voice and confident way of speaking, moving gracefully between colloquial and formal Arabic.

"As a matter of fact, Syrians were the least knowledgeable about using weapons. They didn't even know how to hold a pistol. As for me, no matter what happens, I will never carry a weapon again. I will definitely help the fighters, I will serve in their field hospitals, but carry a weapon? Never again. Why? Well, the reason is simple. About fifteen years ago, I carried a hunting rifle with homemade ammunition, and my brother boasted to his friends about its accuracy. During one of our hunting trips, I saw a bird perched on the grapevine trellis. I took the rifle from my brother's hand and pointed it at the bird. I pulled the trigger and it instantly fell to the ground. My brother's friends applauded and never again did he mock my hunting and shooting skills. I left my rifle with them and ran towards my prize, glowing with pride. This was the first time I had hunted a bird. Under the canopy of grapes in our vineyard, the sparrow was dying. In its beak was a little worm, and above the trellis was a nest of three chicks screeching, chirping softly. One of them was looking down directly at me."

The next volunteer asked to be masked before he began to speak. "Look, we are all poor and we are dying on both sides. Whoever tells you that this war is for the sake of the poor is lying to you. This war is waged against the poor. I miss my comrades in the Syrian army, and I swear I feel for them just as much as I feel for us.

"Syrians are very brave, even those who are with the regime. Sure, I am upset with them, but they are still brave. If it weren't for their courage, Bashar Al-Assad would not have lasted a minute. They also don't have a choice. I am going to tell you something about them, something I witnessed with my own two eyes before I left the battalion in the north and returned to my village.

"Our men once surrounded a Syrian army battalion from all three sides and asked that they surrender. Most of the leaders in the battalion managed to escape, but the rest of the soldiers had no choice but to surrender. We gave them four hours to turn themselves in and assured them that if they were to come out without their weapons and wave white handkerchiefs, they would be safe. After a quarter of an hour, *dabke* songs played over their loudspeakers. They began to mock us. They knew that they had no hope but our mercy as there were over three thousand of us and only about two hundred of them in an exposed location, with no fortification. But they began to sing and dance to *dabke* music. They shouted insults at us, and at Bashar Al-Assad and a leadership that left them to face their fate on their own. They were poor like us, fighters like us, and more foolish than we were. Whenever we called out to them, they responded with bullets and turned 'Al-Hawara' up louder. We could hear their laughter as they danced, and later we found out that they were also drinking arak as they sang. Amongst us were mujahideen who had participated in the jihad in Afghanistan, Chechnya, Bosnia, and Iraq, and they told us that never in their lives had they witnessed anything like what they saw on that day. As the four-hour deadline approached, the Syrian national anthem resounded through their loudspeakers:

'Guardian of the homeland, peace be upon you,
Our proud spirits refuse to be humiliated.
The den of Arabism is a sacred sanctuary,
And the throne of the suns is a preserve that will not be subjugated.'

I swear to you, I shed a tear. I was afraid that someone would see me. I looked at my comrades and they were just as astonished, but the mujahideen, who had come from outside of Syria, did not feel anything. After infiltrating the headquarters and detonating the gates, they surrounded the remaining group that continued to resist until the very last bullet. As we arrived at the battalion, they were all dead. Not one attempted to run away or escape. Listening to music, they resisted until the very last shot. When the mujahideen began to search the corpses, they found that most of the dead were young men under twenty-five. They were from all over Syria, from all the towns and regions, not only minorities as rumor had it. They lived as Syrians, and they died as Syrians. We were not able to celebrate. The cameras came, and I also took photos with a few others, but we couldn't rejoice. They were all children of the same motherland, poor like us, meager like us, and they were oh so very brave."

"I am sorry, sir." He composed himself, wiped his nose and eyes. "Damn those who got us here. OK, that's enough. I have nothing else to say. Fuck this war and those behind it."

He departed in anger. The camera continued to record the space he vacated, and his curses could be heard in the background.

41
Layl

It was not easy for her, but she said it with determination, "I am not traveling. I will stay here." She didn't share any details about her upcoming return to Damascus. The news wasn't painful for Adel, for to him the matter no longer concerned another man wounding his masculinity. However, the decision was painful for Nawwar. As for Mayar, he remained neutral.

Knowing that Layl no longer had any money, Adel felt a newfound sense of self-assurance. He told her, "You can stay for now, and call me whenever you want. We'll wait for you."

She was very grateful for Fidel. It was true that all the memories he had left for her in the apartment were important, even if they ate at her heart, but the most important thing to her was the money he had left her. It spared her the shame of asking, and it empowered her decision. Each of the five 50,000-dirham bundles was equivalent to all the wealth of the world in that moment.

With gloomy faces, they left her, although they had actually left her long before. She cried for them, as was fitting, for the entire day. Two days later, she bid Dubai a final farewell. She headed to Beirut's airport, from which she would travel to Damascus by car. She chose to stay at Semiramis Hotel. She had passed it many times before, but it never occurred to her to go inside. It was in the heart of a city divided by barricades, teeming with mystery, and exhausted by war. After four years, Damascus seemed like it had aged a thousand years on the outside but was pulsating with life on the inside. The ability of its people to adapt was strange yet amazing. Electricity was cut off for more than twelve hours a day, water was barely available, and poverty had swept the city like leprosy, leaving people's faces covered with a thick layer of silence.

She couldn't fall asleep that night until she finally stuffed her ears with cotton balls. The shelling on Ghouta lasted all night. The sound of gunfire was now part of the city's nighttime, and the roar of planes was part of its daytime noise.

Unsure of where to start, she took her time with her breakfast. She was consumed with desire and dread, feeling exposed and vulnerable. She needed to retrain herself to walk the streets of Damascus, to rediscover the place, and to bridge the gap between her memory of the city and its present reality.

As she stepped outside onto the street, she froze. A wave of terror paralyzed her as a mortar shell fell in the city center, causing chaos in the street amid the intense noise of ambulances and army vehicles. Everyone was talking into their phones, reassuring one another. It took an hour for the street to return to its normal pace. Blood was quickly washed away, and the traffic began to move again, as if nothing had happened.

Walking in the city was like drawing a lottery ticket where there was always a chance you will be killed by a falling shell or a stray bullet.

Ashen, she returned quickly to the hotel. One of the employees greeted her with a smile. He brought her a glass of water and said, "You'll soon get used to it." He explained that the shells were coming from armed gangs, and, lowering his voice, he added, "At least that's what they are saying. The more people protest, the more shells fall on them to remind them of the blessing of safety."

She had no interest in talking with a stranger. She knew that even before the revolution, Damascus was swarming with security spies and Mukhabarat agents, and she knew things would be even worse today. It was also more likely the case in a hotel where foreigners and strangers were staying. She thanked him and asked him for the nearest place to buy a SIM card.

"It's not far. They are everywhere in this area," he replied.

She gathered her strength and walked in the direction of Havana Café. It was full of men inside, so she decided not to go in. She continued until she reached the Sham Hotel. She went into its café and sat down in a chair that looked out onto the street. She contemplated the melancholic faces, the caravans of children begging, the misery crawling in the streets. She ordered a cup of coffee, and after regaining her composure, she put the new SIM card in her phone, activated it, and sent messages to Samia and Issa, asking if they could come and see her.

Issa phoned immediately. "I'm coming to pick you up and take you to my home in Dwel'a. Samia will follow us. It will take me a few hours to get to you, depending on the checkpoints. Pack up your things. You shouldn't stay in the hotel."

That evening, she met them like thirsty land meeting the rain.

"We didn't know who they were or what they wanted," said Samia, "We voluntarily chose to go to them, me and two other members of our team. They detained us in an ordinary place for three days without any interrogation. I persisted in my attempts to ask what they wanted from us, who they were, and demanded that they at least allow us to contact our leaders, but all to no avail. On the fourth day, I realized we had been kidnapped when a casual conversation with one of the guards turned into a quarrel and led one of them to slap me. Then they all descended upon me, hitting and kicking.

"They interrogated me the same way they do in the Mukhabarat security branches. They used the same language and methods where they first tried to intimidate me and then tried to entice me with rewards. They wanted all the information about who we were communicating with both inside and outside the country, or at least that's what I had thought. But later we discovered that they had raided our headquarters and obtained all the information that we had. We didn't have anything to hide, but our activities included documenting, managing, and supporting what was taking place in the besieged areas. They simply wanted to hide us, nothing more. I am certain that one of my comrades was killed under torture, and I didn't know what happened to the others until recently. For the last two years, I have been transferred and handed over several times from one group to another. I was then detained in a shelter, uncertain of where or why."

She went on, "I was forgotten, dying slowly. I was on the brink of madness, and contemplated suicide because my captivity seemed pointless and made no sense. I had great anger towards Anees, for after he had sent me a message telling me that he was arrested, I knew that he would crack. Shortly after, we were kidnapped. During the initial investigation, they asked me about him, who he was, what he wanted, how he had entered Syria, what my relationship with him was, and how we got married. I thought he was the reason behind what was happening to me.

"While in solitary confinement, I remembered the film for Riad Al-Turk.[41] I knew that I had to let go of everything on the outside because it was getting the best of me. To think of life outside of confinement was a weak point that caused me great pain. A prisoner first collapses from within, and then diseases begin to destroy the body. The room I was in did not see the sun. I turned it into my own private kingdom and eagerly awaited the meals no matter how bad they were. I kept what I could of leftovers to deal with the fact that time had stopped. I played Riad Al-Turk's game where he would collect leftover lentil grains. I created portraits with them and arranged them at the start of each day. I would then contemplate the finished product for a few minutes before scattering the grains again.

"Despite everything around me telling me to let go of hope and that I was destined to rot to death in the cell, I still found a way to draw my strength and will to survive amidst a decaying world. I drew from people like Riad Al-Turk, who had spent close to twenty years in the regime's prison, seventeen in solitary confinement, and from Sisyphus and Penelope's patience. I couldn't believe it when the guard informed me two weeks ago that I would be released. The news felt like a far-fetched dream. I couldn't believe that I was hearing a human voice again. A week

---

41   Riad al-Turk is a prominent Syrian opposition figure and long-time opponent of the Syrian government. He was born in 1930 in Hama, Syria, and became involved in leftist politics in the 1950s. He was imprisoned for more than seventeen years. In the revolution, Al-Turk was one of the first Syrian political figures to call for peaceful protests against the Syrian government.

later a mysterious man came to me. He stood at the door and said, 'Ms. Samia. Thank God you are safe. I have a message that I need to deliver to you.' I thanked him and asked him what he had to say. He told me that Dr. Anees says hello. That scared me, for as you know Layl, everything here is dubious. I remained silent, fearing that any reaction would lead me into their trap. But I was also afraid that a lack of interest might shut the conversation down. He said, 'Samia, you are free because Anees exchanged his life for your freedom.' And before I could ask him anything more, he disappeared. The magnitude of the loss was greater than anyone could fathom. My personal loss did not matter as it was a result of my own free choice. But most painful is the loss of someone who is not guilty, someone who simply finds themselves standing at the crater of an erupting volcano. After my release, I found that my children were broken. This was an unpreparable and irreplaceable loss. It became my responsibility to at least acknowledge my personal defeat and to rescue my children from complete destruction. I knew that I would stay here, but I needed them to leave."

"I am leaving with her children," Issa said. "The situation is no longer bearable here. If we stay, we are simply awaiting the mercy of a bullet. Layl, I need you to also help me convince Samia to leave, because there is nothing left for us to do here."

"I want to ask you a direct question and I need you to answer me truthfully," Layl replied. "Since you were the ones who incited this revolution and are now leaving, had you known that you would become the bridge over which all criminals would cross over into the country—"

Before she finished her thought, Issa cut her off. "I don't want to interrupt you, but take it easy on us, Layl."

"You have already interrupted me."

"I can use the same logic with you and make the point that you are coming back to judge us after being away for four years! Apart from the revolution, have you even once asked how people are living here? The revolution took place because there was no other way. We did everything in our power and beyond. We worked on behalf of all of us, for you and many other people. Forget about the demonstrations and what things look like from the outside—you should be asking how we will survive the rest of our days, how what's happening in the country is bigger than the country itself, and how if the revolution was just about the regime it would have fallen long ago. For the sake of the blood of the people the system should fall, treaties should be destroyed, and the geography of the place should change. History should be rewritten and what had been silenced should be told and exposed. Blood is being shed for economic and religious struggles and disgusting motives that involve invasions and influence. No one in the world could have ever predicted what would happen, not a fortune teller, analyst, intellectual, or any human being for that matter! Sure, I could stay here and die like a nobody, but do you know what my problem is? Every time I think about death, I think about how much funerals cost, and how I don't want to burden my family and friends. A more reasonable question to ask, Layl, would be what brings you here, not why we want to leave."

"I would never judge you. My problems are much smaller than what you have been through, and my pain is very personal. After everything that has happened, I have made a decision for the first time in my life. For the first time, I am my true self. I was much weaker than people thought I was, but now I have discovered that I am much stronger than I ever thought I was. I am sorry I was not with you from the beginning. I may no longer be able to save anything in the country, but I am sure that I can help one man who is now in the wrong place. I need to save him from himself just as he helped me get myself back. I need you to help me get to Fidel in any way possible."

It was impossible to know what the future held, simply because it did not yet exist. Everything that was going to happen already had, and things were moving backward.

42
Abu Hiddo

He was in his twenties, full of youth and life. Everything in him laughed, except for his gaze; anyone who was caught in it trembled. He possessed the most peculiar eyes in the world. They moved at an astonishing speed and danced in their sockets, watching everything and trusting nothing.

He began by introducing himself. "My name is Muhyiddin. They call me Abu Hiddo." He went on, "In short, bro, I defected from the army because I had no other choice. The entire battalion did, and I followed suit. We went to Homs and protected the protesters. Those were beautiful days. After a while, things began to change. We began to move from one faction to another. I tried to put down my weapon and return to civilian life, but it was no longer possible. What people don't know is that after a human kills another and they feel their life is threatened, nothing returns to normal. I left the country and wandered around Turkey for a few months. But I ended up suffering from depression and insomnia, and discovered that nothing would comfort me other than carrying a weapon again. Something in me had died. It was bigger than me, higher than me. Life's routine was deadly. I had become a fighter. I might have not known who I was fighting against, and I didn't have the faith in God that others did, but what I did know was that I only had one of two choices, either fight or commit suicide.

"Three years passed. I am twenty-five years old but I feel like forty. I listen to people's problems in life, and I find everything pointless. I fought. I watched people's souls depart from their bodies. My friends died in my arms—they took their final breaths in my face. One of them had part of his brain fly out and as I had reached to lift his head, my hand slipped into his hot skull, with his blinking eyes staring at me. I never believed in religion or paradise until the day that Misto was hit by a piece of shrapnel that tore his belly open and caused his intestines to spill out as he tried to put them back in. They were rose-pink, spilled on the ground, mixed with dirt, and had steam rising from them. Ever since that day, I've felt nothing. I am no longer repulsed or disgusted by anything. My soul has died. I am actually dead from the inside.

"Misto died at twenty without ever having been with a woman. Someone on Facebook wrote something that bothered me even more than his death. The animal wrote, 'Misto died while dreaming of the day that Syria would be returned to Syrians.' When I read this, I cursed this person's mother and sister and the mother of the one who created shitty Facebook. I wrote on my page, 'Fuck you and your mother and fuck Mark Zuckerberg's mother. Had it not been for the fucker Mark, you would never have had the space to write about Misto, you son of a bitch. You asshole. Misto died while he was dreaming of tasting the pizza that he had never had before. He used to think that it was the most precious dish in the world. For him, a free Syria was about having a slice of pizza loaded with pepperoni. He died asking me to take care of his mother and paralyzed sister. He asked that I buy them this invention called pizza and fulfill the promise he had made to them. He died without knowing that the people he had entrusted me to help had been buried under the rubble for a week after a barrel bomb crushed their poor home, and that they were trapped for two days in the wreckage without being rescued. I had the misfortune of discovering this by chance under the continuous shelling. Before the dust had cleared, I saw a man, who was a little older, running in the street, screaming, pointing at the rubble in a frenzy. I ran to him. Misto's family home was completely pulverized. A barrel bomb that must have weighed a ton had fallen on it. Five floors were piled on top of each other. I managed to pull out the body of a girl in pieces without blinking an eye. The man who was screaming was able to pull out the body of his son, but it was without a head. He kept talking to him as he held him.

"The layer of lies that I had grown up with and had come to believe were peeled off. Before, I could barely stand to look at a small wound on my finger. Now I can no longer sleep without recalling these images; they are like music played by a devious orchestra that enters my head and plays every night.

"I ran away. I ran away because I felt like I was turning into a monster. Nothing had any meaning or value any longer. I ran away, and I left my unit and weapon behind. I went to Turkey with a forged passport and arrived in Sweden. I applied for asylum, and while at the refugee center, they brought me a doctor who was so damn beautiful. Her beauty was indescribable, to the point where I felt shy even looking at her. It was like looking at God in the face. She had a translator with her who looked like Satan. Anyway, I told her what I had been through in detail. Her face turned pale and she left me with the translator, a sheikh wannabe who asked me flat-out if I was Muslim. I told him to get lost. As for the translator, she began vomiting and I never saw her again.

"They placed me in a psych ward. Everything was neat, organized, and calm. I thought to myself, 'I swear I'm going to go crazy here and die.' I flushed the medicine they gave me down the toilet and made up my mind. I didn't care for Sweden or its charity, and I didn't want to be a refugee. I ran away from them. I ran away from the most wretched label a person can be given—that of refugee—and I returned to Syria.

"I searched for my comrades and was appalled to learn that after I left, they had all become sheikhs. They were broken. We all had aged quickly and felt like we were a thousand years old. Having death as a companion kills the humanity in you. As you look for answers, you find religion waiting for you.

"I talked myself into giving it a try. I repented, cleansed myself, and entered a Sharia camp. I discovered that religion wasn't as bad as I thought it was. Gradually, I became close to God. After two months of the Sharia course, I memorized a few Surahs and began to pray five times a day. I learned some supplications, and the Quran became my companion after having run away from it in the past. I felt purified but also weak. I began to cry like a child, and I suffered. I cried and cried. I was afraid of the punishment in the afterlife. But I also discovered that I had a big family in the world, with siblings from all nationalities. I realized that obeying the orders of my Sharia leader and guardian was the path to my salvation. ISIS became a reality, and its members helped me the most. We were similar to one another, although we were different nationalities from all over the world. We were alike on the inside and it wasn't only because we were interested in Islam. We were searching for something solid that would help bring us together so we could console and help one another.

"After one month, I heard the magical word for the first time: *Inghimasi*.[42] The leaders labeled themselves *Inghimasis*. They would rejoice and congratulate one another. These are the heroes who would infiltrate enemy lines. Their chances of survival did not exceed one in a thousand. But whoever survived would have the honor of choosing to be part of a suicide mission.

"Some of the brothers from the Arab Gulf whose names were on the martyrdom lists would pay great sums of money to anyone whose name appeared before theirs so that they could take an earlier turn and arrive faster in paradise. They were competing to be martyred. I laughed at the naivety of those who thought these people were sick and stupid. They were intelligent and had everything in life, including luxury, high education, and university degrees from London, Paris, and New York. I had never seen anything like it. It was a dream for these people to become human shreds, for Islam did not spread except through shreds of humans. Each part of a martyr, they believed, would then be carried by twenty houris[43] in paradise, who would clean it and transform it from a mortal body into one that would live for eternity.

---

42 The term *Inghimasi* (from the Arabic verb meaning "to immerse") refers to a type of militant fighter who conducts a surprise attack by infiltrating enemy lines and engaging in close combat with the goal of causing chaos and confusion among the enemy forces. *Inghimasis* are known for their willingness to sacrifice themselves for their cause and are often trained to operate independently or in small groups, using stealth and surprise to gain advantage.

43 Houris are beautiful and pure maidens, often mentioned in Islamic texts, including the Quran and Hadith. According to Islamic beliefs, houris are one of the rewards that await righteous men in paradise. The Quran describes houris as "fair females" with "wide, lovely eyes" (Quran 44:54), and "pure companions" (Quran 2:25). The Hadith provides more details about their physical attributes, stating that they have large, dark eyes, a fair complexion, and are free from impurities and bodily defects.

"But bro, I didn't want any of this. I fled and came here, to the place where my people live. I don't want to die, but at the same time, I am fed up with life. And I have no idea what the solution is. I am a fighter and I can no longer live on this Earth except as a fighter, and so killing is just part of it."

Fidel interrupted, but quickly regretted disrupting his flow. "Does heaven not mean anything to you?"

"What heaven are you talking about, man?" he screamed. "Heaven is here and here," he said, pointing to his head and then his penis. "Bro, my mother would be fucked for what I just said. My picture won't be shown anywhere, right? Just turn it off. Turn off the fucking camera."

Before Fidel could respond, Abu Hiddo walked away, leaving the team completely speechless.

The stories told in front of the glutinous lens alternated and multiplied. Journalists and writers usually had to scavenge for good stories, but in this place, all one needed to do to find a shocking tale was set up the camera on the street and choose any random person. The stories accumulated while death continued its daily work like it was part of life's routine.

Fidel was at home when he was surprised by someone knocking on his door. He opened it, and there stood a bearded militant in full gear. He was in his forties and introduced himself as Abu Qutada. After a friendly conversation in which he dispensed religious advice and recommendations, he got down to business.

"The brothers in ISIS are interested in you," he said. "If you feel ready, they have a job for you."

"Are they interested in me or in my work?"

"Honestly, they need a producer like you who knows how to work cameras, speaks good English, and is committed to the Sharia. We have been watching you recently and have seen the example you set as a loyal and committed brother in your work. They will offer you the salary you desire, and you would be responsible for the technical and artistic department and for training the employees there."

"To tell you the truth, I had not planned for that. My intention was to finish a documentary film here."

"The decision is up to you."

"Is it actually safe there?"

"You are a journalist, brother Fadl. Surely, you would have to see for yourself and not listen to rumors. In any case, they are in a bit of a hurry. They have a film in mind and have nominated you to shoot it. When you're ready, we will get you there safely."

"I'll think about it and let you know."

"One more thing, brother Fadl. You would be expected to do this alone, and for your own safety, no one can know about this invitation. Tomorrow morning, I will send one of the brothers to find out your decision. If you agree, we will leave in the evening."

Fidel spent the whole night debating the proposition. Fear gnawed at him even as curiosity excited him. At dawn, he made up his mind. He thought to himself, *it would be foolish to accept or refuse. The right choice lies right in the middle, fifty-fifty.* He held a coin and decided, *if it's heads, I'll go, and if it's tails, I won't.* He flipped it in the air, and it landed in his palm.

43

Anees

He was covered with a thick canvas, curled up amid a pile of rubber tires as the stench of frozen vomit mixed with blood wafted in the air. He was transported by vehicle for almost half of a day towards the unknown.

Why did I resist death? I always knew this death sentence was inevitable. What cowardice made me agree to stay alive? He was overcome by exhaustion, talking to himself and disengaging from reality. With every inhale and exhale of despair, there was still a glimmer of salvation that shone through. Even if his life was in the lowliest of states, he seemed ready to sacrifice everything in order to keep breathing. *Was this the power of life or the arrogance that accompanied humiliation?*

He continued with his self-condemnation to pass the time until he was awakened by a guard ordering him out of his cell. A thick sack was placed over his head and his hands were tied. His body was stiff from the long journey and it was unbearable torment for him to walk.

They brought him to a room, untied him, and brought him a bottle of water, a slice of bread, and a tomato. Then they left. He took a few sips and ate without any appetite.

The day passed by. He thought about nothing, but he listened intently to the continuous noise outside. No one knocked on his door. Intense shelling started to shake the area; the door opened and four prisoners were forced inside. They were in a wretched state.

"If I hear a breath or a sound, blame no one but yourselves," the guard told them firmly.

Initially, they obeyed, and the four retreated into their shells. The biggest one began to sob with his head between his knees. Another was silently clutching his swollen arm and seemed to be enduring intense pain.

At first, Anees viewed them with indifference and some annoyance; their presence had disturbed the solitude he had grown accustomed to. He eyed them with suspicion and doubt, his self-pity greater than any empathy he could feel for anyone in the world.

But as much as he tried to convince himself that he was not obligated to do anything, something inside him pushed him towards them. Despite everything that had happened, it seemed that feelings of empathy and the desire to help every sufferer were still alive in him. He approached the man with the injured arm and whispered, "Let me see it. I am a physician."

The young man looked at him with a confused and terrified look, and stuck out his arm. Anees carefully examined the man's wounded arm. The bones had shifted and urgently needed to be splinted. "I'll put the bone back in its place, but you have to bear the pain." The young man nodded his head, his eyes shining with gratitude. Anees tightly folded up his shirt and said, "Bite on this and try not to make any noise. As they say, better an hour's pain then pain every hour." Another young man approached them and held the man with the broken arm from behind and said, "I can help if you want." Two other men came closer and encouraged their friend to stifle his moans. Even the fourth man, submerged in silence, lifted his head to watch what was happening.

Anees massaged the broken arm calmly, and with one swift motion, he popped the bone back in place. Using two scrap pieces of cardboard that he had found, he made a makeshift splint and wrapped it with torn-up pieces of his shirt. The man muffled his pain and did not scream, but rather his twisted body began to silently convulse. His eyes filled with tears and he almost lost consciousness. The cloth, soaked with his foaming saliva, fell out of his panting mouth. After a short while, he relaxed, thanked the doctor, and then began to tell his story.

"The smuggler instructed us to take the northern route to Turkey and to go from there to Europe. There were twenty-three of us when the bus that was transporting us was stopped at a checkpoint whose faction we didn't know. They detained our group for two days. Among us, there was one Christian man and an Ismaili, and we weren't sure where they took them. Then they began to interrogate the rest of us, wanting to know who we were, where we had come from, as well as our occupations and our family's occupations. Two in the group had brothers who had immigrated and they asked these two for their numbers and began to leverage them for ransoms. The rest of us, the poor whose families did not have anything to bargain, were either sold or handed over to other groups. We had come from rebellious cities and we could not understand why this no longer worked in our favor.

"We stayed in a warehouse for tires. Another group came to investigate us. Abu Mus'ab Al-Najdi asked us, 'Who among you has participated in demonstrations against the regime?' A few men raised their hands. He ordered, 'Come here. Who among you worked with coordinators of the revolution or participated in peaceful protests and contributed to activities like relief efforts, medical activities, or media activities?'

Everyone moved to one side but six of us remained together. We were simple journeymen who were not involved in any of what had taken place. I wanted to join the other men, but I was afraid they would ask me a question I couldn't answer. I said, 'I don't know what a revolution means or what the regime means. I am just an average person who has nothing to do with any of this.'

"The son of bitch lined them up at the wall and shot them one after another. The six of us could not believe what we were seeing. How could these strangers claim that they had come to support the Syrian people and then kill those who wholeheartedly took part in the revolution? We thought that we, the ignoramuses, would be the ones sentenced to death because we had not participated in the revolution, but instead they took us to another barrack.

"A fighter came and apologized to us for our mistreatment and informed us that our friends had been executed because they were deemed part of the apostate awakenings.[44] He said that he liked Syria and its people, and he invited us to belong to the Islamic State because we needed people to guide us, teach us religion, and keep us from going astray.

We accepted his offer and thanked him to appease him. And so he took us to a restaurant to eat and took exceptional care of us. He then invited us to a bathhouse to wash and clean ourselves and get ready. On that unforgettable night, three members of the Islamic State came in threatening us with their weapons. They told us to take off our clothes and gave us a blue pill called Viagra. They asked one of us to fuck one of their members, but he refused, beseeching the mercy of God, the Quran, the Prophet, and the Ka'bah, and begging them to spare him from committing such an act. His pleading did not work and they killed him in front of us. Five of us remained, and they made us take turns on their members for hours. They were worthless, insane people. Then, laughing, they left us. In the morning, we found that Sha'ban had hung himself. He could no longer bear it. Perhaps if they had raped us, it might've been easier. To be forced to fuck another man by force is something that breaks and hurts you, maybe more than being raped, perhaps because it turns you into a victim and a perpetrator at the same time. We remained in this state for one month until two days ago when they were attacked and fled, taking us along with them. I wanted to run away but I fell and broke my hand, and I am here now. I have no idea where I will be tomorrow. At least we are single men, but Mahmoud has children. It's very tough if you have children."

The place was cloaked with heavy silence, and underneath its folds Dr. Anees fell asleep, as if covering himself with it. He wished he could stop hearing anything or anyone. He wished only for absolute and eternal silence.

---

44 The "apostate awakenings," or *Al-Sahwa Al-Murtadah* in Arabic, is a term that refers to a reformist movement in the Islamic world that emerged in the 19th century. It originated in the region of Hijaz (present-day Saudi Arabia) and later spread to other countries in the Middle East and North Africa. The movement aimed to reform Islam by rejecting traditional practices and promoting knowledge, education, and modernization. However, some Islamic scholars and intellectuals criticized the movement and viewed it as a deviation from orthodox Islam.

44
Fadl

Fidel arrived after a smooth two-day journey. As soon as they recognized Abu Qutada, fighters opened the blockades and made way for them to enter. He was transported to a luxurious apartment for senior guests in an area governed by ISIS.

His initial anxiety about this mysterious place gradually became awe as he learned that the building in which they hosted him was a center for recruits from the West. Between fifty to one hundred Westerners came every day from all over the world, carrying various expectations. They arrived after perilous journeys, enduring all kinds of horrors in their efforts to reach the new promised land.

In the restaurant where breakfast was served, there were two sections: one for men and the other for women and children. A mixture of languages from around the world could be heard. French was the second most spoken language in the stronghold of the state. Most of the attendees at the guesthouse were white with blue or green eyes, including Swedes, Finns, Germans, Dutch, and many English. They were of Muslim origin or new converts to Islam. This was where the cream of the crop converged to build this strange dream. It was nothing like what was depicted in the media, but it was also unclear to Fidel what had brought all the people to this place.

While Syrians were fleeing their country and seeking refuge in Europe, Europeans came here to seek glory. The villages and towns came to be known as Little London, Little Berlin, and Little Paris. Everything that modernity strove to achieve and impose in terms of harmony among different human beings was smoothly accomplished in this place.

Over a delicious breakfast prepared by a French chef and a multinational staff, Fidel met four men, from Sweden, England, and Germany—a physician, two engineers, and an economics graduate. He had never met a group as enthusiastic about such a mystifying idea as these intellectuals were about the Islamic State, even though they had not suffered from persecution in their native lands, nor did they lack a profession or a comfortable life in their own countries.

Fidel began to harbor doubts. He wondered if they were agents from international intelligence agencies because the enthusiasm they expressed about taking part in the creation of the greatest moment in history felt exaggerated.

The German said, "These are the happiest days of my life. I feel like I have been reborn."

"You know very well that you may not be able to go back and could easily be killed here," Fidel said.

"I am no longer afraid of death. What I fear today is having to return to that rotten and repulsive existence in which I wasted thirty-five years of my life. It's a divine sign that has been given to us, and we are now destined for triumph in this world and in the hereafter."

It was bewildering for Fidel to witness how things had been turned upside down. The norm was always that people like him, Arabs and Muslims, would have to convince skeptical Westerners. But today, as Fidel sat in the company of acutely intelligent Western men speaking with passion and faith, men who had surrendered to the Islamic call, he was the only one doubting the authenticity of their intentions.

He returned to his room, organized his papers, and charged his camera's batteries. Layl's face crept into his thoughts. Dwelling on her image would mean that he would also start to hear her voice and be hit with a flood of memories. She would besiege him again, opening that well of longing that he could not bear. *I have to distract myself with anything, for these feelings will become completely destructive if I don't learn how to make peace with them,* he told himself.

The call to the noon prayer helped free him from the call of love. He went down to the reception area and asked directions to the mosque. A brother with a friendly face instructed him to wait for a bit and someone would come and guide him.

The mosque was attended by *Al-Muhajiroun*,[45] a name given to all newcomers who arrived from other countries around the world. Its imam was Saudi and his voice was soul-stirring. The place was exceptionally clean, everything in it was orderly and organized. As they lined up for prayer, the newcomers enthusiastically moved to the front rows.

Feeling some satisfaction and much curiosity, he went to meet with Abu Qutada, the forty-year-old leader, who said to him, "I came to bid you farewell. I am leaving on a mission. May God guide you in this place."

He wasn't able to reciprocate the same feelings. He greeted him kindly, and as he headed to his room, a man at the reception desk called out, "Sheikh Fadl, peace be upon you."

Fidel returned the greeting inquisitively.

"Come with us. The Prince wants to see you."

Inside a gaudy office, the Prince sat facing two Apple screens, an iP-hone, and an iPad that rested on a leather base. With his brown and gold cloak, white beard, and black turban, he appeared dignified and lordly. His presence amid such extreme modernity felt paradoxical, as if he had emerged from the pages of history.

"*As-salamu alaykum.*"

"*Wa 'alaykumu s-salam.*"[46]

Fidel couldn't believe his eyes. "Sheikh Ghassan! Could this possibly be?" He threw himself at the man, stretching out his arms. The sheikh stood awkwardly but met him with the same familiarity.

Fidel noticed a group of advisers sitting in the large office, all wearing

---

45 Al-Muhajiroun is Arabic for "the Emigrants." This is related to the Hijra (immigration) when Prophet Muhammad (peace be upon him) migrated from Mecca to Medina in Saudi Arabic in the year 622 CE, marking the beginning of the Islamic calendar. This is also considered one of the most important events in Islamic history, where the Prophet was welcomed by the people, establishing the first Islamic state.

46 As-salamu alaykum is a greeting for Muslims that means "Peace be upon you." The typical response is, "Wa 'alakumu s-salam," which means "and peace be upon you."

perplexed smiles. After the initial surprise subsided, Sheikh Ghassan regained the appropriate distance he had to maintain as part of his new position, but also kept Fidel close enough to send a message to all those present about their relationship.

Sheikh Ghassan then began to speak. "Brother Fadl is one of the best young Muslim men I met at London Mosque. He is a living example of the spirit that the *Ummah*[47] seeks, with a God-given natural talent that makes him one of the finest visual media artists. For many years, I have seen promising signs in him, and have watched his amazing reports. It's true that he may have overstepped the Shariah in some ways, but Fadl happens to be one of those Islamic minds who truly understands the mentality of the West. He has mastered its tools, and is known for his integrity, education, and expertise. I met him in London when he was a young man. He was sad and scared, but his heart was filled with the Holy Quran and a love for Allah. Unfortunately, I had to leave him behind and go to Afghanistan and then Iraq, but he was always present in my thoughts whenever I thought of my days in Britain. Anyway, here we are reunited, praise be to Allah, as it was His will that we meet again on this blessed land that is imbued with the blessed divinity of jihad."

The attendees responded in the expected way during such an interaction: *Masha'Allah, Alhamdulillah,* and Blessed be God the Merciful.[48]

After this dramatic testimony, Fidel was at a loss to come up with some sort of response but was rescued by Fadl, who was feeling so elated by the sheikh's introduction it was like he'd just snorted two lines of pure cocaine. "Your testimony is equal to a thousand testimonies, Sheikh Ghassan, and all I desire is to live up to your expectations," he said.

The warmth and amiability shattered all of Fidel's reservations about the place; meanwhile, the Prince laid out new paths before him and triggered a great sense of curiosity. All of his previous misgivings about ISIS

---

47 The Ummah is an Arabic term that refers to the global Muslim community or nation. It is a term that represents the collective identity of Muslims around the world, who share a common belief in the oneness of Allah (God) and the teachings of the Prophet Muhammad.

48 *Masha'Allah* and *Alhamdulillah* are common Arabic phrases used by Muslims. *Masha'Allah* is the Arabic for "as God has willed" and *Alhamdulillah* is "Praise be to God."

began to melt away in the face of the power of these conversations.

Many riddles sparked his interest, and he listened closely. After everyone had excused themselves, he was alone with Sheikh Ghassan, who hastened to say, "We need you to develop the media department and bring it up to par with our aspirations as well as with recent events. Additionally, we would like to produce some documentary films with the most powerful possible effects. We also would like a whole campaign to be made about the young mujahideen and those seeking martyrdom showing their courage and strength as fierce fighters who are worthy of admiration. The target audience is the Western world, specifically its young Muslim men and women who are in search of true freedom through embracing Islam."

"My dear Sheikh, I would be very proud to contribute to this work, but the equipment that I have with me is not sufficient to help meet your goals," replied Fidel.

Sheikh Ghassan smiled. "One of the brothers will introduce you to the department and its staff. All you need to do is make note of what might be missing and we will bring it to you."

Picking up on Fidel's anxiety and curiosity, Sheikh Ghassan added confidently, "This will be a temporary contract. You can let me know if you don't like it. There may be things that are confusing or do not suit you. We can discuss anything you want."

"I would like to take a tour of the city, or even other cities if possible."

"That's easy. We will organize a tour for you. Sure, the security situation isn't ideal, but it will give you the chance to see things for yourself."

"May I ask you one personal question?"

Sheikh Ghassan's mouth uttered "yes" while his eyes warned "beware."

"Do you really believe in the Caliphate?[49] And where did the Sheikh Ghassan that I knew in London disappear to? Don't you think that the killing and brutality are hurting Islam and its image? And, do you..."

---

49 The relationship between ISIS and the concept of the Caliphate is complex and multifaceted. ISIS, which stands for the Islamic State of Iraq and Syria, declared itself a Caliphate in 2014, with Abu Bakr al-Baghdadi as its self-proclaimed Caliph (leader).

"Take it easy, Sheikh Fadl. Easy. You will find true answers to these questions very soon, but I ask that you keep them to yourself until the full picture is revealed."

The Prince then had the guard send for Abu Abdullah Al-Maghribi. A man about two meters tall, in his thirties, entered with a cold look. He was ordered to take care of their guest and acquaint him with the media department, then take him around the city, making certain that he was provided with all means of comfort. They left the headquarters in a late-model Land Cruiser and passed through busy streets bustling with buyers and sellers. There was a strong security presence, with patrols of masked men in black working alongside Shariah market control patrols that ensured the accurate prices of goods, urged people to pray on time, and held them accountable when they did not abide by the Shariah dress codes for both women and men.

They arrived at a building that used to belong to the regime. A man greeted them and led them to a ground floor, which was crowded with workers; he welcomed and took them to the meeting room and invited heads of departments to join. A group of men entered and greeted them. Among them was a technician from Portugal, a German producer, an American software expert, a Pakistani satellite broadcast and equipment expert, and a Saudi broadcast station manager, in addition to a financial manager, a director of human resources, a director of external regions and correspondents whose nationalities Fidel could not determine but who all spoke heavy, classical Arabic.

The team described their current projects and presented Fidel with general files from the department. Although the department was in its infancy, it possessed enough hi-tech equipment to operate a satellite station the size of CNN. These conversations were mostly in English. He then met with the print team, the advertising team, the internet and social media team, the misinformation team, and the Arab media and global monitoring department tasked with archiving every word written about the Islamic State in any corner of the world.

Fidel told the interlocutor, "I have worked with over fifty major organizations, but I have yet to encounter such a dynamic work spirit."

It was a dream team for any organization, composed of intelligent and skilled professionals with great expertise in production and advertising who understood its subtleties and its power.

He learned that some had joined with their families and children to live under the protection of the fledgling State. Each day, a piece of the puzzle was revealed to him, while he continued to encounter more mysteries and secrets. The most important conclusion he came to was that this was no joke and had to be taken seriously.

There were three different types of *Al-Muhajiroun*: those with scientific and technical expertise in all aspects of life, including physicians, engineers, economists, and management and technology experts; the second type included quality fighters who were experts in modern battle planning and in dealing with explosives, weapons, and booby traps. The third type were those who dreamt of taking revenge against any enemies of Islam; they were everywhere and were the greatest in number. The third type was opportunistic, suffered from boredom, and had criminal records in their countries of origin. They were the most extreme and radical, and acted primarily on instinct.

Everyone had to undergo Shariah courses where, in addition to learning the law, they were assessed for security purposes and placed into different groups. Behind the military efforts, a massive, complex system was at work, where contrary to the stereotype of them as fools and killers, the State had a clear and sophisticated project in place, albeit one not fully understood by any of them or expected to be understood.

As for Syrian locals, Fidel came to discover that their relationship with the State was maintained through coercion and fear. The State assigned its most terrifying and extremist members to live among the residents of the city. Neither side trusted the other, and the State's politics of submission was based on deterrence, intimidation, or bribery and persuasion. Compared to the *Al-Muhajiroun*, the people of the land were the least enthusiastic about the State's ideas. Indeed, a small number of Syrians considered themselves to be part of the State and the rest consisted of people with origins in eighty countries, including most Western ones.

What was strange is that the State considered Assad's regime a secondary enemy, and even one that they could possibly trust and deal with. Each side knew that if they both focused on those who caused hindrances to their projects, they would ultimately protect one another. Their common stumbling blocks were simply the people of the country who belonged to the revolution, its flags, and demonstrations. Those people faced merciless assaults and aggression from both sides. At the same time, the regime released *Takfiri*[50] leaders who had been living in the misery of the country's prisons to provide the Islamic State with iconic jihadist figures who had fought in Afghanistan and Iraq. Additionally, the regime handed over remote areas to ISIS that were far from its strongholds and areas of power, along with tons of ammunition and weapons. In exchange, ISIS provided the regime with supply lines for petroleum, gas, and wheat, at the cheapest prices.

Those who carried out suicide missions usually gave their names voluntarily. They were among those considered to be the least intelligent and least capable of making good decisions. But their decision to blow themselves up were not about houris in paradise; this sort of justification even brought people of average intelligence in the state to laugh. Here, Fidel was able to simplify the most complex of twenty-first century questions—how does one come to blow oneself up? He reasoned that as one tries to make sense of the drive behind blowing up oneself, it is important to understand that the answer is related to the will to believe. The suicide belt represents an emotional relationship with the self; it is about an internal explosion that has taken place as a result of an accumulation of life's disappointments. *How likely is it that ordinary people in the West and East would also blow themselves up if they had a belt?* he thought to himself. It was a simple idea, blessed and encouraged by a group of comrades.

Fidel worked silently and followed instructions. He was given all the equipment he requested, and he carefully selected his team from the

---

50 *Takfiri* is an adjective derived from the Arabic word *takfir*, which refers to the act of declaring someone to be an unbeliever or apostate. In the context of contemporary politics and religion, *Takfiri* is often used to describe individuals or groups who use this practice to justify violence and terrorism against those who they deem to be non-believers or heretics, including other Muslims. *Takfiri* ideology is often associated with extremist and militant groups, such as ISIS and Al-Qaeda.

hundreds of applicants who sought employment in the media. He carefully designed his videos to attract fighters by glorifying their training in the state. He chose images that were captured during battles and put them in promotional clips that would stoke the wild imaginations of the new believers and entice as many as possible. Every week, he and his team were asked to create a new video that could be circulated around the world. And with every video he created, the leaders were more impressed.

Fidel met with Sheikh Ghassan, who was also known by the nickname Prince Abu Hafas. The sheikh briefed him on what they wanted from him. "For the past one hundred years, Hollywood has made films that present us to the world as horrific and violent in order to satisfy the West's agenda of power and control. Here, we must stop producing a backward and primitive picture that serves the agendas of our enemies. What differentiates their work is its quality, but not the ideas. Our ideas are deeper and stronger. We are men who represent a transition to an ideal State, and we must help establish a new generation that carries the spirit of jihad. We are a generation of outrage who will exhaust our enemies through the power of intimidation and shock. We don't care about how the world sees us. What is important for us is that we are at the top of news bulletins and that we do not disappear from the scene. Every condemnation that we receive is in service to our project. The world imposes its arts on us to impose its existence and entity—we will use the same tools to teach it new arts. The coming generation is one that will reinforce the Sharia and will redefine the notion of true human rights."[51]

---

51   This passage is informed by Abu Baker Naji's book *Management of Savagery,* published online in 2004. It is a controversial book that has been widely discussed in both academic and political circles. In the book, Naji, believed to be a senior member of Al-Qaeda or a related extremist group, argues that jihadist groups should focus on creating chaos and instability in order to weaken governments and prepare the ground for their eventual takeover. Naji's central thesis is that societies go through a cycle of savagery and civilization, and that the goal of jihadists should be to push societies back into a state of savagery in order to create an opportunity for the establishment of an Islamic State. He advocates for a range of tactics, including targeted assassinations, bombings, and other forms of violence, in order to create this chaos and destabilization. Naji argues that by creating a power vacuum, jihadist groups can step in, fill the void, and establish their own Islamic State.

45
Layl

After a few days, Layl bid them farewell. Issa arranged to be taken to a northern region that was no longer under the regime's control. He told her, "Someone will meet you at a field hospital where your cover story will be that you are doing volunteer work. From there, you'll have to find a way to reach the area where Fidel lives, which happens to be in the middle of hell."

I want to meet this man again, my other half; a man who has poured in me wine, dreams, and destinations. I want to journey back to yesterday, for there is nothing left ahead for me. What motivates me is thinking about how I can turn back time to its source, a concept understood by no one but the salmon who, like me, long to return to the original springs. How is it that music can bring back such memories? She was about to tell the driver to turn the music off but suddenly realized that what she was hearing was playing in her own head.

Arriving at the liberated, besieged, and destroyed area was like swimming against the current of time itself. Along the way, it was possible that one would be devoured by the creatures who live off those returning to the source of the river—bears and crocodiles, and hungry hunters or pleasure hunters. Yet it was one's faith, a faith like the salmon had, that provided an unexplainable drive. Layl followed the music that accompanied the thought of his absent face, her compass to survival.

Two young men in their thirties welcomed her with wide smiles and reassuring hospitality. They went to one of their homes, and the young man said, "You will be with our families. You should rest, Doctor. We have everything here that you may need. Tomorrow, we'll show you around."

The space had been penetrated by the incessant shelling of planes, yet life also continued. In the house were young girls just starting their lives, and a lonely old woman whose family was either scattered underground in unknown graves or, for those who remained alive, dispersed in different parts of the world. They called her Aunt Um[52] Ahmad.

The situation was far from ideal as there were significant conflicts between the fighting factions. But the youths who led the revolution in its infancy and had escaped death still maintained the same spirit as before.

The place where she now found herself was an entirely different scene from Damascus, as if what separated the two regions was not a distance of three or four hours by car, but rather five years of death that rained down daily from the sky. The airstrikes were part of the everyday routine, with planes distributing their shares of death evenly over villages, towns, and cities. Not a week passed without the hellish downpour of shells and barrel bombs.

During the first night, the home where she was staying was shelled. She went with the family to an underground shelter, which offered no protection but a slight hope for survival. The bombing sounded like the bells of hell and made everything vibrate. The family joined some of their neighbors in the shelter and they all acted nonchalantly. The girls continued to study, while Aunt Um Ahmad doled out eggplant and squash. The sound of the explosion startled her, causing her to puncture the zucchini she held in her hand. "Damn you, you filthy son of a bitch," she cursed. "You have ruined my zucchini, you son of a thief. A kilo now costs a thousand liras!"

In the neighboring room, the young men worked tirelessly to prepare the weekly schedule that they packed with tasks. They sat and enthusiastically discussed an idea that one of them had about creating an open-air cinema, where a large screen could be placed on the wall of the headquarters building, and where they could spread mats and pillows on the ground, serve tea, and invite the locals to watch a film.

Ayman, one of the men who first welcomed Layl, was busy trying to figure out how to obtain a permit for the cinema because the Prince,

---

52 *Um* is the Arabic for "mother of."

who was in charge of the town, would likely not allow it. He said, "We are counting on the support of Syrians among them who would not have a problem with it. I think it will also depend on the subject of the film. We could dedicate the first three minutes to spread awareness and highlight the accomplishments of the White Helmets and include whatever ads they would like before playing the selected film."

Their loud conversations could easily be heard through a curtain that separated them from the women's section. They were speaking with confidence about their tomorrows. On the other side, the women divided chores among themselves, some taught or fed their children while others kept busy making handicrafts to supplement their family's income.

Suddenly, she was living among people who refused to leave their cities and towns, despite facing death from a sky filled with jets that showered them with seeds of death, and on the ground, where they were exploited and violated by jihadists. The jihadists did not reflect the spirit of the place, but after liberating the area they became the authorities.

Ayman said, "We appreciate their courage and they have contributed many good things, but their initiative is different from ours. We don't intersect with the jihadists on anything, particularly those coming from outside Syria. But we can't confront them today while we are being bombed and destroyed. What we are counting on are the Syrians amongst them. They know that we will not accept an extremist Islamic rule; we can accept temporary adjustment to the general situation and within an Islamic framework, at least until relief comes and the war stops." With his shining eyes, he spoke with confidence and determination about the revolution, hope, and life. He was filled with that same inspiring spirit she had first seen and heard in the faces and voices of young revolutionaries during the Umayyad Mosque demonstration.

"May I ask you something, Dr. Layl?"

"Of course. You can ask me anything you want."

"Issa is one of the friends and comrades with whom we've worked in previous years. He said that you can help us in the field hospital by training women to assist with childbirth."

"Yes, that's right."

"He also said you need my help with something else."

"Precisely. It's a personal matter and I will tell you about it shortly."

"Another thing, Doctor. If it's OK with you, in some areas here, it would be better if you wore the hijab. This is a technical measure that will help us avoid clashes with Islamic groups at the blockades."

"Of course," she responded quickly. "I completely understand."

The women finished preparing dinner and invited everyone to eat. It had been a long time since Layl had tasted anything like the food she was served that day. It was cooked with love. A shared meal opened the space for people to enjoy conversation and jokes. The stuffed eggplant and zucchini were exceptional, and Layl noticed that each person had left one last piece on the tray, an altruistic act directed toward anyone who might still be hungry.

The planes continued to circle in the sky, but the shelling gradually subsided. As the cups of fermented tea were passed around, Abdullah grabbed the oud and skillfully began to play, filling the place with music. The charming, deep voice of Aunt Um Ahmad resounded as she chanted along with the music:

O my eye, shed your tears
O heart, stay quiet
My home is ruined by the hour
My child is dying by the hour
Our youth, like roses,
Are carried in coffins.
Mosques are battered,
Homes are destroyed.
O mother, some are now in Turkey and others in Beirut
We've not seen weddings or joys, only funerals in the place.
I swear and shout at the top of my lungs:
I will not exchange Syria for gold or rubies.
Oh the pain.

Silence prevailed; the shelter was awash in a fountain of tears. It was a song that darted from the heart of a woman lamenting the land, leaving nothing unsaid. Their pain was unparalleled; it emanated from roots underground, engulfed the world, covering and exposing everything. The others felt guilty for causing Layl pain, and they began to console her; meanwhile, she felt more suffocated, as if she should be the one doing the consoling.

She witnessed and grieved in this place where death swept over everyone and everything, where when paying a close ear to the shadows of death on the streets, it was possible to hear them say, *Here is the place my father was killed, and at this intersection my friend died; there, at the bottom of the olive tree, my beloved took his last breath*. What had taken place in this country was unimaginable, where the remnants of the departed still bore their marks on the road, their voices echoing in the orchards, their laughter lining the paths, and kneading the fertile red soil with their bones. The people of this land witnessed death, and they would never forget the faces of their killers.

46
Sheikh Ghassan

He made the first film with top-notch cinema cameras and a crew of no less than fifty technicians. The scenario had taken a month to plan and edit, with meticulous attention given to every detail of lighting and sound. It was a stunning production that any producer would dream of executing, but with one difference—in this production, the actors' first on-screen appearance was also their last. Twenty spies were slaughtered in a vast desert after being kept in cages for several days like animals.

At the beginning of this crazy century, a violent United States deployed and showcased its military strength through aerial bombings. Those who were not killed by their smart planes would be taken as hostages, charged with being dangerous and barbaric, and imprisoned in the infamous Guantánamo Bay detention camp, dressed in orange uniforms and regarded as savages.

With every passing day, one sinks deeper into this savage place, a place riddled with contradictions, where the reward is immense and once part of the elite ranks, one feels exempt from all worldly obligations that typically occupy the human mind—a place that offers everything a soul desires, from forbidden cigarettes to cocaine, alcohol, sex with minors, and an abundance of money beyond imagination.

Amid such abundant temptation, Fadl and Fidel worked together for the first time. They needed one another. In public councils, Sheikh Fadl was dazzlingly eloquent, and at work, Fidel accepted nothing less than perfection. They were two separate languages and behaviors, both frightening and conflicting and both from the same man.

Fidel came to fully understand Sheikh Ghassan's words as he witnessed thousands of modern devices, including laptops, the latest smartphones, and cars with post-modern technologies, in the hands of men who seemed to have escaped from the past. Fidel's visits with Sheikh Ghassan became less frequent as Fidel's schedule intensified, the shelling increased, and the city was almost completely shut down to prevent its inhabitants from escaping. In addition to digging tunnels and providing shelters, civilians were also used as human shields. And yet, in spite of it all, the influx of new immigrants never ceased.

Although all the components needed for the state to flourish were present, it was clear that it would not continue. For although the people could not express themselves, their eyes reflected the magnitude of the rejection they felt. Fidel shared these thoughts with Sheikh Ghassan, who replied, "Who told you that this is the State we want?"

"I don't understand. All of this work, and you're not sure that it will endure and expand?"

"I will put aside my reservations about speaking in light of the old, pure friendship and brotherhood that connects us. No, this is not the Caliphate state; it is only a prototype for the true Caliphate. Today, our goal is to manage savagery and train and create a new generation of superior and militant Muslims. We are a polluted generation no matter how pure we claim to be. But this next generation of fighters is pure and creative, and it is through them that Allah's victory and our dream of the promised Caliphate will materialize because this is the will of Allah Himself.

"Our mission today is to learn the arts of management, economics, and media. Empowerment can only be achieved through practical training, not theory. Today we benefit from the contradictions of reality. We compensate for the great loss of the mujahideen in multiple ways. We choose the elite, rehabilitate the cells, and drive a massive movement to plant ideology and faith in the minds and hearts of the people. We also commission the intelligent amongst our European brothers to return to their countries and teach techniques of patience. We do all of this in order to construct a foundation and prepare the necessary conditions for when the time comes. All the hostility today towards Islam is ultimately serving Islam; all the selfishness, greed, superiority, and sterility in the Western world will be met with fertility, readiness for sacrifice, and justice."

He carried on, "The time for the jihad to exist in caves and in isolation has come to an end. Each day we spend in the open air, working as a State and benefitting from the art of management, brings us a step closer to the promised day. Mark my words—this century will not end before Europe is Muslim, and this century will not pass without America heading towards Islam. We know this because of an unbreakable promise that was made to us by the leader of creation and their Master, Muhammad ibn Abdullah. We have made a considerable leap, for we are no longer a party or a secret, restricted movement. Today, we are in the declaration stage, working on all fronts together. We are accumulating wealth and correcting the malfunctions of moderate and Sufi Islam. Indeed, in our project towards liberation, this has been the first enemy we have needed to overcome, for it is conciliatory and coexists with injustice, despotism, and tyrants."

"This is painful," said Fidel.

"Yes, it is painful because we are using excessive force. But at the same time, we are preparing convoys of new empowered missionary Muslims, and not only from Shariah disciplines but also those who have mastered the arts of persuasion and who engage the power of logic. We love the Levant and the land of the Two Holy Mosques[53] for their spiritual and moral strength, but here we will always feel vulnerable to invasions by tyrannical military powers and beholden to banks and blood merchants of the enemies. When we obtain access to the center of decision making and take over contemporary Rome, as is promised by Allah, all of these enormous powers that threaten us will become ours. Throughout history, the Islamic State has always been where issues of power and control are decided. When we were in Damascus, we made it our capital; when we were in Persia, we built Baghdad and excelled in Samarkand; when we were in Egypt, we built Cairo, and after moving to Spain, we went into to Granada and Cordoba; when Constantinople became the center of the world, it became ours. Today, the decisions are made in Washington. However,

---

53   The country of the Two Holy Mosques is a name to describe the Kingdom of Saudi Arabia.

one slap in the face turned their lives upside down. *Alhamdulillah*, they reacted exactly as we had expected and brought along their multitudes of armies into Afghanistan and Iraq, consequently giving birth to our state."

"But the price is high, my dear Sheikh," Fidel interjected, "We have lived in the West, and we know that people there, like the rest of God's creation, are kind and peaceful, and reject arrogant policies."

"But who said that we want to kill them? We are nothing like their lowly leaders," Sheikh Ghassan replied. He took a deep breath and his tone became paternal, "Fadl, I am not foolish or close-minded. I worked in London for years and I know the real London as well as its people better than their own government does. The point is that it is no longer useful for us to beg at their doors or be servants to their ideologies of diversity and coexistence. Yes, there is a great deal that we can take from them—the notion of work ethics, justice, mercy, and protecting the weak. In fact, these are all Islamic values with Western names, and they are missing here in our countries because of their prior support of oppressive governments, as well as their invasions and economic plunder. They construct their privilege on the backs of our misery. Indeed, we've now exchanged roles when it comes to world domination, but we have never looted the people we ruled. On the contrary, we built civilizations, transformed them and were transformed by them. They accuse us of using the sword to force people to convert to Islam. My reply to them is, but why then did East Asian people remain Muslim after the decline of the Caliphate?"

"But if this logic were true, why did the people of Andalusia no longer embrace Islam after the Arabs departed?"

"Because of their massacres," he replied unhesitatingly. "It's because of the massacres they committed against Muslims and Jews to expel them from Andalusia. More important is that we stayed in Andalusia for eight hundred years, mind you, today they mention us in their schoolbooks in less than eight lines. History tells us this, not me. We've ruled the world for a thousand years, and not only did we not rob its people, but we considered them to be our brothers. On the other hand, through colonization, they transferred tons of gold and wealth and created glory from plunder. They killed millions in Africa, transported them on slave ships like animals. Meanwhile, Islam preached equality between Black and white people for fourteen hundred years. We believe in brotherhood among humans, while only sixty years ago, Black people in America were not even permitted to enter the same bathrooms as white people.

"The West ruled for three hundred years, turned weak countries into plundered colonies and built their wealth and civilizations from the blood of the poor. Their greed and selfishness destroyed them, and now they are devouring one another. They hate us because we pose the only threat to their system and greed. All our attempts during the past fifty years to find ways to work with them were in vain because they are the victors. I tell you, what happened in the past hundred years was a turning point that has not yet taken shape, but the genie has awakened and no one can put it back into its bottle. The Caliphate will be a reality before the end of the century, and New York, Washington, London, Paris, and Berlin will be part of its capital cities. London will be a Muslim city, and we will redistribute wealth to the exploited people. This time around, migration will be reversed to our cities in the East, and the dream of the people will be to master Arabic and work in Damascus, Baghdad, and Cairo."

"Where is Israel in all of this?" asked Fidel.

"It is wrong to think that we want to fight the Jews," replied Sheikha Ghassan. "This is only for marketing purposes. We have much more in common with the Jews than what sets us apart. We were both expelled from Andalusia, and the Jews were the ones who suffered most, not only from Christianity but also from the brutality and extremism of the West."

Sheikh Ghassan, or Prince Abu Hafas as he was called, was deeply convinced of this peculiar diagnosis. As for the Syrian revolution, he believed that it posed a greater threat to the Islamic State than anything else. He explained, "The Arab-Muslim people must only rise for Islam. The nation-state and the deep emotions it fosters distract from what we are trying to accomplish. It is critical that the people are not contaminated again with such ideas as they will only cause further delays on the path to empowerment."

"But you are pushing people away from religion. You're also

promoting a false image of Islam," said Fidel.

"In terms of appearance, yes. The reality is that we have to endure this painful period in order to build a global system of jihad leading towards change. When we become empowered and attain the Caliphate State, you will see how we will work for equality, attain justice, and rule by a righteous, mutual consultation as should be the case and as befits us. We are in a state of existential struggle, and everything we have offered to the West in terms of security, understanding, and attempts to convince them of our right to choose our way of life has been met with ridicule and disdain. They want to turn us into a hybrid Islam that caters to their economy and politics and makes it easier for them to destroy us from within. Today, we are experiencing a global awakening, an awakening of Islam. This planet will not see justice until it is governed by the peace that comes from Islam. Democracy and liberalism today are the ruling religions, and Christianity and Judaism have surrendered to them. Only Islam resists. It is a struggle between the spiritual and material, between peace and war, good and evil. The politicization of Islam is supported by the West to serve their agenda of liberalism, which leads to a terrifying brutality that forces people to pursue a materialistic and meaningless life. We are closer to those who say, 'From each according to his ability, to each according to his need,'[54] where the surplus value is offered to the good of the nation and its progress, not for the good of the party or the authority of the tyrant."

"And what about the Sunni-Shia conflict today?" inquired Fidel.

"There is no conflict, because in the end it will serve the main goal. What you see today is a political conflict in sectarian garb."

"But you have declared the Shia to be infidels and you are fighting against them."

"Have you seen us doing anything at all in Iran? We carry out military operations against Shia, or even Sunnis, only in areas of direct conflict and confrontation. It's a political and economic conflict at its core. Historically, we've had a problem with Persians, and not with Shia Islam,

---

54 This famous slogan is often attributed to Karl Marx and is closely associated with Marxist ideology.

315

although we don't object to calling this conflict Sunni-Shia. We are not on either side, but all results will serve the interest of a pure Islam as well as the project of empowering a righteous state."

"But can we deal with the present using the language of the past? Can we really manage the modern world with the language of the Quran, the Sunnah of the Prophet, and the ideologies of the pious predecessors?"

"Of course we can, but this does not mean that we need to reject applied sciences. The jurists of the sultanate tried to do this in their attempts to keep the people ignorant and they failed. This is why I said earlier that the project of the state is a prototype for what is to come. We want managers in all aspects of life, we want to acquire the highest human achievements in science, and we want a generation of warrior-scholars. Meanwhile, we know how to address the public and heal their contaminated hearts. We do not care if the other sees in us only strange *fatwas* and spreads silly rumors about us. We do not care about what others think of us. What matters is what we think of our image and the depth of its impact on the mujahideen. There are many false rumors about us, suggestions that we want to cover a cow's udders or cut down trees, and that we are barbarians and do not care about history and only know how to apply the sword and slaughter—but all of this will help us in terrorizing and intimidating the Other while scholarly, intelligent, and wise people continue to join us from all over the world. Have you ever asked yourself this question: If we were truly barbaric, would so many people have left their paradise of the West and come to us?

"Fadl, I know what you must be thinking right now. Yes, it's true. There is a continuous flow of criminals, fugitives, fools, and even spies. And here we are offering the world a service they could only dream of—to turn these people into fighters for a great cause where they can end up as martyrs and be freed of their sins, instead of wasting money on trying to correct them. Fadl, my dear. I devoutly love you, and I have high expectations for you. I sincerely want to satisfy your curiosity, but I would like to request something from you. You can take your time and think about it. However, this request will provide the keys to access every treasure in life and will guarantee life beyond death."

"Go ahead, my sheikh," Fidel replied.

"In a remote location on the state's land, there is a group of leaders with strong minds, iron wills, and deep faith. They are experts in all fields of life. The door is open for you to become one of them. Who knows? But you must first pledge allegiance to the caliph and declare your loyalty and fidelity. You are here on a temporary contract. Everyone is talking about your wonderful talent. You can finish your work and leave, and I will protect you and provide you with an authorization document from the highest authority here, the Caliphate itself. But since you don't have much time left here, it is my duty to invite you to join us. You are one of those people I trust to be absolutely true about their feelings. At the same time, I pray to Allah that He guides you to the path of truth that has opened before you. If you decide to stay, I will be the happiest person, but if you choose to leave, I will bid you farewell, and we will not meet again."

The message was clear. All the nagging questions that floated around in his mind had now been definitively answered by Sheikh Ghassan. Fidel had witnessed the harsh conditions faced by many of the inhabitants of this state and its affiliates—the transgressions, the oppression, the crimes, and persecution, all at once. He assumed that all of this was temporary, imposed by war.

He left Sheikh Ghassan's place, numb from a conversation that had required such concentration. He felt like he was walking into a trap, stepping into a dark room. Ghassan was essentially saying that he was searching for a nonexistent black cat while blindfolded in a dark room. The call to prayer awakened him from the conversation he was having with himself, pulling him out of that dark room.

A gathering was taking place in the public square, and people were craning their necks upward. There, on the sixth floor, was a blindfolded man—his mouth gagged and his limbs restrained—being dragged by two masked men. As he resisted in vain, a spot of urine appeared on his pants, and then he was thrown to his death for the crime of being homosexual.

47

Sameeh

Ayman took her to their workplace. He brought out massive albums and put them in front of her. They documented the faces of martyrs before they died, hundreds of photos, three quarters of whom were young people in the prime of their lives. Even their dead expressions were full of life, with puzzled smiles drawn on their faces. Most important, their eyes were wide open.

"The eyes are the last to die. Even after the heart stops, one continues to take in the last scene and gazes cling to life as if embracing it," said Ayman.

"I thought the ears were the first thing to work in the womb and the last thing to function at death."

Laughingly, he replied, "I hope we don't have to test this with one another," and he added, "The cherry trees scattered in the orchards were hit by shrapnel and bullets. The shells poured upon us and the shrapnel cut the branches of our family tree, but they could not keep us from growing. During the massacres, our cherries became more delicious."

They visited the neighborhoods and walked roads that had fallen into ruin. Some of the locals cleaned the streets and tried to keep the town uncontaminated. "Being exposed to death by shells does not mean that we surrender or allow disease to spread amongst us. It is our responsibility to remain vigilant about public hygiene. This square has witnessed more than a thousand protests, all of which echoed the one and only word: freedom. We've made it clear that we are here, we are no longer nobodies, and we want our share of this country," he continued. "This is Hajja[55] Aisha, who remembers all the wars of the past century. She tells the stories her mother told her, about how her grandfather took part in Seferberlik, and how he fought everywhere with the French. She recalls every war that took place in the area, including our present day, but she says she has never seen death in such abundance."

He went on, "Here is the city park. This swing is the only thing that remains of it and underneath it is a grave for four children. Aisha screams at the children from inside her room at night, telling them to stop making noise, and she threatens to deprive them of the swing if they continue to misbehave. She imagines seeing them and talks to them. She has memorized the names of all the graves laid out in this park, except for thirteen graves of unknown martyrs. Damascene myrtle has climbed on the tombstones. There are more than two hundred graves; all you have to do is mention a name, and she recognizes who it is immediately. She helped bury all of them, mourned them, and she now guards them. When the bearded strangers arrived, they said that visiting graves was *bid'ah*[56] and wanted to destroy the cemetery. They did not understand how we could bury Christians, *Rawafidh*,[57] Druze, and Sunnis all together. As they entered the graveyard, she was taking care of the graves as you can see, planting roses on top of them and singing. Some of the dead wake up at night moaning, so she scolds them. Some of them cry a lot at night, so she brings them water. Her behavior intimidated the people carrying the

---

55 Hajja is an honorific title used to address an elderly Muslim woman, particularly someone who has made the pilgrimage to Mecca (hajj) at least once in her lifetime.

56 In Islam, *Bid'ah* refers to innovation or novelty in matters of religion that are not based on the Quran or the Sunnah (the teachings and practices of the Prophet Muhammad). It is considered a negative concept because it implies the introduction of practices or beliefs that are not part of the original teachings of Islam. *Bid'ah* is any act or belief that goes against the established teachings and practices of Islam.

57 *Rawafidh* (also known as Rawafid or Rafidites) is a term used to refer to a group of Shia Muslims who are considered to be extremists by mainstream Shia Islam. The term *Rawafidh* means "rejectors" in Arabic and points to this group's rejection of the leadership of the first three caliphs of Islam after the death of Prophet Muhammad, as well as certain Sunni traditions and beliefs.

black flags.[58] One of the *Muhajiroun* who had arrived from Chechnya tried to break a tombstone, so she attacked him, howling, 'Inshallah, your hand will break.' He panicked and missed the tombstone, and as his hammer flew in the air, his hand bent back and broke. He mumbled, seeking protection from Allah and Satan and then he left, followed by his frightened companions. Most of the graves are for young, out-of-town men, soldiers who defected, or activists killed in demonstrations."

As Ayman continued speaking, a young man on crutches came out, greeted them, and then went on his way. Ayman said, "That is Barhoum. He lost his leg to a landmine and visits the grave of his leg that is buried here."

At the center that Ayman and his colleagues oversaw, a little girl engrossed in coloring said to Layl, "I will draw everyone who died so they can come back to life."

Ayman whispered, "This girl lost four of her siblings in a chemical massacre."

Layl moved from one story to another, each time thinking it was the worst thing she had ever heard, and yet each time she heard something worse.

In the center for women's care, she found one local specialized female doctor and a few nurses. One of the legal midwives, a woman over fifty, said, "Doctor, after every massacre, something strange happens. Even women who previously had no chance of getting pregnant are doing so easily, as if men's sperm became stronger and wombs more fertile. This is nature and God's wisdom. The more frequent the massacres, the higher the pregnancy rates."

Amid all of this, smiles flourished, and sarcasm was rejuvenated. Truths were exposed to the sound of roaring laughter. Towns previously unheard of were a reservoir of human joy, creativity, beauty, and illuminated faces; there was a genius of resistance among them and clarity of purpose. Layl came to understand how those who were far away may be confused and not understand the reality of the people, the power of the people. She had made her way to a town inhabited by a mysterious joy, a place like no other, full of handsome youth, attractive men, and women

---

58   Referring to ISIS.

whose presence filled it with breathtaking charm.

Ayman said, "They are organizing a demonstration for the dead today. They'll film it from the cemetery to show that even the dead want to overthrow not only the regime but all systems. And they will write on their signs, 'We, the dead, will haunt you in all places until we bring you all down.'"

For the first time, Layl understood the depth of this mysterious word called revolution. As she was delivering a first aid lecture, a group of masked men entered the place with machine guns and eyes filled with evil. They ordered Ayman to prove that she had permission to conduct the lecture. He informed them that he had obtained approval from the military council and Shariah court. One of them spoke in Arabic but with an accent that was not Syrian, "Do you not know that mixing is forbidden, and that men and women cannot gather in one place?"

"But it's a medical lecture that benefits both men and women," replied Layl.

They took her ID and ordered her to go with them. Ayman and his friends tried to stop them, but they were violently beaten. Layl was dragged to one of their cars, blindfolded, and ordered her to crouch under the seat. Then they drove off in a convoy, firing shots in the air. Everything happened so quickly. Her fear became terror when she arrived at their headquarters.

They interrogated her for an hour, demanding to know why she had come and which intelligence agency she belonged to. They wanted information. One yelled at her, "You are Alawite, and you're either working with the Syrian or Emirati intelligence. You better confess!"

There wasn't a charge that they did not pin on her. She was truthful in all she told them, but chose not to reveal her intention to reach the man who had simultaneously destroyed and rebuilt her life. After three days of interrogation, the commander requested to see her. A guard ordered her to get ready to meet Prince Abu Al-Baraa and took her to his office.

He looked dignified, with long hair protruding from under his turban and a gray and black beard. In a familiar voice, he ordered, "Please, have a seat."

As she sat down, he asked in a trembling, faint voice, "What are you doing here?"

She began to talk, but he cut in, "If you don't mind, fix your hijab." He averted his eyes and turned away. The shawl on her head had slipped and her hair was showing from underneath. Just then, she recognized him—his voice and his mannerisms. The beard could not conceal the familiar features of a face that still burned in her memory. "Abu Al-Baraa? You are Sameeh Al-Ghawarani, aren't you?" she said, as she took off her hijab and let it fall to the floor. He looked away, pretending to be modest and said, "Cover your head, *hurma*."[59]

"*Hurma*? Now my name is *hurma*, Mr. Communist? Before I cover up anything, Mr. Sameeh, first tell me why you ran away." His eyes were on the door, which was still half-open, his head bowed. Indeed, everything that has once been left behind, unresolved, is bound to resurface one day.

Sameeh's betrayal and flight had left her weak. All that had followed had resulted from that betrayal. In the early stages of life, before one becomes immune to pain, the damage caused by emotions can be poisonous, and all attempts to cure it become futile and a blood transfusion becomes a necessity. But in that moment of revelation between Layl and Sameeh, the truth was laid out before them. Fate had brought Layl to this moment. Had she read this scene in a novel, she would have said it was exaggerated. It was the sort of coincidence that could only be invented by a writer. Her situation surpassed a hundred Iliads.

This man's betrayal was not only the cause of her painful experiences and decisions. It was also the best thing that could happen to her. She could now be true to herself and give her life meaning, embarking on the journey of liberation. Having been a worm cocooned in the silk of time, she was now turning into a butterfly, gifted by the power of transformation, following her heart and mind. There, in the clay, was the truth. There, where the fulfillment of her body and soul was—there, with Fidel Abdullah.

It was necessary for her to defeat this cowardly bearded man so that she would forever be liberated from him. She went to the door and closed

---

59   Woman—derived from *harim*.

it. It was as if she had been reborn in light, radiant and beaming with confidence. She walked towards this defeated man, whose eyes were glued to the wall. She whispered to him with a softness that was loaded with all kinds of ammunition, "So Sheikh, you can kill and plant mines in cold blood, but you can't even look into the eyes of a woman you once loved? You were able to argue with ten religious men that there was no God, and now you can't even bear to hear the voice of a woman because she stirs temptation within you? You escaped from the country because you were poor and because Hafez Al-Assad destroyed it, but you still don't see how you've become just like him? You managed to convince me that a hymen was a trivial matter and against women's freedom. Then you ran away after forcing me to have an abortion, and now you can't even bring yourself to look at my hair? We used to talk together for hours about culture, art, and cinema, and now you won't even grant people permission to watch a film?"

Her revelations were like continuous punches that not even Muhammad Ali could have defended himself against, and before her final knockout punch, she changed the rhythm of her voice and said, "In spite of all of this, I excuse and forgive you because this is not your problem alone. You are son to all these disasters. You were raw and at the beginning of your life, defeated to the point that you tried to live a love story that could compensate for your defeat. But love can never triumph with people who are defeated from within. The defeated communist is like a defeated jihadist or a defeated suicide bomber—none of them can offer anything to life other than defeat. But despite all of this, today your words come to mind, the quotes that you were so good at reciting: 'Humans were not created to be defeated; they may be destroyed, but can not be defeated.'"

She picked up the hijab from the floor, calmly placed it on her head, and sat back down in the chair, looking straight ahead. He turned his body to the wall and wiped his face. She couldn't tell if he was crying or was avoiding facing her by pretending to be moved.

"Are you finished?" he asked.

"Not quite. I want you to take me to Sheikh Fadl Abdullah. He is close by, with your ISIS neighbors."

"That will be very difficult—there are conflicts between us."

"Save it for someone else. You are all brothers within the same doctrine, and each of you is playing your own part. I need you to find a way to get me there safely."

"I may be able to get you there, but it won't be easy getting you out."

"I will be grateful."

"Can I talk now?"

"I am listening," she said with a cold smile. She did not listen to anything he said; she didn't care to hear any excuses. She let him speak until he regained his breath, voice, and position. He opened the door again and walked calmly to her. With every step, he regained his masculine power and authority, his new glory. He looked into her eyes and said in that familiar tone she knew so well, "The hijab looks good on you."

"I will consider it a chaste flirtation, Sheikh."

He smiled, jerked away to his desk, and called his assistant. "I need you to take our sister, the doctor, back to where you picked her up from. Then tomorrow morning, bring her back here. Two brothers from the military council will accompany her on a mission."

48

Anees

In the morning, Dr. Anees was transported to another location. The man with the broken arm bid him farewell with extinguished eyes. Anees nodded at him with eyes closed tightly as a gesture of encouragement. They led him to a van and blindfolded him once again. After approximately fifteen minutes, he found himself in a slightly cleaner place.

It didn't wait long before a masked guard entered and ordered him to stand up and follow him to the bathroom. He turned on the faucet and instructed him to shower and shave his beard, and then gave him an orange jumpsuit to wear. Anees assumed that what had happened to the young men would also happen to him. It seemed futile for him to object; his option was either full resistance or total surrender.

They took him back to his room. Another masked guard, who seemed to be a higher rank based on how the guards greeted him, gave him a letter written in English and ordered him to read it.

"You will memorize it without any additions or omissions and recite it before the camera while holding your passport."

"But I don't have my passport."

The guard reached into his pocket, took out the passport and waved it at him, "Now you have it"

I am no one, one of the many who have been forced to undergo this experience against their will, under the wide-open eyes of an indifferent sky. I am no one, aside from having been born in the land of nothingness, the land of ruin and

regret, the land cursed by the universe in the twenty-first century; a land that
I fled a quarter of a century ago because I feared everything. I returned to it,
an ill-fated and unfortunate man, and joined the largest archive of misery and
repudiation in human history. I am like that drowned child, lying on a strange
beach, who no one cares about except for the devouring cameras that violate
his body so that the world can ejaculate its empathy over him. I am all of those
who were killed in cold blood, the surplus of the world's needs, ruining people's
moods as they read their morning papers, forcing them to look the other way.
I am he who has been crushed under the rubble, starved to extinction, killed by
knives, swords, bullets and bombs, the hero of documentaries and news broad-
casts that no one watches. I am the laughter that death cannot stop, the screams
that attract more killers, the one kneeling on two swollen knees that continue to
be beaten up by demons. I am the mirror of this universe and the truth that no
one dares to face. I, along with all screaming, tortured and killed victims in this
accursed place, spit on all of you.

In place of this monologue that festered in Anees's chest, he began to read the prepared statement. "I am Anees Al-Aghawani, a British citizen, and I demand that the prime minister of the United Kingdom step in ..." He had to close his eyes for a moment because of the pain and despair he felt. His face contracted and expanded as he pleaded for mercy and asked, "What have I got to do with setting scores between the world's gangs?"

He read the brief statement while kneeling on a green mat in front of a chroma green background. Then, three giants stood up holding explosive belts, machine guns, and honed knives. They announced that they would slaughter this pig in a matter of days if certain detainees in various countries were not released.

The producer came to put his finishing touches on the performance and asked him to rehearse the required text again. But as soon as Anees said his name, the producer froze, trying to remember where he had heard this name and how he knew this man. Shortly, he remembered that he had spoken with him years ago about filming an archeological site. Fragments of conversations he had had with Layl flooded back, and he remembered that she had also mentioned his name several times. She had told him about his disappearance, but the last thing he ever expected was to see this man here in this place.

Fidel wanted to talk to him and ask questions, but he had to adhere to the organization's strict instructions. He was only permitted to speak with prisoners or suspects through a representative who monitored every word and action.

He told the officer that he needed a different type of lighting and asked permission to approach the prisoner to give him some instructions. The officer said it was OK, so Fidel went to Anees and gave him a set of instructions. Feeling a bit safer, he whispered to him, "Dr. Anees, I know you. You are a friend of my friend." Anees stared at the tall, bearded, long-haired man. He did not recognize him, but before any doubt and confusion could creep in, Fidel added, "I can't talk much, but I am a friend of Dr. Layl. I will try my best to help you in any way I can."

He then changed the subject and shifted to a cold tone, telling him how to look at the camera and how to present himself. In order to stall and in the hope of finding a way out, Fidel pretended that he would need more lighting. When he departed, Anees could hardly believe that a glimmer of hope had finally appeared. Fidel headed directly to the headquarters and asked to see Sheikh Ghassan. Two hours later, his request was granted.

"Ever since I began working here, I've never asked questions that do not concern me. For the first time, I have an inquiry, about the English doctor prisoner who I filmed today," he said.

Sheikh Ghassan was clearly irritated. There was an unspoken covenant that Fidel understood and had never breached, which made the leaders trust and admire his work. Asking this kind of question was strictly forbidden, regardless of the closeness between the two men— especially after Sheikh Ghassan had made it possible for Fidel to work on his own and exempted him from all Shariah lessons and other requirements. They left him alone, in a comfortable apartment in the elite area of the Mouhajiron.

Upon seeing the Sheikh's reaction, Fidel regretted his haste and bad judgement. He quickly wanted to immediately retract his question but the Sheikh spoke first, skeptically asking, "Do you know him?"

"No, not at all. I only wanted to suggest that the shoot take place outdoors."

This made Sheikh Ghassan even more suspicious. "Listen, Sheikh Fadl," he said sternly. "I will find someone else to carry out the task. Any empathy or interference in the affairs of prisoners or convicts carries the penalty of death, and you know that. If you have anything to tell me about this man, I will listen now, but you will no longer be tasked with this particular job."

Realizing the magnitude of his mistake, Fidel could only comply. "As you wish," he said. "To be honest, I only know him superficially from London, but he doesn't know me. I apologize for bothering you."

As he turned to leave, the Sheikh stopped him and said, "Sheikh Fadl. Do take care of yourself, and don't waste what you have accomplished here for nothing."

Fidel nodded his head and left, his mind racing. He knew the time to leave had come and was confident that he was getting closer to filming what he had long awaited—capturing the dangerous mystery. He needed new equipment, which was on its way to him, and he was certain that he would obtain the needed results as he was about to film the execution of four convicts sentenced to death by drowning.

But the face of Dr. Anees continued to haunt him, urging him to violate the forbidden. He could not dismiss the image from his mind. He returned to his apartment and busied himself with work, but he couldn't forget about this man who had brought Layl back to him. He cursed her in his heart and decided to do what he could to help Dr. Anees.

He had many admirers, for anyone who worked in the media and film industry was highly respected by members of the organization. His courteousness, kindness, neutrality, skillfulness, and ability to stay away from matters that did not concern him all helped him establish a loveable image among all who knew him.

Undoubtedly, he would obey Sheikh Ghassan's orders and would not film; however, he had also made a promise to this unfortunate captive. Regret began to gnaw at him as he realized that he had erred in rushing to confront Ghassan.

He got dressed and headed to the detention center. He knew the official in charge of protecting the doctor in the building where he was temporarily held. This person had always tried to flatter him with hopes of joining his department; he was passionate about the media but lacked talent. Rachid Abu Taha was there to greet him in his broken Arabic mixed with French.

"Welcome. May God bless you. Bienvenu. Bienvenu."

Fidel sat with Rachid, who was overwhelmed with joy at being visited by a legend, something that he had least expected. He asked him in French, "Do you want tea or coffee?"

Fidel answered back in French, "Tea would be great."

As they sipped their tea, Fidel began to weave his web. "We need a new team of documentarians to work with us. I saw the experiment that you undertook, Rachid. You are a natural journalist and artist, and all you lack is some training. I came to you directly to ask you before I nominate your name."

In disbelief, Rachid replied, "I am completely ready. Serving Islam has been my lifelong dream, but I haven't yet found the chance."

"Well, the chance found you."

"I am ready. I will do anything for this."

"What I'm looking for is your kind of spirit and passion. I will train you. But I'll need you to promise to keep this a secret between us until you are ready."

"I swear by Almighty God that no creature will know about it."

"Excellent. I'll be busy with a new project and will entrust you with the task of filming the captive that you are guarding for Alberto, I mean Abu Muhjin the Portuguese. But the best I can do is train you directly, and in secret, to deal with the prisoner in your possession."

"But we have strict orders. How will we enter or interact with him without permission?"

"I know, I know. But this is our only chance. It's up to you. The theoretical training is not enough, but I am confident that this will provide you with a great opportunity if we can hold practical training for three days. As for my part, I can come at this same time at night—all equipment is available here. Again, it's up to you."

The joy that radiated from Rachid's eyes disappeared, replaced by obvious anxiety, for he was not only risking his job but also his neck. Involuntarily, he reached for his neck.

At this point, Fidel had to take a gamble, "Listen, Rachid. You're not obligated to do anything. Forget what I said. Thank you for the tea," and he began to leave.

"No, no, no. I trust you Sheikh Fadl. Let's proceed, with God's blessings."

"Let's start now. I just need some time alone with the prisoner first. I need to get him to trust us."

Rachid's intuition told him not to get involved, but he was blinded by his trust and believed that this could be his big chance. So he surrendered himself to Fidel, who went to Anees's detention center after Rachid had relieved the guards of their duties and taken over their shift. The guards were very thankful.

Fidel barged into the doctor's private room. "We don't have much time. I will try to be with you around this time for the next few days. Until now, freeing you from here seemed impossible, but I can be your messenger. My name is Fidel Abdullah. You once spoke with me about filming an archeological site."

"Huddud's House."

"Whatever," he said in English, and then continued in Arabic, "I need to know your story so I'll know what to do."

In calm, measured tones, Anees recounted his story, from the phone call he received in London up to the present moment. Fidel was most interested in the Chef and the "cultural center," asking for the smallest details.

Their conversation was interrupted when Rachid entered in a panicky state. He had clearly begun to sense that he had gotten himself involved in a matter that had nothing to do with his training or with the media. Fidel stepped out with him. "Brother Rachid," he said. "This man is important to me. And you can consider yourself promoted to the propaganda department next week."

"The new guard shift will arrive shortly. You must leave now," said Rachid.

It was not difficult to reach Sami, Dr. Anees's son. The media campaign that Fidel had been leading for the past two years had all the necessary contact information. The hard part was gaining Sami's trust. More important, this had to happen without attracting the attention of the organization's security system.

Sami had been subjected to dozens of misleading calls and blackmail attempts, so he had lost trust in any undocumented information about his father. Fidel had to contact him via Skype. He explained the situation and conveyed all the information he had. In order to dispel doubt and gain his full trust, he secured a direct phone call for him to speak with his father for a few minutes. It was crucial for the father and son to have full confidence in Fidel so that he could proceed.

He told Sami that he would be away for some time but that he would send him an email address and a password when the right time came. Fidel had stored information, images, and videos since the beginning of the revolution. Before leaving, he needed to finish his final project as he had assembled a complete archive that told the truth about what had happened.

In a race against time, he tried to maintain control of his nerves as he completed his final project. Although he was ready to leave, he chose to stay for the sole purpose of trying to get Anees out.

49

Fidel and Layl

He was completely unable to smell.

He sat in his apartment, fully isolated since the last shoot. He no longer left his home. His relationship with Sheikh Ghassan was tense. There were new cold faces at the headquarters. He did not want to be distracted because he felt that he was getting closer to what he had been searching for. They were ignoring him, no longer assigning him any tasks. The rupture had begun. One mistake would be his last and would cost him nothing less than life itself. The continuous chirping of two love birds was what bothered him in that moment, not the sound of the shelling of the planes, which he had become accustomed to.

He did not know who had brought him these two annoying birds. Their chirping was like the pecking of crows on a corpse. He carried them to the balcony and opened the door of the cage. They cautiously flew away to a nearby tree that was so tired and barren it looked like it had been ravaged by locusts. He returned to his computer and became absorbed in rearranging the shots.

He had skillfully crafted the drowning scene. As the inmates, clad in their orange jumpsuits, were lowered into the water and slowly drowned, nine cameras were tied to a crane and positioned directly over the cage.

They provided him with one of the best cameras available, with 12-bit Cinema Raw at 4000 x 2160 resolution. It was unreal how it could capture every moment underwater while fixed on the crane's arm.

Four cameras were positioned underwater, fixed to the PowerShot D2, with a highly sensitive system that combined a 12.1-megapixel CMOS sensor and a DIGIC 4 processor. This was precisely what he needed. If humans had souls and the hour came for these souls to depart, this technology would definitely capture them. And if the image could not be captured, at least its vibration would be detected by the ultra-precise sound sensor.

The four criminals had formed a gang of robbery and terror, kidnapping, raping, and murdering children—at least this was the explanation given in the brief statement that was read before the execution took place.

The European team had proposed this method of execution after a brainstorming session that had impressed the Prince. Those who came up with the most creative ways of killing were honored. Fidel was entrusted with managing the filming operations. The four were injected with sedatives to prevent them from moving; the process of drowning them began after the sentence was read by the court's spokesperson amid a gathering of locals.

In the control room, inside a TV transport van, Fidel ordered the camera crew and the driver of the crane to begin. He felt a slight surge of ecstasy because he was about to film one of the greatest scenes in the history of cinematography. Unknown to everyone else, his true goal was to capture the departing soul at the moment of death.

He contemplated the moments of drowning, one image after another, confident that he would find something. He stared at the faces being tortured with water, unable to hold their breaths any longer and releasing bubbles as they choked. He observed every bubble that came out of their noses and mouths until he accounted for the last bubbles. He then noticed something strange; as he began to enlarge the images, he was seized by a moment of panic, one that didn't have to do with what he was seeing but with the love birds that had returned to their cage and started letting out their rattled tweets. He pounced on the cage, opened the door, grabbed one of the birds, and snatched it out of the cage. The other bird quickly flew away. He held the bird tightly in his fist, ready to decapitate it. But as he looked into the terrified eyes of the bird, he loosened his grip and let it fly out of the window.

He returned to his chair and continued studying the images but found nothing. He opened a small container, poured out a line of cocaine on the surface of a circular mirror, rolled a thousand-lira bill into a tube, and snorted forcefully. A cascade of crystal balls exploded in his head and he felt a burning sensation in his nostrils. Water bubbles were gushing from the mouths of the drowned men. He could hear the stammering of heads that were severed from their bodies. A flock of stars danced in the basin of his skull to Vangelis's "Conquest of Paradise," driving back caravans of faces carried on carpets of ecstasy. A flock of birds lined up on the balcony of the house, nibbling at the place with clattering tweets. He felt like he was drowning in hot mud, unable to breathe, gasping for air. Then everything became calm and the racket stopped. There was a knock at the door. He opened it cautiously. The building's security guard said, "*As-salamu alaykum*. There is a woman who wants to see you."

He needed a few seconds to understand what he had just heard. "What woman?"

She says she is your relative and wants to see you. She is in the reception room downstairs.

"I'll come down in a little bit."

He regained his composure with a little coffee and then he went to the sink and held his head under cold water. All of the Prince's suggestions that Fidel should marry had failed. *A woman!—what a word*, he thought to himself. Over the past months, the idea of that woman had been something distant and strange; the mere thought of her unleashed a fountain of sadness that would not stop bleeding.

And here is my honorable Sheikh, the Prince of this Kingdom, fencing me in with barbed wire and sending a gift to me in the form of an explosive belt, like the one he wears, so that I wear it on my body. As he explained, "It's true that we did not have a choice to come into this life, but this belt is our freedom. We are the freest men in the world, because the only way to silence us is to kill us. We do not surrender ourselves or give up. When the time is right, we will always have this powerful friend. Fadl, people think that we are brainwashed and that the mujahideen martyrs are stupid people who have lost all opportunities in life and blow themselves up for houris. Such people babble about matters they know nothing about; what they don't know is that those who blow themselves up, no matter what the world thinks of them, are the most powerful and freest of men. How many men in the world, and I am talking to you now, do not have the cost of a meal in their pockets and are indebted to the devils of the banks, people who have been expelled from the stockade of society? How many humans spend the night alone, without anyone knocking on their doors or asking about them, waiting for their turn to be assigned work and consequently are stuck in humiliating jobs that offer mere crumbs? Think about what goes on in their minds as they pass by windows of designer shoe boutiques where the price of one pair is equal to a half year of the financial assistance they receive. Meanwhile, crowds of people line up to buy them. This wonderful belt is your only friend in life. No one is stronger than you when you wear it. No one can harm you. No one in this life can enslave you. I am offering you your freedom, my dear."

What nonsense, thought Fidel. *On one hand, the Sheikh talks about salvation, and on the other he sends him a woman!*

He picked up the belt, put it on without hesitation, threw a loose shirt on to cover it, and headed downstairs, determined that if he was the least bit tempted, he would not hesitate to detonate it. But once he saw who was waiting for him—the last person in the world he expected to see—everything inside him exploded except for his suicide belt, which had suddenly become impotent.

Her eyes peered out from behind a burka and struck him with flames. He looked like he was about to collapse. Everything that had previously eluded him now appeared before him, looking him straight in the eye. On either side of her were two armed men gazing at him with suspicion.

When they realized that he knew her, a wave of relief swept over them. He explained that she was his wife and they left apologetically. Only the security guard remained, watching the scene with a skeptical expression until he withdrew and went back to his office.

They had to go upstairs to the apartment quietly. They passed through the corridor in silence, entered in silence, and closed the door in silence. She removed her burka in silence, opened her arms in a whisper, only to collide with the explosive belt.

"Layl, nothing equals your presence here," he said. "But you are late. I am now at the point of no return." She took off the belt silently, and then everything in them began to speak. They were glued to one another for two full days, like a set of conjoined twins, outside of time and place, embracing each other as if any separation would mean the end of one of them.

"You're going to get out of here with me, Fidel, right?" asked Layl.

"Layl, I no longer know who Fidel is. I don't know who I am."

"This is not your place. We're going to leave here together and start anew."

"Start what?"

They were lying in bed. He was entangled in the silk of her body, which brought him back to his favorite smell. He could not stop inhaling her. Occasionally he paused and stared at the ceiling while the thorns of fear grew inside of him. He knew that those scratches, scars, and wounds could not be healed, not even in the purity of her ocean.

"They won't let me go and they won't allow me to leave here. I'm now a part of this, and even if I were to leave this place, I will never be able to live with what I have come to know and with what I have done."

The sound of *takbeer*[60] came from the nearby mosques announcing a new airstrike. The intense shelling had been escalating since the morning. The coalition planes were raining down projectiles on innocent people under the pretense of ridding the world of ISIS.

"If you're scared, we can go down to the shelter," said Fidel.

"No, with you I am no longer afraid," she replied.

The shelling of the planes had not frightened them, but they were jolted by a knocking on the door. He got up and left the bedroom to open the door. There were four officials from the Council along with

---

60   *Takbeer* is an Arabic term that refers to the phrase "*Allahu Akbar*," which means "God is the greatest."

two women from the Khansa policewomen's battalion.

In a stern and condescending tone, he was told, "Sheikh Fadl. You are wanted at the Council urgently, and we will vacate the apartment. And the sister inside will join the sisters."

"Please give a minute," replied Fidel.

"Unfortunately, there is no time," said the officer and he pushed him aside while two armed men entered and took his devices, the suicide belt, and his phone. Meanwhile, the two burka-clad policewomen barged into the bedroom and ordered Layl to put on her burka as they searched her bags and confiscated her phone. They drove them away in separate cars.

The airstrike had destroyed a three-story home that was still engulfed in flames. There were people trying to rescue the wounded from under the rubble while the headquarters known to everyone remained unscathed.

The car carrying him passed by the headquarters and headed to the security square, where the organization's leadership was located. He was placed in an office and ordered to wait. Layl was taken to another office in the same building. There was no mistreatment or accusations, but the waiting period was fraught with anxiety.

One of the policewomen came to the room where Layl was being held and asked, "Do you know French?"

"A little," replied Layl.

She then asked her to fill out a form in both Arabic and French, if possible. Meanwhile, Sheikh Ghassan went to Fadl and told him, "I can no longer protect you. The presence of a woman from the Rawafidh in your home, your absence from attending Shariah classes for a long period, finding drugs and alcohol in your apartment—I could have helped find a solution for all of these things, but contacting British Intelligence and leaking unlicensed videos to them is a grave offense. The only solution for you is to publicly declare your allegiance to ISIS. As for the woman, she will be charged with adultery, and all I can guarantee is that she will not be stoned to death."

"Get us out of here, Sheikh Ghassan. This woman is my wife!"

"Unfortunately, it's too late. The report has reached Mosul, and to-night, or by tomorrow morning at the latest, the committee will come to assess the situation. What will help you and me is for you to declare your allegiance publicly, burn your passport, and broadcast this in English. You will then be transferred to Mosul. And, to prove allegiance, you must execute her with your own hands. Only then will they will take your matter into further consideration."

"So even if I do this, there's still no guarantee? Just let her go. I'll do anything you want."

"The great work you have done could work in your favor, but the report on you is too big to be contained. Anyway, a new prince has been appointed and the matter is settled."

"Help get her out of here and do with me as you wish. You can choose whatever kind of death you want for me, and I am ready. But I implore you with everything you believe in to get her out of here."

"It's very difficult, Fadl, but I will try."

He departed gloomily, leaving Fidel to burn in his inner pain.

The State had achieved the goals it had set for itself—not a single media outlet in the world didn't know about ISIS. But after a few years, the Caliphate had reached its peak and began to decline. The central leadership no longer tolerated mistakes, regardless of who committed them, and any leader seen as weak was replaced by someone who knew no mercy.

The mere mention of the new prince's name, Abu Abd Al-Rahman Mustafa instilled fear, As the leader of a brutal and merciless group of fighters, his fame preceded him from Central Asia. He was practically a legend among the mujahideen. He immediately took the reins of power and organized an execution ceremony and iron-fisted beatings. On Fridays, he spoke of the dignity of jihad and of the importance of cleansing the Levant from all immorality.

Sheikh Ghassan made one attempt to get Fadl released, but it failed before the new authority. But on the morning Fidel was led to his execution, the sheikh managed to provide him with the chance to see Layl one last time. His face was clear, his eyes shone with radiance. He took her hands, kissed them with humility, wiped her tears, and whispered to her, "The secret of my secret you are, Layl. Your smell is with me. The important thing is that your smell is with me."

Her tongue was tied, her face filled with grief, and her eyes took in every detail, every pore on his body. He held her close, inhaling deeply, and whispered, "There is hope. I will catch up with you in another car, and if I am not successful, I have everything documented in an email. The password is 'Huddud's House.'"

These few minutes brought everything into clear focus. He urged her to leave, and when she tried to object, he regained his sternness and said decisively, "Layl, there is no time left."

She touched his face, ran her fingers over his beard, eyebrows, and hair. She had no choice but to obey. Her right hand was the last thing he touched. She huddled in the back seat of the car, looking at her hand as warm tears gently fell on it.

Sheikh Ghassan's final efforts, in coordination with friends of Sameeh, succeeded in securing her release and smuggling her out of the country. She was driven in a private car to the Turkish border. An hour later, it was his turn to leave. He crossed the second checkpoint, showing a permit from the judiciary branch, but at the last checkpoint, fate took a different turn.

Fidel was confronted by Rachid Taha, who had almost been imprisoned because of him and endured the humiliation of having his status as an internal security guard downgraded to that of a checkpoint guard at the dangerous border. He seethed with hatred and vengeance for the man who had deceived him and almost got him killed. Now here stood Fidel with a fake ID and a permit with a different name. Taha knew that uncovering a smuggling conspiracy promised a substantial reward, at the very least a promotion or a return to a safer position. No bribe or threat would have deterred him. He called security, and within minutes they arrived to arrest Fidel and the driver.

They tortured him, but Fidel did not utter a word about the help received from Sheikh Ghassan. The driver, on the other hand, quickly broke and gave them all the information he had.

She was unable to cry; she was unable to die. She was only aging as she walked away and left him to his fate. He recited the *Shahada*[61] aloud and followed it with her name, and he continued to say her name to himself until a bullet pierced his head from behind, exiting through his nose, which still retained her smell. He began to slowly ascend.

The deafening noise turned into hissing silence, and it was as if he were flying, lightly, devoid of pain. He saw his prostrate body gushing blood, quenching a thirsty land. From above, he saw Fadl and Fidel in an embrace, each caressing the other's back; the scene was suffused in pure blue, sparkling and glittering with bursts of light, giving birth to dazzling scents that permeated the air; her smell reached him and he inhaled its ethereal fragrance with deep joy, peacefully submerging himself in a world whose truth he had always yearned to know.

So this is death! He wanted to smile but his trembling lips could not respond as his body was pulled into a state of tranquility.

---

61   *The Shahada* is the Islamic declaration of faith, which is considered the most fundamental statement in Islam. It is also known as the "Testimony of Faith" and is recited by Muslims daily as a declaration of their belief in the oneness of God and the prophethood of Muhammad.

0
Sami

Massive folders packed with the clippings, papers, and news items were arranged on the table, awaiting transfer to the British National Library in London. Registered in his name, they were inaccessible to the general public. A month ago, he created a website where he uploaded all the videos and articles published about Huddud's House, and asked anyone who had any information at all about the house, its residents, or visitors to contact him, whether in Arabic, English, or even Persian or Russian. He picked up the last notebook with his father's name on it and added his own name to it: Sami Anees Al-Aghawani. He was now the final heir. His new mission was to tell this story of war and love and to publish it.

At sea, Issa and Samia's children were struggling, trying not to drown after their boat capsized on the way to Greece.

In the liberated areas, Ayman and his comrades led new protests against the authority of the so-called jihad mercenaries, stripping them of their forged legitimacy. Meanwhile, planes from more than thirty countries bombarded wherever and whenever they pleased.

Aleppo was dying silently as the cameras kept rolling, and the world was silent. In Damascus, the sun rose to the sound of shells from an unknown source, one of which fell on an old house, igniting a fire whose flames reached the sky. The fire brigade desperately tried to extinguish the blaze, and when Samia arrived, she rushed toward the house screaming, trying to push her way inside to put out the flames. This was the fortieth time that this house encountered destruction, but its history testifies that each time it returned greater than before.

Sami received the painful news. Wiping away tears, he sat down to publish it on different sites on the internet.

A video circulated of an ISIS executioner known as Abu Abd Al-Rahman Aljazzar beheading an English physician of Syrian origin, after his government refused to negotiate his release.

Sami further announced, as the son of the physician, that he had transferred priceless documents containing memoirs written by the inhabitants of a Damascene house called Huddud's House, dating back past 1500 BCE.

In a neglected corner of the Syrian Baath newspaper that he had received from an unknown source was a photo of a chef with the inscription, "Dangerous Terrorist Killed, Involved in Organ Trafficking." From the same source, he also received the following news: "In his office, Abbas Jawhar ends his call with Sa'ad Al-Deen, who had hung up on him. Before the officer in charge arrived to arrest him, he opened the drawer of his desk, shredded the sales contract for Huddud's House, and pulled the trigger of a gun he put in his mouth."

Meanwhile Syrian caravans scattered across a Syrian land of hell, carrying shreds of stories about all they had living through on a journey reminiscent of a modern-day Odyssey.

Layl sent the password that Fidel had given her to Sami so he could handle the transfer and digitization of all the materials and convert them to physical and visual documents.

Meanwhile, in her womb was an egg that successfully divided, and a fetus that was beginning to form. Nine months later, she would come to name this child Fidel.

Sami welcomed Layl and her son, and did everything in his power to move her to London to live in Kilburn, Collcott Street, Building No. 3. She would later delight in walking between Kingsbury Cemetery and Willesden Park, where the body of Helen lay and where Fidel had once walked. She also came to know the Brotherhood Society and Mariam, Fidel's ex-wife, who would become her best friend. The two of them would come to visit Helen's grave, next to Edward's, and take a poignant photo of the two graves where the husband's grave caved in and leaned onto Helen's, as if trying to embrace her—apparently, for some, death did not seem to put an end to the desire for an embrace. Fidel Junior became her new solace, and when they asked her about his father's name and origin, she would say, "Fidel Fadl Abdullah, Syrian-British, Arab, Muslim."

She called Sami and told him, "Today is one of the happiest days of my life. I've communicated with my son Nawwar on Facebook, and he and the family are preparing to travel to meet their new brother." Once their conversation ended, Sami had everything he needed to begin writing. On luxurious cotton paper, in dark blue ink, he began to write:

Huddud's House
-A Novel-

1
Fidel

Dubai, the beginning of 2011

Next to Burj Al Arab on Jumeirah Beach ...

--The End--
London, Fall 2016